"I appreciate you helping me out like this."

All those feelings Miriam had tried to command came flooding back—her old hopes and tender dreams. What was it about this man that made her knees turn to wet noodles with one piercing glance? Being Amos's wife would have been lovely, if they'd been more compatible, and if she'd been able to give him the family he wanted.

"*Yah*, it's not a problem," she said, and her voice sounded breathy in her own ears. Then she smelled the scent of bread, and she tapped him aside to pull on her oven mitts. Amos stepped back, his strong arm brushing against hers as he did so, and she swallowed hard, pretending that it didn't feel as sweet as it had.

She'd do her duty by her husband—in the kitchen at least—for these few weeks. And when she left, she'd be certain that he was fine without her. Maybe there was wisdom in *Mammi*'s request, after all.

Patricia Johns is a *Publishers Weekly* bestselling author who writes from Alberta, Canada. She has her Hon. BA in English literature and currently writes for Harlequin's Love Inspired and Heartwarming lines. She also writes Amish romance for Kensington Books. You can find her at patriciajohnsromance.com.

Carrie Lighte lives in Massachusetts next door to a Mennonite farming family, and she frequently spots deer, foxes, fisher cats, coyotes and turkeys in her backyard. Having enjoyed traveling to several Amish communities in the eastern United States, she looks forward to visiting settlements in the western states and in Canada. When she's not reading, writing or researching, Carrie likes to hike, kayak, bake and play word games.

PATRICIA JOHNS

&

CARRIE LIGHTE

Healing an Amish Family

2 Uplifting Stories

Wife on His Doorstep and
An Unexpected Amish Harvest

LOVE INSPIRED
INSPIRATIONAL ROMANCE

LOVE INSPIRED®

INSPIRATIONAL ROMANCE

ISBN-13: 978-1-335-44852-1

Healing an Amish Family

Copyright © 2023 by Harlequin Enterprises ULC

Wife on His Doorstep
First published in 2021. This edition published in 2023.
Copyright © 2021 by Patricia Johns

An Unexpected Amish Harvest
First published in 2021. This edition published in 2023.
Copyright © 2021 by Carrie Lighte

For questions and comments about the quality of this book, please contact us
at CustomerService@Harlequin.com.

Harlequin Enterprises ULC
22 Adelaide St. West, 41st Floor
Toronto, Ontario M5H 4E3, Canada
www.LoveInspired.com

Printed in U.S.A.

CONTENTS

WIFE ON HIS DOORSTEP

Patricia Johns

To my husband, who I love more than anything.

Who can find a virtuous woman?...
The heart of her husband doth safely trust in her.
—*Proverbs* 31:10–11

Chapter One

"*Mammi*, let me get that for you." Amos pulled his grandmother's mug of tea closer to her before she could rise to her feet to reach it. Outside, the day was chilly, the May sunlight drawing out the buds on the trees, but not warm enough for the sick old woman's comfort. She had a shawl around her shoulders, and Amos had put another one over her lap, but her fingers were still cold. He wanted to help…more than help, he wanted to make her well.

The sound of an engine drew their attention, and Amos rose to his feet and headed for the window. It was a taxi, and he couldn't see the occupant, but it was a blue dress that first appeared out the door, then a small traveling bag, and when the woman straightened and turned, bag in hand, his heart stuttered to a stop.

"Who's there?" *Mammi* asked.

He knew the woman very well, and at the sight of her, his breath turned shallow and his heart hammered hard to catch up.

"Amos?" *Mammi* said.

"It's my wife," he breathed.

Miriam Lapp tugged a black woolen coat closer around herself in the spring chill, and she stopped short when she saw Amos in the window. Miriam had changed a little since she'd left him ten years ago. Her strawberry blond hair was pulled back under her *kapp*, but one tendril fell free and it ruffled in the wind. She'd be thirty-five now, and she could still make his breath catch.

"Miriam is here?" *Mammi* asked, and this time she did stand up and her lap blanket fell into a pile at her feet.

"*Yah*, it looks that way," Amos said, and he headed for the door and pulled it open. "*Mammi*, you should sit down," he said over his shoulder, but his grandmother didn't listen.

Miriam headed toward him and came up the steps, then stopped. It was like the last decade just crumbled around him and he was left looking at the wife he'd vowed to love and protect all the days of his life...

"Hello," Amos said quietly.

"Hello, Amos." She didn't smile.

"It's been a long time," he said, his voice tight. He cleared his throat. "A very long time."

"*Yah*, I know," she replied. "You look..." She looked him over in a frank appraisal. "You look good, Amos."

"I've held together," he replied. "So do you."

She looked more than good—she looked beautiful in that way she always had. She'd never been an obvious beauty. Men didn't twist in their buggies to get a second look at her, and Amos had liked that. He'd never wanted a wife that other men gawked at. Miriam had a solidity about her, and a frank honesty that he'd been drawn to from the start. It was why he'd asked her to marry him after only knowing her for four days. They both wanted marriage and *kinner*, and he'd thought she'd make a fine wife. What was the point in wasting time?

"Can I come in?" Miriam asked.

"Yah." Amos stepped back, and he watched her as she came inside the house, unwrapping the shawl from around her shoulders. She'd put on a little weight in the last few years, and it looked good on her. But why was she here?

"Hello, *Mammi*," Miriam said, and she went forward to take *Mammi*'s outstretched hand. "I'm sorry to burst in on you like this."

"I'm glad to see you," *Mammi* said softly. "It's been… a while."

"Yah." Miriam released *Mammi*'s hand and glanced back at Amos. "I don't need to take up much of your time, Amos. I know I'm probably not welcome here—"

"Nonsense," *Mammi* interrupted. "You're Amos's wife, dear. You *belong* here."

Amos could hear his own breathing, and his head felt light. He'd had enough shocks for one day, and he eyed Miriam uncomfortably. Technically, *Mammi* was right, but the goodwill of extended family hadn't been enough to keep them together.

"Why have you come?" he asked at last.

"My *daet* passed away." Her lips quivered with repressed emotion. "Last week. A stroke."

"I'm sorry," he said. "I didn't hear." He looked futilely toward the folded newspaper, *The Budget*, that lay on the kitchen table. He hadn't opened it yet, but that was the best way he'd learn of anything happening in Miriam's hometown of Epson, Pennsylvania, where her father had lived and owned his businesses.

Miriam nodded and blinked back some tears. "*Gott* knew best." For a moment, there was some awkward silence. "Anyway, *Daet* left everything to my brother, Japheth."

"Everything?" Amos asked. "He didn't hold something back for you?"

She shook her head. "I thought he would have—"

So did Amos, for that matter. Her father, Leroy Schwartz, was a wealthy Amish businessman, and he had never made any attempt to help Amos and Miriam reconcile—at least no attempt that allowed Amos to have any self-respect. Leroy thought Amos wasn't a good enough provider for his daughter, and if he'd kept his married daughter home with him, enjoying a life that Amos couldn't hope to provide, then the least the old man could have done was leave her something in the will so that she could continue in comfort.

"Are you coming back, then?" Amos asked, uncertain how the question sounded, but it had to be asked. Her father was dead, and Leroy had been the one providing for her. As her husband, Amos was the one responsible for providing for her now, if she needed help.

"No, I'm not coming back to be a burden on you," Miriam said, and color bloomed in her face. "But when you and I got married, *Daet* gave us that commercial property in Epson as a wedding gift, and—" Miriam stopped. "And since *Daet* was running the place, anyway, all these years—it was only in our names on paper—"

"You want it back," Amos said.

"*Yah...*" She shrugged weakly. "I know it's crass, Amos, but it's the way I'll support myself, if you'll let me. Otherwise, I'd become your problem."

Miriam smiled slightly, and Amos's gaze moved toward that small travel bag. She hadn't come prepared for a long stay, so it seemed as if she were partway joking. Amos hadn't heard anything about that strip of stores since she left. Her father had put them into both of their names, but he'd continued to manage them—not that Leroy Schwartz would have trusted him with it. That was more of an insurance for his daughter in the old man's eyes.

"Yah..." Amos shrugged. "It's yours, Miriam. Do with it as you like. Your *daet* wanted you to have it, anyway, and I've never had anything to do with that property."

Besides, Amos had his own thriving carpentry business, and he wasn't a vindictive man. He and Miriam had both suffered enough.

"Do you know where the papers are?" Miriam asked hopefully. "I need to show them to Japheth and prove that strip mall belongs to me. He's already changing things, and he was about to evict some tenants, and—" She stopped. "I need to prove it's mine."

"They might be in the safe-deposit box at the bank," he said. "I don't remember if that was where I put them or if they're still around here somewhere—but the bank is already closed for the day."

Miriam's face flushed again, but she didn't ask him if she could stay. She dropped her gaze, then nodded twice.

"I'll come back tomorrow, and maybe we could go to the bank together, then," she said. "I'll get a room in town, and in the meantime, if you'd be willing to look through your papers here—"

"Come back?" *Mammi* interrupted. "Why would you go to some hotel in town when your home is right here?"

"*Mammi*'s right," Amos said. "You can stay here until this is sorted out. It's your home, after all."

Even if she'd never appreciated it. Even if she'd been so anxious to get away from it that she'd left important documents behind in her rush.

"Thank you," Miriam said, and she glanced around uncomfortably. "I'll try not to be in your way, Amos. I'll do the cooking and cleaning while I'm here, of course, and—"

"Amos, would you go see to the chores outside?" *Mammi* said, her voice silencing Miriam.

Amos met his grandmother's gaze, irritated. Was she really trying to get rid of him?

"If you don't mind, dear," *Mammi* said, softening her tone. She cast him an apologetic look.

"*Yah*, of course," Amos replied.

"I need a word with you alone, Miriam," *Mammi* said, and her voice firmed. "This requires some privacy between women."

Miriam and Amos both looked back at *Mammi* now, and Amos couldn't help but wonder what *Mammi* had to say that he couldn't hear.

Amos pulled his coat on and headed outside without another word, but as he shut the door behind him, he couldn't help but cast another curious look over his shoulder. *Mammi* had never been the take-charge sort around his house, and the last several years, he, Noah and Thomas had been taking care of her in her old age. She didn't have the same strength or even eyesight anymore.

What could *Mammi* have to say to Amos's estranged wife at this late stage? Miriam was his wife in *Gott*'s eyes, and in the community's, but she hadn't been a wife to him in a very long time. Whatever *Mammi* had to say to her could be said in front of him, couldn't it? Unless *Mammi* didn't want to embarrass Miriam any more than she had to when she lectured her about her moral, wifely duties. Who knew what passed between women when men were out of earshot?

Amos sighed and headed in the direction of the stables. He might as well muck out some stalls.

Besides, having Miriam here for a day might help with *Mammi*. She'd need some care that only a woman could provide, and both Noah's wife and Thomas's had small *kinner* of their own to care for. If Miriam could pitch in, it would help.

Gott, heal my grandmother, Amos prayed in his heart as he pulled open the stable door. This was the same prayer he'd been raising up since that doctor's appointment yesterday morning. They were all in *Gott*'s hands, but right now Amos needed *Mammi*'s sensible advice and gentle ways more than ever.

Because Miriam had just arrived, and that had sent his heart for a different kind of tumble.

Miriam looked toward the closed door, then toward the old woman. *Mammi*, or Mary Lapp as the rest of the community knew her, looked smaller somehow, and more fragile. But at her age, frailty could creep up faster than any expected. It had been a long time since Miriam had been in this house or even looked into this old woman's face…and she fully expected a lecture.

Miriam was not a good wife.

"Sit down, dear," *Mammi* said.

Miriam pulled up a chair opposite *Mammi* and sat,

perching on the edge. Miriam pressed her lips together, bracing for the onslaught.

"I'm sorry for your father," *Mammi* said quietly.

"Thank you." Miriam felt the tears rise again. Her father's death had been a shock to everyone. "We didn't see it coming."

"No, we don't tend to," *Mammi* said. "You know, at my age, you look at me and see a withered old woman. But I don't feel old. My joints feel old, and my hips sure do, but my heart doesn't. I look in the mirror, and it's like I see a stranger with wrinkles and white hair. In here—" she placed a hand over her chest "—I'm as young as you."

Miriam nodded. "They say time flies."

"It does," *Mammi* replied. "It feels like yesterday your Amos was a little boy at my apron. Now he's your husband."

Mammi looked at her meaningfully. Here it was— the lecture.

"*Mammi*, I know this didn't turn out the way anyone hoped," Miriam said. "But it's complicated. I'm not some horrible woman who uses and abuses her own husband."

"Then help me to understand," *Mammi* said. "Why can't you and Amos be together? It isn't like either of you can remarry and try this again. He's the only husband you have."

"We don't get along, *Mammi*," Miriam said quietly. "He wants *kinner*, as all Amish men do, and I'm afraid to have them. The thing is, I was just as eager for a family as any other woman when we got engaged, but you know that my mother died delivering me. It was when my sister died with her second baby two weeks before the wedding that I got really scared… I didn't want to die giving birth like she and my mother did. Is it so wicked of me to think that I might have value aside from giving birth?"

Mammi shook her head. "Of course you have value in and of yourself. *Gott* created you in His image. And I had a good deal of trouble having babies, myself. You know about that. So I do understand."

"But Amos thought I'd get over it—he thought I was just grieving a sudden death in the family. He wanted me to have more faith—but it wasn't his life that was in the balance, was it?" Miriam's voice trembled. It was an old argument, but it felt fresh. "And I'm too bold and forthright for him. It was a good thing when I came looking for a husband in Redemption, but not once we were married. I was supposed to change who I was."

"That first year is difficult," *Mammi* said.

"More than difficult," Miriam replied. "He couldn't get along with my father, and I couldn't be the woman he wanted. I'm good with numbers, with business, and I learned a lot from my father—none of which Amos wanted from me. He wanted *kinner*. He thought I was someone different when he married me, and I take responsibility for that. All the same, we made a mistake. We jumped into marriage because we were both lonely, and we thought it would be enough. It wasn't."

"And yet, you're still his wife," *Mammi* said seriously. "And there are certain duties—"

"I'm not sacrificing myself to have a baby!" Miriam burst out.

"I'm not asking you to," *Mammi* said. "But there is something I need you to do, and it's important."

What would it be now? Some ploy to bring them

back together and show them that a lifetime of tolerating each other under the same roof was better than what they had now? Miriam wasn't a good wife. She couldn't settle into the Amish rhythms of marriage, babies and motherhood. But she did have other plans.

"*Mammi*, please, this is between me and Amos, and—"

"I'm dying."

The words hit Miriam in the chest. She blinked. "What?"

"I'm dying," *Mammi* repeated. "We found out yesterday. I've been going for tests and I have some very aggressive cancer."

"You could still beat it," Miriam said with a shake of her head.

"It's very advanced." *Mammi* pressed her lips together. "No, I think it's best to accept the inevitable. This is bad, Miriam. And I only have a couple of weeks left."

Somehow, Amos's grandmother had seemed like she'd outlive the rest of them. She was always so strong—emotionally and physically. But then, Miriam's father had been a strong, barrel-chested man, too, and he'd died. Human beings were all more fragile than they might like.

Miriam shook her head. "I don't know what to say. I'm so sorry... I—"

"*Gott* doesn't make mistakes," *Mammi* said gently. "Isn't that what you said earlier? *Gott* counts out days. He lays them out before us, and when our time to go home to Him comes, we go."

Miriam met the old woman's watery gaze, and for a moment, they were both silent.

"Are you scared?" Miriam asked weakly.

"A little," *Mammi* replied. "I've never died before." The old woman smiled at her own gallows humor. "I don't know what that will feel like. But I do know that I'm in *Gott*'s hands, and I feel confident in that. I'm looking forward to Heaven. I'll see my own dear husband again, and the babies who died in their infancy—I'll finally hold them again. I didn't have an easy life, my dear. All of my children died before me, so I'll be grateful to see them again."

"I hope I have your courage when the time comes," Miriam said.

"This brings me to my request," *Mammi* said. "Right now, I have some strength to dress myself and wash myself, but the days are coming very quickly where I will need a woman's help. I know I could ask any number of relatives in Ohio or Florida once I tell them the news, but they're far away, and it wouldn't be easy on them. Besides, I'm asking you."

Miriam felt her heart skip a beat, and she licked her dry lips. This was a heavy request—one she couldn't deny if she were part of the community here, but she wasn't any longer. "Why me, *Mammi*? I'm not exactly part of the family anymore."

"Technically, you are," *Mammi* replied. "But more than that, my grandson needs your support, too. I've been the woman caring for his home these last ten years, and I've helped him in raising two teenagers to manhood. I've been the one to encourage him and remind him that *Gott* loves him still, even when life is hard. And I'm about to die. He needs support through this, and I want you to help him."

He'd raised teens—she'd heard the rumors about that. Her husband had taken in two boys.

"Would *he* want that?" Miriam breathed. "Because I don't think he looked overjoyed to see me, *Mammi*.

It's been a long time. I'm sure there are other people who are closer to him."

Mammi was silent, her blue eyes meeting Miriam's until Miriam dropped her gaze uncomfortably.

"You left him, Miriam," *Mammi* said firmly. "*Yah*, marriage was hard. It was hard for both of you, but you left this home, and you doomed that man to a lonely life without a wife by his side. He didn't leave you. There is a distinction there."

Guilt welled up inside of Miriam's breast, and she swallowed. "I tried, *Mammi*."

"I know, dear." *Mammi*'s voice softened. "And I'm not asking you to come back and live as his wife. All I'm asking for is that you stay for two weeks—maybe three—and you help Amos through my death. That's all. As his lawful wife, I think you could do that much for him." *Mammi* deflated back into her chair. "But you can decline. I'll understand, and I'll never mention it to Amos."

Miriam sucked in a breath. The old woman watched her fixedly, and Miriam knew that what *Mammi* asked was reasonable. This was how the Amish community survived—they pitched in and helped to care for each other. They didn't have old-age homes, they had family, and Mary Lapp didn't have any living children to step in. Marriage was a lifelong commitment, and there was no divorce permitted. *Mammi* was only asking her to do her Amish duty in a time of need.

"I'll need my own room," Miriam said. "I know we're married, but Amos and I can't share a room."

Mammi smiled at that. "Of course, dear. I'm not asking you to keep up appearances, just to support Amos. That's all."

There were footsteps outside, and the side door opened. Amos came back in, and he glanced at them, then went to the mudroom sink to wash his hands.

"Am I all right to come back in?" Amos asked.

"You're the man of his house," *Mammi* replied softly. "You come and go as you wish."

Miriam smiled weakly at that. *Mammi* had always been a strong spirit whose words were sometimes a little closer to the Amish ideal than her actions. She'd most certainly booted Amos out of the house for the conversation.

"*Mammi* has asked me to stay," Miriam said.

Amos eyed her for a moment, then his gaze slid toward his grandmother. "What?"

"For two or three weeks," *Mammi* said. "I need help that only a woman can provide, Amos. And I've chosen Miriam."

Amos nodded, but worry creased his brow.

"*Mammi*, if this is some attempt to reunite Miriam and me—"

"Nonsense," *Mammi* said with a small shrug. "Do you really think I'd use the last few weeks of my life to meddle in yours?"

"It had occurred to me," he said with a faint smile. "But we're adults who know what we're doing," Amos added. "We've tried this, *Mammi*. More than once."

"Sometimes things change," *Mammi* said quietly. "That's all you can really count on in life, isn't it?"

Amos looked over at Miriam and they exchanged an uncertain look. Even knowing what *Mammi* was very likely trying to do, how could Miriam turn down a dying old lady who'd always been nothing but kind and good to her? And as much as she hated to admit it,

Amos was going to need help getting through this—
Mammi wasn't wrong there.

"I'll stay in the guest room, if it's available still,"
Miriam said. "And we're understood that there is no
pressure here. I'm just here to do my duty by you both
and help for a little while. Then I'll take my paperwork
and go back home. You don't have to worry about that."

Amos cleared his throat. "So *Mammi* told you what
the doctor said?"

Miriam nodded.

"Okay, then," Amos said with a sigh. "I guess it's
decided."

Miriam looked toward the kitchen. There were
dishes to wash, and dinner would come soon enough.
She grabbed a blue apron from a peg on the wall and
tied it around herself.

"I'll cook and clean while I'm here," Miriam said.
"So you won't have to worry about that. I'll even get
some food put aside into the freezer. You still have one
in the basement, don't you?"

"Yah," Amos said.

Other people would come by with food, as well.
Amos would be fed after his grandmother passed.

"I'm ready for a nap, if you two don't mind," *Mammi*
said.

"Let me help you to bed," Amos said, and as *Mammi*
pushed herself to her feet, he went to her side, steadying
her.

Miriam was back in her married home, and it was
strange how little had changed around here. Granted,
she could see the corner of a bed in the sitting room,
making things easier for *Mammi*, but the rest of this
house remained the same.

She touched a blue, chipped teapot on the counter, and her mind swept back to the day she'd moved into this old house as Amos's wife. She'd been full of hope back then, and that blue teapot had been new—a wedding gift. She'd unpacked it, washed it and made their first pot of tea as a married couple. Amos had brought whoopee pies—the chocolate kind with the white, whipped centers. She loved them, and he knew it. Their first meal together in that house had been whoopee pies and hot tea.

Ten years ago, she'd still thought that *Gott* had blessed her with a home of her own, and that her talents would be celebrated by this quiet, new husband of hers...

Miriam picked up the warm teapot and emptied it into the sink. The teabag fell to the bottom of the sink with a splat.

Ten years ago, Miriam had still thought that those wedding vows guaranteed some sort of special blessing onto the well-meaning couple—a hedge of protection, or a deeper well of wisdom...but she couldn't have been more wrong.

Miriam had made a mistake to marry Amos, and as a good Amish woman, there was no way to undo it. But she could help now—for a couple of weeks while they needed it most.

Chapter Two

"*Mammi*, what are you doing here, asking Miriam to stay?" Amos asked as he helped his grandmother lower herself onto the side of her bed.

The stairs had gotten increasingly difficult for her in the last couple of months, so Noah and Thomas had helped him to bring her bed downstairs. There was no extra bedroom down here, so the sitting room had turned into her private room for the time being, and it saddened him to think that when the sitting room was returned to its proper purpose again, *Mammi* would be gone.

"I'm doing what I should have done a long time ago," *Mammi* said. "I'm trying to help you two reach some peace."

"So you admit to meddling?" he asked with a tired smile.

"It isn't meddling exactly," she replied. "It's making you face each other. I have no power over what conclusions you'll come to, but you need to face her, Amos."

Amos sighed. His grandmother might be right.

"Now?" he asked sadly.

"If not now, when?" she asked. "I wouldn't have written to drag her back here, but she showed up on the doorstep, and that felt…providential. Sometimes *Gott* is working in mysterious ways, and you have to let Him."

There was no arguing with *Mammi*. She was convinced that *Gott* was always working, always moving, and every little coincidence was orchestrated from above. And after his parents passed away—first his father, and when he was a teenager, his mother—*Mammi* had been the one to take him into her home and raise him. So he knew his *mammi* very well, and to try to convince her that, just this once, *Gott* wasn't up to something…it wouldn't work.

"Do you need anything, *Mammi*?" he asked. "A glass of water?"

"No, no," she said, lying down on her pillow. "I took my pills earlier. I'm fine. I just need rest."

Amos looked back at *Mammi* for a moment, and she looked so small, so thin. She used to be a plump grandmother who plied all the kids who came over to play with Amos with pie and sweet, Amish peanut butter sandwiches. When he'd been struggling with his father's gruff, overly strict ways, it had been *Mammi*'s softness that had been a respite for him. She'd made him believe that there was still beauty in the world, despite the difficulties in his home. She used to be a source of quiet wisdom, which included some memorized scripture or a line from a hymn.

But the years had caught up to *Mammi*, and for all she'd done for him in years past, she needed him now to take care of her. But she was trying to do something good before she left them all—he just wasn't convinced that she was doing the right thing. She could focus on someone else, or even use these last weeks for herself…

Would she die disappointed? That thought gave his heart a squeeze.

When he emerged into the kitchen, Miriam looked up from the sink full of dishes she was doing.

"I know this is awkward," she said, then turned back to washing out a pot.

"Yah," he agreed. "But I don't think I could turn *Mammi* down right now."

"Me, neither." Miriam didn't turn toward him again. She continued scrubbing, her shoulders hunched up as she worked.

Amos stood there for a moment, wondering if he should go find some work outdoors, but he couldn't quite bring himself to leave just yet. There was something about seeing his wife's familiar figure at the sink that had him rooted to the spot.

How many times had he dreamed of this—one more chance to fix their relationship? But it was different in the light of day.

"Miriam," he said.

"Hmm?"

"What are you going to do?" he asked. "After you leave, I mean."

"I told you," she replied. "I've got a strip mall in Edson that brings in an income." She glanced back. "If I can find the documents that prove it's mine."

"Ours," he qualified.

Some color touched her cheeks. "Yes, ours."

Amos sighed. "Dry your hands. Come on."

He headed for the staircase and didn't even wait to see if she followed him, but he heard her footsteps as she caught up, and they hit the top stair side by side. Amos opened his bedroom door and headed straight to his closet. He pulled down a cardboard box. When he turned back he saw Miriam standing tentatively in the doorway.

"You're my wife," he said. "I imagine you could step foot in here without fear of scandal."

Miriam smiled faintly at that, then stepped inside. "It feels strange. That's all."

It felt a little weird to him, too. This used to be their bedroom together, and even when they were fighting and going to sleep back-to-back, as far from each other as possible, it had still been theirs. He put the box on the bed and sat down next to it.

"Are the documents in there?" she asked.

"I don't know," he replied. "But I haven't gone through it since you left, so…"

He still remembered that horrible day when he'd come back from the shop and found the house cleaned to a shine, and a letter on the kitchen table. His stomach clenched at the memory. It had been four days before he'd been able to cry over his loss, and that had happened in the stable, sitting on a hay bale and sobbing his heart out into his own calloused hands.

Miriam's gaze dropped to the box, and she sank onto the bed on the opposite side of it. Amos opened the flaps. Inside, there was an envelope and he opened it and slid out their marriage certificate.

"There's that," he said, passing it over.

Miriam took it wordlessly. He rummaged through and found an old tax return, and a few pens with their names and the date of their wedding printed on the side. For what that was worth now.

There was an old *kapp*, a little dusty, and a few hairpins. He passed them over, then pulled out a comb that had been hers, too.

"You kept all this?" she asked at last.

"It didn't feel right to throw it out," he said, and his gaze dropped to the *kapp* in her hands. "It was still perfectly good, that *kapp*. And the hairpins. I mean... they were still—" he was just repeating himself now, but she'd always left him a little tongue tied "—they were still good."

As if that explained why he'd kept it all. Whatever their marriage had become, when Amos had married Miriam, he'd been full of hope, and those last feminine touches around his home had reminded him of the life he'd dreamed of but never got to enjoy with her.

The last item in the box was a half-finished wooden box. He'd started the engraving on the edges and never finished it. Miriam picked it up and turned it over in her hands.

"It was going to be for our anniversary," he said.

Miriam nodded. "Where did we go wrong, Amos?"

"We're just very different people," he replied with a shrug. "And I drive you crazy."

She smiled faintly at his humor, and they fell silent for a moment. She'd driven him crazy, too, for the record. She hadn't understood how he thought or what hurt him any better than he'd understood her. It was like everything she did was geared to prove him less of a man somehow. But had she meant to do it, or were they just horribly matched?

"The papers I need aren't here," she said.

"I haven't thrown anything out," he said. "They're around somewhere. We'll keep looking. And we can check the safe-deposit box at the bank tomorrow."

Miriam nodded. "Thank you."

"When you find them…and when you go back," he said, "will you be happy?"

"I think so," she replied. "I want to build up my business. My *daet* started with one store—did you know that?"

"*Yah*, you told me," he replied. Repeatedly. Her *daet*'s story was like a legend for her.

"Well, he built it up—store by store—until he owned most of the street. And I want to do that—start with the strip mall that I have, and manage it well so that I can buy another business to actually manage. The secret is in having more than one business—more than three actually. Leasing out the strip mall is my first, but if I can make a decent profit, I'd like to buy something more traditional."

"Like?" he asked warily.

"I don't know—something truer to our Amish roots. I was thinking of opening a fabric shop, or a bakery. Maybe a carpentry shop. I could buy another piece of property on another street. I don't have to be there to physically run the new business, but I could manage it—I can hire people for the day to day operations. But I'd need to choose the type of business carefully so that I could make enough to give decent wages. That's important to me—that people are able to make enough."

"I pay my guys well," he said.

"That's a good thing." She nodded. "If you were ever looking to sell—"

Amos pushed himself to his feet. "Sell? You think I'd give up Redemption Carpentry?"

The business that *he'd* grown from the bottom up? Was he supposed to give up, or something?

"No, just—" She shrugged. "I was just saying. I didn't mean anything by it."

"If I was ever looking to sell, you'd be the last person I'd sell to," he added.

"Why?" she demanded, rising to her feet to match him. "Because I'm a woman?"

"Because you spent every single day of our marriage comparing me to your father," he snapped. "Your *daet*, the business genius. Your *daet*, the respected entrepreneur. Your *daet*, who was a humble, Amish man despite the fact that he owned a good chunk of that town."

That last part was meant to be ironic, because her father hadn't been humble in the least, but people had been forced to make him feel like he was. He owned too much—they depended on him. Charities went to Leroy Schwartz first, because his support would be the most crucial. Miriam had been used to a certain amount of deference that came from being Leroy's daughter, except Amos hadn't deferred to her. He'd been her husband, and he'd expected her to trust him.

"My carpentry shop never did measure up to your father," he said.

"That's not true," she replied. "You were only starting out. Of course you wouldn't have what he did."

"It certainly wasn't enough for you," he said. "You didn't marry me for the man I was. You married me for the man you thought you could make me into."

"I married you…" She sucked in a breath and her eyes snapped fire. "I married you because I was an idiot who thought marriage was the answer to everything. I was wrong about that."

They both were. He'd thought that a decent Amish woman in his home would bring happiness, too. He'd thought that if he could find a woman of faith like his *mammi*, that he could sidestep the misery his parents had endured. He and Miriam had both been naive.

"My father was a good man," Miriam added. "And he left big shoes to fill."

"Your brother will be fine," Amos said with a sigh. "He's inheriting enough that he can afford to make a few mistakes and not suffer from it."

"I was talking about myself." She met his gaze with a glittering glare. "I'm stepping into his shoes."

"You're going to try to be like him?" Amos asked in disbelief. "That's a man's role. What about your home?"

"Here?" she asked uncertainly.

"Anywhere. Your kitchen. Your quilts—"

"I'll do both," she said, then she shook her head. "Maybe I won't quilt, Amos. I live in my father's house with my brother and his wife, and we've managed to keep house so far."

"And that's enough for you?" he asked. "A shared house with your brother, and a sprawling network of businesses that call you 'ma'am' like some Englisher woman?"

"Englisher?" She seemed to hear the insult in that word. "You call me that? I'm a Schwartz. My family has been Amish since we came over from Switzerland. Being successful doesn't make me any less Amish!"

And he wasn't as successful, just a small-business owner who made enough to pay his workers and a little extra to set aside for retirement. That was the hint, but he wasn't going to do this. They'd fought enough to last a lifetime.

"I'm not trying to argue," he said, moderating his tone. "I'm sorry."

Miriam crossed her arms over her chest, not seeming to have heard his apology. "I won't have *kinner*, Amos, but I'll still grow something that will outlive me. I'll still contribute to my community with jobs and quality goods, and I'll make a space for myself. Sometimes that space takes a little money in order to carve it out. That's just life. But I won't be ashamed of success, my own or my father's."

Amos ran a hand through his hair. "We're Amish! It isn't supposed to be about money!"

"Money is a tool, Amos," she said. "It isn't supposed to be about the *love* of money. There's a difference."

Was there, though? He didn't exactly think that poverty was a virtue, but Jesus had talked about the wealthy and eyes of needles, hadn't He?

"I don't want to fight with you," she said.

"*Yah*, me, neither," he said, but his words sounded angry, even in his own ears. What was it with this woman that could rile him up this way? He was normally a calm and reasonable man, but staring Miriam down like this, he felt like all of his rational ways deserted him.

Miriam had a deeper, more challenging kind of attractiveness. Her eyes had a depth to them that he'd never seen in another woman. And the way she angled her chin when she was holding back an opinion had always stuck with him…

Funny how their disparate personalities had led to as many kisses as arguments—as unhealthy as it seemed to be, their attraction was linked to the fighting. That wasn't Amish, at all. He caught her gaze, and her flushed cheeks brought out a glitter in her eyes. There had been a time when he'd been able to kiss those pink lips…but not now. Fighting and making up couldn't support a relationship for any length of time. Amos's parents seemed to find a balance of arguments and then gentleness, but he couldn't have called his mother happy exactly. And it wasn't like he wanted the relationship his parents had had—he was trying to avoid it.

"If we keep up like this, we'll only upset *Mammi*," Miriam said.

She had a point, and Amos let out a long breath. "*Yah*. Let's stop fighting about all the old problems and get along for a couple of weeks."

"Okay. I agree," she said.

He held out his hand, and she took his. Her hand was slim and soft, and he shook it gently. "And don't worry—we'll find your documents."

"I hope so."

"They're here, Miriam." He glanced around. "Somewhere."

Couldn't she trust his word with just one thing?

"Now, I have to go see Noah and Thomas," he added. "They know about *Mammi*, but we need to discuss some things together, and they'll want to come see her. Can I let you take care of things here while I do that?"

"Of course," she replied. "I'll make a big enough dinner that if people come they'll be fed."

"Thanks…"

And just like that, he had a wife in his home again. For all Miriam drove him crazy, he was grateful to have someone here to help him, even if she did stir up a stew of powerful emotions. But that had to stay safely beneath the surface until she'd left again. He didn't have the strength to face both his grandmother's passing and his unrealistic hopes at the same time.

His heart had never been safe with Miriam.

Miriam peeked under a clean dish towel at the rising little domes on the baking pan. She was making a batch of buns to go with a large pot of beef stew. It would stretch to feed extra people, and it generally tasted good.

But Miriam had never been a fantastic cook like her friends had been. She'd been the one who could do math in her head faster than her brothers could on paper, and her father had proudly used her as his "Amish calculator." She'd had other skills, even back then.

And it was hardly fair that her *daet*, who had encouraged her in this, who had been so proud of her business acumen, hadn't left her anything more than the property bestowed on her at her wedding. She was thirty-five years old, and if her *daet* had wanted her to become more feminine and focus on the cooking and cleaning, he shouldn't have focused on teaching her the family business skills. She wasn't a pet to teach to do tricks—she was a woman who'd believed that she had her father's respect. That will that left everything to Japheth had been *Daet*'s judgment from beyond the grave—he'd cut her down to size, just not to her face.

Miriam took the lid off the bubbling pot and fished a piece of beef out to test its tenderness with a fork. It wasn't soft enough, and she dropped it back in.

"Did I sleep long?"

Miriam looked up to find *Mammi* in the doorway, her *kapp* a little askew.

"A few hours," Miriam replied. "Here—I'll help you with your *kapp*."

She crossed the room and adjusted *Mammi*'s *kapp*, pulling out the hairpin and replacing it gently.

"Thank you, dear," *Mammi* said. "Where did Amos go?"

"To see Thomas and Noah," she replied.

"Ah. Yes." *Mammi* didn't say more than that.

"I heard some rumors about my husband taking in some boys," she said.

"*Yah.* They're the sons that Amos never had."

Miriam felt a stab at those words—the sons she'd been unwilling to provide apparently.

"They're grown now," *Mammi* added. "He took them in after you left, when they were teens in need of a proper Amish home. They were so scared. So alone."

"Where were their parents?" she asked.

"Their father died, and their mother went English. She wanted them to go with her, but those boys were devout and they wanted to stay. So she agreed so long as they stayed with Amos. She trusted him. So Amos stepped in, and he raised them the rest of the way. Their mother visited, and she eventually came back to the community. But we all became a family by choice."

"That's…quite lovely," Miriam admitted.

"Yah," Mammi said. "We love those boys—well, men now—very dearly. And they're both married and growing their families."

As Amish people did. Or as Amish people were supposed to do. There were always a few who didn't follow the mandate to be fruitful and multiply. Miriam rubbed her hands down her apron.

"*Mammi*, I'm going to bring a more comfortable chair into the kitchen for you," Miriam said, and she headed into the sitting room to gather up one of the upholstered chairs that had been shoved against a wall to make room for the bed. She dragged it out to the kitchen, then fetched an ottoman to go with it.

Mammi sank into the chair and allowed Miriam to pull the ottoman closer. Then the old woman looked wistfully toward the kitchen. "You look like you're cooking for a crowd."

"People are going to want to see you, *Mammi*," Miriam

said. "They love you. I'm just preparing…in case people come by."

Mammi nodded. "Funny how quickly the time passes. I still feel like I could be thirty-five, you know. Well, maybe not thirty-five. That's how old you are, isn't it? And you seem almost like a baby to me." She laughed softly. "I feel like I could be fifty, though. Eighty-eight creeps up when you don't notice."

"You're eighty-eight?" Miriam asked. She'd never known *Mammi*'s age before.

"Yah." *Mammi* turned toward the window, and her gaze grew sad. "You don't want to get to my age and have regrets, Miriam. You want to take hold of these years and live them to the full. There's no going back. Once they're gone, they're gone."

"Do you have regrets?" Miriam asked.

"A few," *Mammi* said, and she looked toward Miriam. "I wish I'd enjoyed my husband a little bit more. I didn't realize I'd lose him so young. And I wish I'd argued with my sister less. I wish I'd known how to help my son, who was addicted to drink and gambling… I just didn't know. Nothing I tried worked."

Miriam was silent. Perhaps no one was completely free of regrets. She had a few of her own, the biggest one being her wedding. Miriam went back to the counter, checked the rising buns and decided they were ready for the oven. She added a few more coals to the fire, and then slid the pan of buns inside.

"There is a customer who won't pay Amos," *Mammi* said.

"What's that?" Miriam closed the oven and straightened.

"At the shop," *Mammi* said. "There is a customer

who won't pay him. They promised to pay up, and never did. Amos keeps thinking that because it's a big company ordering furniture for a show home that they can be trusted."

"Why are you telling me this?" Miriam asked with a shake of her head.

"Because I thought you might have some insight for him," *Mammi* replied. "While you're here, you might help him out a little bit."

Miriam chuckled softly. "*Mammi*, if only you knew how much Amos would hate to have me meddling in his business."

"Oh, I know just how much he'd hate it," *Mammi* replied, and a smile flickered at the corners of her lips. "It would still be good for him."

The women exchanged a smile and Miriam rolled her eyes. "You're not sounding like a good Amish woman, *Mammi*."

"Ah, but I'm a very good grandmother," she countered.

Outside, Miriam heard the crunch of buggy wheels and the clop of hooves. She went to the window and looked out. That wasn't Amos, or at least the first buggy wasn't Amos. It was a younger man with a blond-haired woman at his side. There was a little girl peeking over their shoulders, and the woman seemed to be talking to the child very seriously.

People were coming, but so was some help in the kitchen. Another buggy pulled into the drive behind the first one with another couple, the man's marriage beard still short, and the woman had a baby in arms. Was Amos really leaving her alone to host people she didn't know? Her heart sped up, but then she saw the third buggy—and it was Amos.

He sat tall, and his dark gaze was locked ahead of him. He always had been a good-looking man—those broad shoulders, the strong hands. He held himself with more confidence now, and she found it hard to tear her gaze away from him.

But she did, and she commanded her heart to stop that hopeful pattering. She might be able to feed people, but that was where this ended. This was Amos's life, and Amos's chosen family.

A few minutes later, the women came inside with the little girl and the baby. They gave Miriam a brief hello, and then went to *Mammi*'s side, bending down to speak with her quietly. Miriam watched them—there were some tears, some reassurances, and *Mammi* kissed the baby, and the little girl tried to crawl onto *Mammi*'s lap, but her mother stopped her.

Then the door opened again and the men came in, the buggies now unhitched, it would seem. They were all somber and quiet, and when Amos looked across the kitchen, he caught her eye and held it.

"I would also like to introduce you to my wife," he said, raising his voice so that it reverberated through the room.

The kitchen silenced, and all eyes turned to her. At first, no one moved, then the woman with the little girl rose to her feet and crossed the kitchen.

"It's nice to meet you at long last," she said. "We've heard about you."

Nothing good, no doubt. Miriam gave her a silent nod.

"I'm Patience," she added. "Thomas's wife."

Then one by one, the others came by to do the

same—Thomas and Noah, and then Noah's wife, Eve, with their baby boy, Samuel. The little girl was named Rue, and she stared at Miriam with wide, wary eyes.

"Come, Rue," Patience said, holding out her hand. "Come say hello."

Rue came to Patience's side and whispered loud enough for Miriam to hear, "She's the bad lady…"

Patience's face flooded red. "I'm sorry, she sometimes says things—"

"It's all right," Miriam said. "I'm sure people have talked. I understand."

This was what she'd agreed to, wasn't it? She'd said she'd stay for a few weeks, and that would entail running into people who would have heard about her. Women who left their husbands were considered dangerous, on pretty much every level.

"Let us help you with the food," Eve said, and she passed the baby over to her husband.

"Rue, you can help set the table," Patience said, casting the little girl a smile.

Miriam looked at the other two women uncertainly. Would they hate her? Make sure she felt just how wicked she was in their eyes?

Amos came by the stove, his large frame filling up the kitchen. The women moved to the side, slipping away to give them momentary privacy. Amos lifted the lid of the pot to look inside the bubbling, savory depths, and Miriam watched him uncertainly.

"It looks really good, Miriam," he said, his voice low enough for her ears alone. He replaced the lid. "I appreciate you helping me out like this," he added. "Truly."

And all those feelings she'd tried to command came flooding back—her old hopes and tender dreams. What was it about this man that made her knees turn to wet noodles with one piercing glance? Being Amos's wife would have been lovely, if they'd been more compatible, and if she'd been able to give him the family he wanted. But he'd found a way around it, and he'd had that family without her.

She should be glad for him.

"*Yah*, it's not a problem," she said, and her voice sounded breathy in her own ears. Then she smelled the scent of bread, and she tapped him aside and pulled on her oven mitts. Amos stepped back, his strong arm brushing against hers as he did so, and she swallowed hard, pretending that it didn't feel as sweet as it had.

She'd do her duty by her husband—in the kitchen at least—for these few weeks. And when she left, she'd be certain that he was fine without her. Maybe there was wisdom in *Mammi*'s request, after all.

Chapter Three

Amos led the family in worship that evening around the kitchen table. It was comforting to be all together, sharing the sadness and the prayers as a family. They all took turns praying for *Mammi*, even little Rue. They prayed for healing, and for comfort, and for reassurance for her that whatever happened, *Gott*'s will would be done and that *Mammi* would be protected from pain. *Mammi* asked them to sing her favorite hymn, too, and when they were done, *Mammi* was tired again and the women, Miriam included, helped her to get into her nightclothes for bed.

The men were left alone in the kitchen, Noah holding his infant son in his arms. Samuel was asleep, nestled against Noah's chest. Anyone just seeing this young father for the first time would never guess that this baby wasn't biologically his. He'd met his wife when she was eight months pregnant, but for Noah, there was no difference, and *Gott* had knit them together into a family more truly than DNA ever could. It was similar to the way *Gott* had made Amos, Noah, Thomas and *Mammi* into a family, too, and Amos had been so deeply thankful for what *Gott* had given him these last few years.

The men rose from the table and moved toward the windows. The sun had set, and the first few stars were piercing through the dusk.

"I don't know what I expected from Miriam, but she seems nice," Thomas said.

Amos looked over at the younger man. Thomas had a reddish beard and a more confident way about him now that he was a married man.

"That was never the problem," Amos replied. "She's a decent person."

"What *was* the problem, then?" Noah came up next to them, gently patting his son's diapered rump.

Amos sighed. "We're very different, and we just couldn't seem to get along. She didn't want *kinner*, either, and—"

"She didn't?" Thomas's eyebrows went up. "Really? Even now?"

"*Yah.* She's got a family history of trouble in childbirth, and it scares her," Amos said. "But it wasn't that, even. I mean, we could have adopted. She's from a wealthy family, and I don't think she realizes just how privileged she was. She was always trying to improve me, and I...hated it." He felt some heat hit his face. "I'm not explaining this well. We didn't get along. That's all that matters, and without *kinner* in a home, there isn't much reason for us to stay together and drive each other crazy, is there?"

"Do you think you might try again to make it work with her?" Thomas pressed.

"No." Amos shook his head. These men were both

young, and they'd married women who were well-matched to them.

"She came back, though," Noah said. "She could have left again if she didn't care."

"I think she does care," Amos admitted. "She wouldn't have agreed to stay and help *Mammi* if she didn't, but it doesn't change the complications between us. I tried to fix things a year after she left. I wrote her some letters, and I went to speak with her father."

"And?" Noah asked.

"And…it didn't go well. Her father thought I was beneath Miriam and he said that he'd encourage her to go back to me if I could prove I was a better provider than I'd been," Amos said.

"A better provider." Thomas's lips turned down.

"I had the carpentry shop, and I was building it up," Amos said. "That wasn't enough for a Schwartz, it seems."

"Did Miriam know what he said?" Noah asked.

"I told her. She defended her father. Even when that man was fully in the wrong, she would defend him and insist that I respect him. I couldn't keep fighting and pushing for something that would never work. I told her if she wanted to come home, she knew where I was. She never came."

"Until now," Noah said softly.

"She came for some papers," Amos said with a shake of his head. "Not for me. It was *Mammi* who asked her to stay. We know where we stand, Miriam and me, and we don't need to keep breaking our hearts afresh every decade."

The men fell silent. Amos didn't have any reassurances to give to Thomas and Noah.

"You two married the right women," Amos said. "I

made mistakes, and so did Miriam. But you two can learn from us, and love your wives well. Don't let bitterness take root in your marriages—do whatever you can to keep things sweet between you."

"It's good advice," Thomas said quietly, and they all seemed to sink into their own thoughts.

Patience was the first one to come back into the kitchen with Rue at her side. Patience slid a hand into the crook of Thomas's arm and the couple exchanged a sad look.

"We'd best get home," Thomas said, and he shook hands with Amos and then Noah. "Rue here needs her bed."

As if on cue, Rue's mouth cracked open in a big yawn and she rubbed her eyes.

"*Yah*, of course," Amos replied.

"I'll go get our buggy hitched, too," Noah said. "Are you okay tonight, Amos?"

"*Yah*, I'm fine," Amos said. "The doctor gave *Mammi* pills to help her sleep, and Miriam is here, so…"

Noah and Thomas both looked toward Amos at mention of his wife, but this time there was just sad acknowledgment. The best of intentions weren't always enough.

When the buggies were hitched, Amos watched as they made their way out into the evening dusk, their headlamps bouncing as they went over some bumps and headed up to the main road. Noah and Thomas would be fine—they had wives to comfort them, and *kinner* to remind them of the next generation. This difficult time would be a little gentler for them because of the women at their sides.

"Are you okay?" Miriam asked, and it jolted him out of his reverie.

"Yah." He nodded.

"Mammi's sleeping now," Miriam said. "She seems comfortable."

Amos looked down at Miriam and let his gaze move over her face. He wanted to remember her like this—when she'd stayed for a little while to help them.

"Thank you for this," he said. "I'm not sure how I'd be dealing with this without you."

"Someone else would be here—a family member from Ohio, one of those women who were here tonight, perhaps."

"Still, it was you who was here, and I'm grateful," he said.

Miriam smiled at that. "You're welcome."

She passed him and headed to the counter. She began piling up dishes, and Amos joined her. They started the water in the sink, and Amos got a dish towel to dry while she washed.

"People are going to talk now that I'm here," Miriam said.

"Yah," he agreed. "They already are."

"Oh?" She glanced up at him, and he noticed the wariness in her eyes.

"Mostly they want to know why we aren't together," he said. "They like you."

She rinsed a bowl and handed it to him. "What did you tell them?"

"That we've gone through all of this before, and we don't need to do it again every decade," he replied.

"I like that." She cast him a tired smile. "That's a good answer."

"Do you still not want *kinner*, Miriam?" he asked. "Even at this age, when we don't have much time left to make it happen?"

Miriam sighed. "I've seen specialists. I was having some medical issues, and they were connected. I asked about the likelihood of me suffering from the same problem my mother and sister did—it was curiosity mostly. They said they recommended that I not get pregnant. That wasn't a problem. I wasn't with my husband, anyway, was I?"

She rinsed another bowl, then a plate, and piled them on the dish rack next to him.

"So you were right in being scared when we got married," he said.

"Yah."

Amos was silent. He'd spent a great deal of time and energy trying to convince her that she didn't need to worry and that they should start their family. He'd been so sure that he'd been right, too. Apparently, that had been foolish on his part.

"I'm sorry about that," he said. "I don't think I took it seriously."

Miriam shook her head. "It's fine."

But was it? If he'd reacted differently, would they have found a way to stay together? He'd been so sure that she was just overreacting to a family tragedy. He'd known he should have taken her more seriously in general—at least, that was the conclusion he'd come to over the years. When a woman said she wasn't happy, a man should take that as seriously as a fire alarm.

"If I hadn't pressured you to start a family—" he started.

"Don't do that to yourself, Amos," Miriam said.

"This wasn't about *kinner*. We could have found a way to adopt—you certainly did."

"Then what was it about?" he asked.

"We're very different, you and me. And I didn't realize how different when we got married. I mean, would you have really wanted me involved in Redemption Carpentry?"

"I built up that business from nothing," Amos said. "I started it in my shed in the evenings while I worked a day job at a factory. I worked until I could barely stand some nights, getting a job done so that I could keep my reputation. I didn't need help, or advice. I didn't need you reporting back to your *daet* to have him judge me from Edson."

Miriam nodded, but didn't answer.

"Are you saying you wanted to help out at the business?" Amos asked. "That would have made you happy?"

Miriam turned and fixed her gaze on him. "I'd have liked to be the manager."

Of *his* shop. She gave him a rueful smile.

"Right now, I have a strip mall to lease out and plans for a business to start up," Miriam went on. "I won't have to ask permission to run it as I will, and *that* makes me happy. I'm my father's daughter, Amos. I have business in my blood, and I want to see what I can do when I'm not being held back by well-meaning men."

"Like me," he said.

She shrugged. "Maybe. And like my brother."

"You think you'll do better than your brother?" he asked.

"I know it." She didn't sound like she was bragging, either, just factual.

"Your father seemed to want you to take on a more

feminine role," he countered. "Why else would he not give you any more in the will?"

"I agree," she said, and rinsed another dish, then pulled a fresh pile of dirty dishes into the sink. "He did seem to want that. But I don't."

Amos sighed and took another dish to dry.

"So stop beating yourself up about all those years ago," she said, and she smiled over at him. "Even if you'd been a little more sensitive back then, I'd still have driven you crazy."

"Is that supposed to comfort me?" He chuckled.

"Yes," she said, and she smiled. "Oh, Amos. We're ten years older, ten years wiser, and life hasn't gotten any simpler, has it?"

"It doesn't seem like it," he agreed.

"If I had met you under different circumstances, I think you and I might have been friends," she said.

"You think?" he asked doubtfully.

"Actual friends," she said. "No threat of marriage on any horizon. I think we might have debated things and disagreed and stomped off…and still respected the other's opinion. Maybe if we had neighboring shops or something."

"Would you have married a different kind of man?" he asked.

A richer man was what he meant. A more successful man.

"Me?" She laughed softly. "I wouldn't have been marriageable anymore, Amos. I refuse to have *kinner*, and I'm too stubborn in everything else. No, I would have stayed single." She glanced up at him. "You would have married, though."

Miriam was right. He would have. He'd have found a

sweet woman who wanted babies and family and faith… and he would have loved her dearly for all of his life, and been grateful for the home he went back to every day. And the deeply ironic thing is that even if he'd married a different woman who would have made him happier, he would have thought back about the serious daughter of that Amish businessman and remembered the depth in those dark eyes… Even if he'd never married Miriam, she would have been in his head.

Miriam rinsed the last dish and handed it to him, then pulled the plug and dried her hands.

"Let me show you to your room," Amos said.

What they might have done no longer mattered. They'd locked themselves into this marriage, and no amount of what-ifs made any difference at all.

The next morning, Miriam stood at the kitchen counter with individual containers of hot stew in front of her. Amos had left early for work since he'd wanted to finish up a project, and he'd eaten a small breakfast with the promise that Miriam would bring them a hot lunch later in the courting buggy Amos kept for *Mammi*'s use. She and Amos would also take the opportunity to go to the bank's safe-deposit box and check for those documents. She'd feel better when they were in her possession once more.

She was already feeling rather domestic in her duties here at the house, but her mind kept skipping ahead to the carpentry shop. She was curious about it—the kind of business Amos had built for himself.

"How well does the shop do?" Miriam asked *Mammi*, who was seated in her comfortable chair pulled up next to the window.

"I wouldn't know exactly," *Mammi* replied. "Amos doesn't tell me those things."

"Right…" He wouldn't. That was the men's world, and they took care of those burdens alone. "But the business has a good reputation around town?"

"The best," *Mammi* replied. "Those men are very skilled. Amos made all the furniture in this home."

Miriam smiled. "*Yah.* I remember. Just before we married."

"That's right," *Mammi* said. "Amos's shop is known for their beautiful work. You should be proud of that." *Mammi* cast her a meaningful look.

"It isn't my work to be proud of," Miriam replied. She knew what *Mammi* was getting at—trying to give her a personal connection here. It wasn't so simple to patch things up, though.

"Where do they advertise their business?" Miriam asked. "On the local radio? In magazines?"

"They don't. They hardly need to," *Mammi* said. "Besides, most Amish people around here don't trust ads. They trust friends and family. That's how you spread the word—let it go naturally."

That didn't apply to the Englishers, though—how could they hear about the shop if there were no ads? Englishers would travel for an Amish-run shop that delivered quality goods. But it wasn't her business—literally or figuratively.

Miriam dropped her gaze. "As long as the business is doing well. That's all that matters."

"Well…" *Mammi* paused, seeming to measure her words. "I do worry sometimes…"

"About what?" Miriam asked.

"I mentioned those customers that are giving Amos

trouble about paying," *Mammi* said. "Most people are honest and willing to pay the agreed price, but some aren't." *Mammi* lifted her gaze. "Some push and pressure and complain so much that a decent man like Amos, who is dealing with a sick grandmother, might just give in."

Mammi stared at Miriam hopefully, and Miriam met her gaze, frowning. *Mammi* had apparently picked up more than she wanted to readily admit. The men's responsibilities might not be the women's business, but everyone was affected by them.

"What's going on?" Miriam said.

Mammi sighed. "I shouldn't meddle. I know that."

"But it's bothering you, all the same," Miriam said gently.

"The order they're working so hard to complete today—that is the one that hasn't been paid in full, and the customer was late in getting them the down payment," *Mammi* said. "Amos has been particularly worried about it. I overheard him talking to the boys—sorry, Noah and Thomas—and they all agreed it was a problem. It's a big enough order that if they don't get paid, they can't pay back some of their own creditors."

"How big is the order?" Miriam asked.

The number that *Mammi* said made Miriam suck in her breath.

"And you think they won't pay?" Miriam asked.

"Amos thinks so," *Mammi* replied. "Me? I just listen to them talk. But with my illness, I'm not sure Amos is at his best. If they don't get paid for this one, it'll be hard for Amos. Very hard. I know this isn't what matters at a time like this—money certainly isn't a faithful person's priority—but Amos has worked too hard to have his business driven under by unprincipled people. I'll be with *Gott*, but he has to face the coming months. He's a man with ideals, and he lives by them…but I worry."

"What would I do about it?" Miriam asked.

"I don't know," *Mammi* said, and she shrugged weakly. "Maybe nothing. But could you perhaps pray on it while you're driving out to deliver their lunch?"

Miriam took the courting buggy down the still-familiar roads that led to the town of Redemption. The afternoon was warm, and Miriam couldn't help but enjoy the grass-scented breeze. Bees buzzed around the wildflowers that grew up in the ditches at either side of the road, and beyond the barbed-wire fences, cows grazed and looked up at her passing buggy with large, liquid eyes.

Mammi had asked her to pray…

Lord, I feel like I haven't prayed enough to ask for Your guidance. I came out here to find the documents, and I didn't even bother asking what You thought of it. And now I feel like I'm getting entangled in Amos's life all over again, and I can't tell if I'll only make things worse.

Because when she left the first time, she'd ripped both of their hearts to shreds, and she'd promised herself she'd never do that again. Whatever they'd hoped marriage would be, they'd both been wrong. But in her own defense, she'd gotten a lot of advice from older married women telling her that if she just followed expectations, all would be well. A good man—any good man—would be a good husband, she'd been told.

Just don't nag him.

That little piece of advice had come from a very

happily married aunt, and it had turned out to be the most difficult to follow. Was it nagging to tell him her opinion about things? Was it nagging to point out what she'd learned from growing up with an entrepreneur father? Was it nagging to mention when he could save some money, or take advantage of a deal? Even if it wasn't, that never seemed to do well for their relationship. Amos had been sensitive about his shop and about her father's opinions about him, and if she had to be honest, *Daet* had been rather terse and curt. But he was like that with everyone—and they'd respected his words because he was a man who knew what he was talking about.

Except for Amos. Amos had taken everything so personally, and he seemed to expect things from *Daet* that others didn't. And from her, too…

"I'm sorry I wasn't a better wife, Lord," she prayed aloud. "But maybe I can help him now…in his time of sorrow. Maybe You can use me to ease his burdens a little bit, and maybe make up for not enough praying before I married him."

Because if she'd prayed hard back then and listened intently, God would have found a way to show her that this marriage wasn't His will. She was sure of it.

The town of Redemption had grown since she'd last lived here, and there were more Englisher tourists than she remembered, too. A group of women stopped on the sidewalk and took a picture of her passing buggy. She smiled and nodded at them, and they beamed back at her. If Edson could draw in more of the tourists, she could make use of this amount of passing foot traffic on a sidewalk…

But this wasn't about her, it was about Amos. Her

own business plans could wait until she got back with her documents. Maybe *Gott* had brought her to Redemption for a reason... Maybe he needed her for a little while more than he realized.

Miriam parked her buggy behind the carpentry shop with her horses under a tarp erected for shade. A few yards away, there was a large box truck, the windows open and the driver eating a fast-food burger from the driver's seat. She eyed him as she got down from the buggy, then put her attention into her own business. There was a trough of water, and after the horses had drunk their fill, she gave them their feedbags. Then she looked toward the back entrance of the shop. Did she dare go in that way?

She sucked in a wavering breath.

No, she'd go in the front.

Miriam gathered up the wooden crate that contained the towel-insulated containers of stew, and she made her way between the buildings toward the front of Redemption Carpentry. An Englisher man passing on the sidewalk noticed her attempting to open the door, and he pulled it open for her. She smiled her thanks and headed inside.

Amos was at the counter, and two young Englisher men stood there with angry stances. They wore blue jeans and dirty T-shirts. One had a trucker's cap pushed back on his head.

"Our boss is waiting," the first Englisher was saying. "And we have a truck rented and waiting out back. This is costing us money. Who's going to compensate us for that?"

"I need payment," Amos replied.

"Our boss will send the check," the second Englisher replied. "But he wants to see the furniture himself and make sure the order is right before he pays you. It's only fair."

Amos sighed and rubbed a hand over his beard. "He could have come himself and seen to that."

"He's obviously busy with other things," the first man snapped. "Now, if you aren't going to release our goods, we're going to be letting other businesses know exactly how we feel about your shoddy service. That could tank a business of your size."

Miriam's heart pounded hard and she met Amos's gaze over their shoulders. She went to the counter and deposited the crate of food, then angled her head to the side.

"Excuse me," Amos said, and followed her a couple of yards away. "Everything okay?" he asked her.

"At home, fine," she replied. "But you can't release that furniture to them."

"Miriam, this isn't your business," he said.

"I'm just saying—they'll never pay. Their boss, or whoever is cutting that check, is not going to pay up."

"They'll pay," he replied. "It's just the way Englishers are sometimes—"

"Amos, listen to me," she said, reaching out and catching his arm. "I've seen this before with my *daet*. He always said that an item loses value in the customer's eyes once it's in their hands. The invisible boss won't pay the full amount—I can guarantee that."

"What makes you so sure, knowing absolutely nothing about this customer?" he demanded.

"*Mammi* filled me in," she replied.

"Forgive me, Miriam, but we don't worry *Mammi* with these things," he said with a sigh.

"Well, she worries all the same," Miriam shot back. "And according to her, you've been worried, too. I've seen this before. An item is worth the quoted price to a customer as long as that item has not been attained. The minute they have it in their possession, the value decreases for them—it's an emotional thing. They no longer feel the pressure, or the yearning for it, and they don't see why they should have to pay top dollar anymore. They'll offer you something less, and since they've already got the furniture, you'll have no choice but to accept it."

Amos shook his head. "He's paid the down payment."

"Can you afford to lose the rest?" she asked.

"I know what I'm doing," Amos said, and while his tone was even, she could see the annoyance flashing in his eyes. He pulled his arm free and headed back over to where the men stood, their backs to them. They appeared to be making a call on their cell phone now.

"...won't hand it over," the first man was saying into his phone. "What am I supposed to do, then?"

"So *Mammi* asked you to help with this?" Amos asked, looking back at her.

"Yah." She shrugged. "It's a tough time for you, Amos. It isn't shameful to accept help. Maybe I'm the last person you want it from—and I do understand that—but I'm here. And I'm offering. For whatever that's worth to you."

Amos's expression turned stony, and he paused for a moment, considering. Then he turned to the Englishers.

"I need the payment before I release the furniture," Amos said, raising his voice. "I have to insist."

Miriam couldn't help the smile that tugged at her lips.

"My boss is going to be furious," the first Englisher said, warning in his tone.

"It's just business, my friend," Amos said simply. "I can't let that furniture go without payment. When you can sort out the payment, then we can load up."

"We'll be back," the man growled, and they headed out of the store, the cell phone still at his ear.

Miriam eyed Amos cautiously. "That was the right thing to do."

"If it wasn't, I just lost a major sale," he said.

"If he's an honest businessman, he won't be offended at you expecting payment," she countered. "I'm sure he expects payment for his services, too."

Amos ran a hand through his hair, then sighed. "I didn't know *Mammi* was worried. And I'm a little offended that she thinks I need help."

"She wants me to be a supportive wife," Miriam replied. "And in my opinion, that includes the business."

Amos regarded her thoughtfully for a moment. "You don't trust me."

"Your grandmother is dying," Miriam replied. "You're not at your best. That's understandable. *Mammi* wants me to help you, too, but I can't do that unless you'll let me."

Amos nodded slowly. "She could have asked anyone else…"

"We know what she wants," she said softly. "She wants to reconnect us, and while we both know it isn't that easy, if she knows that we're working together during this difficult time, she'll be comforted at the very least. She's worried, Amos, and if that relieves her worry…"

Their gazes met, and Amos sighed. He pressed his lips together, then dropped his gaze.

"All right," he said. "For *Mammi*. Will you help me out around here, Miriam?"

"Yah." She felt her eyes mist. "I'd be happy to."

"But you can only speak to me about your ideas privately. Never in front of my employees or the customers."

"Of course, Amos."

She'd get her husband through this difficult time, and maybe it could be penance for the rest of her mistakes. While they hadn't been a good match romantically, Amos was still a good man, and he deserved support.

Maybe You brought me here at this time for a reason, Gott, she prayed. *Gott* sometimes worked in the strangest ways.

"Let's go to the bank," Amos said. "We'll check the safe-deposit box for those documents."

Those documents were her escape. When all of this was finished, she had a life and a business waiting for her in Edson. But when she left, she would feel better for having done her duty.

Chapter Four

Amos held the door for Miriam as they headed out of the shop and onto the sidewalk. It still felt like a dream that she was even here—close enough that he could smell the faint scent of vanilla in her hair from a morning spent in the kitchen as she passed through the door ahead of him.

He'd dreamed of her over the years while she was gone... Some dreams were just his frustration working itself out. He would dream of their arguments, of him stomping out the door to try and find some peace outside, and he'd wake up in a sweat, relieved that he wasn't actually pitted in some week-long mental struggle with his own wife.

Noah and Thomas used to tell him that he talked in his sleep—loud enough to be heard through the walls. He hadn't done that since he was a boy, and he'd been filled with all the anxiety of his mother's unhappiness. She'd been sad a lot—and sometimes as a child he'd watch her just standing there in the kitchen, motionless and so weighed down by unhappiness she looked like she might crumble.

"It's not your fault," she used to tell him. "It isn't your *daet*'s fault. I just have this cloud that seems to find me... That's all. It's just a cloud."

Back when his mother was consumed by her cloud and had crawled into her bed after her work was done to lie alone there, his cousin who slept over sometimes used to tell him that he talked in his sleep, too. There was something about the sadness he couldn't fix that had worked its way into his dreams back when he was a boy, and it seemed to come back again after Miriam had left.

But other dreams of Miriam had been softer and sweeter. One night, not too long ago, he'd dreamed of holding her hand, and feeling the softness of her skin, and smelling that feminine aroma of baking and sunlight that clung to her clothes and hair... He'd woken from that dream with such an ache of loneliness inside of him that he'd been forced to get up a full hour before sunrise, just to try and shake it.

And now Miriam was here, still smelling faintly of baking and sunlight. It was almost cruel that his dream of her had matched the reality so well. Couldn't *Gott* make this easier on him?

But maybe Amos didn't deserve easy. He'd married the wrong woman, and now he would pay. What a man planted, so did he reap. Did Amos have any right to ask *Gott* to change those rules on his behalf?

A man in a passing buggy leaned forward to openly stare at Amos and Miriam, and Amos sighed. That was Isaiah Kemp, a local farmer who lived on his grandfather's land.

"We've been spotted," Amos murmured.

"I noticed that," she replied. "Sorry."

"It's okay. It was bound to happen sooner or later."

And people would ask questions. That kind of gossip would fly around town—Amos's runaway wife was back in town. They'd be wondering if Amos and Miriam were reconciling at long last, and then they could all discuss it afresh when she left again. As much as Amos hated being the topic of local gossip, he was glad he had a community that cared.

"What will you tell people?" she asked, glancing toward him warily.

"That we had some business together," he said. "It isn't really their business. What do you want me to tell them?"

"That we have some business together is fine," she said.

"Do you miss any of them?" he asked. "I mean—do you miss any part of living here in Redemption?"

Miriam's expression turned wistful. "I miss our first few weeks of marriage. That was a nice time."

Amos tried to remember those first few weeks. They hadn't known each other well, and there had been so many guests, so many invitations to honor after their wedding. Every Amish new couple was inundated with friendliness.

"We were so busy," he said.

"Too busy to fight yet," she said, and she shot him a smile. "I miss that—when people were happy for us, and the women were teasing me about learning to cook for you, and…and no one was mentioning babies quite yet."

"Yeah…" Come to think of it, maybe he missed those first few weeks, too, before either of them realized that this was a monumental mistake.

The bank was three blocks east of Main Street, and as they walked along side by side, away from the busy Main Street, Amos felt some of his tension fade. There were no buggies on this particular street, and the people who stopped to stare at them were tourists. He could handle the curiosity of strangers. Amos glanced over at his wife.

"So, do you have anyone discussing the fact you came to see me?" he asked. "Did you start any gossip in Edson by coming out here?"

She shrugged. "I might have. My brother knows I'm here, and he knows why. I called from the phone shanty yesterday so he wouldn't worry and left a message with an Englisher business. They'll pass it along—to more than my brother, I'm sure."

"He's really going to insist that you prove you own that strip mall?" Amos asked. It seemed petty, especially when Japheth had inherited everything else.

"Yah." She shrugged. "He thinks I should do my duty and come back to you."

Amos raised his eyebrows. "Really?"

Amos hadn't had a terribly warm relationship with his brother-in-law.

"Japheth said that *Daet* was wrong about giving you such a hard time, and that I should have come back and learned how to be a proper wife," Miriam said. "He said I should be minding a home, not a strip mall."

"Did he always think that way?" Amos asked. How long had Amos had support from her side of the family and not known it?

"Japheth never would cross *Daet* when he was alive," she replied. "But that isn't the first time my brother told me to come back to you. You should be grateful I don't let my brother bully me, or I might have been on your doorstep sooner."

Amos hadn't known that his brother-in-law had been encouraging her to go back to him—that was news.

He tried to smile at her humor, but he wasn't sure he managed it. It wouldn't have been terrible to see her sooner…if she'd wanted to be a proper wife to him again.

"Maybe he meant well," Amos said quietly.

"I tried to be the wife you wanted, Amos," she said. "It didn't work. It's harder to change yourself than you anticipate. And my brother wants me involved in his business just as much as you want me in yours. That's all this is—I'm in the way."

Amos dropped his gaze. He couldn't argue with that. She had absolutely refused to stay in the home, and Amos took his role as man of the home seriously. It was his job to run the business and provide financially for his wife. Whatever it took to bring home enough money to keep them comfortable and pay his employees, he'd do it. She needed to trust him, just as he needed to trust the running of the home to her. He'd never tell her what to cook, or when to plant the garden, or when to harvest the vegetables. He'd never tell her how to arrange her own kitchen or when to air out the bedding. That was her realm.

Except they'd hardly known each other when they married, and she *hadn't* trusted him to take care of things.

Redemption Credit Union was on the corner, and Amos let his wife go inside ahead of him. There were no Amish people in the bank that afternoon, which was a relief. And they waited in the snaking lineup to get to a teller.

"Hi, Mr. Lapp," the teller said with a smile.

He didn't bother reminding her that she could just

call him Amos. The Englishers had their own way, and she meant it as respect.

"I just want to get into my safe-deposit box," he said.

"Of course. Just a moment," the teller said with a smile. "I just have to sign out the keys."

"Do you...need to see inside the box yourself?" he asked Miriam, his voice low.

She cast him a small frown. "I trust you, Amos."

With this, perhaps. But she hadn't trusted him to provide for her.

"Mr. Lapp?" the teller said, coming back. "Just this way."

Amos went into the little sterile-feeling room beside the bank vault and he accepted his box from the woman with a nod of thanks. He put it on the table and opened it. He didn't keep too many things in the safe-deposit box—some business documents, some land deeds... And when he sorted through them, he didn't find the documents for Miriam's strip mall. He went through them again slowly, just to be sure, but they weren't there.

Where would those documents be? He hadn't seen them in years, and he never would have disposed of them.

When Amos relocked his box into the wall of the vault and came back out, he turned to the teller who had helped them.

"Thank you," he said. "Have a good day."

Miriam was silent, but she did look down at his empty hands and her disappointment was evident.

"They weren't there," he said as they came back out into the sunlight. "I'm sorry. It was worth checking, though."

"Do you have any proper filing system?" she asked.

"Of course," he replied.

"I mean for your personal documents," she said. "Because my *daet* always had a carefully organized personal filing system that was just as meticulous as his system for his businesses. He always said that—"

"Miriam." Amos's curt tone cut her off. "I know where *my* personal documents are. These are yours."

The distinction mattered, because he couldn't be blamed for misplacing her papers. She'd been the one who left so fast she'd left them behind, and he wasn't taking the blame for that.

"Fine." She pressed her lips together.

"Are you sure you don't have the documents with your own things?" he asked.

"I went through everything," she replied. "They aren't there. Trust me, it was the first thing I did. I didn't want to come here."

He felt the cut in those words. But this was hard for her, too, he realized. And now she'd given her word that she'd stay for a few weeks.

"We'll keep looking at home," he said.

She nodded. "At least we know they aren't in the safe-deposit box. That's something."

As they headed back toward Main Street, Amos looked over at her. The breeze was cool, and she rubbed her bare arms. His first instinct was to put an arm around her—it was what he would have done years ago if she were cold, but he mentally chastised himself for even thinking of it now. She might be his wife in name, but that was all.

"I'm sure we'll find the documents," he said. "It'll just take doing some searching together. We'll look when I get home tonight."

"Thank you, Amos," she said.

Amos was silent for a moment, and then he added, "I've done well with my business, I'll have you know."

He needed her to know this—that he wasn't some floundering fool, no matter how those unprincipled Englishers had made him look. He might not be the man to make her happy, but he was a man.

"Hmm?" Miriam's mind must have been elsewhere, because she looked over at him, mildly confused.

"I did well with my business," he said. "Since you left here, I've built up a three-carpenter operation. I'm well respected, and I pay my employees well. I believe in that, too—making sure Noah and Thomas can support their families on one job. I don't want them to have to look for work on their evenings in order to make ends meet."

"That's really good," she said with a gentle smile.

And he felt like a fool for even mentioning it.

Miriam's mind was on those documents as she made her way back to the buggy parking lot. If she couldn't find the document that signed that piece of property over to her, she *would* be Amos's problem. That hadn't been a joke earlier. Japheth had the official sales documents from when their father acquired the commercial property, and there were no copies of the papers that signed it over to her.

Was this her father's plan to send her back to Amos, after all? It didn't seem likely. *Daet* had been frustrated with her choice in husband. He might have liked Amos more if he'd been more deferential to *Daet*. But Amos was a man who stood tall—he was respectful, but he didn't take advice easily, and he didn't seem overly impressed with *Daet*'s accomplishments.

Not that *Daet* had wanted Amos to be in awe of him exactly. But Amos could have tried harder to win him over. Instead, Amos had simply gone about building his business the way he wanted to. With *Daet*'s advice, that carpentry shop could be three shops by now. But whenever Miriam had suggested that her father might have some ideas to help him, Amos would freeze up and refuse to hear her.

Miriam reached the buggy and stroked the gelding as she came up toward his head to remove the feed bag. She walked him to the water trough to let him drink before the ride home and waited as he did so.

"Miriam Lapp?"

Miriam turned to see a woman shading her eyes. She stood just behind the fabric shop, then she waved. It was Fannie Mast, one of Miriam's friends from that first year of marriage. She wished she could just duck out of sight, but she'd been spotted now. Miriam waved back.

Fannie headed in her direction, walking quickly with a smile on her face.

"Miriam!" she said as she arrived and enclosed her in a hug. "You're back! Praise *Gott*! We've all been praying for you and Amos to reconcile, and I have to say, my faith had gotten weak on the subject—"

"It's good to see you, Fannie," Miriam said.

"When did this happen?" Fannie asked, shaking her head.

"It…hasn't," Miriam said with a wince. "I'm here to find some paperwork, and I'm staying long enough to help Mary in her time of need."

"What time of need?" Fannie frowned. "Is she all right?"

"She's dying," Miriam said softly. "She doesn't have much time, and she asked me to help her until…until…"

Fannie's eyes misted with tears.

"Oh…" Fannie breathed. "I had no idea…"

For the next few minutes, they talked about *Mammi*'s illness and all the sadness that came along with it. Mary Lapp was a beloved member of the community, and everyone would want to help her, including Fannie.

"So you aren't home to reconcile?" Fannie said softly.

"No…"

Fannie nodded and swallowed.

"How are you doing, though?" Miriam asked.

"I'm good," Fannie said. "We have four children now—two boys and two girls." She smiled. "When you and I met, I was pregnant with Adam, and Silas was making our first cradle out in the workshop, remember?"

"I never did meet your son," Miriam said.

Silas was Fannie's husband, and they'd been quite newly married when Miriam and Fannie had met and struck up a friendship.

"Time has certainly marched on," Miriam said. "That's wonderful. *Gott* has blessed you."

"I've worried all these years…" Fannie paused. "We used to…vent…to each other…"

Miriam knew what her friend was referring to, and she batted her hand through the air.

"Fannie, it's fine. We used to complain about our husbands to each other. Your secrets are safe," she said.

"We were wrong to do that," Fannie said. "I never breathed a word of it, except to Silas, of course—I tell him everything. But we should never have spoken of

them that way. They're good men—honest, hardworking, faithful. We never should have complained about
their messy ways or the times they were thoughtless. I
wasn't a perfect wife, either, you know! And after ten
years of marriage, I have a better appreciation for the
difficulties of that first year."

Miriam felt a wriggle of guilt.

"Fannie, we might have complained to each other,"
Miriam said. "But we also encouraged each other. You
made me feel stronger—"

"Strong enough to leave him?" Fannie asked seriously.

"That wasn't your fault," Miriam replied. "Fannie,
you fell in love. Silas adored you for years before he
was old enough to court you, and you both fell in love
with each other."

"So did you and Amos," Fannie countered.

"No," Miriam admitted. "We wanted to. We thought
we would after we got married. We saw such wonderful
potential in each other, but it just…it never happened.
We drove each other crazy. We thought if we arranged
things just right, we could have what you and Silas
had—what other couples had. We wanted it, but we
were wrong in getting married as quickly as we did. If
we'd taken our time, we'd have seen the problems before we said the vows. So stop blaming yourself—this
wasn't your fault. You made my life sweeter for being
in it. I promise."

"You didn't last a year," Fannie said.

"Almost a year," Miriam said, as if that distinction
even mattered.

"Can I tell you something?" Fannie said. "This is important, and I have been thinking about it the last ten

years. I've been asking *Gott* to forgive me for my role in the breakdown of your relationship with your husband."

"Fannie…" Miriam said.

"The first year is the hardest," Fannie went on. "It just is. A wife will be upset because her husband isn't acting the way she expects him to act, and she might think that means he doesn't love her well enough, or that he's being selfish, or that he's choosing to ignore what she needs in the marriage. But that is seldom the case. Marriage is like any skill—like canning or quilting or gardening. It takes time to learn."

"*Yah*, I could see that," Miriam said uncomfortably. She wasn't looking for marriage advice, but it looked like Fannie was intent on giving it.

"That first year or two of marriage is incredibly hard, and no one talks about that," Fannie went on. "The older couples just give you your space to figure things out between you. But I had to change, too. I had to learn how to bend for Silas. I was just as stubborn as he was!"

"What changed things for you?" Miriam asked.

Fannie was silent for a moment, then she sucked in a breath. "When you left."

"Oh…"

"*Yah*. When you left Amos, I felt just sick. The thought of leaving Silas made my stomach hurt to even think about, and it rattled me back to my senses."

So her life had been the morality tale to shock Fannie and Silas into each other's arms. Miriam wasn't sure she even wanted to know that.

"And then when Adam was born, we looked down at him, and we knew that we had to do better in our marriage…for our family," Fannie went on. "We sat down and we talked things out. I said what hurt my feelings, and he said what hurt his, and we both promised to do our best not to hurt each other ever again."

A baby—the one thing that Miriam wouldn't give Amos. It was bitterly ironic that a baby was their answer, but maybe that was appropriate. Silas and Fannie had been in love—the real kind of love where they got kind of mushy around each other. Amos and Miriam had been married—and love hadn't found them yet. It was all out of reach for them.

"I'm glad you sorted it out," Miriam said, and she felt a lump rise in her throat.

"That first year *is* hard," Fannie repeated. "If you'd waited longer—"

"I wasn't having *kinner*," Miriam said.

"I know you *said* that, but—"

"Doctors advised against it," Miriam said curtly.

"Oh…" Fannie nodded quickly. "I'm so sorry, Miriam."

But she was a mother of four children, and she'd never know what it was like to be a woman without them. Some sympathy didn't count for much. Back in their early days of friendship, they'd both been newly married and on equal footing. But children changed that dynamic between them. Fannie was a mother, and Miriam was not.

"It's all right," Miriam replied. "I've made my peace with it."

They were both silent for a couple of beats. Fannie kicked a little rock across the dusty ground.

"You said you and Amos weren't in love," Fannie said quietly.

She wasn't going to let this go… Miriam had agonized over it for long enough, and she'd answered so many questions in her own community over the years. She didn't want to discuss it any longer!

"We weren't," Miriam said firmly.

"We sometimes tell ourselves stories to make ourselves feel better," Fannie said.

"The fact that we didn't love each other doesn't comfort me, believe me," Miriam said with a sigh.

"You need to know this, Miriam. When you left, Amos was crushed," Fannie said earnestly. "Really crushed. He lost weight—we all worried about him, and Mary cooked all she could to fatten him back up again… But he was just…empty. Until he took those boys in, and then he had someone to care for again. They brought him back to life."

Miriam swallowed, silent.

"It broke his heart when you left him," Fannie went on. "So you claim you didn't love each other, but I daresay that Amos loved *you*." Fannie smoothed her hands down the front of her dress. "I'd better get back. I left the *kinner* with my *mamm* while I went for errands, and the littlest one, Priscilla, was just wailing when I left, so I need to get back."

"Of course," Miriam said.

"I'm glad I saw you," Fannie said. "And I'm going to be honest with you—I'll be praying that you and Amos reconcile. I won't be praying behind your back."

Miriam smiled faintly. "It was nice to see you, too."

When Fannie left, Miriam got up into the buggy and flicked the reins. She was eager to get away from here, back out onto open road where there was no more threat of meeting well-meaning old friends.

The balance between Miriam and Fannie had certainly changed. Back when they'd been confidantes,

Miriam had been the stronger one of them. Miriam had been a few years older, she'd had a stronger personality, and she'd come from a family that had been very successful. Fannie had been younger, meeker, and she'd looked up to Miriam in a lot of ways. They'd both been new wives, and somehow, Miriam had been the "expert" on life.

Fannie didn't seem to look up to her anymore... She was now the mother of four—with both marriage experience and advice. Miriam was the one who'd failed.

The horse moved onto the road, and she urged them toward the traffic light. It was green, and she leaned forward to look both ways as she came to the intersection, and then flicked the reins as they continued forward.

Forward—always forward. That was how she lived her life.

Fannie had said that Amos had been heartbroken. And while her own heart squeezed in response to that mental image of big, strong Amos losing weight and growing thin, it didn't have the effect that Fannie would hope.

Miriam wouldn't come back home to Amos, because she knew something that Fannie refused to accept— Miriam and Amos weren't good together. And if she came back the way Fannie was praying for, then she would only end up breaking Amos's heart all over again.

She *did* care about Amos's happiness. She did... enough to never attempt to reconcile. He deserved some peace.

Chapter Five

Amos headed back into Redemption Carpentry, a frown on his face. Miriam's opinion of him had always been a sensitive spot for him. Back when they'd gotten married, he'd wanted her to see the able provider he could be, but all she ever seemed to see were the places where he might be able to improve.

The ridiculous thing was, he was the most successful he'd ever been right now. His business was doing very well, he had Noah and Thomas working full-time with him and he was well-respected in the community. Amos had nothing to be ashamed of, yet faced with his own wife, he still felt like he had something to prove to her. And every time he tried to show her what he'd accomplished, it fell flat.

If he were smart, he'd just stop trying.

Amos headed through the empty showroom and into the back shop. Noah and Thomas were both bent over some sanding, and they looked up when he came in.

"Is our customer's truck still back there?" Amos asked.

"No, they left," Noah replied. "Are you sure about sending them off like that?"

"Not really," Amos replied, and he felt a wave of irritation. "Miriam said that her father had dealt with people just like them, and this was the way to handle it."

"And she'd know?" Thomas asked, squinting.

"She'd know how her father handled things, *yah*," Amos said as he put his hat onto a peg on the wall.

"That's a lot of money to be playing with," Thomas said. "If the buyer doesn't come back—"

"It's a lot of money to play with if he decides not to pay us the full amount, too," Amos replied. "She's right. If they decide not to take the order, then we'll sell the pieces individually. We'll get paid for it, just a little more slowly."

Still, he'd been anticipating that large check—he couldn't deny it.

"Wollie Zook put in an order for a kitchen storage cupboard," Noah said, turning back to his sanding.

Wollie Zook was a friend of Noah's back when they were *kinner*, and Wollie had gone English some years ago when he married an Englisher girl. They had four *kinner* of their own, and now they were living in the Amish area again.

"So Natasha is really converting to Amish?" Thomas asked.

"*Yah*, it would seem so," Noah said. "Last time I was there, she was in a *kapp* and apron. Her mother-in-law was teaching her how to sew dresses for the girls."

Amos let out a low whistle. No one had seen that coming—when a man went English for a woman, he didn't normally bring his whole family back with him.

"It's not easy for her," Noah went on. "Natasha is an

English speaker, and the Dutch isn't coming very naturally to her. She's trying, though."

"How can she do the baptismal classes if she can't speak it?" Amos asked.

"Wollie went with her at first and was translating, but that was disruptive," Noah replied. "So the bishop is doing that particular baptismal class in English for her sake."

"That's nice of him," Amos said.

"If you want to bring someone into the fold, you have to make room for them," Noah said.

"Amen to that," Thomas murmured, and Amos glanced at the younger man. Thomas was sensitive about making a welcoming place for Englishers—his daughter was an Englisher girl and Dutch was her second language, too.

If they wanted to bring Wollie Zook back into the Amish community, then they had to make room for Wollie's wife. She was so very English...everything about her was different—the way she spoke, the way she stood, the way she looked at people so directly. The way she parented was just...louder. An Amish mother could murmur a remonstrance and have her child obey, but Natasha could be heard giving a lecture to her *kinner* all the way from the road.

"Patience is teaching her some basic Dutch," Thomas said. "But Rue keeps trying to compete with her, and I don't think it's fun being shown up by a five-year-old."

Amos chuckled. "Maybe she just needs friendship."

Noah and Thomas both nodded at that.

"This might sound crazy..." Noah looked up. "But I think that Miriam and Natasha might actually get along. I think they both could use a friend."

"That's not a bad idea," Thomas agreed. "Sometimes the oddest combinations can make for lifelong friends."

Amos rubbed a hand over his beard. Was Miriam lonely? The thought tugged at his heart.

"She hasn't been back in Redemption for years, right?" Noah said. "Does she want to connect with any old friends?"

"She's been avoiding them," Amos admitted.

"Then she might appreciate a new friend," Thomas said.

"She's not staying," Amos reminded them. "She's here for a couple of weeks, and then she's going back."

Still, the thought of his wife's potential loneliness had softened a part of his heart. She'd always been a little bit on the outside of things. When they were married, they'd been arguing a lot, which meant that she didn't have that soft, comforting home with him. She had a few friends, but she didn't know anyone well—the friends she'd grown up with and her family were in Edson. Add to that, she was so different—something he only really noticed properly after they were married. She was stronger, more focused, more stubborn than the other women seemed to be. Miriam was more of everything.

"Are you sure you want her to leave?" Thomas asked.

Amos sighed. "It isn't about that."

"How is it not?" Thomas asked. "She's your wife. If you wanted her to stay—"

"It isn't that simple," Amos said. "Besides, she wouldn't want to be at home. She'd want to run the shop."

The men exchanged a look. So they were finally understanding what he was getting at.

"Like, she'd run the front of the store?" Noah asked. "That might not be a bad idea. As it is, we have to run back and forth to serve customers and take orders while we're working. If we had someone who could stay out front and help customers, someone who couldn't be pushed around—"

"She'd want more than that," Amos said. "She'd want to change how I run things."

"What makes you so sure?" Thomas asked.

"I know *her*."

Amos wasn't in the mood to debate this. He knew his wife far better than Thomas and Noah were giving him credit for. He and Miriam had already fought battles that these young men had no knowledge of.

Maybe they were right about one thing, though. Maybe Miriam could use a friend while she was here— someone to distract her from his life a little bit.

The bell above the front door tinkled, and Amos headed for the showroom. When he got there, he saw the owner of the show homes standing with his arms crossed over his chest, looking around with a frown. He was a portly man with a cowboy hat and a large buckle, and when Amos came into the room, his gaze snapped up.

"Hello," Amos said.

"Mr. Lapp," the man said with a tight smile. "I'm not happy to have to come down here myself, I'll have you know. When I sent my men to pick up the order, I expected you to release it."

"I expected payment," Amos replied quietly. "I'm running a business here, Mr. Boone. I can't release the furniture without payment."

"You and I had an agreement," the other man said irritably. "I came to an Amish business because I thought my handshake would mean something here. I came for the old-fashioned moral fiber."

Amos didn't answer. He wasn't going to argue the morality of a handshake right now. A handshake only meant something when two men knew each other.

"Fine." Mr. Boone sighed, and he pulled a money order out of his pocket. "Here it is, in full. But I'll need to take a look at the furniture before I hand this over."

"Perfectly fair," Amos said. "Right through here. We have everything ready to load up. Do you have the truck here?"

"It's waiting around back."

Miriam had been right, it seemed. This Englisher businessman was ready to pay up, if Amos put his foot down with him. And looking at him now, Amos had a suspicion that once the man got the furniture, the payment wouldn't have been quite so prompt. Amos pulled out the paperwork for the order and nodded his head toward the back door.

"I have the order outlined right here," Amos said. "We can take another look at it together."

As Amos ushered the man through the back, he felt a wave of relief.

Thank You, Gott, he prayed. *We needed this.*

And maybe, just for today, he'd needed Miriam, too.

That evening, after they closed up shop, the men stood in the back room, their hats on their heads and the crate of rinsed, empty dishes from Miriam's hot stew all ready to go. It had been a productive day, and with that payment from the big order in the bank deposit envelope, Amos felt like they'd be all right. At least he'd be able to tell *Mammi* that she need not worry about it anymore.

"I'm tired," Noah said. "I'm looking forward to Eve's good cooking." He winced. "We could bring you some dinner, Amos."

"No, no," Amos replied. "My wife will have cooked."

The words came out more casually than he'd even intended. It had been so long since he'd been able to say anything like that, and he felt his face heat.

"Give *Mammi* our love," Thomas said.

"And ours, too," Noah added.

"Of course," Amos said. "I'd better get back. *Mammi* gets really tired in the evenings, and I want to be able to spend as much time with her as I can tonight."

"We're praying for her," Noah said. "And for you."

"Thank you." It meant more than the younger men might know, but in times like this, Amos wasn't expecting healing so much as he was longing for *Gott*'s comforting presence. "I'm going to go to Blueberry Bakery before I leave so I can bring *Mammi* some whoopee pies," he added.

"She'd like that," Thomas said.

"*Yah*, she would."

"We'll hitch your buggy so that you can leave right away when you get back from the bakery," Thomas said. "It's the least we can do."

Amos felt a lump rise in his throat. These were good men, and he was glad to claim them in his makeshift family circle.

So Amos started up the road at a brisk pace, his heart heavy in his chest. He wanted to bring *Mammi* whoopee pies to make her smile, but these weren't only *Mammi*'s favorite treats, they were Miriam's, too. The first night they spent in their own house, Amos had made sure to have a box of whoopee pies from Blueberry Bakery, because Miriam loved them. He could still remember how she'd looked with a touch of cream at the corner of her lips and her eyes sparkling with happiness.

He pushed back the memory. *Mammi* loved whoopee pies, too. What Amish person didn't? If he brought those pastries home, would Miriam think he was trying to remind her of something?

He felt a tickle of nervousness at that thought. Maybe he was...

Regardless, Amos owed Miriam his sincere thanks today, and he ruefully acknowledged that *Mammi* might enjoy his humbled position with his wife even more than she'd enjoy the whoopee pies.

Dear, sweet *Mammi*.

She always was a matchmaker at heart. If only her last attempt at bringing a couple together could have some hope of working out, because *Mammi* would really enjoy that.

Amos would have to make do with whoopee pies.

Miriam stood at the kitchen counter peeling potatoes. It was a job she could do without even thinking, her fingers knowing the work so well that the pile of peels grew steadily without her hardly noticing.

On the porch, *Mammi* was sitting in the rocking chair chatting with a neighbor, Doris, who had stopped by to see her. The two older women's voices came filtering back through the house with the grass-scented breeze, soft and warm. They were talking about people the used to know years ago... "That Yoder boy, the one with the leg brace," and "the King family from Indiana—the

ones who sang so beautifully." Miriam smiled wistfully. It was good that *Mammi* could have time with her
friends remembering the richness of her life.

Outside the kitchen window, a neighbor boy was cutting the lawn with a push mower, the blades whisking
through the grass. He ducked his head as he worked, his
straw hat pushed back so that his glistening forehead was
exposed. She watched him work for a couple of minutes,
in the way she watched all children these days. If *Gott*
had given her a different constitution, she might have
had a strong, strapping boy like this of her very own.

But *Gott* didn't make mistakes, and she wasn't going
to waste her time railing against Him. So she turned
back to her cooking. Dinner tonight would be chicken,
mashed potatoes, gravy and some canned green beans
from last year's garden. Tonight she had a feeling they
could all use a little comfort on their plates, and nothing
seemed to feed heavy hearts better than chicken dinner.

The visit with Fannie had been on Miriam's mind
all afternoon. Fannie and Silas had obviously worked
out their difficulties, and there was a disparity now between Miriam and Fannie. Miriam had been strong back
when she and Fannie had been friends—she'd been confident, sure of herself…and she'd been very sure that
Amos was wrong. Fannie had been less certain of herself, more worried about what her new in-laws thought
of her, and more heartbroken every time she and Silas
had an argument.

And in Miriam's humble opinion, Silas had been in
the wrong, too. He hadn't been taking his young wife's
feelings into account. He'd been demanding and unwilling to bend. But they'd sorted things out appar-

ently. They'd finally found a way to understand each other, after all.

Today, Fannie had been the stronger one, more sure of herself, and perhaps for good reason. The goal had been to have a happy marriage, not to go back to her father's home in disgrace, even if she did help grow a business. Comparing herself to her old friend, she felt embarrassed. How many diatribes had Miriam gone on that Fannie would remember now in a much different light? How many silly things had Miriam said about what made a marriage work that Fannie would shake her head about?

That was one problem with being opinionated and talkative—the Bible said that "In the multitude of words there wanteth not sin: but he that refraineth his lips *is* wise." In the multitude of words this time, there had been a whole lot of foolishness, and Miriam's face felt hot even now thinking about it.

Outside, she heard the clop of horses' hooves and the crunch of buggy wheels along the gravel drive. She looked out the window to see Amos's buggy pull up next to the stable. Amos said something to the boy with the push mower, and the boy grinned up at him and nodded. Amos always had been good with children. They liked him.

Miriam turned back to peeling potatoes into a big black pot, the strips of potato peel dropping to a bucket on the counter next to her. By the time Amos had finished with the horses and his footsteps sounded on the steps outside, Miriam had finished with the potatoes and set the pot on the stove to boil.

The side door opened, and Amos came inside, a bakery box balanced on one palm. Miriam put the lid onto the pot and shot him a hesitant smile.

"It smells good," Amos said.

"Thank you," she replied.

He put the box onto the table, and then went back into the mudroom. The water turned on as he washed his hands, and she stood there, eyes on the box, waiting for him to come back out.

"So, how did it go at the shop?" Miriam called.

Amos came out of the mudroom, still drying his hands. He tossed the towel into a hamper by the door.

"Fine," he replied.

"The business that owed you money—I imagine the manager called you?" she said.

"No, he didn't call." Amos met her gaze with that calm, reasonable way he had that had always driven her crazy. He knew what she was asking.

"Oh… No?" Had she gauged that wrong?

"They did come back and pick up the order," he said.

"Did they pay?" she demanded.

Amos smiled. "*Yah.* They paid."

Was that so hard to tell her? She shot him an irritated look. "Good. That's what I wanted to know. The full amount?"

"What if it weren't the full amount?" Amos asked, crossing his arms over his chest. "What would that mean to you?"

"It would mean you were taken advantage of," she replied. "And I'd ask for his phone number to speak to him directly. That would be unethical business, and if he wanted to play fast and loose with businesses in this area, he can find himself with a very bad reputation in these parts. As it is—"

"He paid the full amount." Amos picked an apple from the fruit bowl on the table and took a crunching bite.

Was this a game for him?

"Why wouldn't you just tell me that?" she said.

"Why does it matter so much to you?" he asked. "I've kept myself in business for the last twenty years without your help or input. I'm sure I can continue on my own."

"It's the principle," she said. "I don't like seeing rich men taking advantage of a small business. It's not right. Of all the people who can afford to pay, it's a big company like that. My father always paid his bills early—every single little bill. Even the small ones that didn't seem like they mattered, because he knew that those small bills paid kept small businesses running—"

"So you're comparing the big business with your father, and I'm a little business, just struggling to keep myself afloat," he said, his gaze locking on to hers. She knew that tone—she'd offended him again.

"Amos, I'm not the one who said you needed that payment," she said. "And now you have it. I thought you'd be happy."

"It's how you see me, Miriam," he said. "It's how you've always seen me. I'm not some man struggling to begin. I'm respected in this community, you know. Well respected."

"*Yah*, I know!" She turned away, irritated, then turned back. "I'm not insulting your position in the community, Amos. I'm not suggesting that you're unable to run your own business. But I do think you could do with a little more respect from the Englisher businesses you sell to. How many of them have short-paid you? How many have expected deep discounts in order to do business with you again? *They* don't respect you nearly enough!"

"Let me ask you this," Amos said, his gaze narrowing. "How many businesses have you actually run all by yourself?"

She blinked at him. "My father owned—"

"I'm not asking about your father," he said. "You. How many have you owned and operated, making all the decisions yourself, accepting any consequence that came from them on your own shoulders without any hope of someone bailing you out? How many?"

Was he trying to embarrass her now? She felt the blood drain from her face, and she pressed her lips together. This was why they'd always fought. Because he couldn't see when she was helping! He refused to see when she was right!

"You think watching my father run a veritable empire taught me nothing?" she asked curtly.

"I think watching something done and doing it yourself are two very different experiences," he replied. "And until you've run your own business, you have no right to give advice as if you were your father. You aren't Leroy Schwartz. He might have taught you, but he didn't put those businesses into your hands."

Because her father had never intended for her to run them—that was the thought that was running through Miriam's mind, and it settled like a rock in her chest. Her *daet* hadn't left her even one business to run on her own. He'd given everything to Japheth, even after ten years of her working tirelessly by his side. He'd never given her the chance to prove herself.

Miriam felt her chin tremble with emotion, and she looked up to see *Mammi*'s friend Doris standing in the doorway to the kitchen. She must have come through the front door, and they hadn't heard her.

Amos's ears turned red, and they both instinctively angled away from each other.

"I just wanted to let you know that I'm heading back

home to start my own dinner," Doris said, glancing between them. "I don't want to leave Mary alone out there. She needs help to come back inside."

"Thank you for telling us," Amos said. "I'm sorry about—" He glanced toward Miriam. "We, uh, we were just having a discussion. Everything is fine."

"Hmm." Doris raised an eyebrow, and Miriam felt the judgment. This time, it might be deserved. *Mammi* needed a supportive and loving environment, not two people who fought like a couple of magpies.

"I'll go help her inside," Amos said, and he headed back through the house toward the front door with Doris on his heels.

Miriam stood there for a moment, her heart pounding in her chest. Amos always had known how to cast a barb that hurt. He didn't even know he was doing it, because she'd never told him how deeply her father's choices had stung her. He was doing what he did best—making a point.

She turned toward the table and saw the bakery box sitting there. She moved toward it, and plucked the lid open. Inside there were three plump, chocolate whoopee pies with white, whipped centers.

Tears welled in her eyes. Whoopee pies. Had he remembered that first meal alone together, a pot of tea between them and a box of whoopee pies? She looked in the direction Amos had gone, and there was the sound of the front screen door slamming shut and the murmur of voices outside.

She shut the lid to the bakery box.

Amos had probably forgotten that little detail about their history. Because if Amos had any fond memories at all of their brief time together, they hadn't softened him one bit.

Chapter Six

Mammi sat in a rocking chair on the porch, her hands folded in her lap. She had a blanket over her legs despite the warm weather, and she looked up as Amos came outside and gave him a gentle smile. Jeremiah Miller, the boy mowing the grass, had finished his work and he waved as he headed back up the drive. Amos had hired the boy to do the mowing for a set amount each month, and so far, he'd been doing a good job.

"Doris said you're ready to come in," Amos said to his grandmother. "It was nice that she came by."

"*Yah*, I was glad to see her. I treasure these times now even more than I did before. But I'm not quite ready to come yet," she said. "Why don't you sit?"

The only other place to sit was the swing, and Amos settled onto it, leaning forward onto his elbows to keep himself stationary.

"It's a lovely evening," Amos said.

"*Yah*," she agreed. "How did things go with that big order?"

"Uh—" He wasn't sure how much his grandmother had overheard from inside. "It went well. They paid in full."

Mammi smiled. "So your wife was of some use."

Amos nodded and gave his grandmother a rueful look. "*Yah, Mammi,* she was."

"Did you tell her that?" *Mammi* raised her eyebrows.

"I—" Had he said it in so many words? "I told her that they paid."

"That didn't sound like a grateful spirit inside there," *Mammi* said.

So she had heard. He felt his face heat. "Did you all hear that?"

"*Yah,* I'm afraid we did," *Mammi* said softly. "I won't lie to you, Amos."

Amos scrubbed a hand over his beard and looked in the direction that Jeremiah Miller had gone. The boy looked over his shoulder, then picked up his pace. Amos felt a wash of shame. He had no business arguing with Miriam like that—even if she saw him as beneath her. What must young Jeremiah think? And very soon the Millers would be discussing what happened here today.

"I'm sorry about that, *Mammi.* Miriam and I—" He cleared his throat.

"You know how to pluck each other's last nerves," *Mammi* said. "I know, dear. I don't mean to make this harder on you. You are a calm and sweet man, and Miriam might be the only woman capable of getting a rise out of you."

"She might be," he agreed, and he looked at his grandmother in misery. "What do I do with her?"

"You might get further if you stopped insulting her late father," *Mammi* said frankly.

"I'm not insulting him—" Amos started.

"You are," she said. "Leroy Schwartz may have been a difficult man, and I know that he did nothing to help you and your wife reconcile. He was proud—forgive me for pointing it out—but he was also her *daet*. And she isn't going to see his faults, especially now. How do you think it helps to point out the things that hurt her most?"

Amos sighed. He had every reason to resent her late father. Leroy had been obstinate and had encouraged his daughter to stay away from her marital home. He'd expected Amos to somehow raise himself up to a higher level to be worthy of Leroy's youngest, his much-loved daughter. Leroy had set impossible standards for Amos to achieve in order to gain his respect, and that had left Amos angry and resistant. But that adored daughter would see her father differently.

"Your *mamm* and *daet* struggled to get along, too," *Mammi* said. "Your *daet* was not a gentle man. But you aren't like him—"

"And Miriam isn't like my *mamm*, either," he countered.

"No, she isn't," *Mammi* agreed. "Still, growing up you didn't have a good example of a happy marriage at home. I don't know why your *daet* was so hard on your *mamm*. Your grandfather had many a stern discussion with him about it, too, I can promise you. It wasn't right, Amos."

"I know that," he said, feeling a rise of defensiveness. "I know that better than anyone. Do you think I want to end up like my parents?"

"Of course not," *Mammi* sighed. "May I give you some advice, Amos?"

"It couldn't hurt," he replied, his voice tight.

The last thing he wanted was to end up like his father. His father was the one who made their home so nervous and unhappy—he'd been clear on that all this time.

"Be the change you want to see in your relationships," *Mammi* said softly. "It feels ever so justified to point out where someone else is going wrong, but dear boy, you have to look at the plank of wood in your own eye first. And we all have one. So treat your wife with the consideration you would like her to give you." *Mammi* smoothed her hand over the blanket on her lap. "I was married for a good many years, Amos. I know that it works."

"Was *Dawdie* ever difficult?" Amos asked. "Like my *daet* was?"

"Sometimes, but not for long," she said, and she smiled over at him. "In a long marriage, people learn how to bring out the best in each other. We're all capable of sinking to our worst, Amos. But with a husband and wife, they have to learn how to find the best in the other and draw it out. Because we're all capable of goodness, too. And maybe we need to be willing to let someone draw out the best in us, too, or you just get caught in a stubborn circle. That was a lesson in life that your *daet* never took to heart."

And maybe that was the secret to the next few weeks. Amos needed to change his approach to Miriam. He needed to be a better man.

"I'll try, *Mammi*," he said. "Thank you for the advice."

Mammi smiled and held out her hand. "Help me up. We should go inside now."

Amos rose to his feet and took his grandmother's frail hand. He steadied her as she stood up, and put an arm around her to help support her weight.

"The food smells wonderful," *Mammi* said. "Miriam has worked hard. Don't forget to acknowledge that."

"I won't forget, *Mammi*," he said with a faint smile.

* * *

Mammi ate very little at dinner, but she beamed in appreciation of the whoopee pie for dessert. She took a small bite and nodded her thanks, but she didn't eat much more than that.

"I'm ready to take my medication and go bed now," *Mammi* said. "I hope you two don't mind."

Miriam helped *Mammi* to change, and then Amos lifted her into bed. He sat on the edge and read some of her favorite passage from the Bible while her eyes drifted shut.

"'The Lord is my shepherd; I shall not want. He maketh me to lie down in green pastures: he leadeth me beside the still waters. He restoreth my soul: he leadeth me in the paths of righteousness for his name's sake—'" He paused and looked down at his grandmother's slow breathing. She was asleep, but this next verse was for his own comfort. "'Yea, though I walk through the valley of the shadow of death, I will fear no evil: for thou art with me; thy rod and thy staff they comfort me...'"

Mammi looked peaceful in her slumber, and he closed the Bible and put it down on the bed next to her.

Gott, be with my grandmother, he prayed, and he rose to his feet and headed out of the front room, now dim with the shut curtains, and went through the hallway to the kitchen. All was silent and still. The dishes were done, the table cleaned off and the scent of dinner still hung in the air. He spotted the open bakery box on the end of the table—there was one whoopee pie left.

Amos closed the box and carried it with him outside. *Mammi* had been right—he needed a better start with Miriam this time around. These few weeks together didn't have to be misery. They could respect each other, and maybe Miriam felt disrespected by him, too.

He let the side screen door clatter shut behind him, and as he walked around the side of the house, he saw the chains of the porch swing moving back and forth before he spotted Miriam behind a veil of lilac bushes.

Had she come out here to avoid him? And if she had, did he blame her?

Amos cleared his throat as he came around to the front of the house, and Miriam stopped swinging.

"There's a whoopee pie left," he said, holding up the box.

"You go ahead," Miriam said. "I don't mind."

"Do you want to share it?" he asked.

Miriam's cheeks pinked. "It's okay, Amos. You don't have to smooth things over with me."

"I think I do," he countered. "I haven't been entirely fair to you. *Mammi* pointed that out, for the record. And she was right. I'm being hard on you for things you had no control over."

Amos came up the steps and Miriam moved over on the swing.

"If you come with dessert, you can sit," she said with a small smile.

Amos sat down next to her and they resumed the slow swinging. He opened the box and held it out to her. Miriam broke off a piece of the whoopee pie and, using one hand to catch crumbs, she took a bite.

Amos did the same—and finally the dessert felt like the treat it was supposed to be.

"I was being sensitive," Miriam said quietly. "My *daet* didn't leave me anything to run. You don't know how that feels. He left it all to Japheth, and left me nothing. After working with him more closely than my brother did!"

"Really?" Amos looked over at her. "I thought Japheth—"

"Oh, *Daet* let him oversee a few businesses himself," Miriam said. "So I guess there is that. But I was the one who was at *Daet*'s side. I went with him when he checked on his management, and I went over financial statements with him, and double-checked numbers from the bank. I was the one listening to all of *Daet*'s advice. I was there."

"I didn't mean to rub that in," Amos said.

"I know…" She took another bite. "But I'm sensitive about it, all the same."

Amos nudged her arm with his. "I'm sorry he did that."

"Thank you." She took another small bite.

"Do you remember that first meal we had when we got married?" he asked.

Miriam's gaze flickered up to meet his. "I thought you'd forgotten."

"Of course not," he said. "Whoopee pies were your favorite, and I wanted to make you happy. That's why I bought them this time—you and *Mammi* both love them and I hoped that it would… I don't know…make us all feel some happiness."

"It was thoughtful," Miriam said. "I had a tough day today."

"You had a victory today," he replied. "I should have thanked you properly for your help with that big order. You were right about them. If I'd done it my way, I would have lost money. So thank you."

Miriam smiled. "You're welcome. Am I allowed to mention that my *daet* taught me that?"

"You already did mention it earlier, and I'd rather not get into it again," he said, and he laughed softly. "Miriam, you can take the credit for having seen a situation that needed a different approach. That was you."

Miriam nodded. "I know you didn't get along with him, Amos, but I miss him. He might have been gruff and ornery, but never to me. He was always kindness and patience with *me*."

Even old Leroy could be softened by his youngest daughter, it seemed.

"It must still be a very fresh grief," he said softly.

"*Yah*. Very fresh," she whispered.

"I'm so sorry for all you lost when your *daet* died," Amos said. "I know how you loved him."

Miriam's chin trembled and she looked away to hide her emotion, but she didn't need to do that with him. He was her husband, after all, and if she couldn't cry over her father's death here, then where could she do it?

Amos reached out and took Miriam's hand in his. He ran his thumb over the tops of her fingers and then gave her hand a gentle squeeze. She squeezed his hand in return.

"No one loves you quite like your *daet* does," Miriam said, her voice thick with emotion. "I feel almost... orphaned." She pulled her hand back and wiped her cheeks with the palms of her hands.

Amos had lost his parents young, and that adrift feeling of not having a *mamm* and *daet* here in the land of the living to encourage him and be proud of him had never quite gone away. But he'd never had a warm relationship with his own father, so maybe he was envious that she'd had that.

"I know I'm not quite what you wanted, Miriam," he

said. "I know our relationship isn't any kind of ideal, Amish or English. But I want to make things easier for you—for what I'm worth."

And he meant it. They might end up with a strange friendship forged over years of supporting each other from a distance, but he would always be her husband—for the rest of their lives.

Miriam took another bite of the whoopee pie, and the sweet cream mingled with chocolate cake. White paint flaked off the porch floor where her shoes touched, and she let her gaze move out to the freshly mown yard with the neat rows of grass clippings. She loved this scent—one she hadn't stopped to enjoy in far too long. She'd always been so busy with *Daet*.

It was strange to be swinging with Amos like this... almost like a regular married couple, enjoying a spring-time evening after dinner. Maybe she'd spent so much time with *Daet* because she'd been able to avoid see-ing other happily married couples, like Japheth and his wife, Arleta. Being with *Daet* let her forget what she was missing out on, because he'd always been peculiar, and he'd never remarried.

"You can have the rest," Miriam said, nudging the box in Amos's direction. He took the last piece of whoopee pie, and for a moment, they ate in silence.

"There has to be a way for us to be happy," Amos said.

She shot him a wary look.

"Not living together," he clarified. "I mean... No one else is going to understand our arrangement, but there has to be a way that we can be friendly toward each other and both live the life that gives us the most contentment."

"So what would be different than what we've been doing the last ten years?" she asked.

"Maybe we could...stay in touch?" He looked over at her. "Write letters. Visit from time to time. I do wish you well. I wouldn't mind seeing your strip mall in Edson one day."

Did he mean it? Sitting here with him on this swing, it almost felt possible that they could have some sort of workable relationship that kept them friendly.

"Maybe we could try that," she said.

"I don't want to see you unhappy, Miriam," he said quietly. "Especially not because of me."

"I'm okay, Amos—"

"No, it's more than that," he said. "I never told you much about my *daet* because he didn't match up to yours...at all."

"Oh?" She felt her breath catch. It was true, he'd never spoken much about him. But he'd passed away when Amos was a boy, and she'd assumed that was the reason.

"My *daet* believed that the Bible was the answer for everything," he said.

"It is," Miriam said frankly.

"But the Bible doesn't mention every single thing that a person might encounter," Amos said. "There might be situations where we have to extrapolate an answer from the Bible. My *mamm* was depressed. I don't mean she felt blue or a little moody sometimes. I mean that she struggled with feelings so miserable that she would take to her bed for a week at a time." He licked his lips and glanced over at her. "One winter, when she was in one of her bad stretches, she wandered out into a snowstorm, and she would have frozen to death out there if *Daet* hadn't gone after her."

The thought chilled her, and they stopped rocking. He'd held all of this inside?

"You were embarrassed to tell me?" she asked.

"*Mamm* and *Daet* were already gone," he said. "And quite frankly, I didn't want to give you anything more to look down on than you already had."

Miriam blinked at him. "Amos, I wouldn't have looked down on you."

"You already did," he said. "But I don't want to argue about that. The point is, my *mamm* suffered from depression, and after that snowstorm my *daet* brought her to a doctor. The doctor prescribed some medication, and when *Mamm* took it, she felt a lot better. She was more like herself. She'd get up and cook meals and talk to us about our days at school. She'd mend our clothes, and plan for the weekends."

"So, it helped," Miriam said.

"It did," he said. "The problem was, my *daet* didn't like the idea of the medication. He said if taking some pills made her act normally, then she could act normally without them. He said she should pray more and try harder. So he took the pills away."

Miriam frowned. "That sounds cruel. If a doctor said—"

"We don't agree with everything an Englisher doctor says," he said. "And *Daet* drew a line. I often thought it was the expense—they had to pay for every bottle of them, and if *Mamm* needed them daily, well, that would add up. Anyway, *Mamm* stayed off her medication for a long time. She struggled through her sad times, and she did her best to keep taking care of us when she was so unhappy that I was afraid she'd go walking out into a storm again. But I'd seen what life could be like when she took those pills, and it was wonderful! It was happy in our home again… But *Daet* wouldn't allow her to do the one thing that would make her happy."

Amos looked over at Miriam, sadness swimming in his dark gaze.

"Oh, Amos…" she murmured.

"I promised myself I'd never do that to a woman," he said softly. "I told myself that I'd never stand between my wife and happiness."

Miriam's breath caught. "You don't!"

"I'm glad. I want you to be happy, Miriam. And even if what it takes to make you happy goes against my view of what ought to be, or how things ought to work, I won't stand in your way."

Miriam felt a welling of sympathy for her estranged husband. There was so much he'd never told her…so much she'd never even imagined lay beneath the surface. She slipped her hand into his warm, calloused grip.

"I appreciate that, Amos," she said.

His hand tightened around hers, and they started to swing again, back and forth, his strong hand moving gently over her fingers. He was a handsome man, and sitting here holding his hand, she could imagine so much more between them… But that would be selfish of her. She knew her true personality, and she knew how little Amos wanted her meddling in his carpentry shop. Some respect and sympathy between them didn't change who they were at heart.

In a way, it was easier to resent him than to respect him, because then she had to admit how much she was missing out on with this marriage—how much she was letting go. What must the other women in the community, like Fannie, think of her now?

"Are people talking about us?" she asked.

"A few," Amos replied.

She nodded. "I saw Fannie Mast on the way home today."

"Oh?" He looked over at her. "You two used to be good friends."

"Sometimes I think that *Gott* might be trying to teach me some humility, Amos," she said quietly. "Of all the things I was proud of, *Gott* has stripped them away. I was proud of my family, and my *daet* is dead. I was proud of our businesses and our ability to grow them successfully, and they have all been left to my brother if I don't find those papers. And once, years ago when I was young and idealistic, I was proud to have a husband."

"You still have a husband," he said.

She smiled at him faintly. "In our way, I suppose. But not in the way anyone else would approve of. Fannie used to fight with Silas so bitterly. Did you know that?"

Amos shook his head. "No. They seem so happy—"

"It's private, so you can't say anything. This is a secret I'm telling you as my husband. She did the same with Silas," she said. She knew Amos well enough to know that she could trust his discretion.

"Okay…"

"Apparently, they are happy now," she said. "But when they first got married, they were like anyone else and they had to adjust to married life. Silas wasn't very affectionate. He expected Fannie to do her duty, put the meals on the table, to clean the house and take care of the garden, and he never once thanked her for any of it. She was…" Miriam thought back to the young, newly married Fannie. "She was very sensitive, and kindhearted, and hopeful."

"What improved things for them?" Amos asked.

"I left." Miriam looked over at him.

"No…" Amos shook his head.

"I'm serious," she replied. "I was a wake-up for them. I used to encourage her to tell Silas how she felt, and to stand up to him. He could be such a bully…"

"And when you left, it scared them, seeing what could have happened to them if they carried on that way," Amos said.

"I think so," Miriam replied. "That, and she no longer had me there to encourage her to revolt."

"Did you?" he asked.

She felt some heat in her cheeks. "A little."

Amos chuckled softly. "No harm done. They're fine now. They have all those *kinner*, and seem very happy when I see them on Service Sunday. Silas and I get along quite well."

"Is he…nice?" Miriam asked. "He didn't seem very nice to Fannie back then. Is he kind? Does he respect her?"

"Yah," Amos said. "He loves her dearly, Miriam. He talks about her all the time. Fannie's baking, Fannie's singing, Fannie's garden… You'd think there was only one woman on the earth."

So Silas *had* loved her… Was it possible that Miriam had been stirring up trouble for that couple when what Fannie had needed was a little encouragement? If so, she hadn't meant to, and she felt truly sorry for it now. Back then, she'd thought that most women must be just like her—chafing at the restraints, eager to do more than women's work or run a small shop, to wrap her brain around some new challenge that could really excite her. But that didn't seem to be true. Most women in their communities loved their time at home, their time with their *kinner*, evenings quilting with friends...

Other women were content.

"I was foolish back then," Miriam said quietly. "And Fannie now knows it."

"How so?" Amos asked.

"I thought that Fannie was just like I was," Miriam said. "I thought she just wasn't strong enough to stand up to her husband and tell him what she really needed. I used to encourage her to have it out with Silas, to tell him what she really thought of how he acted toward her. I thought she deserved better treatment. Maybe the one she wasn't strong enough to stand up to was me."

Amos was silent, but he cast her a sad look. Her strong personality had always been her biggest weakness, and there was no getting around it. It was what had kept her single in Edson, too.

"It doesn't matter now," Miriam said, and she pulled her hand back from his warm, comforting clasp.

"You weren't the terrifying storm you seem to think," he said quietly.

"No?" she said. "Then why didn't anyone come after me to talk me into coming back?"

There hadn't been any women coming by to talk to her about forgiveness or to give her advice about making up with her husband. There hadn't been any visits from elders and their wives to give some advice to a woman who'd run away from her husband.

"Because your father was particularly imposing," Amos replied, but he smiled as he said the words, taking the sting out of them.

"That's true," she admitted ruefully.

Her *daet* had certainly had a way about him. He

could use a single look to cow an Englisher businessman trying to drive down a fair price. And he'd used
that look in protection of his daughter.

"Miriam, you were nothing like I expected," Amos
said. "But we're okay. We're both living happy lives.
I've got Noah and Thomas, who treat me like family,
and *Gott* has been good to me. I feel blessed with the
life I lead. I really do."

Miriam looked over at him—the calm, content man
she'd married. And she was so far from content, so far
from happy with how her life had turned out. But if
she'd learned something on this trip back to Redemption, it was that her own frustration couldn't be put
onto others.

Her husband had built a happy life without her, and
she couldn't upset another life just because she felt unsettled and not quite fulfilled.

"I'm glad," Miriam said. "I'm going to take a walk,
I think. I could use a little time alone."

Amos nodded. "Sure. Thank you for sharing the
whoopee pie with me."

They stopped swinging and Miriam stood up. She
needed to walk and pray, and see if she could find a
portion of that trusting contentment that her husband
had found. If *Gott* could give Amos that kind of peace,
maybe He would grant it to her, too.

Chapter Seven

The next morning, Amos went out early to gather eggs from the chicken coop and then muck out the stables where their three horses were housed. The air was cool, and dew hung heavy on the grass and the small, barely sprouting garden plants. He paused at the outside row of pea plants and touched the coiling springs.

He glanced back toward the house. There was a light on in the kitchen, and he saw Miriam pass in front of a window, her arms full of wood for the stove. He stood there, motionless, letting the moment wash over him.

His wife was home.

It felt strange…uncomfortably good. He couldn't get used to this obviously. She wasn't staying. But *Mammi* had been right that some help around here while she was so sick was incredibly welcome. Just recently, the outdoor chores as well as the cooking and what he could manage of the cleaning had fallen to him. *Mammi*'s health had started failing rather abruptly.

The sun was peeking over the horizon, glowing pink in the mist that hung over the fields. Mornings like this one had always made him feel closer to *Gott*. He'd often thought about the fact that *Gott* had given them sunrises and sunsets. He could just as easily have created a world where the sun came up and went down with the same regularity and no fanfare. But *Gott* splashed the sky in color twice a day.

And that same *Gott*, the one who loved them enough to give them beauty for the sake of beauty and did not make mistakes, was going to bring *Mammi* home one day soon. Amos trusted *Gott*, but that didn't stop his heart from breaking. *Mammi* had been a beautiful spot in his life. She was like a splash of sunrise.

The rumble of an engine drew Amos's attention, and he walked toward the drive to see a pickup truck coming up to the house. He knew the vehicle well—this was Wollie Zook.

"Good morning!" Amos called as he sauntered toward the truck.

Wollie turned off the engine and hopped out. He was dressed in Amish clothes, which looked odd coming out of the driver's side of a vehicle.

"Good morning, Amos," Wollie said.

"How are things going?" Amos asked. Wollie wasn't coming by for a chat, he was pretty sure. There was something wrong.

"I didn't want to disturb you all, but I've got a problem over at my place that I need a hand with."

"Oh?" Amos said. "What's wrong?"

"It's an axle on my buggy," Wollie said. "It got knocked out of alignment going over a pothole, and I can see the problem, but I need a hand fixing it."

"Is that why you're back driving the truck?" Amos asked.

Wollie's face colored a little. "*Yah*, well… I didn't

have a lot of time. I wanted to come find you before I headed to work, and..."

Some conveniences were hard to let go of. If Wollie were living a fully Amish life, he'd have walked to his nearest neighbor, not driven to his neighbor of choice.

"It's okay," Amos said with a shake of his head. "I can help you out. How much time do you have before you leave for work?"

"About three hours," Wollie said. "My shift doesn't start until ten."

"I can help you this morning. Noah and Thomas have keys to the shop—I can be a little late," Amos said.

"That would be great," Wollie said. "Thank you."

"For sure." Amos nodded again, and he eyed the younger man. "It's not easy, is it?"

"Coming back Amish?" Wollie let out a breath. "It's supposed to be easy for me—I was born to this life. But it's not as easy as I thought. I got used to things—Englisher conveniences that just saved time. Like the truck. I told myself I wouldn't drive it again, but I kept it, just in case of emergency. I've got four *kinner*, after all, and Natasha is expecting again. We haven't told anyone yet, so don't tell people, if you don't mind."

"Congratulations," Amos said. "That's great news."

"Thank you," Wollie said. "But all my other *kinner* were born English, and...things can go wrong. I'm feeling cautious."

"*Yah*, I know," Amos said.

Wollie pursed his lips. "It's not easy for Natasha, either. She's been trying to use the woodstove that we had installed a couple of months ago, and she's having trouble with it—burns just about everything she cooks. As for sewing—my *mamm* is still sewing my shirts for me, because it's too much to ask Natasha to do." Wollie dropped his gaze. "I've started to wonder if I was wrong to ask her to live an Amish life with me."

"Wollie, you married an Englisher woman who was willing to try to be Amish with you. That's something extraordinary right there," Amos said seriously.

"True, that isn't common, is it?" Wollie's gaze flickered toward the house. "Your wife is back, isn't she?"

"*Yah*, for a little while," Amos said.

"Not for good?" Wollie asked.

Amos sighed. "Our marriage is complicated. Be thankful for a wife who can live with you English or Amish. You are a blessed man, Wollie."

Wollie smiled. "*Yah*, I am."

His smile faltered. He looked worried.

"Miriam isn't really a homemaker," Amos said. "So I don't think she'd be the right one to teach your wife how to keep an Amish home."

"I think she needs a friendly face, more than anything," Wollie said.

Miriam had a soft spot in her heart for struggling wives, it seemed. "Maybe she'll be willing to show her some basics. I mean, she's a good cook…"

"Do you think she might?" Wollie said. "I think my wife would appreciate the social contact. She's so frustrated."

"I can ask," Amos said, and felt a sudden wave of misgiving. Volunteering Miriam for something she didn't want to do would only cause more friction between them. He was overstepping; he could feel it. But the words were already out.

"Tell you what," Amos said. "Let me finish up here,

and I'll come by your place. If she can help, I'll let you know."

Wollie smiled and bounced the truck keys in his palm. "Thank you, Amos. I'll see you later on, then."

Amos watched as Wollie pulled his truck around and headed back up the drive. He glanced toward the house. Wollie might have the challenge of trying to reintegrate his family into an Amish way of life, but at least he had a wife dedicated to staying by his side. Amos had a wife home with him for a little while longer, but there was an unrooted, unsettled feeling to this arrangement, and he envied Wollie just a little bit.

Amos headed up the steps, and when he went inside the house and washed his hands, he saw Miriam cranking the windows open to catch the morning cross breezes. A pot of oatmeal bubbled fragrantly on the stove, and *Mammi* was already settled in the easy chair.

"Was that Wollie Zook?" Mammi asked.

"*Yah*, that was him," Amos replied. He went over to where his grandmother sat and kissed her on the cheek. "How did you sleep, *Mammi*?"

"Oh, as well as I seem to sleep these days," *Mammi* said.

"What does that mean?" he asked.

"I wake up a lot," she replied. "But nighttime is a good time for prayer, Amos. When you can lie in the darkness and seek the Lord."

"Were you in pain?" he asked.

"The medication helps with that," she replied. "No need to fuss over me, dear boy."

He'd always be a "dear boy" in *Mammi*'s eyes, and the endearment brought a lump to his throat. He nodded and turned toward the kitchen.

"Wollie needs a hand fixing his buggy," Amos said. "That's why he drove the truck."

Miriam looked up from the biscuits she was cutting out on the floured counter. "A truck?"

"I know how it looks," Amos replied. "Wollie left the community to marry an Englisher woman. They had a bad fire and started reconnecting with us again, and they've decided to try to live an Amish life. The problem is, his wife is Englisher, and she doesn't see things the same way."

"She's a good Christian," *Mammi* said quietly.

Amos looked back at his grandmother.

"She is," *Mammi* said. "I saw her at the grocery store once, and she was in line to pay with her *kinner* all in the cart, and talking and reaching for things, and…" *Mammi* shook her head. "But there was this woman ahead of her in line who didn't have enough money to pay for her whole order, and she was going to start taking things out—things like milk and bread and meat. Things that would properly feed a family. And even though the Zooks lost so much in that fire, Natasha Zook handed the woman enough cash to cover her bill. Just handed it over. And when the woman said she'd pay her back, Natasha said not to worry about it. Just like that. And then she paid for her own order, and do you know? She had to put a few of her own things back because she didn't have enough. Some of the treats for the *kinner*."

Amos stood there in silence. He hadn't heard about that, and the thought of the good she'd done to that other woman, even though it meant she wouldn't have enough for her own grocery bill, was moving. That was the kind of Christian love that their Amish community tried to show.

"She's a good woman," *Mammi* said firmly. "And she's trying hard."

"It sounds like it," Miriam said quietly.

"Wollie mentioned that, uh—" Amos cleared his throat. "He mentioned how frustrated Natasha is right now. She grew up English, so doing things our way is hard for her. Cooking on a woodstove is a real challenge, and so is sewing. She's also lonely. I think she feels isolated. I—" He winced. "I know this is out of line for me to do, but I suggested that you might have enough time to help her—maybe just be friendly."

Miriam pressed her lips together. "I've got to be here with *Mammi*."

"Have her come here," *Mammi* said. "Sometimes all the help a woman needs is a little kindness. Tell her to come visit us today, and we'll show her how to do some basic sewing."

Amos looked over at Miriam. "Is that okay?"

"Yah." She nodded. "I'd be happy to show her a few things."

Miriam went over to the stove and stirred the pot of oatmeal a few times, then she pulled it off the heat and closed the damper on the stove. She moved with confidence around the kitchen, but he could see the sadness in her eyes.

Amos crossed the kitchen to keep his words with her private, and he lowered his voice.

"I'm sorry that I offered up your time like that," he said. "I knew it was too much the minute it came out of my mouth."

"It's okay." She shook her head and cast him a rueful smile.

"Having you here—" He swallowed searching inside of himself for the words. "It's been nice."

She looked at him, silent. He'd been expecting a joking comeback, or a roll of her eyes. Instead, she just looked at him.

"It's all too easy to fall into treating you like—" He dropped his gaze, not finishing.

"Like your actual wife?" she asked softly.

Amos looked up. *"Yah."*

Miriam picked up the pot with pot holders. "I am your wife, Amos. And until I leave, you can let me help you like a wife would do. If showing Natasha a few things will make things easier for you, I'm happy to do it."

She brushed past him with the hot pot of oatmeal toward the table, and he felt the old sadness come back. Miriam was being kind by helping out the way she was, but getting used to her presence, to this unnatural calm and peacefulness between them, wasn't good for him.

It would only hurt more when she left again.

"I'd better hurry up," he said. "I said I'd help Wollie with that axle, and then I have to get into work."

Sometimes it was better to focus on the day ahead instead of the hesitant, unrealistic hopes that had started inside of him.

Miriam had just finished pinning the last wet towel to the clothesline when a truck turned down the drive and came rumbling up to the house. Miriam recognized it from that morning—it was the Zooks' vehicle. A blonde woman in Amish garb was driving, and after she parked, she opened the door and got out. She looked hesitantly toward Miriam.

"Hello!" Miriam called, and she headed down the

steps toward her. "You must be Natasha. I'm Miriam Lapp."

"Hello." Natasha glanced over her shoulder as her children came tumbling out the back seat of the truck. They were all dressed in Amish clothing, as well—two boys and two little girls, all beneath the age of ten.

"Welcome," Miriam said with a smile. The children smiled back, but hung close to their mother. Natasha tucked a stray tendril of hair behind her ear.

"Your husband is helping mine repair that buggy," Natasha said. "Thank you for that. Wollie's determined to take it to work today."

"He's happy to help," Miriam said. "I'm glad you made it."

"Me, too," she replied with a smile.

"Have you ever played horseshoes?" Miriam asked the kids.

"Our *daet* showed us how," the older boy said.

Daet. She noticed that he'd used the Pennsylvania Dutch word. She smiled at that. *Kinner* could adjust quickly to changes, and moving to a life of farming and outdoor activities would be an adventure for them—at least during the summer.

"If I got you the game, could you set it up?" Miriam asked.

"*Yah*, I can do it," the boy said in Dutch.

"That was very good!" Miriam said. "Nicely done."

"My *mammi* taught me that," he said, switching back to English. "I can say a few things."

"All right, tell me another thing you can say in Dutch..."

It didn't take long to get the *kinner* enjoying some outdoor play, and Miriam led Natasha inside where *Mammi* was dozing in her easy chair. They could see the *kinner* out the window, tossing horseshoes and laughing. The smallest girl lay next to the garden, and she was pushing little rocks into the soil as if she was planting.

"Oh, I'm sorry—" Natasha started toward the window.

"She's fine," Miriam said. "It's how they learn. She's not hurting anything."

Natasha smiled shakily. "This is very nice of you to have us over like this. I appreciate it."

"Have you started learning to drive a buggy yet?" Miriam asked.

"I'm afraid of the horses," Natasha said. "I almost got kicked once, and I haven't learned how to hitch up. Besides, we only have one buggy right now, and my husband needed it for work. But honestly, even if we had another one, I'm not sure I could manage driving it."

Miriam nodded. "There are a lot of changes to get used to."

"I'm not doing terribly well, to be honest. The kids know more Dutch than I do at this point, and I burn everything I cook." She laughed uncomfortably.

"Sit down," Miriam said. "Let me get some cookies."

She brought a plate of shortbread cookies to the table and sat down opposite the other woman.

"Can I ask you something?" Miriam said.

"Sure," Natasha replied.

"Why are you doing this?" Miriam asked. "Don't get me wrong—everyone is so happy that you are. You're very, very welcome in this community, and I've been told that your husband's parents are overjoyed to have you all come to the Amish faith together..." Miriam leaned forward. "But why did *you* choose this life?"

"For him," Natasha said with a weak shrug.

"How is your family taking it?" Miriam asked. "Your parents and siblings, I mean. They're English, I take it?"

"Yes, they're… English." Natasha smiled faintly. "And they aren't taking it well. They think we're crazy and my parents are worried about the kids getting enough schooling, and having a future, and…" She sighed. "So, it has been tense with them."

"And you did all this for Wollie?" Miriam asked.

Natasha was silent for a moment. "I met Wollie at a baseball game. The Amish young people were playing against our church's youth group, and Wollie and I started talking, and…it all just came together. I think we fell in love that very day. We talked for hours, and he was just the kindest, gentlest man I'd ever met. And when he looked at me, I could see exactly how he felt about me, and I'd never experienced that before."

Miriam held her breath. Neither had she, for that matter…

"And you decided to get married?" she asked.

"Not right away. We started seeing each other. He came with me to some church events, and we'd go out for drives together in the car. Once he brought the buggy, but we drew a lot of attention with the buggy, so we stopped that." Natasha glanced toward *Mammi*, whose eyes were still closed. "We got married because we loved each other too much not to get married. I truly believe that God created us for each other, and I could see how He'd brought us together. Back then, his parents had wanted him to marry a strict Amish girl, and I wouldn't have been acceptable, anyway. And my parents were very happy to show Wollie the English way of living, so we went to where there was more support. Being together was what mattered most to us."

Miriam nodded. "I do understand that. Your family was more supportive of the marriage... That makes sense. But now?"

"Coming back to the Amish faith is for Wollie," Natasha said. "I hadn't realized how much he'd given up by turning his back on the Amish culture. Over the years we talked more about why you all do what you do, and I saw the beauty in it. Besides, I could see my husband's yearning for the way he was raised, and it was draining away a part of him to be away from this life. So when our home burned down, I agreed that the time might be right to learn how to live Amish." Natasha smiled, her face lighting up. "Do you believe in people being created for each other?"

Miriam didn't know how to answer, but thankfully Natasha didn't seem to require one.

"I believe that God created Wollie and me for each other, and that no other man could make me as happy as Wollie does," Natasha said. "And Wollie thinks the same thing. We do things together or not at all. That's how we do everything."

"You don't think there might have been other men you could have been compatible with?" Miriam asked.

"Compatible? Maybe..." Natasha took a bite of a cookie. "But there's a difference between being brought together by God's own hand and stumbling across someone you have compatibility with."

"I suppose..." Miriam sucked in a slow breath.

She hadn't experienced either... She and Amos weren't even compatible, it seemed.

"My problem," Natasha said. "My biggest problem, at least, is that I'm not like you Amish women. You're all so good with your hands, and smart when it comes

to practical matters. You're good cooks, good seam-
stresses, you take care of animals, know how to hang
laundry!" She gestured out the window toward the flut-
tering towels on the line. "And all my life, I've never
been good at those things. I've had other talents."

"Like what?" Miriam asked.

"I'm artistic," Natasha said. "I'm good at painting
and drawing. I'm good at handling money—which I
suppose is useful anywhere. I'm actually quite good
with computers and gadgets, too. But that's no help
here, is it? I'm just different."

Miriam nodded. "Me, too."

"What?" Natasha looked sincerely surprised.

"I'm very good with numbers and business," Miriam
said. "I'm different, too."

"But you seem so—" Natasha glanced around the
kitchen "—competent."

"I am." Miriam chuckled. "Natasha, can I tell you
something?"

"Please!" the other woman said.

"We're not perfect and we're not all the same. Being
Amish means believing in the same faith and the same
values," Miriam said. "You don't have to be the same.
You will be you, and you'll bring your strengths to the
community, and you'll contribute. Maybe not with computers and the like, but you'll find a way to pitch in."

"But the canning, and pickling, and sewing, and gardening, and…" Natasha's voice trailed away.

"You'll learn," Miriam said with a shrug. "And
maybe you'll never be terribly good at those things.
But you'll find your place. You'll see. Don't put so much
pressure on yourself."

Natasha's expression relaxed. "You're the first person to tell me that."

"Am I?" Miriam asked. "I'm sure I won't be the last."

"Since I'm here," Natasha said. "I'm having trouble cooking on my woodstove. Could you walk me through how you do it? Wollie's mother has shown me all of this, and I feel so silly asking her again and again. If I could cook just one meal for my family without burning it, I'd feel like a success."

"Of course," Miriam said, pushing her chair back. "Come—I'll show you some tricks."

An hour passed while Miriam showed Natasha how to cook with a woodstove, how to dampen the heat and how to get the perfect glow for baking bread. *Mammi* woke up from her nap and she gave a few tips of her own about how to run an Amish home.

And after the children had come inside for some pie and tall glasses of milk, Natasha thanked Miriam for her kindness and sent the kids out to the truck, as it was time to go home for lunch.

"Thank you for taking the time for this," Natasha said earnestly. "I'm looking forward to starting the fire in my own stove for lunch. It'll be different this time, I'm sure."

"You're very welcome," Miriam said. "It was so nice to meet you."

When their guests had left, Miriam cast *Mammi* a tired smile.

"She's very nice," Miriam said. "I can see why her husband fell in love with her."

"*Yah*, I told you," *Mammi* said. "But I think you might have given her some bad advice."

Miriam shot the old woman a look of surprise. "What? When?"

"When you told her that she didn't need to worry about being like the other Amish women and that she could be different," *Mammi* said. "I woke up a few times there, and I was listening to you two talk…it was nice. But I don't think that advice was quite right."

"What would you have her do?" Miriam said with a shake of her head. "She can't change who she is! She'll have to find a way."

"She will," *Mammi* said softly. "But you're coming at this from a very different position than she is. She speaks very little of the language, knows very little about living an Amish life and knows very few people in our community. It's not going to be so simple for her."

Miriam was silent.

"You could be different because you've got Amish pedigree all the way back to Switzerland," *Mammi* said. "No one will question how Amish you are. You might not like the life of an Amish wife, but you know the work because you've been taught it since you were tiny. And as for your affinity for business, it might be very useful if your husband will listen to your good instincts, but another woman wouldn't be able to do what you are doing and still be accepted. You come from a strongly Amish family and were raised by a wealthy Amish father who was revered in the community. It's different for you. You have some privilege and you get away with a whole lot more."

"I suppose it might be a little different," Miriam said after a moment.

"More than a little, dear," *Mammi* said frankly.

"If Natasha had a friend who could stand up for her—"

"But you aren't staying," *Mammi* said meekly. "So it can't be you."

Right. She was doing it again—dishing out advice that was in no way helpful to the woman who was looking to her for support. She rubbed her hands over her face.

"It's okay," *Mammi* said gently. "I think you encouraged her all the same. She has a mother-in-law to set her straight on the rest."

"I do try, *Mammi*," Miriam said with a sigh.

"I know," *Mammi* said with a tender smile. "And that's why I love you so."

Miriam went over to where the old woman sat and bent down, giving her a hug.

"I'm just going to go pick up the horseshoes," Miriam said. "I'll be right back."

As Miriam headed out into the noon sunlight, she felt another wave of regret—this one having nothing to do with Natasha or Fannie. This one was for her husband.

Miriam had expected more of Amos—it was true. She'd expected more growth in his business, and more strength in standing up to her father. But Amos didn't come from a family like hers, and her father was the kind of man who would not be moved once he'd made up his mind about something.

Miriam had expected Amos to be like her father—his business sense, his narrow focus, his effectiveness. But Amos wasn't her father. And he didn't have generations of accumulated land and businesses at his fingertips. He hadn't been raised by businessmen who'd taught him everything they knew.

Had Miriam's expectations of Amos…*her father's* expectations of him…been unfair?

Chapter Eight

Amos spent the first few hours of his day with Wollie, fixing that wagon axle. It took longer than they thought, and it still wasn't completely finished by the time they called it quits for the morning. But Wollie could finish it on his own that evening. Amos dropped him off at his work and then had to head all the way back to Redemption Carpentry, which took more time still. But there was no helping it—these things happened sometimes. As he rode, his mind kept slipping back to that unfinished box he'd found in his bedroom closet—the one he'd been carving for his and Miriam's first anniversary.

He'd never finished it. When she left, it hardly seemed like a priority. He couldn't bring himself to throw it into the stove, either. So it had sat up there for the better part of a decade, simply collecting dust.

But if things were going to be different for him and Miriam now—if they were going to be friends of some sort—then he felt like the change in their relationship deserved to be acknowledged between them. Maybe it was time to finish carving that box and give it to her, after all.

Would that be too much? Would he make things

weird between them? But somehow, leaving that small box unfinished felt wrong now, and he couldn't quite explain why. But he needed to do something about it.

Amos arrived at the workshop a little after noon, and Noah and Thomas both looked up at his arrival. He nodded to the men as he hung up his lunch satchel on a peg by the door and dropped his hat on top.

"You made it," Noah said. "Is everything okay at home?"

They were asking about *Mammi*. *"Yah, yah..."* Amos nodded. *"Mammi* is doing okay. Every day she seems a little more tired, but she's okay."

Noah straightened and brushed the wood dust from his forearms.

"Wollie came by this morning," Amos went on. "He needed help with a damaged axle on his buggy, so I dropped by his place to help him fix it. It took a lot longer than I thought—one thing after another seemed to go wrong. It's not quite finished, but Wollie can do the rest on his own. So I drove him to work, and he figures he can get a ride back with a coworker. That's why I'm late."

"How's he doing?" Thomas asked.

"Pretty well," Amos replied. "He's finding it harder than he thought to readjust to Amish life, though."

"He is?" Thomas said, surprised. "I understand it being difficult for his wife and *kinner*, but—"

"He got used to their ways," Amos replied. "Like having a truck. He said they kept it for emergencies, and when the buggy broke, he came to find me in his truck."

The men exchanged looks. None of them had extra Englisher vehicles for hard times. Amos knew how to be Amish, and it wasn't by having backup plans that went against the *Ordnung*. Marriage was supposed to be the same—vows and a life together, no divorce, no separation, no backup plan. Maybe Amos wasn't much better than Wollie right now.

"Once you've jumped the fence, coming back isn't so easy, is it?" Noah said quietly.

"It will take more time, I suppose," Thomas said. "Our *mamm* found it hard coming back, too. It isn't just the rules and giving up the Englisher conveniences. It's the friendships that have changed, and the way the community sees you. Our *mamm* really struggled with that coming back. She still does, somewhat."

"Still?" Amos asked.

"Coming home again means facing judgment," Noah said, his voice low.

Amos's mind went back to sitting on the swing next to Miriam, her soft hand in his. Miriam was facing judgment—from friends, family, people who'd only ever heard about her and hadn't even met her. And she'd felt safe enough with him to open up about it...

Things were changing, and Miriam had started to trust him, of all people. He hadn't expected that.

"Amos?" Noah said.

Amos realized he'd been lost in thought, and he looked up. "Sorry, what?"

"The bank statement arrived with the mail today," Noah said. "It's on your desk in the office."

"Thanks. I'll go take a look."

Amos headed in the direction of his office while Thomas and Noah turned back to their work in shaping a sleigh bed. Their voices mingled with the swish of the planer, the scent of freshly cut wood accenting the air.

The office was just off the side of the showroom. It

was a small room with a large, plain desk and a bank of filing cabinets. One long, narrow window let in a shaft of sunlight, illuminating a white envelope on his desk. That would be the bank statement.

Amos sat down at the desk and pulled out his ledgers. He kept careful track of his work, the payments, expected payments…and for the last couple of months, his accounts had been off. He kept hoping that they'd rectify themselves somehow before the next bank statement… He'd check again today.

Amos opened the envelope and cracked open his newest ledger. For the next few minutes he scoured the columns, looking for the missing money. He'd made a mistake somewhere, obviously, because there was no way that Noah or Thomas were stealing from him. Still, he needed to know where he'd gone wrong, and he went over the numbers carefully, cross-checking as he went.

Two hours passed that way, and when there was a tap on the door, he roused himself.

"Come in," he called.

Noah opened the door and looked inside. "Everything okay, Amos?"

"We're out about five hundred dollars," Amos said.

"Out?" Noah frowned.

"I've made a mistake somehow, and I don't know where." Amos straightened his shoulders and rolled his neck. "I might just have to write it off and we'll carry on."

"You could ask Miriam," Noah said.

Amos eyed the younger man for a moment. "I did ask her to help me out a bit while she's here…"

"Well, then?" Noah said.

Amos sighed. It was the tally of numbers that held

him back… If she never knew the actual amount of money that moved through his business, then he could let her believe he was more successful than he was. If he opened his books to her, then there would be no more room for inflated assumptions.

"It's my own pride," Amos said quietly. "Her father was a wealthy man, and this business would have been small potatoes for him…and for her."

"You aren't ashamed of a successfully run carpentry shop!" Noah said.

"No, I'm not." Amos shook his head. "And she did offer to help, so I'll ask Miriam to look at it."

Noah and Thomas wouldn't have any idea how hard this was for him to open up to Miriam, but she'd laid her own insecurities bare the night before, and perhaps it was only fair for him to allow her to see a little bit of his true situation, too.

Their marriage wasn't going to include sharing a home or romantic hopes, but with her father gone, he could feel that things were changing between them. Leroy's influence was fading away, and maybe they could move forward in their relationship with a little more trust and mutual respect.

Fannie and Silas wouldn't see their relationship as a success…and neither would anyone else in this community. Noah and Thomas both knew what happy marriages looked like now that they had their own. But it could be an improvement for Amos and Miriam.

Maybe *Gott* could bless them with a single step forward.

When Amos got home, he brushed down the horses and sent them out to the pasture. Then he gathered up the ledgers and headed into the house. It smelled of fragrant beef pie and home-baked bread—the aroma making his stomach rumble in response to it.

The women weren't cooking, though. *Mammi* was seated in her easy chair, which was pulled up next to a window overlooking the backyard, and Miriam sat at the kitchen table with one of his work shirts on her lap, sewing a split seam with a needle and thread. They both looked up as the screen door bounced shut behind him.

Amos paused in the doorway, and when Miriam saw him, some color went into her cheeks. She looked down at the shirt on her lap and continued sewing.

His shirt in her hands felt strangely intimate. He hadn't wanted her to be doing anything extra around here. Cooking and cleaning was fine, and obviously *Mammi* would need her help, but having her going over his clothing and mending the tears and worn spots—that felt like the work of more than a woman in the home. That felt like a wife's tender care, and he didn't want to be left with her neat, tight stitches in his clothing when she left again—a reminder of all the feminine, gentle contribution that he couldn't expect anymore.

"*Mammi* asked if I'd mend it," she said, as if she needed to explain herself. Maybe she felt the intimacy involved with the chore, too.

From where she sat by the back window, *Mammi* shot Amos an exaggeratedly innocent look. "It needed mending, dear."

"Thank you," Amos said. "Did *Mammi* also tell you that I sew up my own seams when they split?"

"No," Miriam said, and her gaze flickered toward the old woman.

"He sews like he's hoeing hard ground," *Mammi* said

with a short laugh, miming the action. "He hacks at it. So *yah*, he closes a seam, but…" She shook her head.

Miriam started to laugh, and Amos was forced to join in.

"I'm not that bad," Amos said, and *Mammi* just shook her head again.

Amos put his ledgers down on the corner of the kitchen table, and then went back to the mudroom to wash his hands. When he returned, Miriam was just snipping the thread. She shook out the shirt and looked it over.

"It's in good shape now," she said, and she passed it over to him. "Dinner's ready. I just need to set the table."

Miriam paused at the ledgers, glancing down at him. He could see her piqued interest at the sight of them.

"Do you have more work to do tonight?" she asked. She reached out and touched the corner of the top ledger, and then pulled her hand back.

"I do," he said. "There's some discrepancy in my tallying, and I need to find it."

"Are you going to ask Miriam to help?" *Mammi* asked pointedly.

Amos bent down and kissed his grandmother's cheek.

"I was going to, *Mammi*," he said quietly. "I was just getting to it."

Mammi smiled at him gently. "There is no harm in needing her, dear. Helping each other is what our whole community is based on."

But it had never been what his marriage with Miriam had been based on… Their marriage had been more of a power struggle as he tried to prove to her that he was man enough to take care of her.

"Do you think you could look at the books for me, Miriam?" Amos asked, raising his voice. "*Mammi*'s right—I do need the help. I can't find this error."

"I'd be happy to," Miriam replied, and she shot him a smile. "I miss getting my hands into some financial statements. It's as satisfying as bread dough."

She always did have a way of expressing herself, and she'd never been quite like any other Amish woman.

"Thank you," he said. "I appreciate it."

All the same, his stomach knotted up. She'd find the mistake, he was sure, and it would undoubtedly be something he'd recorded improperly. So she'd be seeing his error. She'd also see exactly how successful he was—no more and no less. And when she saw how close they came to the line each month, he had a feeling that she'd look at him just a little bit differently.

Maybe this was good for his own character—letting go of his pride and desire to appear more successful than he was to earn his wife's respect. This would have to be part of their new dynamic. If she didn't respect him as the man he was, no amount of money would change it.

Maybe *Gott* was teaching him to stop trying to be something that he wasn't.

When dinner was finished, Miriam did the dishes with Amos's help. She told him he didn't need to, but he'd ignored it, and gone about cleaning off the table and bringing dishes to the sink, anyway. When they'd finished cleaning, *Mammi* dozed in her easy chair again, a breeze from an open window cooling her face, and Miriam and Amos settled down at the kitchen table with the stack of ledgers.

Miriam had been looking forward to this—she'd never had such an up-close look at her husband's business before. She'd wondered about it in the past, and her *daet* had had a few opinions about Redemption Carpentry, but Amos had never given her anything more than a cursory tour of the shop in their first year of marriage. He'd kept quiet about anything else to do with his business.

"So what's the problem?" Miriam asked.

"I'm out about five hundred dollars on paper and I can't find where I made the mistake," he said.

"Can I take a look?" She put hand on the top ledger.

"I'll show you where—" He opened it, flipped back a few pages, and she noticed his hesitation before he put it in front of her.

The lines of numbers were all neat and color-coded. She was able to easily follow the rhythm of the money coming in and out of this particular account. She worked for the better part of an hour mentally tallying up the numbers until she spotted the sudden loss of money. It was a calculation error—an expense that was written down for an order that had never been picked up, and somehow, it hadn't been included in the running tally.

"There—" she said. "I found your problem. Five hundred dollars for wood and various parts that never made it into the tally."

"Where?" Amos bent down, and his strong arm brushed hers. He smelled warm and faintly of wood. He was so tall and strong, and something inside of her longed to just lean her cheek against the solid muscle. The sudden, unbidden thought surprised her, and she felt her face heat. She reached past him, underlining the item in pencil.

"Right… I can't believe I missed it. I must have gone over that section ten times!"

Amos looked down at her, and she felt her breath catch as she tipped her chin up to meet his gaze. Those dark, intense eyes, his thick, dense beard—she dropped her gaze.

"Do you keep track of your expenses every month?" she asked, clearing her throat. This was territory she was more comfortable with.

"I have a general idea of what it costs to run the place," he said.

"So not a tailored monthly expense report?" she asked.

"No."

She nodded. "Because if I look from the beginning of last month—" She flipped back and picked up a pencil and pad of paper, jotting down numbers as she pulled a finger down the tallies of numbers. When she got to the end of the month, she nodded. "*Yah*. That's what I thought."

"What?" he asked.

"Here—" She did some quick arithmetic in her head and added it up. "This is what it cost you to run your shop last month. And this is what you made." She circled the second number. "You didn't make enough to cover your expenses."

"*Yah*, but the month before we were paid out for some big projects, and we had money left over," he replied.

"Let me take a look at the last six months—" She reached for another ledger and Amos put his hand over hers, stopping her.

"I don't need help with that," he said firmly.

"Amos, the fact that you have stayed in business all this time and have a steady flow of clients says that you are good at what you do," she said. "But even the most talented craftsman can be run under for a lack of attention to detail. My *daet*—"

"I didn't ask for your father's words of wisdom," he said curtly.

"Then what about mine?" she asked. "I can tell you what I see! Do you care about that?"

Mammi woke up from her sleep. She sucked in a breath and pulled herself up a little straighter in the chair. Miriam and Amos both looked in her direction, and Miriam couldn't help but feel like they were a couple of *kinner* getting caught for squabbling.

"Are you two spatting again?" *Mammi* asked, her voice tired.

"No, *Mammi*," Amos said quickly. "Of course not. We're just…"

"…talking business," Miriam concluded for him, and he cast her a rueful smile.

"So you are," *Mammi* said, and shook her head. "Do you think you could put a pin in that, and help me get ready for bed? I need my pills…"

"*Yah*, of course." Miriam stood up and put her pencil down next to the pad of paper, then went to *Mammi*'s side. She helped her to stand, and together they went into the sitting room where *Mammi*'s bed was. Miriam glanced back over her shoulder before they left the kitchen, and Amos stood there by the table, his hands limp at his sides. He looked deflated—was that her fault?

"At a time like this, he needs all the help he can get," *Mammi* said as Miriam helped her to sit down on the side of her bed.

Miriam went to a chest of drawers and took out a clean nightgown.

"He sees my opinions as a threat," Miriam said. "I don't think he'll take my advice."

"He sees your old *daet*'s opinions as judgment," *Mammi* replied.

"My father was a brilliant businessman," Miriam said.

Mammi caught Miriam's gaze and held it. "My dear girl, I am about to follow your father in the direction he went, so trust me when I tell you that I have infinite sympathy for your loss, and for your father's. No one is ready to die. Your father might have been a brilliant businessman, but he had a habit of treating everyone like a business deal. And people, Miriam—" *Mammi* let out a slow breath "—people are not so easy to line up. And they don't all cooperate like employees."

Miriam helped *Mammi* dress for bed, then pulled the covers back to allow her to lay down in crisp, clean sheets.

"My father was very loving," Miriam said softly. "I don't know what you heard about him—"

"To you," *Mammi* said. "He was very loving to you... Was he equally understanding for Amos?"

Miriam was silent. No, her *daet* was not. But he had a daughter to protect, and he'd wanted the very best for Miriam.

"I can't solve your issues with your husband," *Mammi* went on, "although I would dearly love to. But think about what I've said. Maybe it will help."

Miriam sat on the edge of *Mammi*'s bed and looked at *Mammi*'s pale face.

"When so many people respected him so deeply," Miriam said, "I don't understand why Amos didn't."

"Because they wanted something different from your *daet*," *Mammi* said. "They wanted his business advice to help them achieve a portion of what he had during his life, or possibly they wanted a donation to their charitable cause. It is very easy to show deference and respect when you stand to gain."

"And Amos didn't stand to gain from him?" Miriam asked with a short laugh. "He could have learned so much from my *daet*!"

"He didn't want what they wanted," *Mammi* said, and she reached out and nudged a Bible closer to Miriam. "He didn't want his business advice. He said he wanted your father's respect, but as his grandmother, I knew his heart a little better than that. What Amos wanted from your *daet* was love."

Miriam paused, staring at the old woman. "Love?"

"My son, Aaron, had problems of his own. He was very gruff, and his wife suffered from depression. He withheld his wife's medication because he didn't believe in it. Didn't Amos tell you about this?"

"A little," she admitted.

"Amos had to grow up a little faster than other children, and he never did have a kind, solid father to show him the way," she went on. "And when my husband died, he didn't have a *dawdie*, either. A boy needs a father…" *Mammi*'s voice caught. "Your husband didn't want advice or judgment from his father-in-law. He wanted love." She was silent for a moment, and then she nudged the Bible again. "Please…just open it at random and read whatever your eye falls on."

Miriam's father was a tough and crusty old man, and even his own *kinner* had to read beyond his brusque demeanor to see how he really felt about them. They had longed for some of the same affection Amos had missed out on, too. And given her father's personality, Amos might have wanted something that was too much to ask.

Miriam did as *Mammi* asked, and the Bible opened to the end of Proverbs.

"'Who can find a virtuous woman? for her price is far above rubies. The heart of her husband doth safely trust in her, so that he shall have no need of spoil. She will do him good and not evil all the days of her life…'"

The words were familiar ones—words her own *daet* had raised her on. Leroy Schwartz had shown his daughter how to run a business, how to make money grow, how to think ahead to possible pitfalls and how to throw her heart into her work. A good woman worked hard, and used her intelligence.

You have both of those attributes, Miriam, her father used to tell her. *I couldn't be more proud.*

"'Many daughters have done virtuously, but thou excellest them all. Favor is deceitful, and beauty is vain: but a woman that feareth the Lord, she shall be praised. Give her of the fruit of her hands; and let her own works praise her in the gates.'"

Miriam looked up from her reading as she came to the end of the book of Proverbs, and she found *Mammi*'s eyes still open.

"I think you were a wife like this," Miriam said.

"We all try," *Mammi* replied. "We all fall short."

Except Miriam had fallen much shorter. She'd been hardworking, smart, dedicated to the task at hand, and yet she hadn't been able to hold their relationship together. If making a man happy were simply about a woman's willingness to work hard, she would have been fine. But there had been more to it.

"I'll let you sleep," Miriam said softly.

"Good night, dear," *Mammi* replied.

Miriam tiptoed out of the room and back to the kitchen. The ledgers were all picked up again, and Amos sat at the table, a cup of water in front of him.

"Can I work out a budget for you?" Miriam asked, pausing at the table.

Amos looked up at her, pressed his lips together. "It's okay. I'll figure it out."

"Amos." She pulled out a chair and sat down. "Let me help you." She could see the old stubbornness in his jaw. "Let's leave my *daet* out of this, okay? *Mammi* explained that maybe I…push my father onto you more than I should."

"You do, a little," Amos said.

Miriam nodded. "I'm sorry. He could be difficult, and if it's worth anything, even us *kinner* had to guess at how he felt for us sometimes. It's just the way he was. But if you spent enough time with him, his love made it through, and you knew…"

Amos nodded, silent.

"The thing is, Amos, regardless of who taught me, I know how businesses thrive, and I know how they fail—"

"My business is not failing," Amos said quietly.

"No, but you are running very close to the line!" she countered. "You need to either raise your prices, or get more business. Raising your prices can be risky. You can raise them a little to match inflation—people understand that. But a better way to get more business is to advertise."

"People know about us," Amos said. "We're the best Amish-run carpentry shop in this area."

"*Yah*, a certain number of people know about you. How do you grow that?"

"I let our work speak for itself," he replied.

He was so noble, so good…and so unwilling to bend!

"That won't work," she said. "Has it so far?"

"We've been steadily growing," he replied.

"Not fast enough to make up the difference," she replied. "You have two full-time employees as well as yourself, and your expenses keep growing, because your supplies cost more every year, too. Amos, you have to look broader. You have Amish customers, but you need the Englishers."

"I've dealt with Englishers!" he snapped. "They're always pushing for a deal!"

"Then push back!" she said. "You have a business to run! And if you're going to get the word out to the Englishers, then you need to get some radio ads."

"Radio?" he frowned. "No. That's not our way."

"But it's their way," she said. "You have to put ads where you'll find your customers, and local radio is a great place to do it. Englishers listen to it while they drive, my *daet*—" She stopped herself. "Forget who told me about it. But I've seen those radio ads work wonders. A few days after they first were aired, there was a spike in new customers—all English."

Amos stood up. "I don't need more advertisement."

"Everyone needs more advertisement," she said. "Some can't afford it—"

"I can afford it just fine!" he said. "Miriam, I have run this business my way all these years, and I've done just fine."

Miriam met his gaze, and instead of that warmth she'd seen earlier, there was glittering irritation. This wasn't about her *daet* anymore, and she felt tears rise in her eyes.

"Do you know the verses I read to *Mammi* tonight?" she asked, her voice wavering.

"I heard them," he said, his voice low. "The wife of noble character from Proverbs."

"She worked hard, and she was smart," Miriam said earnestly. "She did her husband good all the days of his life. Let me do you good, Amos…"

They were silent, and Amos broke the eye contact first, looking down at his work-roughened hands.

"She also lived with her husband," Amos said quietly. "It's not the same with us."

Miriam's heart sped up, and she blinked back the tears.

"We might have a different way, you and I, but I am very much your wife, Amos Lapp!" she snapped. "Just try and marry someone else, and you'll find out how very married you are. And do you know what I think? You don't *want* a wife of noble character who can help your business thrive. You don't want a smart, talented woman at your side. You want to do it on your own and prove to me that you never did need me!"

"I have been doing it on my own!" he said. "And what is so wrong with a man wanting to be a man? I want to be the one who provides! I want to give my wife a proper life, to let her live without worry about money or debt, and I want her to trust that as her husband I have things under control!"

"Do you want me to just turn off my brain?" she asked, shaking her head.

"I want you to have a little faith in me!" he retorted.

It was difficult to have faith in a man who refused to let her see anything. It was difficult for a woman to put her entire future into the hands of a man who knew less about business than she did, and wouldn't let her see any of the details that would let her benefit him. But he was right—they weren't living together. So it was different.

Miriam nodded. "Fine. I'll back off."

Amos picked up the pile of ledgers, and his jaw tensed. "Thank you for finding the error. I appreciate your help."

"*Yah*. No problem," she breathed.

That was all the help that he wanted—one clerical error. She had so much more to offer, and the men in her life never seemed to see it. Amos had even accepted her offer of help earlier, and he wasn't using her to her full potential.

"Would you let me look for my papers?" she asked, her throat tight.

"*Yah*." He nodded. "Of course. I've gone through this one box a few times looking for other documents, and I haven't seen yours. But you never know. I can help you—"

"No," she said with a shake of her head. "You have a restful evening. I can look alone."

Her last hope of providing for herself with any amount of dignity at this point in her life was to find those papers that proved the strip mall was hers.

Chapter Nine

When Amos went to bed that night, the kerosene lamp was still lit in the kitchen, and Miriam was standing in front of a stack of papers, sorting through them and putting them into separate piles. He hadn't asked her to organize those papers for him, but she was doing it, anyway.

He couldn't sleep yet, and he didn't want to go downstairs and argue with his wife again. She was only trying to help, and she wasn't doing any harm. Besides, she needed to find her documents.

He'd hurt her feelings tonight—he could see that much—but he wasn't sure what piece of uncomfortable truth had been the culprit.

Was she angry that he didn't want to use her idea for advertising on the radio? She made it seem so simple, but how on earth was he supposed to make that happen? He didn't have any of the technology that Englishers used for such things. Did they just…talk into their phones? Did they have computer programs that did it? That wasn't an option for an Amish man! They had small businesses and small farms, and by not getting too big, they stayed closer to their communities, and closer to home. He'd never questioned that before. There was no shame in staying small!

But now, Miriam was suggesting growth using Englisher media that he wasn't comfortable with, and sitting in his bedroom just over the kitchen, he wasn't going to sleep. So he got up and he sat in a little chair next to the window with his Bible on his lap.

She might not like a husband who was the traditional man, who cared for his wife and didn't expose her to worry. She might not like that he wouldn't give up control in his own company, and he might irritate her something fierce just by existing.

But that was okay. He was still the man of this house and would sit up until he heard her go to bed. Then he'd go to sleep. Call him old-fashioned, or call him too stubborn, but he felt in his bones that protecting the women in his home was still his responsibility.

He opened his Bible, and an underlined passage stood out at him. It was in First Peter: *Likewise, ye husbands, dwell with them according to knowledge, giving honor unto the wife, as unto the weaker vessel, and as being heirs together of the grace of life; that your prayers be not hindered.*

This was a verse that he'd read over and over again during that first year of marriage, and in the years since she left. These had been accusing words—ones that drove him to his knees, asking *Gott* to change him, and forgive him, and show him how to do better. In fact, he'd read this passage and prayed the same prayer only a few weeks before Miriam arrived.

He could see the meaning in the verse very clearly— if he wasn't honoring his wife, and if he wasn't treating her as an equal, then *Gott* wasn't going to be listening to his prayers. There was no righteous confidence for a man who didn't have peace in his own home.

Lord, he prayed. *I don't want to be a difficult husband, but she isn't an easy woman to understand. Show me how to do this...*

He put his Bible aside and went back to his closet. He pulled down the partially carved trinket box, and he ran his fingers over it. He still felt a surge of guilt at never having finished it. He carried it over to where his lamp sat on the windowsill, and he pulled out a knife.

It had been nearly ten years since he'd worked on this box, but he could remember the exact pattern he'd been working on, and he could see the finished product in his mind's eye. He started to carve, the sharp knife biting into the wood. He didn't know how to honor his wife. He was better than his *daet* had been to his *mamm*, but it wasn't nearly good enough. Maybe finishing this gift at long last could be a start.

An hour later, Miriam's footsteps went up the stairs and into her bedroom. Her door shut with a soft click.

He continued carving, his hands sure as he worked out the vines and thorns of the rosebush twining around the outer edge. He wanted to be right with *Gott*, and he knew he wouldn't be, unless he was also right with his wife.

The next day at work went smoothly enough, but Amos's mind was on those numbers that Miriam had pointed out. If he had to be completely honest with himself, he'd be more comfortable if he had a little more wiggle room in his budget. If he could sell some smaller items every day, the sorts of things that cost less to make and could bring in a bigger profit, that would be incredibly helpful. With more Englisher customers buying things like spice racks, ornamental mailboxes, quilt racks and jewelry boxes, he could have more money left over for emergencies, or for putting toward retirement. A man might not want to retire, but his body might insist upon it.

If he asked *Mammi*'s opinion, he knew what it would be—listen to his wife. But *Mammi*'s priorities weren't completely locked on his business success. She wanted to bring him and Miriam back together under the same roof. What she didn't realize was that having Miriam here, having her help, her cooking, her mending his shirts…it wasn't making things easier on a heart level. Because he had never asked his wife to leave—she'd left on her own, and he didn't think that she'd willingly come back just because of a couple of weeks of getting along.

After they'd closed up the carpentry shop for the day and Thomas and Noah headed home to their own wives and *kinner*, Amos hitched up his buggy and set out for home. When he arrived, he took care of the horses, and then he came up the steps, past some laundry hanging on the line, and into the mudroom.

He glanced into the kitchen and *Mammi*'s chair was empty. His heart gave a little jump.

"Where is she?" he asked.

"Sleeping," Miriam said. "And hello."

"Sorry," he said. "Hi. Let me just wash my hands and get my boots off."

Miriam came to the mudroom door and leaned a shoulder against the frame as he soaped up his hands.

"The doctor came by today," she said.

"What did he say?" Amos asked.

"He said that she'll be sleeping more often now," Miriam said. "And if she needs more pain medication, we should give her whatever she needs to be comfortable."

Amos nodded, dried his hands and exchanged a sad look with Miriam.

"I'm glad you're here with her," he said. "I'm going to take tomorrow off to spend some time with her, I think. If she's sleeping more, I hate to lose time with her."

"I think she'd appreciate it," Miriam said with a nod, her eyes misting. "Come in and have dinner. I made chicken pie with some salad on the side. If you're still hungry, I also made some apple crisp."

It sounded delicious, and he nodded his thanks and followed her into the kitchen.

"Did *Mammi* eat?" he asked.

"She had a little apple crisp," Miriam said with a smile.

That was good to hear. He peeked into the bedroom to see *Mammi* sleeping peacefully, her thin, weathered hand resting on her Bible. Then he went back to the table.

Miriam dished up two plates of food, and then sat down with him. She looked at him expectantly, and he bowed his head. This was his home, and it was his place to ask the blessing.

"For this food we are about to eat," he prayed, "make us truly thankful."

The problem was, he *was* thankful for the food, for the woman who'd cooked it, even for the heartache that she brought back up for him. He was thankful for all of this—the time with his grandmother, and for the faith that he clung to in these difficult times. It was letting go of it all that was going to hurt the most.

He raised his head and plunged his fork into the

flaky crust, chicken gravy pooling over his plate. He nodded as Miriam offered him some salad on the side. He'd worked hard, and he hadn't eaten any lunch today, his mind being on other things, so he was hungry now.

"I wanted to ask you," Amos said. "If I were to...do a radio ad...how would I do it?"

He kept his eyes on his plate and took another bite. He wasn't sure how she'd react—condescension, a story about her *daet*'s superior business skills...

"Are you really thinking of doing it?" she asked.

He glanced up, and to his surprise, he saw genuine happiness in her face.

"It's a good idea," he admitted. "And if I could make a little extra, it would make saving for retirement a little easier."

She smiled at that. "*Yah.* That's the thing. You do a lot of large items that have high overhead cost to build, meaning that you're putting a lot of time and energy into pieces that aren't going to make you as much profit. Smaller pieces that use less material and time could make up the difference, and Englisher tourists as well as Englishers living in the area are your perfect customers for this."

"Hmm." He chewed, listening to her talk. She had more ideas—not just the radio ad. She thought he should put up ads for his shop at the bus depot where the tourists arrived, showing pictures of the smaller items, touting them as genuine Amish.

"That sounds silly," he said. "I suppose anything I touch is genuine Amish."

"Isn't that great?" she said. "It's all about getting word out, and there are plenty of people who would love nothing more than to buy Amish-made merchandise. Honestly, Amos, what I wouldn't do for this kind of foot traffic in Edson!"

Her happy smile faded, and she put down her fork. For a moment, she sat in silence.

"What?" he said.

"Oh, it's nothing." Miriam rose to her feet and picked up her plate. He watched her go to the counter and deposit her plate there.

"Miriam," he said, and she turned toward him.

"It's just an emotional time," she said. "I'm fine."

But she wasn't. He could see that plain as day. She'd been happy talking about marketing his business up until she'd mentioned going home. Did she not want to leave?

"I found my papers," she said. "They were down the side of the box, under a flap."

"Oh, good…" He felt his earlier optimism start to fade, too. "I'm glad you found them."

"I'll have my own strip mall to run," she said. "It's a start. And I am serious about opening a new business, too."

"With your marketing sense, you'll be jumping ahead in no time," he said.

"*Yah*, it's…ideal." But her voice caught, and his heart tugged toward her in response.

Amos rose to his feet, the food forgotten. He crossed the kitchen and caught her hand. She looked up at him, her eyelashes wet, and without thinking better of it, he pulled her into his arms and against his chest.

It was a long-buried instinct with her—pulling her close—and she fit in his arms in just the same way she used to. He was afraid to look down at her, but he tightened his arms around her, and rested his cheek against her hair and *kapp*.

"Miriam," he murmured, and when she looked up, he followed another long-buried instinct, and he bent down, covering her lips with his.

They'd always had such passionate kisses after arguments, and there had been something about the relief of falling into each other's arms all over again that felt the same.

Except they hadn't been fighting this time.

They'd been getting along...

Amos had a way of looking at her just before he kissed her that made her stomach tumble...and ten years hadn't changed that a bit. Feeling his restrained strength in his gentle touch, her heart skipped a beat.

Miriam felt the warmth of Amos's strong arms as he pulled her closer against him, and up onto her tiptoes. His beard tickled her face, and she felt all the frustration and tension inside of her melt away. There always had been something about Amos's kisses that had scrambled her mind and left her a little weak in the knees, and feeling his arms around her again felt more familiar than she had a right to. It had been a good many years since they'd shared a kiss, but it was like no time had passed at all, and they'd simply fallen back together.

His touch, his breath, the feeling of his lips against hers... It was like the time between that tumultuous first year and today had collapsed together like a folding fan.

Standing here in the kitchen with his arms around her, the heat from cooking still hanging in the air and that same old feeling of wild relief coursing through her, she didn't want to move. It was a relief to be in his arms again, to feel his touch, his breath on her face, to smell that musky scent of sunshine and woodworking.

She didn't want to think, or move, or disturb the moment so that it would flutter away.

Amos pulled back, and she blinked her eyes open. For a moment, neither of them said anything, and Miriam held her breath. Then when Amos leaned toward her again, she felt a surge of misgiving. There were so many reasons not to kiss her husband, and she shook her head, and pulled out of his arms.

"We can't do this, Amos," she said. Her voice sounded too loud.

"We're married," he replied with a rueful smile. "Of all the people who have the right to kiss each other, I think we do."

That wasn't what she was talking about, and he knew it.

"We've done this before," she said, softening her tone. "We fight, we argue, we make up, and we do it again. I can't do this anymore!"

"Except we weren't fighting," he murmured. "Not this time."

"Only because we're trying our best to make this a peaceful time for *Mammi*," she said. "If it weren't for her, we would be."

Amos licked his lips, then took a step back. "Maybe I shouldn't have kissed you, but I do care about whatever it was that made you look so heartbroken a minute ago."

"I'm not heartbroken..." She swallowed, and as if to prove her wrong, tears misted her eyes.

"You are..."

She looked around the kitchen, at the newly familiar table and chairs, the cupboards that used to be hers, the chipped blue teapot that sat on the counter, still warm with leftover tea.

"I'm going back to Edson to run my own business,"

she said softly, and she looked up at Amos, then wiped an errant tear from her cheek. "That's all."

And she'd be forced to walk away from this house all over again—put it behind her, and go start over in Edson, where people knew and respected her, and where there was no husband to cook for, no old woman to care for... No one who needed her.

"You wanted that life in Edson," he said. "Don't you?"

"I still want it," she said. "But I suppose coming back has reminded me of all the things I'd wanted when we first got married—all those silly, girlish hopes I had for our life together."

"I had a few hopes, too," he said quietly.

"Oh?" Was this where he told her where she'd let him down?

"I'm just saying that when you leave, it's going to be hard for me, too," he said. "But I won't apologize for kissing my own wife. There was no sin in that."

Kissing him had always been easier than talking to him. It had been easier than facing their differences, or finding solutions. Of course, a married couple should have a life filled with affection and love, but they hadn't used married love to tie them together—they'd used it to forget their last fight.

"Amos, I can't do this," she whispered. "I'm tired and I'm sad. I'm dealing with my father's death, and your grandmother's illness, and—" She swallowed. "I'm not at my strongest."

Because when she was at her strongest, she could see her way through all of this. She could see the other end—when she got past the heartbreak again, and she realized that while neither of them had dreamed of this separate life, they were happier apart.

"I know. Me, neither," he said. "But having you here is nice all the same."

For now. But for how long? Their relationship didn't have what it took to last, and it was easy to forget that in emotional moments like this one.

"Natasha Zook was telling me why she was willing to become Amish," Miriam said. "Because if you get to know that woman, her becoming Amish makes no sense! She's not even Mennonite! She's English to the core, and yet here she is dressed in Amish clothing, burning her food on a woodstove and driving around in a pickup truck." Miriam shook her head. "And she's determined to be Amish. Why?"

"The Amish faith is pure and she can see the Christian love we have here—"

"The Amish faith is many wonderful things," Miriam said, cutting him off. "But that's not why. Her decision was far from theological, Amos. She said she was willing to do it because she loved him. But more than love, she said she truly believed that *Gott* had created her and Wollie for each other. She says no other man can make her happier than Wollie can, and she's willing to uproot her entire life, alienate her family, who thinks she crazy for doing this, and start this brand-new life that she knows very little about."

"For him," Amos said, his voice low.

"For him." She nodded. "Did you ever think that *Gott* looked down on this planet some thirty-five years ago and decided to create the perfect woman for you in the form of…me?"

Amos blinked at her, and she felt the heat in her face.

"Have you ever considered that?" she pressed. "You and I decided that we wanted to get married—

we wanted to *be* married. It wasn't about us being such a perfect match. It was about us both being left over!"

"Maybe *Gott* was working with that," Amos said.

"Then you must also think that *Gott* isn't a very good matchmaker," Miriam said. "Because you and I are terribly matched. We were just too foolish to see it, and we didn't ask for anyone else's opinion before we insisted that we were ready to marry. We thought we could make our marriage something beautiful with sheer willpower."

Amos was silent.

"We are married, Amos," she said. "But we aren't like Wollie and Natasha. We aren't like Fannie and Silas. I married you, but I wasn't willing to have *kinner* with you. I wasn't willing to risk my health to grow our family."

"I understand that now," he said.

"Yah," she said. "But I also realized that my logical approach to all of these things tells me a lot, too. There was a lot I *wasn't* willing to do for our relationship. And I think what you are willing to do is just as telling as what you aren't."

Because she hadn't been willing to take any leaps of faith with Amos. And when she'd heard Natasha talk about her love for her husband, Miriam had felt something she hadn't felt in a long time—envy.

It was easy to be around people who'd married for logical reasons and were kind and decent to each other. She didn't feel so different from them—she'd married for similar reasons, even if it hadn't worked out as positively. And then she heard the story of a woman who'd married a man from a completely different culture because she'd fallen in love with him. And she'd poured herself into his culture because she believed that *Gott* had created them from embryos to be together.

Some people might mock that kind of romantic view, but Miriam couldn't bring herself to. She couldn't make fun of it, because she did believe in a *Gott* who cared about the details. She did believe that *Gott* guided their steps and showered blessings upon them. But somehow, Miriam had missed *Gott*'s guidance with the most important decision of her life.

"I don't know what to say," Amos said at last.

"It's okay," she said. "We weren't in love with each other, Amos. And we thought it wouldn't matter."

Amos stayed silent, and she felt tears rising inside of her. She wouldn't cry over this—not in front of him.

"I'm going to check the horses," she said, standing up.

It wasn't her job, but keeping busy was easier than focusing on the happiness she may very well have given up because she was in too much of a hurry and had wanted to make things happen on her own.

Miriam headed for the door.

She didn't need her husband's kisses, or his sympathy. She needed to get her balance back.

Chapter Ten

Amos drove to the shop the next morning to tell Noah and Thomas that he wouldn't be working that day, and as he drove his horses down the familiar roads, his mind was stuck on the kiss from the night before. He wasn't sorry, and he wouldn't apologize for it. They'd doomed each other to a life without romance, and if all he had to think about at night was a single, honest kiss that they'd shared; then he'd hold on to it.

And yet, he knew that brief moment of weakness would come with its own punishment. The most honest moments of his life always did. Like when, as a ten-year-old, he'd finally demanded that his father pay for his mother's medication after she had taken to bed in depression. He'd told his father that she would have her pills, or Amos would start telling anyone who would listen what was happening behind those walls. Let the bishop and the elders come—Amos would tell them an earful! And his father had believed him. He pulled out his wallet and handed the cash over. But his relationship with his father had never been the same. His *daet* had never been the same, either... He was more cowed.

More wary. He stopped thundering and booming when he was angry, too.

When *Daet* died the next winter during a bad bout of the flu, Amos had felt like he was partly to blame. He knew that he'd broken his father's spirit, and while he'd meant it for good, there were a whole tangle of consequences.

His *mamm* had never felt quite right about taking the pills again, either. If Amos had reined in his emotions and dealt with it differently, would his mother have taken her medication without guilt?

Amos arrived later than usual, and Noah was just flipping the sign in the front window to Open.

"I'm not staying today," Amos said. "*Mammi* is getting weaker. I wanted to take a day with her while I can."

"*Yah*, understandable," Noah said. "Is she in much pain?"

Thomas came out of the woodshop and leaned against the door frame.

"The medication helps with the pain," Amos said. "But it also makes her sleep a lot, and…maybe that's a blessing, but—"

Thomas came into the showroom, and they all stood in silence for a moment.

"It's good that you'll have time with her," Thomas said. "How are things with Miriam there?"

"Miriam is great," Amos said. "She's helpful, she's efficient, *Mammi* just loves having her back in the house and…" He sighed. "I'm not saying that it isn't complicated. You're both married men now, so I'm sure you understand. Miriam is my wife—she's not just a woman in the home. She's…*my wife*."

Did they understand all the emotion that was locked

in those two little words, *my wife*? Because he'd taken vows before *Gott* and his community that he'd love and care for her. She might not have wanted either of those things in the end, but it didn't stop that he'd vowed to do it. There was something about a wedding—a woman in her wedding apron, a bishop to give the blessing— that locked things down inside of a man whether it was good for him in the long run or not.

"Do you think she might stay, after all?" Noah asked quietly.

Amos shook his head. "No. I don't. We both know how this is going to end. It just isn't easy. That's all."

And it was his burden to bear.

Thomas shuffled his feet uncomfortably, and Noah and Amos looked over at him.

"Patience and I have a meeting with an adoption agent today," Thomas said. "I know this is bad timing with *Mammi* being so sick, but we still long for *kinner*, and this is a chance at growing our family. If I could leave a bit early that would be really helpful. I can come back later on and get more work done in the shop if we're behind—"

"Don't worry about it," Amos replied. "A meeting with an adoption agent is really big. Is there any news? A baby, perhaps?"

"This is a long process," Thomas said. "They told us to expect it to take a while, so we aren't getting our hopes up just yet. I don't want Patience to get disappointed again—" Thomas glanced toward his brother, and Noah froze.

That was a complicated history between the brothers. The first child that Patience had thought she would adopt had been Eve's, and Noah had married Eve and was raising her child as his own. Patience still didn't have another baby in her arms…

"I don't mean it like that," Thomas said. "Samuel is your son now, Noah, and there are no hard feelings there. But when we thought that we were going to adopt Samuel, Patience had her heart in it completely. And if this little boy ends up going to another home, I just don't want her heartbroken again."

"So there is a child?" Noah asked.

"There is a little boy who needs a home. He's two years old, and he's been in the foster system for a while. He has food allergies, and he has some attachment issues because he's been to a few different foster homes already—" Thomas sucked in a breath. "He'd need stability and love—that's what the agent said—and we have that in great supply. He's been through so much upheaval in his young life already that he just needs a home that won't change on him again."

"I'll be praying for you," Noah said earnestly. "Eve and I both will."

"Thank you," Thomas replied. "Patience and I have been praying for the child *Gott* has for us, and I just feel—" Thomas shrugged. "I feel like *Gott* is working in this. But only *Gott* knows what He has in store for us."

"*Mammi* would say that *Gott* is working in every little detail," Noah said.

The men all smiled sadly at the mention of *Mammi* and for a moment they fell silent. Amos looked at the young men he'd raised in his home with *Mammi*'s help, and he saw the emotion brimming in their eyes. They loved her, too.

"She's a woman of faith," Amos said. "She's been praying all this time for both of you—I'm sure she'll be glad to pray for this, too. When you need to leave, you can just put up a sign saying that we're closing early today, and we'll see people in the morning. Family first." Amos patted Thomas on the shoulder. "Always."

"Thanks," Thomas said with a nod and a grateful smile.

"I'd better head back," Amos said. *Mammi* was waiting.

On the way, Amos prayed silently for Thomas and Patience. They'd been through a lot already. When Eve Schrock came to Redemption to give birth to her child and give it up for adoption, they'd thought they were getting an answer to their prayer to adopt a baby. But when Noah and Eve fell in love, Thomas and Patience had tearfully handed the infant back to his mother and stepped back to allow Noah and Eve to raise her son. That had been heartbreaking for Thomas and Patience, but they'd put family first—that was the Amish way. That was *Gott*'s way.

And now, they had another chance to grow their family, and Amos prayed earnestly that *Gott* would grant the deepest desires of their hearts and give them this little boy into their care, if it be *Gott*'s will.

It was always hardest to add that last little bit to a prayer: *If it be Your will, Lord.*

There were other prayers deep in Amos's heart that he was afraid to even bring out into the light. Like this growing hope that Miriam might decide to stay, after all. He wouldn't say it aloud. He'd never tell Noah or Thomas…or even *Mammi* for that matter. Sometimes a man's hopes were so fragile that he didn't dare let anyone else see them.

But having Miriam here had shown him what it could be like if they lived together…what it could be like if she were truly his wife again, in his heart and in his arms. And that kiss last night had settled deep into his heart. Was it stupid of him to hang on to it like that? Probably, but he couldn't help it, either.

When Amos turned into the drive, he saw Miriam arranging a wicker chair underneath a cherry tree, an old, faded quilt spread over the grass nearby. She didn't turn right away, her attention on the job in front of her, and when he reined in the horses, he watched her work for a moment.

There was something about her presence at the house again that softened him. When she turned he hopped down from the buggy and circled around to unhitch the horses, and Miriam looked up and met his gaze. She didn't smile, or wave, but the eye contact made him catch his breath.

"What are you doing?" he called.

"*Mammi* wanted to come out and enjoy the beautiful weather," Miriam said, angling her steps in his direction. "So I'm making it comfortable for her."

The sun was already warm enough that the dew had burned off. A butterfly flitted over the tiny, growing plants in the garden, and Amos pulled off his hat and wiped his brow. It would be the kind of spring day that gave them a taste of summer.

Miriam put her hands on her hips, looking up at him as he got down from the buggy.

"Did you know that your grandfather used to take your *mammi* out on picnics every summer, just the two of them?" Miriam asked.

"Uh—" He stopped, eyed her for a moment. "I seem to remember that..."

Mammi had been telling stories that morning, it seemed.

"She said he proposed marriage on a picnic by the creek," Miriam said, and her expression was thoughtful. "On the Service Sunday their intentions were announced, she made him a picnic, and they ate it in the backyard on an old blanket. She said it was the most delicious meal she ever made."

"She has good memories," Amos said.

"I'm almost envious," Miriam said.

He smiled faintly. "I don't think my proposal to you was as good as my *dawdie*'s. I asked you to marry me on a Service Sunday, on bench at the back of the barn after everyone had left to go eat."

Miriam had been visiting some friends—an older couple, who had since passed away. It was a veiled attempt to meet a single man, truthfully. He'd known it.

Miriam's cheeks pinked. *"Yah."*

"I could have done better," he said.

"You were very serious. I still remember what you said," she replied.

"I don't," he admitted. "I was so nervous I blurted out something...that you agreed to."

"You said we were very much alike, both of us strong and deeply committed to the faith," Miriam said quietly. "And you thought we could be very happy together if we decided to be, and you wanted to know if I would be willing to marry you."

Amos looked over at her, feeling foolish at the memory. It hadn't been terribly romantic, but then, they'd hardly known each other, either. He'd been envisioning a life that never materialized—one where they had babies and raised them to be well-behaved boys and girls.

He imagined dinners as a family, worship time before the *kinner* were sent up to bed…

"I'm truly sorry," he said.

"For what?" Miriam asked.

"I was obviously wrong about us being happy together if we wanted to be," he said.

Because he had wanted it…so badly.

"Oh, Amos." Miriam put a gentle hand on his arm. "We were both wrong. And we both tried. But I still have the memory of a very sweet proposal and a lovely October wedding. No one can take that from me."

But what was it worth, when they couldn't manage to live under the same roof? *Mammi* had her memories of *Dawdie*'s proposal, of their little farm wedding and of the babies they'd had who hadn't survived and the one and only son who had, and even through that heartbreak, they'd weathered it side by side. She had memories of growing old with her husband… And then *Mammi* had the bitterly sad memory of burying him in the same graveyard as the babies who had passed away so early. They'd had a true and complete life together— the good and the bad. What could Amos and Miriam say? Their lives had been lived separately.

Amos looked toward the house.

"*Mammi* is waiting for you," Miriam said.

"I'll take care of the horses and then go get her," he said.

"Sure. I have a few things to finish out here," Miriam said.

She turned and headed back toward the picnic area she'd been putting together, and Amos watched her go. Then he tore his gaze away from his wife, and started to unhitch the horses. Whatever was happening inside of a man's heart, whatever pain he was trying to tamp down, work didn't stop.

When Amos was finished, he headed up the steps and into the kitchen. *Mammi* sat in her comfortable chair and her whole face lit up when she spotted him.

"How are you feeling, *Mammi*?" he asked.

"Much better!" she said. "I can't quite stand up, but I do feel better than I have in weeks."

"Yah?" He shot her a smile. "I'm glad."

"We're having a picnic—" *Mammi* motioned weakly toward the window. "But I need help getting out there. I've been longing for some sunlight, and some fresh air."

"Shall I carry you out?" he asked.

"Yes, please." Her smile was sweet, and she leaned forward in her chair.

Amos bent down and scooped his hands under her frail legs and lifted her up in his arms. She hardly weighed anything these days, and her dress was so loose.

"Thank you, Amos," *Mammi* said, patting his shoulder gently as he carried her out the side door and into the warm spring air. "There's nothing quite like a spring day to make you feel closer to Heaven, is there?"

Amos carefully made his way down the stairs, and Miriam hurried over to angle the chair for him so that he could place *Mammi* down in her spot in the shade under the cherry tree. He settled her in the wicker chair, and Miriam brought a pillow to put behind her back. *Mammi* looked around herself with a smile on her face.

"Would you like some strawberries, *Mammi*?" Miriam asked. "The neighbors got them from the supermarket, and I whipped up fresh cream to go with them."

"No, but thank you, dear," *Mammi* said. "I'm just not hungry. But, Amos—"

Amos bent down toward her.

"Sit down," *Mammi* said. "Let's enjoy some warm weather together."

Amos sank down to the quilt on the ground and he stretched his legs out, resting on his elbow. From where he lay, he could see the beginning of cherries on the tree above their heads, little green fruit. By the fence, he spotted a rabbit nibbling on the lush grass.

"The strangest bits of Scripture come back to you when you're at this stage of life," *Mammi* said softly.

"Oh?" Amos asked. "What verse are you thinking of?"

"'I am come into my garden, my sister, my spouse,'" *Mammi* said, her voice quiet. "'I have gathered my myrrh with my spice; I have eaten my honeycomb with my honey; I have drunk my wine with my milk: eat, O friends; drink, yea, drink abundantly, O beloved…'" *Mammi*'s voice trailed away.

"Song of Songs," Amos murmured.

Mammi smiled. "I miss your *dawdie*, Amos. We had a good life together. A good, good life…"

For *Mammi*, it seemed like her days of marriage and motherhood, of love and living deeply, were only a breath away. When Amos was *Mammi*'s age, when he was looking back on his life, would he be feeling resplendent with satisfied memories like *Mammi* was? Or would he have regrets?

Miriam stood back a few paces, watching Amos and his grandmother talking quietly in the shade of the cherry tree. *Mammi* looked even smaller today, but she was brighter, somehow, happier. Maybe it was the sunshine, or having her grandson home with her during the day like it was a holiday just for her.

Looking at Amos lying on the blanket, she could remember what he looked like eleven years ago when he'd proposed so earnestly. He was still tall and handsome, although now he had the thick, bushy beard of a married man. His chest was still broad, and his arms roped with muscle from the physical labor he did every day.

She really had thought that a man as good as Amos couldn't help but be a good husband…or maybe the fault had been hers. She'd refused to have *kinner* after her sister's death. She'd always thought that after she married, she'd be able to settle into raising her *kinner* and keeping house. It was a huge amount of work to occupy a woman's time, but without the *kinner* in her future, somehow her hopes for running a business, the competition of coming out on top, came creeping back in. Maybe they would have, anyway.

Which was wrong. She wasn't even arguing that. An Amish woman wasn't supposed to compete. She was supposed to be content in the role of wife and *mamm*. But Miriam hadn't been able to.

"Where did Miriam go?" *Mammi*'s voice came to her on the breeze.

"I'm here, *Mammi*," Miriam said, and she came over to where they sat. "Can I get you anything?"

"Sit, sit," *Mammi* said, gesturing to the blanket. "I was about to tell a story."

Mammi's mind seemed to be on her late husband these days. Miriam had never met *Dawdie*. But she'd heard stories here and there about him. He had saved his brother from being crushed by a load of hay bales when he was a teenager, single-handedly lifting fourteen bales off his brother, and pulling him to safety. She'd also heard a few funny stories about *Dawdie* getting confused in *Englisher* shops, or *Dawdie* coming back with a funny quip when his brothers used to needle him. Miriam settled down on the blanket next to Amos, who shifted his legs to make room for her.

"I remember when Amos was just a little boy," *Mammi* said. "He was about as tall as the tie on my apron, and he was a rascal…"

Miriam looked over at Amos and chuckled.

"Wait—this is a story about me?" Amos said. "I thought we were going to hear about *Dawdie*!"

"So did I," Miriam said. "But this might be just as good."

"Oh, hush," *Mammi* said, a smile twinkling in her eyes. "Amos was an only child. His mother had some difficulties in his delivery, and she wasn't able to have any more, and we had neighbors with children his age, so he'd come to visit and play. Anyway, one day, Amos was visiting us, getting a chance to play with other kids, when we had an *Englisher* traveling salesman stop by. They were much more common back then. This one was selling encyclopedia sets. And when he knocked on the door, he looked so bedraggled and tired that I invited him in for tea and pie. While he was eating, a storm opened up outside, so he had to stay a little longer."

Amos frowned. "I don't remember this…"

"No?" *Mammi* said. "Well, you weren't very old. Anyway, I knew I wasn't buying any encyclopedias from that man, but the man didn't know it, and he kept trying to make his sales pitch. But I didn't want to send him out into the storm, either. So I let him talk."

"I think I do remember this," Amos said. "I remember the kitchen being dark and rain coming down in a torrent and a man in an overcoat sitting at the kitchen table..."

"*Yah*, that would be the one," *Mammi* said. "Little Amos didn't like this Englisher stranger pushing me to buy something, and he seemed to think that I needed help. So he stood up just as tall as he could stand, and he said, 'My *dawdie* is working in the field, and my *daet* isn't here, so that makes me the man of this house. You leave my *mammi* alone, or I'll have to ask you to leave!'"

Miriam looked over at Amos, while *Mammi* was laughing softly to herself. Amos's cheeks grew pink, and he pulled off his hat and rubbed a hand through his hair.

"I thought I was bigger than I was," Amos said. "I remember being older than that."

"Oh, no," *Mammi* said. "You were all of five or six."

"So your nobility started young," Miriam said.

"Apparently." Amos rolled his eyes. "If you could call insulting a grown man nobility."

"I'm going to tell you something," *Mammi* said, sobering. "And I know I've told you a little bit about my son, Aaron, but there's more."

"*Mammi*—" Amos started.

"She needs to hear this," *Mammi* said. She looked a little paler now, and she sucked in an uneven breath.

"No, I don't think she does," Amos replied. "*Mammi*, please trust me on this—"

"Amos, you'll have to trust *me*, this time," *Mammi* replied. "She'll only understand you better if she understands your *daet*. Now, I don't have much strength, and perhaps you'll insist upon me keeping quiet... You are the man of this home..."

Amos rose to his feet now, and he looked from

Mammi, then down at Miriam. She could see the battle on his features, and *Mammi* was right—Amos could insist upon this secret being keep, as the man of the home.

"I wouldn't give you any orders, *Mammi*," Amos said, his voice tight. "You know me better than that."

Miriam caught her breath and looked back at the old woman. She was watching her grandson with a somber look on her face, and then she continued, her voice quiet.

"My son, Aaron, wasn't a good husband," *Mammi* went on. "He didn't provide well. He used to gamble and drink, and the money he made was often spent by the time he got home on the evening of payday. I sometimes blamed the fact that I couldn't give him siblings for how he turned out. He never did have to share..." She shook her head. "But Amos was an only child, too, and he turned out to be such a wonderful young man that I suppose I'm forced to admit that it wasn't me. It was drink. It was addiction..." She sighed. "So Amos felt the immense pressure very early. Amos didn't have anyone to share with, either, but there was much less to live on. He and his mother had to find ways to hide money from Aaron to keep him from gambling it away."

"But you were so little," Miriam said softly.

Amos didn't answer. He pressed his lips together and stood braced as if for a blow.

"He didn't think he was little," *Mammi* said. "And he certainly didn't stay little. He was big for his age at ten. Aaron's drinking and gambling got worse as he got older, not better. We tried everything to get through to Aaron that he was ruining not only his life, but his wife's and son's, too. We even talked about having him shunned, but his wife did her best to keep on raising

Amos on the little bit of money she could scrounge up from odd jobs and charity then hide from Aaron. And we kept bringing over groceries and doing our best to help out."

"One day, when I was about ten," Amos said, his deep voice taking up the story, "my *daet* got home from gambling, and he owed a great deal of money. They'd roughed him up, and he was looking for the deed to our acreage so that he could sell it, I think. I'd already started confronting my father about things in our home, and I wrestled that deed out of his hands—it wasn't hard. He was drunk, and I—" Amos swallowed. "I hit my father in the face with a water pitcher, knocking him out cold."

Miriam sucked in a breath and stared at him in shock. Amos—sweet, gentle Amos, hitting his own father?

"And my mother took over the family finances that day," Amos said. "I worked odd jobs, and my *mamm* and I pooled what we could make in a bank account together. She took over paying the bills, and I even put a little bit of savings aside for emergencies. My mother and I learned together, and we kept our home. My father was never allowed access to that bank account."

"*This* acreage?" Miriam asked, looking around at the familiar garden, the house, the trees.

"*Yah*, this one," Amos said. "My parents both passed away. My *daet* got a bad flu the very next year and my *mamm* had a stroke a few years after when I was about fourteen. She went into the hospital and didn't recover."

"You took good care of your *mamm*," Mammi said quietly. "You're a better man than your father was, and I'm proud of you. So proud."

Amos met his grandmother's tender gaze, and she saw tears mist his eyes.

"Miriam," *Mammi* said. "There are always reasons why people react the ways that they do. And your husband is no different in that. We tried to make our family look a little better for your benefit. We were embarrassed. We didn't want people to know our problems…"

"I understand," Miriam said softly. "It's okay."

"Maybe we should have told you all of this sooner," *Mammi* said. "But all the same, when I die, I won't be harboring secrets. I don't think the Lord can bless that."

They were all silent for a few beats; the birds overhead were the only noise that interrupted the stillness between them.

Amos sighed. "I think that's enough stories for now. I'm going to go check on the horses."

And he bent down, giving his grandmother a kiss on her cheek before he strode away toward the stables. Miriam watched him go, her heart hovering in her chest. The horses were fine—he was running away.

"That's why he longed for my *daet* to love him," Miriam said, tears rising in her eyes.

"Yah," Mammi said softly. "That's why."

Because his own *daet* hadn't loved him properly, and he'd been hoping that her *daet* might fill some of that emptiness. There were good reasons why Amos was the way he was, and none of those reasons were because he wasn't man enough or strong enough, or smart enough.

At last, she understood him, and that was a gift in itself. *Mammi* was right that secrets only made things harder, but it didn't change who they both were, and what they both needed.

Amos needed a dutiful wife at home who would trust

him. Her trust was the key to his heart. And Miriam needed some freedom, some adventure, to have a voice in growing their business to its full potential.

Their needs didn't change, especially not Amos's. He'd needed a very different kind of woman, and the fact that he'd married her, the very opposite of what would fulfill what his aching heart needed most, made their marriage all the more tragic.

Chapter Eleven

"Are you upset with me, Aaron?" *Mammi* asked.

"It's Amos, *Mammi*," he said softly.

"Oh…yes…"

She was propped up in her bed, her eyes half-shut, but she struggled to open them all the way to look at Amos as he sat down on the edge of her bed. The room was warm, but *Mammi* had wanted an extra blanket over her legs. An open window let in some fresh air, the sound of birds twittering coming in with the early-evening sunlight. On the bed next to *Mammi* was a bowl of the strawberries from the supermarket with some whipped cream, but she refused them.

"Are you upset with me for telling Miriam what I did?" *Mammi* asked.

"No, *Mammi*," Amos said softly. "Of course not."

"You can say if you are," she whispered. "I can take it."

No, she couldn't take it, but even so, he wasn't angry with her. How could he be? His grandmother had been one of his biggest supporters growing up, and on the day he and his mother had opened that bank account, his grandmother had given him a hug and told him that he was a good boy. She'd been the difference between despondence and hope. She'd been a ray of sunlight. His throat tightened with emotion.

Mammi had tired herself out today. He could see all the signs. She'd been weaker than ever before, and she was in bed long before sunset. Noah and his family had come to see *Mammi*, and they'd all prayed together for Thomas's hopes of adoption. *Mammi* had prayed so eloquently for all of them, mentioning them each by name. She had been bright and cheerful, but all her energy seemed to be gone now. He reached out and took her hand. It was cool to the touch, despite the warm room.

"I'm not angry, *Mammi*," he said. "It's probably better that Miriam know it all. The truth will set us free—isn't that what the Bible says?"

"*Yah*, it does." She smiled faintly.

"I don't feel like a good man, *Mammi*," he whispered.

"It isn't your feelings that matter," *Mammi* said, opening her eyes with a struggle. "You *are* a good man. It's a fact. You can trust me, dear one."

Amos looked up to see Miriam standing in the hallway, watching them with tears in her eyes. He gave Miriam a reassuring smile, and she turned away again.

"Do you think she'll stay?" *Mammi* asked.

"Here? With me?" he asked. He didn't have to ask who she meant. They both knew. Miriam was the one they were both thinking of tonight.

"*Yah*. She's your lawfully wedded wife, Amos."

"*Mammi*..." Amos swallowed. Must she push this? Must she force him to tell her the truth? "Miriam and I are very different people. Her understanding why I'm the way I am doesn't change *who* I am. Or who she is."

"I know…" *Mammi* sighed. "But you're such a good man, Amos. You have such a heart. I'd just hoped…"

And how Amos wished he could tell his grandmother otherwise and flood her old heart with joy. But it wasn't just for her joy that he wished he could say she was staying. Because having her here had been a relief in so many ways. He hadn't realized how much he'd missed his wife—even arguing with her! But that wasn't reason enough for her to stay. They had made mature and reasonable plans for their own futures. He looked up, but the hallway was empty.

"I'll be okay, *Mammi*," he whispered. "I will. I have Noah and Thomas and their families. I'm like a grandfather to those *kinner*."

"God's fingerprints are on everything," *Mammi* murmured, not seeming to be put off. "He's working still. Don't you doubt that. He's working…"

Mammi's eyes were still shut, and she breathed more slowly than seemed natural. Was she still holding out hope for his reunion with his wife? If only she'd give up, he wouldn't feel quite so guilty as he did. Miriam deserved a happy life, even if that meant she would live it away from him.

"Amos…" *Mammi*'s voice was quieter still. "Would you read me… John 14?"

Amos released *Mammi*'s hand and he wiped an errant tear from his cheek. These times sitting on the edge of his grandmother's bed, reading her Bible passages, had become so precious over the last weeks. He was sharing her hope—and oh, how he needed it tonight.

He picked up *Mammi*'s worn Bible, and he opened to the passage. She'd underlined the first few verses in pencil, and he started to read.

"'Let not your heart be troubled: ye believe in God, believe also in me. In my Father's house are many mansions: if it were not so, I would have told you. I go to prepare a place for you. And if I go and prepare a place for you, I will come again, and receive you unto myself; that where I am, there ye may be also…'"

He read slowly, enunciating the words the way she liked him to do, and then he paused, looking down at his grandmother's face. She still looked peaceful, and her eyes were shut, but something had changed. Her chest was still, and Amos could feel in his heart what had just happened.

Mammi was gone.

Amos stood up and went into the kitchen. Miriam was at the kitchen table, a cup of tea in front of her. She looked up as he came in.

"I think that…uh—" Amos looked helplessly toward Miriam. "I think that *Mammi* has passed away."

Miriam straightened, the blood seeping from her face. "What? When?"

"A few minutes ago, while I was reading the Bible to her," Amos said, and his voice broke.

Miriam went into the bedroom, and Amos stood immobile in the kitchen. She returned a couple of minutes later.

"Oh, Amos…" Miriam whispered, and she crossed the kitchen and stopped in front of him. "I'm so sorry…"

She stood there, her dark gaze meeting his with such deep sympathy that Amos felt the tears rise up in his eyes. His grandmother was gone, and his heart was full to breaking. He didn't know what to say, but Miriam saved him from trying to find it. She reached up and put her arms around his neck, tugging him down so that she could hold him. He slipped his arms around her waist and pulled her against him. He couldn't cry, though. While his throat was tight with unshed tears, and his chest felt so full of emotion that it might crack right open, he couldn't let it out.

Somehow, he'd been putting off feeling this impending loss—focusing on Miriam's presence, on his work, on the silly battles he and his wife always seemed to wage against each other. And maybe it had all been a way to avoid the heartbreaking truth that his beloved *mammi* had been dying. But there was no way to avoid it any longer.

Miriam cried in his arms, her tears soaking into his shirt. Having Miriam here, so close, was the most comforting thing he could imagine right now. *Mammi* had been right. And maybe she had been meddling in his life, hoping to make a reunion happen that really had no hope, but she had been right that having his wife here with him during his grandmother's death was exactly what he'd needed.

Even at the last, *Mammi* had been thinking of him...

Amos pulled back and Miriam wiped tears from her cheeks.

"We should call the doctor," Amos said woodenly.

"Yah." Miriam pulled a slip of paper out of her apron with the doctor's number on it. "And we need to let people know so that the funeral arrangements can begin..."

"Miriam—" He caught her hand. "Will you stay for the funeral?"

Because he couldn't face the thought of her leaving. Not yet.

"Of course," she said, and her chin trembled. "I promised *Mammi* I'd get you through it."

And perhaps he needed to get her through it, too. *Mammi* had meant so much to all of them, and Miriam had always had a special place in *Mammi*'s heart, even after the miserable breakup, after the community had judged her, and Amos did his best to forget her. Miriam deserved to mourn for *Mammi*, too.

But after the funeral, Miriam would go home. It had been the plan all along. Maybe it was best to simply be thankful for the time they'd had together, for this chance to truly connect as two human beings. *Mammi* had wanted them to get back together, and Amos had started to hope for the same impossible thing.

Gott, *thank You that Miriam's here today...*

That was all he could think to pray.

The funeral was put together by the community. *Mammi*'s friends and extended family worked in unison on the preparations so that Amos and Miriam had very little to do. Amos went through some of *Mammi*'s things—she didn't have much. There were some dresses, some *kapps* and aprons, an unfinished needlework project of a Bible verse and a box of little collectible animal figurines she'd bought over the years when she and *Dawdie* would travel together.

Noah and Thomas came by the house early to help Amos carry *Mammi*'s bed and the chest of drawers back upstairs to her bedroom. Miriam swept out the room, mopped it, wiped down the surfaces, and they moved the couch and chairs back to where they belonged. It felt suddenly very empty in that sitting room, and very, very lonely.

Mammi was buried in the community graveyard, and

there were sermons, singing, a large meal put together at Amos's house that everyone contributed to.

The songs they sang were about Heaven, and their hope of eternity with *Gott*. Miriam had stood on the women's side, and Amos had stood shoulder to shoulder with Noah and Thomas on either side of him. The family from Ohio and Indiana had come, too, but when he looked up, it was Miriam's steady gaze that gave him the most strength. Whatever happened during wedding vows, while they didn't seem to guarantee happiness or a peaceful home, they did connect a man and a woman in an undeniable way.

Mammi's funeral was long, as all Amish funerals were. Amish funerals gave people time to accept the loss, and to hold the sadness in their hearts together. Mourning took time, and so did comfort. That was part of the Amish way—they took their time to do things properly, to feel them deeply. They didn't rush. Grieving was never done alone when one had a community like Redemption.

"She was the only grandmother I knew," Noah told Amos sadly, his infant son in his arms. "And she was so full of wisdom and hope."

"Yah..." Amos nodded. "She was very loved."

His mind kept going back to her final day—the one spent outdoors where she insisted that she was feeling better, and she kept telling stories. He knew that *Mammi*'s life hadn't been perfect. She'd buried her only adult son after that one terrible winter, but it could be argued that she'd lost him years before to addiction. She'd lost babies and had never had the house full of children she'd prayed for. *Mammi* had spent a lifetime praying, and not always seeing the results. Her life wasn't perfect, but somehow, when *Mammi* was looking back on her lifetime, she saw sweetness and beauty because she'd had her dear husband at her side.

The funeral passed by in a blur, and when the funeral day was done, and all the baking and casseroles had been left in his kitchen by kind neighbors, Amos knew that life would start to return to normal in degrees.

And he felt that his goodbye to his grandmother had been complete.

The next morning, Miriam stood in the kitchen dishing up bowls of oatmeal. After Amos had gone out to do his chores, Miriam had stripped the guest room bed, remade it with fresh sheets and swept the floor so that the room was as neat as she'd found it.

This house, so familiar, was not hers. This wasn't her home, even if she was starting to feel like she might have some claim to it after all they'd been through these last two weeks. It was almost like the honeymoon period after their wedding, when she felt that powerful tie to the man she'd vowed to love. And here she was, feeling that too-strong claim on Amos and this home, all over again.

Miriam was the one who kept feeling too much, needing too much. If she were just like the other women, she could quietly find contentment in keeping her home and supporting her husband. But Miriam wasn't like the others, and she'd grown to accept that. She wasn't the wife Amos needed. And this life in his home as his wife, as beautiful as it could be, wouldn't be enough for her. It was better to leave now, and deal with the heartbreak all at once. Because if she stayed longer, when she left they'd both be bitter and angry, and that would be worse.

Amos's boots resounded on the steps outside, and the door opened. She listened as his boots thunked to the floor and the water turned on for him to wash his hands.

"Good morning," he said, appearing in the mudroom doorway.

"Good morning," she replied, but the words felt tight in her throat.

"It felt good to get outside," Amos said. "It seems to help."

Miriam nodded. It likely did help, but she'd be outside soon enough when they were on their way to the bus depot. And then there would be a two-hour bus ride where she'd be holding back tears, and when she finally did get back outside again in Edson, she would find somewhere private, and those tears would fall.

But not until then... Amos might be looking for relief right here and right now, but her relief would have to wait.

"Breakfast smells good," Amos said, but as the words came out, his gaze landed on her travel bag, and he froze. He looked up at her, his eyebrows climbing. "You're leaving today?"

She hadn't meant to ask for the ride quite like this, although how she saw that going, she wasn't sure.

"If you'll drop me off at the bus station on your way into work," she said. "I've made us breakfast, and you have enough baking and extra food here to last you a month—" She forced a smile. "I think you'll be in good hands."

Just not hers. And that tugged at her heart. There had been other hands to show him compassion and care for the last ten years. Why should this hurt more now? He glanced over at the food on the counter—bags of muffins, loaves of bread, piles of produce.

"I thought you might stay a few days longer," he said, turning back to her.

"I'd only sit in this house alone," Miriam said, and she shook her head. "I don't think I could handle that."

"I like having you here," he whispered. "I like coming home to your cooking, and hearing your voice around the house."

"I've missed you, too, Amos," Miriam said. "But we have to be realistic now."

"Realistic," he said hollowly.

"Yah!" Was he going to force her to do this? "Amos, the longer I stay, the harder it is for me to go—"

Amos crossed the kitchen and he tugged her solidly into his arms. His lips came down over hers, and for what felt like a blessed eternity, he kissed her.

Amos pulled back, and Miriam sucked in a wavering breath. She wanted him to kiss her again, to let her forget that her bag was waiting…

"Don't go yet," Amos whispered.

Her heart squeezed in response. "Amos, don't do this to me…"

"Do what?" he asked, shaking his head. "I'm just asking you to stay a little longer."

"Why?" she asked helplessly. "What is there to be gained?"

"Maybe we could have some time to figure this out," he said hopefully.

"We went through all of this ten years ago!" she said, her voice starting to rise. "We figured it out then, Amos!"

Amos's dark gaze met hers solemnly. He'd always been so noble, so calm... "We could change our minds, you know. You could stay here. We could make a life together—try again."

"You don't really want that," she said.

Because she hadn't changed—she was the same woman who drove him crazy.

"Maybe I do," he replied.

"You say you do," she countered. "But what you want is to come home to me. You want me here, keeping your home, cooking your food, spending the evening together reading *The Budget*. You don't want the reality of what having me here would actually be!"

"It could be just like you described," he said. "We could vow to stop arguing."

"It didn't work," she said. "Not even for *Mammi*. This doesn't come naturally to either of us. Why can't you see me for who I am, Amos? I wouldn't be a patient and meek wife, waiting for you to figure out the radio ads. I'd go find out how to do them myself! And put together some ideas, and even make a budget for it," she said. "I'd want a hand in your business. I'd want to run it *together*."

He pressed his lips together in a look she recognized.

"I can see the look on your face," Miriam went on. "You don't want that life, but that's who I am. I've got a strip mall that will provide some income, and I've got ideas for that other shop, too. It's not like other women don't run businesses!"

"Other women do it with less ferocity," he said with a small smile.

"I'm not like them!" Miriam rubbed her hands over

her face. Talking about this more wasn't going to change anything. Letting her emotions out wasn't going to help.

"Why can't you just stay a little while?" Amos asked quietly. "I'm not asking for forever yet. I'm just asking you to stay with me…see if you might like it—"

"No!" The tears Miriam had been working so hard to hold back started to flow.

"Why?" he demanded, his own agonized gaze locked on to hers. "Give me a good reason why not, Miriam! You're my *wife!*"

"Because we've done this before!" she sobbed. "We've done it, and it tore me into pieces when I had to leave! And it'll only be worse this time!"

"Worse?" He threw his hands in the air. "How on earth could it be worse?"

"Because *I love you!*" The words came out before she could think better of them, and Amos suddenly stilled, his expression shocked. But she did…she was only really realizing it now. That's why her heart kept pulling toward him. It was why she kept falling into his arms, and why he could hurt her like no other. She loved him. She'd fallen in love with her husband, and it wouldn't help them one bit. Loving a man didn't make a relationship work! Loving him only made it more painful when they hurt each other.

"Yah…" she breathed. "I love you. And I shouldn't… I'm not what you need, and I can't change who I am. If I don't go home now, I'm not sure I'll survive this. You *have* to let me go!"

Chapter Twelve

Amos stared at Miriam, his heart lodged in his throat. She *loved* him? After all these years of wondering if she ever had, now she loved him? Her eyes sparkled with unshed tears, and a tendril of hair had fallen loose from her *kapp*. She was petite next to him, and all of that pent-up energy inside of her usually made her seem taller than she really was. She used to intimidate him, if he had to be brutally honest. But right now, looking into her eyes, looking for answers to that way his heart was yearning toward her, she didn't look any bigger than life anymore. She looked fragile.

"Miriam—" His voice caught.

Miriam shook her head. "Don't make it harder, Amos."

"What do you think I'll say?" he asked.

"You'll tell me that I'm being foolish. That what I'm feeling is connected to a death of someone we both cared about. That given some time, I'll get my footing back, and—"

"Seriously?" Amos asked. "You think that's what I'd say when you tell me that you love me?"

"It's what you should say." She swallowed.

And maybe it was. Maybe that would help them both get past this, but it wasn't what he felt. He'd been running from this for ten years, but he'd never said the words to her before.

"I love you, too," he said, and he caught her slim hand in his calloused grip, looking down into her tearstained face.

"You don't have to say that—" she started.

"Miriam, stop it!" he said, and he shook his head. "I love you! Okay? I'm not saying what I think is appropriate. I'm telling you how I feel. I think about you constantly. I have for the entire time you were gone. It would be easier not to love you! Much easier. Because you're leaving again, and I'm going to be left alone in this house trying to hold on to some little detail—like the way you smell so soft and sweet, or the sound of your laugh. But I'll forget—ever so slowly, it will slip away, and that feeling of forgetting will be worse than torturing myself with memories. So this isn't convenient for me, either."

Amos tugged her close, his gaze locked on to hers. For a moment, he wasn't sure what to do, but then he slid his arms around her waist and lowered his lips over hers. Miriam rose up onto the tips of her toes to meet his kiss. She wasn't what he needed, and he wasn't the kind of man who completed her, either. But his heart didn't want to listen to reason. He wanted to hold her close and kiss her senseless, and never think ahead to the future when they'd inevitably break each other's hearts all over again.

If Amos couldn't love his own wife, then who could he love? There was no moving on for an Amish couple. They were married until death parted them, and he couldn't look for another woman who might be a better fit. When he'd promised to be hers ten years ago, he had signed his entire future into her hands.

Miriam pulled back first, and Amos looked down at her plump lips. She was so beautiful...but she wasn't truly his.

"I'm not what you need," she repeated. "And that matters. If *Mammi* showed me anything, it was that you're a good man with a tender heart. There is nothing wrong with you wanting a wife at home who will trust the business to your capable hands. Nothing! But I'm not that woman. You don't want all of this energy focused on you and your business," Miriam said. "Just accept that. And we can go about our separate ways. And if we're ever in trouble—if one of us is sick or hurt, or in need of help—"

"I'll be here," he said, his voice low and deep. "Always."

"And I'll take care of you," she said earnestly. "If you need me, all you need to do is send me a message and I'll drop everything. You still have a wife. You'll appreciate me more if you see less of me."

Did she feel the same about him? Was he easier to appreciate when she saw him once a decade? Were they better supporting each other through the hard times, and then taking their distance again?

Miriam took a purposeful step away from him, dropped her gaze and wiped her face. Then she walked toward her bag and picked it up. She hadn't noticed the hair that had come loose, and when she looked back at him, she looked bedraggled and sorrowful.

"Would you drive me to the bus station, Amos?" she asked quietly. "I need to get home."

Her voice caught at the last word: *home*.

This was her home, and Amos wanted to shout it at her, to make her hear it! *He* was supposed to be her home—his arms were supposed to be her protection. But whatever marriage was supposed to be, they'd always seemed to miss the mark.

"If that's what you want," he said, and he caught her eye, waiting for her to see what she was so determined to walk away from. "If it's what you really, truly want."

Would she change her mind?

"Thank you, Amos," she whispered. "I appreciate it."

No, she wouldn't. She always had been stronger than him in spirit. She was tougher, more determined, more convinced of her own views. No one changed Miriam Lapp's mind on anything.

Amos let out a slow breath and nodded. He'd watched his mother be miserable trying to make his father happy. He'd watched her deny herself of the things she needed most desperately, just to try and please her husband. And maybe medication wasn't the same thing as what was most necessary to Miriam's happiness, but regardless, Amos would never do that to his wife. Amos wouldn't beg her to come back, or change herself, or to give up one fraction of the life she longed for. Not for him.

He went outside and hitched up the buggy. As he worked, he wondered if Miriam weren't right. This was painful now, but she was right that they were so very different. They wanted different things from life, from marriage, from love… And when Miriam was happy and bright, shimmering with energy, that was when she was meddling in his business, giving him unasked for advice or staring down one of his customers.

She didn't want to be a wife at home, trusting her husband to provide. She wanted to be pushing him forward, making him better, putting her fingerprints all over the business he'd built up from scratch. She was so much energy, so much good intention, so much forward motion…

They drove each other crazy.

Gott, how did we get here? he prayed in his heart. *How did we end up loving each other, but completely incapable of living together?*

No one would understand this if he tried to explain. Noah and Thomas would nod, and then exchange perplexed looks with each other. *Mammi* was the only one who came close to understanding the complexity of his relationship with his wife, but even she had been bent on trying to reunite them.

Amos brought the buggy to the side of the house, and then took her travel bag and put it in the back. Miriam didn't wait for a hand up. She settled herself on the bench, and he went around to the other side.

He'd drive his wife to the bus station, and then he'd have to let her go.

She was right. If they did this later—in a month or two, in another year—it just might tear out his heart, too, and he couldn't be sure he'd recover.

When the bus pulled away from the station, Amos couldn't see Miriam's face. All he could make out was the white of her *kapp*, and then just as the bus came past him, he got a flash of her face, and her hand suddenly pressed against the glass.

He stood there as the bus rumbled away, his heart hovering in his chest as if it was afraid to beat again.

She was gone.

He suddenly remembered that carved box. He'd finished it the night before, and he'd forgotten to give it to her. Even in their goodbyes, he seemed to be messing this up.

He swallowed hard and turned back toward the station. His horse and buggy waited in the parking lot, and he pushed past an Amish man he knew, refusing to look up. He couldn't face friendly banter right now. He couldn't pretend he was fine when inside of him he was falling apart.

When he got to the buggy, he hoisted himself up into the seat, his vision blurred by unshed tears. They wouldn't fall, but they hung there in front of his eyes, making it impossible to see anything clearly.

His shop was waiting for him. Thomas and Noah would be starting to worry...

He'd go back to work. He'd pour this heartache into his craft, and he'd work long hours so that when he got back to his empty house, he could simply drop into bed and melt into the oblivion of sleep.

His heart would heal...eventually. And *Gott* would give him something else to live for. Before, it was Thomas and Noah who came into his life. Maybe there would be someone else who would need his battered heart and his best intentions.

Just not a wife.

Life was long, and as *Mammi* always said, *Gott* worked in the details. *Gott* still had something for him to do, a way for him to brighten his corner. He'd just have to wait for the Almighty to put it in his path.

Gott might be preparing mansions for them in Heaven, but He didn't forget his *kinner* on earth, either.

* * *

Miriam carried her bag into the family farmhouse. The Schwartz farm was large, even by Amish standards. The house had seven bedrooms, and a summer kitchen that extended off the south end for cooler summer cooking. Japheth's wife, Arleta, was peeling potatoes into a large pot, and she looked up with a tired smile.

"You're back," Arleta said.

"*Yah*, I'm back." Miriam set down her bag.

"Your brother thought you might stay with your husband," Arleta said. "I confess, I thought you might, too."

Miriam shook her head. "I only stayed as long as I did because Amos's grandmother needed my help in her final days."

"*Yah*, I'm sorry for your loss," Arleta said. "I know you loved her. What with your father's passing, and now Mary Lapp—"

Miriam nodded. "It's been a hard season."

Miriam glanced around the wide kitchen. The table seated twelve, easily, and there was space enough for a row of storage cabinets that held bulk ingredients.

Once upon a time, this house had been full of extended family and visiting friends filling up all this extra space, and now it was Japheth's family, his wife and four children. Her brother was nowhere to be seen, and she wondered if he was in his office, or away from the house. She pulled out the envelope that held the documents she needed to prove that she owned the strip mall. This was her most important task right now.

Overhead, Miriam could hear one of her nieces sweeping, and out the kitchen window two more of her nieces were bent over in the garden, weeding. The baby was in a cradle in the corner of the kitchen, and

Arleta was pregnant again. She'd had no trouble with childbearing.

"It might be a good time to reconnect with Amos..." Arleta said hesitantly, and Miriam's mind was tugged back to her sister-in-law.

"Are you anxious to get rid of me?" Miriam asked with an uncomfortable laugh.

"Of course not." Arleta shook her head. "But I really think your father did you wrong by meddling in your marriage the way he did, and your brother and I never agreed with that. We couldn't counter him, of course. That would have been wrong. But Amos Lapp is a good man. He might not be as successful as we are, but he's still a good man. I'm sure you don't want to be keeping house with me. I mean, I'm good company, but I'm not enough." Arleta shot her a teasing smile.

That was what most everyone would assume—that Miriam had finally gone home to her husband. But it wasn't an option.

"I won't be getting in your way," Miriam said. "I found the documents I went to look for. My *daet* signed a certain property over to me, and I'm going to use that income to start a new business that I can run."

"Which property?" Arleta's tone sharpened.

"The strip mall on Main Street," Miriam said.

"Hmm." Arleta turned back to the potato peeling, but her movements were sharper now, and the peels whisked into a bucket.

"What did I say?" Miriam asked.

Was Arleta angry at her getting even that much? Arleta stopped peeling and looked up.

"And you think that's the right move for you?" her

sister-in-law asked pointedly. "You think you should run a business and forget about keeping a home?"

Miriam glanced around the spotless kitchen. This *was* her home. She'd been born in this house.

"Do you want me underfoot?" Miriam asked.

"I'm not asking you to leave if you're determined to stay. We all have to choose the life we want, and if this is it, then who am I to argue with you? But this is a big house!" Arleta said. "There's enough work to share! My girls and I can keep it running, but we have a whole garden we let go to seed because we don't have enough time in the day to take care of it! And you want to go start your business like you're some child playing games with her *daet*. And Japheth doesn't need the help, if you're thinking of working with him! He's the man. He can keep it running. No one wants a woman coming to them for lease payments, anyway. Your father spoiled you! He let you play like a little girl, going with him to take care of business when you should have been here at the house doing your duty. Let Japheth take care of the men's work. What about doing the work you're *supposed* to be doing? If you won't do it for your husband, you can do it here."

Miriam stared at her sister-in-law in surprise. She hadn't realized that all this bitterness was under the surface. When her *daet* was alive, he ruled this house and he dictated that Miriam should go with him to understand the business. Miriam had pitched in when she was at home, but that wasn't the majority of her day.

"My *daet gave* me that business," Miriam said, her voice tight. "And I will need it to provide for myself. Maybe I'll end up getting a little place of my own—"

"You have a husband to provide for you," Arleta said.

"You have a home with him. I don't know why you refuse to go back."

"Because I don't make my husband happy!" she blurted out, tears springing to her eyes.

Behind her, Japheth's voice reverberated. "Should I go have a word with him? I don't care if he's happy or not! You're his wife!"

Miriam turned to see her brother in the doorway. Japheth stood there with his arms crossed over his chest, his eyes ablaze. He didn't have his hat on inside, and his hair was slightly askew.

"No, I don't need you to go shout at Amos," she snapped. "I'm perfectly capable of speaking for myself. Amos and I understand each other very well. We're just...different."

"As are all men and women!" Japheth retorted. "Miriam, our *daet* didn't do you any favors by chasing away your husband. I'll tell you that much. I thought if you went back to see Amos, you'd see reason, too."

"*Daet* didn't chase him away..." she said. "If anyone had ruined things, it was me and Amos. We were adult enough to make a marriage work or tear it apart."

"*Yah*, *Daet* did," Japheth replied resolutely. "*Daet* made you into the son he always wanted, and that didn't prepare you for married life."

Miriam exchanged a tired look with her brother. This was an old conversation. Their father had taken more interest in teaching Miriam the business because she'd caught on to it more quickly. It was second nature to her. The numbers came easily, the equations made sense. And she had an instinct for what would make a business work that Japheth had always lacked. Their *daet* had been so very proud of Miriam's ability…just not proud enough to leave her a proper inheritance.

"Japheth, I can't apologize for who I am," Miriam said. "I'm tired of doing that."

Japheth rubbed a hand over his thinning hair. "Come to my office. Since you're here, I need you to look at some ledgers for me. I can't make sense of them."

"Arleta needs help here," Miriam said.

"She's fine. Come on." He started out of the room and Miriam cast her sister-in-law an apologetic look. "Your husband might not need your business sense, but right now I do."

"I was hoping she could help me with that garden," Arleta said, raising her voice after Japheth, and there was a tension in her voice that meant Japheth and Arleta had discussed this before.

"I *will* help you with it, Arleta," Miriam said. "I'm sorry I didn't help more before. I'll do better. I'll get started this evening, in fact."

Maybe some hard work would help to distract her from her own heartbreak today.

Miriam followed her brother down the hallway to the office that used to be their father's. She paused at the door as Japheth went inside. He moved easily around the room, confident in his new ownership, it seemed.

"How long has Arleta been upset with me?" Miriam asked.

"What?" Japheth shook his head. "She's fine."

"She's not fine," Miriam replied. "She's angry."

Japheth sighed. "You have to see that it wasn't fair the way *Daet* treated you. If *Daet* had given me half the tutoring he gave you, I'd be more ready to do this."

"He let you run a couple of businesses," she countered.

"But he showed you how to run all of them at once," her brother replied.

"I don't think he expected to die so soon," Miriam said.

"True." Japheth met her gaze. "So we have to talk about this seriously. I know that Arleta wants your help around the house, but I'm going to need some help with running things until I get a better handle on all the properties."

The prospect of staying involved with the business should spark some excitement in her. She paused, waiting to feel something, but she couldn't quite summon up the enthusiasm. She was emotionally empty.

"Okay," she said after a beat of silence.

"I'll need you to show me what *Daet* taught you," he said. "Maybe you could come around with me to the different properties. But don't say anything in front of people. We'll talk about it in the buggy."

The same thing Amos had asked of her—help out, give her opinion and let the man look like the one who had thought of it all. When could she take the credit?

"I can do that," she said. It didn't matter, anyway.

"I can help you with the strip mall," he added. "The renters might respond better to a man. *Daet* was pretty tough, and that kept things orderly."

"I don't need help with it," she replied.

Japheth shrugged. "That's fine. I wanted to take Arleta to see some of her family in Indiana. If you'll be here, maybe you could take care of things with the businesses while we're away. That would be helpful…"

Things would continue as they had with *Daet*. She'd

pitch in, offer her advice, scan the ledgers for inaccuracies and look for ways to improve the efficiency. It had been exciting when *Daet* was alive—but helping her brother would be a different dynamic. She would no longer be the daughter learning, she'd be the sister teaching. This was a chance to prove herself, and if her brother would be willing to accept her input in the running of things, she could help to build the Schwartz legacy even further. Even if that legacy was almost entirely in her brother's name.

And yet, it wasn't quite as exciting anymore, and she couldn't put her finger on why. Was it that she'd gotten a glimpse of another life…one she thought she didn't want…?

"Miriam?" Japheth said, softening his voice. "Are you okay?"

A tear had slipped down her cheek, and she hastily wiped it away. "*Yah.* I miss him…"

"Me, too. It's not the same coming into this office and not having *Daet* tell me to stop messing with his filing system." Japheth smiled sadly and put his hand on a stack of invoices yet to be filed.

But her brother had misunderstood. While she did miss *Daet* dearly, it was Amos her heart was aching for.

She'd known there would be a cost to staying in Redemption for as long as she did, and she was paying it now. Would she stop loving Amos over time, or would she just learn to live with this ache of loss? She wasn't sure. But walking away from Amos this time was the hardest thing she'd ever done.

Chapter Thirteen

The visit with the adoption agent was more productive than Thomas had dared to hope, and Amos and Noah were incredibly happy for Thomas and Patience. If *Mammi* had only been able to see their prayer answered, because Thomas and Patience were adopting a little boy. The process had moved more quickly than any of them had expected, and tonight a two-year-old child was being introduced to his new, adoptive family for the first time.

Amos gave his horse a last stroke down his long nose before he headed out of Thomas Wiebe's stable for the house.

There was a minivan in the drive, so it appeared that the adoption agent was still there. Thomas had asked Amos to come that evening and meet their new son, and he wondered if he should have come a little later…given the family more time alone before coming to say hello. He'd assumed that Noah would be there, too, and their mother, Rachel. But there were no extra buggies. Not yet at least. Maybe they were on their way.

Amos had had a lot of invitations to dinner over the

last few days from families in their community. With *Mammi*'s passing, the community had pulled together to not only keep his kitchen stocked during his time of grief, but to make sure he wasn't lonesome, either. But it wasn't friends and extended family who he was missing most right now.

He was missing his wife. It was supposed to get easier without her—it hadn't.

Amos headed up the side steps and he pushed the screen door open. He could see Thomas and Patience at the kitchen table with an Englisher woman who looked to be in her forties. As he came all the way in, he spotted Rue sitting cross-legged on the floor with a toddler next to her. The little boy held a blanket that appeared to have a cartoon mouse on the front of it—very un-Amish. Rue reached forward and smoothed a hand down his hair lovingly. The little boy leaned toward her, and Rue wrapped her thin arms around him tenderly. Amos couldn't help but smile.

That little boy had just found the most loving home imaginable, and he had no idea yet how blessed he was.

"Amos, you made it!" Thomas said. "Come in, come in."

Amos glanced around. The adoption agent, deep in conversation with Patience, was a middle-aged woman wearing a pantsuit. She was plump and looked pleasant enough.

"I feel like I misunderstood an invitation?" Amos said uncertainly.

"Not at all," Patience said, looking up. "We invited you purposefully. That's Cruise, over there, getting to know his new sister."

Amos smiled wistfully. "He's really cute."

"He's got a Mickey Mouse blanket!" Rue said. "He loves it a lot."

"And he will keep it for as long as he wants," Thomas said, perhaps a little more firmly than necessary. "We're just so glad to bring him into our family. Rue seems to be his favorite so far."

"That's a wonderful sign actually," the Englisher woman said. "Oftentimes, the sibling relationships can be the toughest. I'm glad your daughter is so open to having a little brother."

"Oh, I was praying for a brother," Rue said with a wide smile. "And sometimes *Gott* doesn't give you the one you think you'll get. Sometimes he's got a brother waiting somewhere else. And Cruise is *wonderful*."

Cruise—a very un-Amish name, too, but no one in this room seemed to mind a bit, least of all Amos. Thomas was getting a son tonight, and Amos's heart was full of joy on his behalf.

"This is Nancy Cross," Patience said, pulling his attention back. "She's an adoption agent. When we talked to her last time, she had mentioned a rather special situation, and we thought of you right away."

Patience's gaze moved toward Cruise on the floor. She slipped away from the table and went over to where the *kinner* were playing. As she crouched down next to them, she ran a protective hand over the toddler's wispy blond hair.

"You thought of me?" Amos pulled up a chair and sank into it.

"I'll just let Nancy explain," Thomas said.

"Hello, Mr. Lapp," the woman said with a warm smile. She offered him her hand, and he shook it.

"Just Amos is fine," Amos said. "Nice to meet you."

"Likewise," Nancy said. "When we were doing our adoption interview, Thomas told us about how you took him and his brother into your home and raised them like they were your own. It was a really touching story, and I was moved, truly."

Amos smiled awkwardly. "I was more than happy to do it."

"Well, I wanted to tell you a story about four boys," Nancy said, pulling out a file folder and removing some color school photos. "This is Michael, Jack, Vince and Colby. Their parents were killed in a car accident six months ago, and boys this age can be hard to place separately, let alone together. These brothers need a stable home and they need to stay together. They were raised Mennonite, but they don't have any extended family to take them in. They're in different foster homes right now, and it's stressful for them."

Amos looked down at the last photo of the boys together. The tallest boy looked like he might shave already. The younger boys all looked similar—the same curls and big, brown eyes.

"That was taken just before they went into foster care," Nancy added.

It was the sadness in their faces that tugged at him the most. He looked over to where Patience crouched next to Rue. She held her arms out to Cruise, but the toddler leaned toward Rue instead. She let her hands drop, but her face showed that she had the ability to wait and win the little boy over. She sank down all the way onto the floor, tucking her legs underneath her.

"And you want me to be their new home," Amos surmised.

"Well, sir," Nancy said. "We were hoping you'd consider it. It takes a really special person to be able to raise boys well, to love them, to make them feel secure. And these boys need that badly. I don't mean to pressure you in any way. I just wanted to let you think it over."

Four boys who needed a *daet* and a home... The last time he'd done this, he'd had *Mammi* to help him out, to be the woman in the home, to cook the meals and mend the clothes...

"It's a big responsibility," he agreed.

"This is my card," Nancy said, passing it over and rising to her feet. "If you are interested, please give me a call. But again, no pressure."

"*Yah*. I'll think it over..." He put his finger on the photo. "Could I keep that?"

He shouldn't. The Amish didn't have photos in their homes, but somehow he wondered if Gott would forgive him this little lapse... It was a very unique circumstance.

Nancy smiled. "Absolutely. You can keep all of the photos if you like—"

"No, just one." He pulled the photo closer and then gave her a smile. "I'll pray on it."

Nancy said her goodbyes, shook hands with Thomas and Patience and then she took her leave. Amos stood up then, too.

"I'll let you have some privacy as a little family," Amos said.

"You're part of the family," Thomas said. "And you've got another grandson."

"I couldn't be happier," Amos said, and he leaned in and gave Thomas a hug and a slap on the back.

"Let me help you with your buggy," Thomas said.

The two men went outside together. The sun was

starting to set, but it was still light enough to be able to
be able to work without a lantern.

"What do you think?" Thomas asked.

"About the boys?" Amos sucked in a slow breath.
"I don't have *Mammi* here to help me out anymore. It
wouldn't be quite the same."

"You've got all of us, though," Thomas said. "And
you're not half-bad in the kitchen, you know."

Amos smiled sadly. *"Yah..."*

They brought the horse out to the buggy, and as the
men hitched him back up, Amos looked toward the
house. The kerosene lamp light inside made it so that
he could see Patience in the window. She was standing
and holding Cruise in her arms now. She smiled tenderly at him, and he stared at her, wide-eyed.

"Your wife is a wonderful woman," Amos said quietly. *"Gott* blessed you with her."

"Yah," Thomas agreed. "She makes me a better man,
too. I don't know if you remember, but when Rue came
to live with me, I took away her suitcase of Englisher
clothes, and I just about broke her heart. With this little
boy, we knew he had an Englisher name, and Patience
warned me that he'd come with his own little treasures
that comforted him. It was Patience who told me that
he needed to keep his name and his treasures."

"You won't change his name?" Amos asked.

"No." Thomas shook his head. "His name was a gift
from his biological mother, and we won't take that away.
He'll be Cruise Wiebe, an Amish boy with a strange
name, but we'll give him a middle name, though. I was
thinking Amos would be nice."

"Really?" Amos looked at Thomas, stunned. "After
me?"

"You're the father who taught me how to be an adoptive *daet*," Thomas said, and he dropped his gaze, rubbing a hand over his reddish beard.

"I'm honored," Amos murmured.

He looked down at the picture of the boys in his hand. "Did Patience really change you that much?"

"Yah..." Thomas shrugged. "But that's marriage, isn't it? We all become more flexible, and we're better for it." Thomas seemed to realize what he'd said, and he shot him an apologetic look. "I didn't mean—"

"No, no," Amos said. "It's fine."

"The thing is, I was a good man before her," Thomas said. "But I'm a better father with her...if that makes sense."

It did make sense. Because looking down at the photo of four boys so desperately in need of a home, Amos was sorely tempted to take them in. But he wasn't imagining doing this by himself anymore. In his mind's eye, Miriam was at his side, and they were raising a houseful of boys together.

He missed her desperately, but a life with Miriam would involve some considerable change on his part. He'd have to accept her influence in his home and in his business. And he had a feeling that Miriam could make him into a better version of himself, too, if he'd just be willing to let her past his defenses. Thomas was a better man with Patience, and a better father. And Miriam could do the same for him. He wasn't going to be so stubborn as to claim he couldn't improve.

Was he really considering this?

"You just made up your mind, didn't you?" Thomas said, eyeing him with a small smile.

"Yah." Amos shot Thomas a grin. "But it begins with a trip to Edson first thing in the morning."

Thomas's smile broadened. "I'll be praying you come home with Miriam."

"I need all the prayer I can get, Thomas," Amos said. "Now let me get home. You go on in to your family."

Miriam stood outside her strip mall with a pad of paper in one hand as she jotted down notes of things that needed to be improved over the next several months. One shop—a florist—had a water leak that hadn't been reported, and that would be a more expensive fix. She'd already had some firm words with the owner of the business about reporting these things promptly or having his lease canceled.

She didn't need her brother's help in delivering that kind of reprimand, and the leasees would simply have to get used to reporting to her. According to her records, they hadn't raised lease prices in the last five years, so she would revisit those numbers, but she didn't want to be unfair to the businesses there, either. She'd have to look at all the details first.

"Ma'am?" The florist came out of his shop, and he shot her an uncomfortable look. "I want to apologize for my attitude before. I shouldn't have argued with you, and I can promise that I'll be checking those hoses from now on."

"Thank you," Miriam said, and she softened her tone. "I appreciate that. We have a cell phone for emergency calls, so please only use it then. You can leave a message and we'll get the right people in to fix things like water leaks. Those can't be left."

"Right." The man nodded. "I'll do that."

He headed back into his shop, and she smiled faintly. She'd been called "ma'am." She liked the sound of it—

even if it was rather fancy. Then her smile slipped. There was something Amos had said... *Do you want to live in a house with your brother, and have a sprawling network of businesses that call you "ma'am" like some Englisher woman?*

She'd have these people's respect, and within a matter of months, she'd have them giving her the same deference they'd given her father... She might have to find a little home to live in alone, though, if her sister-in-law didn't like the current arrangement. Japheth and Arleta would need a family home to themselves. Marriages oftentimes needed a bit of space... That was ironic, because her marriage seemed to need more than most!

"Whoa..."

Miriam looked up as her brother reined in his buggy, but she froze when she saw who was with him.

"Amos?" she breathed.

Her husband was already rising to his feet as the buggy came to a stop, and Amos jumped down and gave Japheth a nod of thanks, then he turned his drilling gaze onto her. Miriam smoothed her hands down the front of her dress.

"What are you doing here?" Miriam asked, and her voice trembled just a little more than she wanted it to.

Amos crossed the distance between them, and it was like everything around them disappeared.

"I missed you," he said softly.

"So you came to visit?" she asked feebly. Were they going to include this in their relationship now, too? Somehow, she couldn't complain.

"Not exactly," he said, and he caught her hand in his. She squeezed his fingers just as tightly in return. "I came to ask you to come home..."

Miriam blinked at him, and her gaze flickered over to where her brother still sat in the buggy, trying to pretend he wasn't watching.

"Did my brother ask you to do this?" she asked falteringly. "Because—"

"This is me," Amos said quietly. "I showed up at the house looking for you, and your brother said he'd give me a ride to find you."

"Oh..." she said faintly.

"Miriam, I love you," he said. "And I know you love me. I've been a fool. I wanted you to be someone else—to be meeker and quieter and less of everything that you are. But that was wrong. You're intelligent, and beautiful, and I want you to come home and be a part of everything."

"What?" She squinted up at him. "Amos, you can't mean that."

"Why not?" he asked.

"Because I drive you crazy!"

"*Yah*, sometimes." A smile flickered at the corners of his lips. "But I need you. I need your help, and I think *Gott* is showing me just how much I need it."

"What changed?" she whispered.

"I missed you so much my whole chest hurt," he said. "I went to bed at night and missed you. I went to work and I missed you. I tried to pray and I missed you... I was starting to get the message that I needed you back at home with me, because I don't think getting over you is even an option." He swallowed, and his gaze met hers. "And then I got the chance to fill my home with *kinner*..."

"What?" she breathed.

"It's a little sudden," he said. "But in my experience, the best things seem to be."

He pulled out a photograph of four boys, and she looked at those sad faces and her heart nearly broke. They needed a mother...

"They need a home, and I've been asked if I would adopt them," Amos said. "I've got a bit of a track record with older kids because of Thomas and Noah. And, well... Thomas and Patience are adopting a little boy, and they heard about these *kinner.*"

"You want to raise them?" she asked. "Is that what you're saying? You want to adopt these boys?"

"That's exactly what I'm saying. It would be a big job," he said. "They aren't Amish born, these boys. But I don't know... I look at those faces, and I think that I could offer them something—stability, faith, a real home. And for me...for us...it would be a chance at a house full of love and laughter."

"I'll still drive you crazy," she said, shaking her head. "I'd still want to know about the business, and want to grow it in spite of you."

"Good." He nodded earnestly. "Good! Miriam, I'll need all your energy, and intuition, and business sense. Because if you and I adopt these boys, they'll take up a lot of time and dedication. If you'd be a wife to me, and a *mamm* to them, and...a manager at the shop..."

Miriam felt tears well in her eyes.

"Really?"

"Thomas said something that made me think. You have to bend for a wife. And the right woman can make you a better man."

Miriam was silent, and she fingered the photo of the

boys. Her heart was already reaching toward them, and she sent up a prayer.

Gott, is this Your will? Can I go home now?

"You haven't contacted anyone about the radio ad, have you?" she asked with a teary smile.

"Not yet," Amos admitted. "I'm not great with that stuff. But you and I together, Miriam, we could do this... If you wanted to."

"I've missed you," she whispered.

Amos bent down and covered her lips with his. His kiss was soft and enveloping. When he finally pulled back, he murmured, "Come home with me..."

She nodded. "I'll have to help my brother a little bit, though."

"I'll be willing to share your expertise, Miriam," Japheth called from the buggy, and she laughed softly at her brother's grin. Had he heard all of that?

"*Yah*, Amos," Miriam said, looking up into her husband's hopeful face. "I'll come home with you, and I'll be a wife to you, and we'll adopt those boys together."

Because it felt right. In her heart, she could feel *Gott*'s smile on this.

She'd be a *mamm*... It hardly seemed real, and as she looked down at the photo again, she felt her heart open just a little bit wider. Yes, she'd be a *mamm*!

Amos slid an arm around her, and she tipped her head onto his shoulder. She knew exactly where her home was, and it wasn't here in Edson any longer—it was wherever her husband happened to be.

Mammi had been right, after all, it seemed. *Gott* had been working.

Epilogue

On a chilly morning in September, when the leaves were just starting to turn yellow on the trees outside, when the mornings were getting cooler, and the garden was turning brown outside the kitchen window, Miriam tucked a package of banana bread into the last lunch bag and handed it to Michael. He was the oldest, and he stood there—broad shoulders, a dusting of a mustache on his upper lip. Michael had been the hardest to reach the last couple of months. He'd been so quiet and stoic... almost like there was Amish inside of him, after all.

"I think you'll like your lunch, Michael," Miriam said, casting him a smile. "I'm giving you a little extra—growing boys need to eat."

The boys all wore their new school clothes—store-bought pants and suspenders, and hand-sewn shirts that Miriam had made herself in the evenings since they'd arrived in their home. Several women from the community, including Natasha Zook, came over to sew with her to get the boys ready for school that fall. And they each had four fresh new shirts, and three pairs of pants to last them the winter. If they didn't get torn... Boys tended to wear out clothes before they outgrew them—at least, that was the advice she'd received from Fannie Mast. And Fannie would know.

The last few months Miriam had been feeding her new sons food they loved, food they'd never tried before, and discovering their favorites. Babies bonded with milk, but big boys like these needed shoofly pie and fried chicken. A *mamm* fed her boys—and she'd been reveling in this new role of wife and mother.

Outside, Amos had just hitched the buggy, and the horses shifted their hooves impatiently. Miriam glanced out the window at Amos, who was leaning forward, waiting for them.

"Are you ready for your first day at school?" Miriam asked brightly.

"We don't know Dutch," Jack, who was twelve, said nervously. He'd been mentioning the same thing over and over for weeks. It was his personal worry.

"That's okay," Miriam said for the hundredth time, it felt like. "The teacher understands. You'll be fine. And you'll meet some other *kinner* your age—" She paused, winced. "Kids your age," she amended. "And you'll be back home before you know it. I'll make sure there are some warm cookies, if that helps."

"Okay." Jack smiled faintly. He still looked nervous.

Vince was ten, and he peeked into his cloth lunch bag, rooting around. Michael nudged him.

"Wait until lunch, Vince," he said.

"I was only looking…" And Vince glanced up at Miriam with a small smile. They all knew Miriam well enough by now to know that she wouldn't get upset over them eating. If anything, Miriam took great joy in feeding these growing boys. *Her boys.* Her heart flooded with love just looking at them.

"All right," Miriam said. "Off you go. *Daet* is waiting. Have a good day."

The boys seemed okay with Dutch names for *mom* and *dad*, because they were different enough not to overlap with their memories of their birth parents. But just sending them off today…it didn't feel quite right.

Michael opened the front door, but before he could push open the screen, Miriam said, "Boys!"

They turned, and her heart sped up. She wasn't used to making speeches, but before they went out the door to school for the first time, she felt like she needed to say something important.

"Boys, I want you to remember something," Miriam said earnestly. "I love you all. I know this is different and new, and I know we'll all stumble a little while we figure out how to be a family, but one thing you'll learn about me is that I'm very stubborn. I might drive you a little crazy with it sometimes, but the good part about me is that nothing you do will ever shake my love for you. Ever. I'm just too stubborn to change my mind once it's set, and I love you. Do you understand? I'm your *mamm* now, and I will love you until the end of time. That's how this works."

It hadn't been quite what she wanted to say, but it would do.

Colby, who was the youngest at nine years old, came back into the kitchen and wrapped his arms around her waist in a tight hug. She put a hand on the top of his hat on his head, and then he headed back to the door as quickly as he'd hugged her.

"Bye, *Mamm*," Colby said. "See you after school."

Michael shot her a shy smile, then opened the screen, and the boys all tramped outside toward the buggy where Amos waited.

This was it—their first day of school. And they were plenty old enough to handle it just fine, so why was she feeling this strange flutter of anxiety at the thought of it? Maybe this was just part of being a *mamm*.

Amos smiled over their heads at her. He'd drive the boys to school for the first day, and they'd walk home. It wasn't far, but the first day seemed like an important day to get a ride with their new *daet*.

Amos's smile warmed his eyes and made her cheeks grow warm in response.

"Have a good day at work, Amos!" she called.

"Yah." He blew her a kiss. "You're coming by the shop later, right?"

"I'll be there!"

Then Amos flicked the reins and they were off.

Miriam watched the buggy head down the drive, and when she went back inside to the kitchen, the screen door bounced shut behind her before she closed the door. The house was silent, except for the ticking of the kitchen clock. But she wouldn't be lonely or bored on her own today. She had dishes to do, breakfast to clean up and a stack of ledgers waiting for her attention on the counter. And next to the ledgers sat that beautifully carved box that her husband had spent a decade finishing for her. She was using it for her recipe cards because she liked looking at it every day. It reminded her of how much her husband loved her, and that reminder was just as sweet today as it was the day she'd come back home.

Miriam stood in the kitchen in absolute silence, her

heart soring upward with a silent prayer of thanks. *Gott* had given Miriam the deepest desires of her heart that she'd been too afraid to even ask for. She had her husband, who she loved deeply; she had four sons to call her own, two businesses to grow with the man she loved and a beautiful array of days spreading out in front of her to fill...

She was finally home.

* * * * *

AN UNEXPECTED AMISH HARVEST

Carrie Lighte

To my faithful readers, with much gratitude.

But he answered and said, It is written,
Man shall not live by bread alone, but by every
word that proceedeth out of the mouth of God.
—*Matthew* 4:4

Chapter One

"You're so thin!" Susannah Peachy's stepgrand-mother, Lydia, exclaimed as they embraced each other. "I hardly recognize you."

It had been nine months since twenty-three-year-old Susannah had visited the small but growing Amish district in New Hope, Maine. At that time, she'd weighed about forty or forty-five pounds more than she did now, so her figure had been much rounder. Her face had been fuller, too. But she still had the same caramel-brown eyes, long, straight nose and thick brunette hair that was so curly that not even pulling it back into a bun could tame it. By the day's end, it always seemed to fluff up from her scalp, lifting her prayer *kapp* and making her appear slightly taller than she had in the morning. So it was a bit of an exaggeration for Lydia to say she hardly recognized Susannah, although she supposed it was a surprise for the older woman to see her so much thinner.

"I might look a bit different but I'm still the same person I was before," Susannah assured her. "Being thinner doesn't make me any different on the inside.

Kind of like wearing that cast on your arm doesn't make *you* any different."

"I wouldn't be too sure of that. Having this cast on my arm makes me a lot *grumpier*," Lydia confessed. "Not because I'm in pain, but because I want to accomplish more than I'm able to, which frustrates me. I feel so restless. When I get into that kind of mood, I have to stop and remind myself how blessed I am that I only fractured my wrist when I fell. I could have broken a hip! So I have nothing to complain about—especially since you've *kumme* to help me."

Susannah suspected there were a number of young women in New Hope who could have assisted her maternal grandfather's wife, but clearly Lydia preferred Susannah's company. Her grandfather, Marshall Sommer, had always doted on his only granddaughter, too. And, of course, Susannah loved them both very much, as well. But if she'd had her way she wouldn't have come to visit her grandparents in Maine. Instead, they would have returned to Dover, Delaware, to visit Susannah and her father, along with her brother and his family.

However, when Lydia broke her wrist and asked Susannah to come and keep house and cook for the farm crew during harvest season, she couldn't say no. It would have been unthinkable to refuse to help a family member in need, especially since her grandparents were getting up there in age. Only the Lord knew how many more opportunities Susannah would have to spend time with them.

Besides, it wasn't as if she was going to be overwhelmed with work. The crew consisted of only four men; two were local and the other two were Lydia's fourteen-year-old twin great-nephews, Conrad and Jacob, who were coming from Ohio. Which meant Susannah would actually be cooking and keeping house for fewer people here than she usually helped her sister-in-law cook for back in Delaware. So in a way, coming to her grandparents' farm might feel like a holiday visit by comparison. Especially since Susannah shared her grandparents' fondness for Maine.

Yet she was already counting the days until she could go home. Today was Friday and the crew was scheduled to begin harvesting on Monday. They'd spend three or four weeks picking potatoes, depending on how often it rained during that time. That meant at a minimum, she'd see her former suitor, Peter Lambright, at least two or three times in church, which met every other week. But as far as she was concerned, that was two or three times too many.

"You must be *hungerich* after being on the road since the wee hours of the morning," Lydia said, interrupting her thoughts. "I made a peanut-butter pie. I had to hide it in the fridge behind the lettuce so your *groossdaadi* wouldn't see it and ask me for a piece before you arrived. Let's have a slice with tea before supper. You can fill me in on all the news from Dover."

Susannah hesitated. "*Denki*, but I'm not *hungerich*. I'll wait until supper to eat, but I'll have tea with you."

Lydia lowered her silver, wire-framed glasses and peered at Susannah. "But I thought peanut-butter pie was your favorite? That's why I made it. It might be a little lumpy because I had to mix it using my left hand, but I think you'll still enjoy it."

Susannah didn't want to explain that she'd gotten into the habit of only eating dessert once a week. Usually she ate it following a light meal, not in the late afternoon before she'd even had her supper. But she appreciated how much time and effort it must have taken for Lydia to make the pie with one arm in a cast. She figured this one time she could indulge in a taste...especially since she was serving it, so she could cut herself a little piece. "Your pie is always *appenditlich* and it was thoughtful of you to make it for me. I guess a smidgen wouldn't spoil my supper," she said. "If you go sit in the living room, I'll be right in with it."

After putting the kettle on the gas stove, Susannah removed the pie from behind the lettuce on the bottom shelf of the diesel-powered refrigerator. As soon as she saw the white creamy custard topped with a crumbly peanut-butter-and-powdered-sugar mixture, her mouth watered.

She set it on the countertop, remembering when she'd spent the summer in New Hope a year ago, Lydia would make a peanut-butter pie at least once a week because she knew it was Susannah's favorite. Lydia didn't like the pie nearly as much as Susannah and Marshall did, so the two of them would more or less split it over the course of a couple of days. The only other person who could make such a delicious peanut-butter pie was Susannah's mother, who had died four years ago.

Mamm *didn't take very* gut *care of her health*, she thought sadly. Neither had her father. That's why last winter Susannah had changed their diet. Her father was overweight, too, and he'd briefly been hospitalized for complications from his diabetes. The *Englisch* doctor indicated if he didn't get his blood sugar under control, he could suffer kidney, nerve or eye damage, or cardiovascular problems.

At first, Susannah's efforts to help improve his health were met with resistance. Surprisingly, the pushback didn't come from her father; it came from her sister-in-law, Charity, who had remarked, "How can bread be unhealthy when I make it myself? It's not as if it's store-bought and full of preservatives. And the *Lord* made corn and potatoes, so they must be *gut* for us."

Susannah had shared what she'd learned about eating whole grains, nonstarchy vegetables and protein, as well as "good" fats and dairy. And all of it in moderation. But Charity continued to turn up her nose at the dishes Susannah prepared until she saw how the pounds seemed to slide right off her and her father's blood-sugar readings stabilized. Then Charity helped Susannah peruse cookbooks from the library for healthier meal ideas and recipes, too.

"I'm *hallich* to be losing weight because now I have more energy," Susannah had told her. "But I'm especially *hallich* that the *dokder* said if *Daed* keeps these habits up, he might be able to stop taking his medication."

Still, there were a few members of her church district who were worried about Susannah's weight loss. She'd been mildly overweight for most of her life, so some people initially assumed she was ill. Others expressed concern that she was focusing too much on external appearances, or was becoming *hochmut*. Highminded. Proud. Not merely about how slender she had become, but also about the knowledge she had gained, even though she never flaunted her weight loss or offered nutritional advice unless someone asked her for it. However, after the novelty wore off, they became accustomed to how she looked and what she ate or didn't eat for lunch after church or during other community events. And eventually they stopped making comments, much to Susannah's relief.

But it seemed she'd have to get used to hearing similar comments all over again, because as they were enjoying their sweet treat, Lydia remarked, "Wait until Dorcas sees you. She's going to be astonished at how *gut* you look."

Susannah pushed a big forkful of pie into her mouth so she wouldn't respond brusquely. Ideally, Amish people didn't place an undue importance on superficial appearances, which was the very reason some had been critical of her when she first started slimming down. Yet she frequently noticed that even though *she* was discouraged from focusing on her weight, other people had no qualms about drawing attention to it. Regardless of whether their comments were positive or negative, the fact that they made more than just a passing remark about it seemed hypocritical to her.

She attempted to redirect the conversation, as she'd become adept at doing. "I'm really looking forward to catching up with Dorcas in person again. Although we probably won't spend too much time together, since she'll be working at Millers' restaurant."

When Susannah stayed in New Hope last summer, she had quickly formed a close friendship with Dorcas Troyer. The two young, single women had enjoyed each other's company again when Susannah returned to New Hope for a week at Christmastime, and they'd written to each other frequently throughout the last year.

In fact, Dorcas was the only person that Susannah had confided in when Peter asked to be her suitor the previous summer…and the only person Susannah had told about their breakup last January. She still remembered teardrops splashing onto the stationery as she wrote,

Peter wouldn't give me any reason for ending our courtship, other than to say he doesn't think we're compatible, after all. But I know it's because I've gained so much weight since last summer.

Her friend had written back,

I've known Peter for years and I can't believe your weight is such an issue for him. Are you sure that's why he broke up with you? Could it be that he just finds it too difficult to carry on a long-distance courtship?

Susannah highly doubted that. After she'd left New Hope the first time, Peter's biweekly letters had been filled with proclamations of his affection for her. The couple had called each other at their respective phone shanties at three o'clock every other Sunday. Even after two hours of talking, they'd never run out of things to share and laugh about. And although they had only been able to sneak off for an hour with each other when Susannah came to New Hope last Christmas, they'd agreed their time alone together was the best part of the holiday.

That's why it was so confusing that four days after she got home, Peter called and said he had decided to end their courtship. The change in his attitude was so abrupt it made Susannah feel as if he was an utter stranger. As if someone else had been pretending to be him on the phone and in his letters. Had been pretending to fall in love with her the way she'd been falling in love with him.

"Why?" she had cried, as bewildered as she was devastated. "I don't understand."

"We're just not a *gut* match."

"But *why* aren't we a *gut* match? What has changed all of a sudden?"

"I'm sorry to hurt your feelings like this, Susannah, but I don't want to discuss it further. Please accept my decision."

Afterward, she went over it and over it in her mind, trying to figure out what could have possibly changed to make Peter end their relationship. The only thing she could come up with was that once he'd seen her again, he was no longer drawn to her because of how much heavier she'd gotten. Maybe that was why he'd held his tongue about his reason; he hadn't wanted to hurt her feelings by telling her the truth. But whether he said it aloud or not, she'd been crushed to discover that Peter valued how she *looked* more than who she *was*. That he was rejecting her because of her weight gain.

Likewise, in the following months she was disappointed when certain other men *accepted* her because of her appearance. During the past spring and summer, she'd had no fewer than four bachelors in Dover ask to court her. Susannah would have felt honored, if it hadn't been for the fact that they'd all known her for at least ten years and they'd never expressed an interest in her until she was slender. So it insulted her and reflected poorly on their priorities when they'd asked to walk out with her once she was thin.

Nor did she consider it a compliment just now when Lydia suggested, "Hopefully you and Dorcas will have a chance to go to a singing together. You look so pretty that I wouldn't be surprised if half a dozen young men ask to be your long-distance suitor before you return to Delaware."

If they did, I'd say no, Susannah thought. If there was one thing she had learned about men this past year, it was that their feelings for her fluctuated along with the needle on the bathroom scale. And she'd rather be single than be loved for her appearance.

Just thinking and talking about suitors and courtships made Susannah anxious and she again avoided responding to Lydia's comment. "*Denki* for making the pie for me. It was *appenditlich*," she said.

"You're welcome, dear. But you hardly had a sliver. Are you sure you don't want another slice?"

Susannah glanced down at her empty plate and suddenly she felt rather empty inside, too. "I suppose a little more wouldn't hurt. Just this once."

After Peter Lambright helped his brother, Hannes, load the picnic table into the *Englischer*'s truck, Hannes closed the tailgate.

"Wait a second—we haven't loaded the benches," Peter reminded him.

Hannes chuckled and reopened the gate. "I'm so used to making A-frame tables, I forgot the benches weren't attached to this one."

Peter waited until they'd put the benches in the truck and the customer drove away, then said, "You've got to pay closer attention to what you're doing, Hannes. If you can't be trusted to remember something as basic as giving the customer the furniture he paid for—"

He clapped his hand against his cheek. "Oh, *neh*—I forgot to collect payment from him."

"Hannes! You've got to be kidding me."

"Jah." He grinned. "Collecting payment is the first thing I do."

Peter wasn't in the mood for his brother's shenanigans. "Quit horsing around. I need to know I can count on you this next month."

Hannes's grin melted and he replied solemnly, "Of course you can count on me."

"Gut. Then get back to work. I'm going over to the *haus* to check on *Mamm* and then I'm going to pick up Eva from *schul*."

Peter began walking toward the house, which was located a couple of acres east of the workshop. Twelve years ago, when the Lambrights had moved from Illinois to New Hope, his father had deliberately built the workshop as far from the house as possible. He was starting up a business—making picnic tables, porch swings and other wooden lawn furniture—and he didn't want customers driving too close to his children.

Their father had always been overly cautious around *Englisch* vehicles. That's why it still baffled Peter that one fall evening five years ago, his father apparently had forgotten to light the required lantern that hung from the side of the carriage. Or else the flame had gone out. Either way, the man driving a lumber truck behind him hadn't seen the buggy until it was too late to stop and he collided with the carriage, killing Peter's father.

His family had been devastated, of course, especially Peter's mother, Dorothy. But she faithfully relied on the Lord for comfort and strength. With His help and the help of her community, she was able to shepherd her children through their bereavement. Eventually, joy returned to the Lambright household…until late last autumn.

That was when Dorothy first experienced a significantly low energy level and an even lower mood. When it got to the point that she was staying in bed until noon, she finally consulted a doctor. He didn't find any physical cause for the change in her emotions and activity level, and diagnosed her with moderate depression, which she found both embarrassing and confusing.

"But I don't *feel* depressed about anything, except that I don't have more energy," she'd said afterward, instructing her children not to tell anyone about her diagnosis. Instead of accepting the prescription the doctor offered, she experimented with natural supplements and herbal remedies, to little avail. Hoping fresh air might help, she made it her goal to stroll with Eva, then twelve, to school each morning. But that only exhausted and overwhelmed her all the more.

It wasn't long before her friends noticed that Dorothy was less active in the community, her house was unkempt and she was often either weepy or irritable. Concerned, they suggested she visit a doctor, which she didn't want to do again. Some people in their district implied she was unwell because of unconfessed sin in her life. No doubt they meant to be helpful, but they did her more harm than good.

"I keep asking *Gott* to examine my heart and show me my sinful ways, and I keep trying to change," Dorothy had cried to Peter one Sunday after the church leaders had visited their house. "But I just can't seem to pull myself out of this. I'm so ashamed. And so, so tired."

I can't believe she's felt like this for almost an en-

tire year, Peter thought as he walked up the porch steps and into the plain two-story home. He found his mother sitting in the rocking chair in the living room, a shawl wrapped around her shoulders and an unopened Bible resting on her lap. She rubbed her eyes as if she'd been sleeping. Or crying.

When he greeted her, she replied, "What are you doing home? Is it suppertime already?"

It wasn't—not that it would have mattered; his mother rarely made supper anymore. She rarely *ate* supper anymore, either. But it was hard to say whether that was because *she* had no appetite or because the meals thirteen-year-old Eva made from a box or a can were unappetizing.

"*Neh.* I just came to see if you need anything from the store. I'm going to go stop at the Sommers' *haus* on my way to pick Eva up from *schul*," he said. The school was close enough that his sister usually walked home, but he thought he'd surprise her by giving her a ride. "I need to ask Marshall if he needs me tomorrow or if we'll wait until *Muundaag*."

"Needs you for what, *suh*?"

"I'm helping him with the harvest, remember?" Peter had told his mother several times that he was going to help Marshall Sommer harvest his potato crop this autumn. But when her cheeks reddened and her eyes brimmed with tears, Peter realized he must have sounded impatient. When she was especially tired, Dorothy couldn't concentrate and she was sensitive about her forgetfulness.

"Oh, that's right. But I still don't understand why you wouldn't send your *bruder* instead. Picking potatoes is something a *kin* could do."

She had a point—children much younger than Hannes did the potato picking on the weekends on New Hope's other potato farm, owned by the Wittmer family. And in the *Englisch* communities up north, students had a three-to-four-week break every autumn, so the high schoolers could help with the local harvest. Not just picking, either—he'd heard of sixteen-year-olds driving trucks with upward of 50,000 pounds of potatoes on them. But here in New Hope, potato farms were an anomaly. The Amish children didn't get a break from school to bring in the crop, although sometimes they helped out on the weekends. So there would be another man, someone from the nearby Serenity Ridge district, who also would be joining the crew.

"I'm going to do more than pick—I'll be transporting potatoes to the potato *haus*, too. There's a lot of heavy lifting involved, so I'm better suited for it than Hannes is." While it was true that his brother had a slighter frame, that wasn't actually why Peter was the one who was helping Marshall on the farm. But Peter couldn't tell his mother the *real* reason, since he and Marshall had agreed they wouldn't discuss the matter with anyone else.

She smiled wanly. "Well, it's very kind of you to give him a hand, especially without pay. You're like your *daed* was—a *gut* provider to your *familye* and a *gut* helper to your neighbor. You'll make a *wunderbaar* husband and *daed* one day, just as soon as you meet the right *weibsmensch*."

Helping Marshall has nothing to do with kindness, Peter thought as he guided his horse down the road a few minutes later. *And I'm not nearly the* mann *my* daed *was.* As for meeting the right woman, Peter had already met her: Susannah Peachy, Marshall's granddaughter...

A horn sounded behind him, startling Peter from his thoughts. Then the car accelerated and passed him on the narrow, curvy country road, a risky maneuver. He shuddered as he recollected his brother's behavior in an *Englisch* vehicle last New Year's Eve, when the seventeen-year-old had driven an SUV off the side of an icy hill, flipping it twice and landing it in a ravine.

Blessedly, Hannes had emerged from the wreckage with nothing more than a few bruises and a sore shoulder, but the vehicle had been rendered undrivable. Because the accident had happened on their private property, the owners—parents of an *Englisch* acquaintance Hannes hung out with during his *rumspringa*— had agreed not to involve the police. In exchange, they required immediate reimbursement for the cost of the expensive vehicle.

Peter had to withdraw all of their shop's savings from the bank. But he'd still come up a few thousand dollars short of paying for the SUV. And there hadn't been a dime left over for immediate household and business needs. Ordinarily, Peter would have sought advice and possibly financial help from the church leaders, but there hadn't been enough time, since many of them were still out of town, visiting their families for the holidays.

Besides, he knew they would have insisted on discussing the matter with his mother and that was shortly after she'd been diagnosed with depression. Peter had been concerned that she'd sink even lower if she found out about Hannes's accident, especially considering how her husband had died.

Desperate, Peter had known he was going to have

to ask someone for money. The Amish in their district virtually never borrowed from *Englisch* banks or creditors, except when making a big land purchase. Instead, they sought loans from other community members, who generally considered it a personal obligation and a demonstration of their faith to help district members who came to them in need. These loans were handled with the utmost discretion and they were always interest-free.

Peter had turned to the one person he knew was in town and who could afford to help him: Marshall Sommer. It was humbling to ask a nonfamily member for money, but Peter had been in a long-distance courtship with his granddaughter, Susannah, and he hoped to marry her one day. So he felt a kind of kinship with the older man.

Understandably, when Peter made his request Marshall asked why he needed a loan. "My—my *familye* has r-run into some unexpected expenses that need to be addressed immediately. Expenses our b-business profits won't cover," he'd stuttered nervously. While vague, his answer was also truthful.

Marshall must have assumed he meant their business was in the red, because he'd lectured, "I'm surprised you haven't saved enough to take care of your *familye's* basic needs when sales are down."

Peter had felt humiliated, but there was nothing he could say in his own defense without disclosing his brother's situation. And he was afraid if Marshall knew that part of the money was going to be used to recompense *Englischers* for the damage his brother did, he would have suggested Hannes suffer the consequences. As Marshall had continued to chastise him for not being a good steward of the resources the Lord had provided,

Peter's face grew hot. If it hadn't been a violation of the *Ordnung*, he would have rescinded his request and borrowed from a bank, instead.

"*Jah*, I'll give you the money you need," Marshall had finally agreed when he was done delivering his discourse. "But instead of repaying me in cash, there are two things I expect from you. First, I need you to help me harvest next fall, since Lydia's two *seh* can't *kumme* next year."

His proposal seemed a fair exchange of money for labor. Since the fall was a slow sales period for lawn furniture, Peter figured Hannes could mind the shop by himself. "*Jah.* I'll help with the potato harvest. What's the second condition?"

"I want you to break off your courtship with my *kinskind*."

Peter had been so stunned that just thinking about it now made his stomach cramp. He'd had no idea that Marshall knew about their courtship and even less of an idea why he'd want to interfere in it. His response was a single word. "Why?"

"Because a man who isn't responsible enough to manage a *gut* income like yours isn't a man I'd want my granddaughter to consider for a husband," Marshall had bluntly replied. When Peter didn't—when he *couldn't*—respond, the older man reiterated, "I don't want you to court Susannah. If I can't convince you to end the relationship, I'll do my best to convince *her* you're not right for each other. Given what I know now, I believe she'll agree with me."

He'd understood. Even if Peter refused the loan, Marshall was still going to tell Susannah how irresponsible he thought Peter was and then *she'd* end the relationship. So, Peter had thought he might as well take the money and end their courtship himself. Once again, he'd been speechless.

"Do you need a few days to think about it?" Marshall had asked.

I didn't have a few days. I barely had one day. And there was no one else I could turn to, Peter rationalized to himself for at least the hundredth time since the day he'd accepted the old man's offer. *Marshall had been determined to break up Susannah and me. So what* gut *would have* kumme *from jeopardizing my* bruder*'s future and my* mamm*'s health by refusing the loan?*

At least by accepting it, Peter had kept Hannes out of trouble with the police. And while Dorothy's health hadn't improved, it hadn't worsened, either.

Yet try as he might to justify it, Peter still felt guilty. Only in retrospect did he fully realize that asking for a loan didn't make him a poor match for Susannah; it was breaking her heart in exchange for money that made him unworthy of her love. Unworthy of *any* woman's love.

As he journeyed the final mile toward the farm, Peter thought, *Within a month, harvest season will be over.* He had no hope of putting his mistake out of his mind completely. But maybe, just maybe, once he'd fulfilled his obligation to Marshall, Peter would be able to stop thinking about the pained, bewildered tone in Susannah's voice the day he'd called her and ended their courtship without so much as a word of explanation.

Susannah felt so drowsy after the long trip—and her second slice of pie—that she was tempted to take an afternoon nap while Lydia was resting. But she knew what she really needed was a walk in the brisk autumn air. She had just retrieved a sweater from her suitcase when she heard a buggy coming up the lane. *Groossdaadi!* she thought.

She raced outside and hopped down the porch steps, running up behind the buggy that had stopped just shy of the barn behind the house. Since her grandfather apparently hadn't seen her, she decided to sneak up on him, the way she used to do as a young girl. She knew now that she'd never really scared him, but she loved it that he always pretended to jump back in surprise, first throwing his arms in the air and then wrapping them tightly around her.

"Boo!" she exclaimed, springing forward once he'd climbed out of the carriage.

But as soon as the man turned, she immediately realized her error; although he was tall and broad-shouldered, he looked nothing like her grandfather. This man had wavy brown hair beneath his straw hat, his eyes were gray-blue and there was a small bump on the bridge of his nose. This man was Peter Lambright, her ex-suitor. She nearly stumbled backward in surprise.

"Hello. I'm Peter Lambright. You must be Lydia's niece," he said, smiling. She used to love that smile; it could keep her warm for hours, but now it turned her insides to ice.

Clearly, because of her weight loss, he genuinely didn't recognize her; it wasn't just an expression, like Lydia had used. *You didn't see me for who I really was when I was heavy, so I guess I can't expect you to see me for who I am when I'm thin*, Susannah thought bitterly.

"Neh. I'm Marshall's *kinskind*, Susannah," she retorted sarcastically, as if they'd never met. She crossed

her arms and lifted her chin in the air, waiting for the realization to sink in. His mouth dropped open and he appeared dumbfounded, so she asked, "What are you doing here?"

"I—I... I'm helping Marshall harvest this year. I came to ask whether he needs me tomorrow or if we're going to begin on *Muundaag*."

Susannah felt a surge of dizziness. She couldn't believe her ears. "*You're* helping with the harvest?"

"*Jah*. He—he asked me last winter if I'd help out since Lydia's *seh* couldn't *kumme* here this year." Redfaced, Peter fiddled with the reins, since he hadn't hitched the horse yet. "How long are you visiting?"

Susannah didn't want to chat; she wanted to flee, but it was as if her shoes were pegged to the ground. "Until Lydia's wrist heals."

Peter wrinkled his forehead. "Her wrist?"

"She had a fall and she broke it. I'll be cooking meals and keeping *haus*."

"I'm very sorry to hear that," he said grimly.

"Pah!" Susannah sputtered. She suspected he meant he was sorry to hear Lydia had broken her wrist, but it came out as if he was sorry to hear that Susannah was going to be staying throughout the harvest season to do the cooking and housekeeping. And *no one* was sorrier about that than *she* was. "My *groossdaadi* isn't home, but Lydia did mention that harvesting is still scheduled to begin on *Muundaag*, unless it rains."

"Okay. I'll *kumme* back then," he replied, yet instead of leaving, he lingered a moment longer, as if he wanted to say something else. Or maybe he wanted *her* to say something else. But she had absolutely nothing more to say. She tapped her foot against the ground impatiently and he swiftly scrambled back into his buggy.

As his horse trotted away, Susannah felt like weeping. *I didn't know how I was going to see him every other* Sunndaag *in* kurrich *without getting upset,* she thought. *How am I going to handle knowing he's right here on the farm six days of the week?*

Chapter Two

Peter felt light-headed as the buggy sped away from the Sommer farm. He'd been completely taken aback when he'd heard a female voice shout and then a woman had leaped out at him. Susannah Peachy was the last person he'd expected to see, so his brain didn't immediately register her face. He'd nervously introduced himself before he'd gotten his wits about him. Of course, once she spoke and he looked into her eyes—those beautiful, unforgettable almond-shaped eyes—he'd realized his mistake.

She must think I'm baremlich, *acting as if our relationship meant so little to me that I can't even remember her*, he thought. Which couldn't have been further from the truth; their relationship had meant the world to him, despite how he'd ended it. But the shame he felt for breaking up with her and the shock of seeing her again had overwhelmed him and he was stunned speechless.

Considering the circumstances, Peter would have appreciated it if Marshall had let him know Susannah was going to be at the farm during harvest. That way, he could have been praying the Lord would help him know what to say to her. Instead, he'd added insult to injury by behaving like a complete *dummkopf.*

Maybe he didn't tell me because he's afraid that I won't keep my promise—that I'll try to resume my courtship with her again, Peter thought. *Knowing him, he's doing his best to keep as much distance as he can between Susannah and me. Including waiting until the last possible minute to tell me she's here on the farm.*

Apparently, Marshall hadn't informed Susannah that Peter would be helping with harvest, either. It was possible the old man was worried that if she knew he was going to be on the farm almost every day, she wouldn't have come to New Hope. And to be fair, Peter wouldn't have blamed her, not after the piteous way he'd ended their courtship.

Nor did he blame her for looking at him so disdainfully a few minutes ago. Well, maybe she wasn't disdainful. Maybe it was disappointment he'd seen in her eyes. Or maybe Peter was just reading that emotion into her expression because that's how *he* felt about his own behavior. Regardless, he was aware that it had to be much more difficult for her to see him than it was for him to see her. *She* was the wronged party; he was the one who had wronged her.

I'll have to try my best to stay out of her sight while she's here—for her sake, as well as for mine, he decided as he pulled into the yard of the one-room schoolhouse.

Whenever he picked up Eva, he tried to arrive at the very last minute before school was dismissed so he wouldn't have to make small talk with the parents of the other students. It wasn't that he was unfriendly; it was that they inevitably asked about his mother and it was wearisome trying to answer truthfully while still respecting her wishes to keep her health situation private.

Not half a minute after he stepped down from the carriage, the school door opened and a crush of young children scurried down the steps, followed in close succession by the older scholars, as Amish students were called. Eva was one of the last to come out and she was hugging a cardboard box to her chest. Peter waved to get her attention and when she lifted her blond head and spied him, she smiled and quickened her pace.

Once they were out on the road, he pointed to the box between them and joked, "Is that your homework?"

"*Neh*. It's the youngest scholars' spelling tests and math worksheets. The teacher asked me to correct them tonight."

It wasn't unusual for the older students to help the teacher with the younger students' assignments during class and to correct their papers after school, but Eva was always volunteering to take on even more responsibility. Peter suspected she hoped that sometime in the future she could replace New Hope's current teacher if she resigned to get married and start a family. Eva provided the teacher a valuable service and she genuinely enjoyed correcting papers, but in the next few weeks, Peter was going to need her help at home more than ever.

"It's *gut* that you're willing to assist your teacher, but don't forget, starting on *Muundaag*, I'll be working on the Sommers's potato *bauerei* in the evenings for the next four weeks," he said. "And Hannes may have to work late if he can't keep up with the orders, so I'll need you to keep *Mamm* company."

"I haven't forgotten. But *Mamm* usually goes to bed

a lot earlier than I do so I'll have plenty of time to help the teacher with her paperwork."

"Perhaps if you suggested doing an activity together—quilting or playing checkers—*Mamm* might stay up later."

"But whenever I ask her to do something like that, she says *neh*, she's too tired," Eva argued. "You've been right there in the same room—you've heard her yourself."

Usually his sister's tone wasn't so flippant and Peter reacted impatiently. "There's no need to get *schmaert* with me, Eva. I know *Mamm* usually says *neh*. But that doesn't mean you should give up trying. I'm counting on Hannes to take care of the shop and you to take care of *Mamm* and the *haus* while I'm away. Understand?"

Almost immediately, Eva's eyes brimmed with tears. "Don't *you* understand? I *have* been taking care of *Mamm* and the *haus*. And I'd love it if she wanted to do something with me after supper. Even if all we did was sit on the porch and talk. But she never does…" She dissolved into tears, so Peter directed the horse onto the wide sandy shoulder of the road and came to a stop.

First Mamm, *then Susannah and now Eva—I sure know how to say all the wrong things to* weibsmensch *today*, he thought. He put his hand on his sister's shoulder as she cried. It was unlike her to be so tearful and it made him realize how deeply his mother's illness was affecting her, too. She'd been doing her best to take over all of the household tasks at home, without ever grumbling. Nor had she ever complained that her mother no longer engaged in activities—or even in conversation—with her, but Peter recognized now how much it must have saddened her.

When she stopped weeping, he said, "I'm sorry that right now *Mamm* isn't able to do the things she used to do with you. And I do appreciate how much you've taken over in the *haus*. I should tell you that more often."

"I don't mind doing the cleaning and cooking myself. But I can't *talk* to myself, the way I used to talk to *Mamm*." Eva sniffed. "I know she's still in the same *haus*, but it feels like she's a million miles away. What's wrong with her, anyway? Do you think it's really that she's depressed?"

"I don't know," Peter answered honestly. "But the Lord is our Great Physician, so I keep asking Him to heal her."

"I do, too." Eva heaved a sigh. "And I ask Him to give me more patience because it feels like forever since *Mamm* was—was *Mamm*."

Peter winced to hear his little sister describe exactly how he felt about their mother, too. "I have an idea. Let me get through the harvest first, and then if *Mamm* still isn't her old self, I'll convince her to go to the *dokder* again."

"How are you going to do that? You've asked her to go to the *dokder* as many times as I've asked her to work on a quilt or play a board game with me. She always tells you *neh*, too."

Peter had no idea how he'd finally persuade his mother to make another doctor's appointment, but he'd have plenty of time to think about it on the farm. Picking potatoes could be as boring as it was backbreaking, so having a challenge to think about would keep his mind occupied. "Leave that to me—and meanwhile, keep praying, okay?" Eva nodded but she still looked so forlorn that he suggested they should pick up a pizza for supper. "This way, you won't have to cook and you can grade those papers. I'll visit with *Mamm*, if she's up to it. And Hannes can take care of the animals."

"That would be great. Let's get the kind with ham and pineapple," she suggested, visibly perking up.

Relieved he'd finally made *one* female smile that day, Peter instructed the horse to giddyap. Unfortunately, he had a feeling it was going to take a lot more than a Hawaiian pizza to keep a smile on his mother's face. And as for making Susannah grin? Peter figured there was virtually no chance of that happening. *But at least if I avoid her, I won't make her frown*, he thought.

Susannah's meal was so salty she couldn't seem to drink enough water to quench her thirst. She and her grandparents were eating supper at a picnic table outside an *Englisch* diner in town because Lydia had insisted Susannah shouldn't have to cook her first night there. Susannah thought that was silly, since cooking was such a routine part of her life and she actually found it relaxing.

But then Lydia whispered that she wanted an excuse to get an extrathick milkshake before the restaurant closed on September 30 until Memorial Day of the following year. So Susannah had played along, telling her grandfather that yes, she really would enjoy eating out. And she would have enjoyed it, too, if everything on the menu wasn't fried or previously frozen. But since she didn't want to seem ungrateful, she ordered a burger with coleslaw instead of fries.

"I didn't realize Peter Lambright was one of the *menner* helping you with the harvest this season," she remarked to her grandfather in what she hoped was a casual voice. She had never told her grandparents about her courtship with Peter before and she certainly didn't intend to let on about it now.

Marshall finished chewing a large bite of fried chicken before replying. "How did you find that out?"

"He stopped by to make sure you didn't want him to start work tomorrow instead of *Muundaag.*"

"Hmpf." For some reason, he seemed disgruntled. "Since Lydia's two *seh* couldn't *kumme* this autumn, I had to recruit two other *menner* to help. Peter Lambright is one of them."

"Peter is a *wunderbaar* young *mann.*" Lydia's straw made a loud slurping sound as she finished the last of her milkshake. She set the empty paper cup on the tray. "Once he sees you again, I wouldn't be surprised if he asks to be your suitor."

Embarrassed that Lydia was discussing such a topic in front of her grandfather, Susannah looked down at her plate and picked at her coleslaw with a plastic fork.

"Don't be *lecherich*. She didn't *kumme* here to find a suitor." Marshall's gruff reply to his wife surprised Susannah. "She came to help *us.*"

Lydia persisted, "But there's no reason she can't help us *and* find a suitor, is there?"

Jah, there is a reason. A very gut *reason*, Susannah thought. *And that's that I'm not interested in a suitor and I'm* especially *not interested in Peter.* Susannah didn't answer aloud and neither did Marshall, but he hastily collected their used paper plates and cups and carried them on the tray to the recycling station.

"Your *groossdaadi* is so protective of you," Lydia whispered. "I don't know if it's because you remind him

so much of your *mamm* or if it's because he doesn't realize that you're no longer a young *maedel*."

The comment was almost amusing coming from
Lydia, since she also had a tendency to fuss over Susannah as if she wasn't a grown woman. "It's okay.
He's right—I didn't *kumme* here to find a suitor." Susannah tried to sound as resolute as her grandfather had
sounded, but she couldn't seem to get through to Lydia.

"If you're not interested in Peter, the other young
mann who's coming from Serenity Ridge is a bachelor,
too. Benuel Heiser. He's the one who's picking up the
buwe at the bus station."

Susannah thought the other crew member was local,
not from Serenity Ridge, so she was surprised to hear
Lydia mention there would be an extra horse on the
farm. "Benuel's staying at the *haus*?"

"Of course not—your *groossdaadi* would never
allow that, not with you here!" Lydia exclaimed. "He's
staying with his relatives just down the road. My great-
nephews, Jacob and Conrad, will be the only ones staying with us…which reminds me, I didn't make up their
beds yet. You'll have to do that for me. Now, do you
have room for dessert?"

This time, Susannah didn't give in. "*Denki*, but I'm
so full my stomach hurts."

Hours later, as she was lying in bed, her stomach *still*
hurt. Whether that was from the amount or type of food
she'd eaten that afternoon, or because talking about and
seeing Peter had upset her, Susannah couldn't be sure.
But she knew if she continued eating and feeling like
she had today, she'd regret it physically and emotionally. So before falling asleep, she resolved she'd start
the next day with prayer and an early morning walk.

Unfortunately, she overslept and was woken the next morning by the smell of sausages frying. She got dressed and hurried into the kitchen. Lydia was standing in front of the oven, where two large cast-iron pans were sizzling on the stovetop.

"How did you ever manage to lift those singlehandedly? I'm sorry I slept in—you should have woken me." Susannah looked into the pans. One contained thick slabs of ham and several sausages; eight eggs were frying in the other. Seeing the amount of food, she asked, "Did Jacob and Conrad get here already?"

Lydia looked confused. She backed away and sat down at the table so Susannah could finish preparing the meal. "*Neh.* They aren't coming until suppertime. Why?"

Susannah didn't want to point out that the breakfast was enough to feed half a dozen people, instead of just the three of them. It would have come across as self-righteous, considering it wasn't that long ago when she wouldn't have blinked at eating a breakfast this size. So she said, "I just want to be sure to make their beds up before they arrive."

After Marshall came in from the barn and they'd eaten their breakfast, Susannah washed and dried the dishes and then carried a stack of sheets and quilts to the open, unfinished loft upstairs. The beds weren't actual beds; they were borrowed mattresses lying on the floor. But after Susannah made them up, swept away the dust and washed the windows to a shine, she surveyed the room and thought, *It looks really cozy and comfortable up here. Especially for two scrappy fourteen-year-old* buwe *like Jacob and Conrad.*

She'd met the twins when she'd come to New Hope

the previous summer, and at the time, they'd been just about her height, so when they arrived shortly before supper, she was surprised to see they were now taller than her grandfather. And they were taller than Benuel, the sinewy auburn-haired man from Serenity Ridge who'd given them a ride from the bus station.

"You've really grown!" Susannah remarked as they all crowded into the kitchen.

"Jah," Conrad acknowledged with a lopsided grin. "And you've really shrunk!"

She supposed she had invited his remark and she would have dismissed it lightly, considering the last time they were together she and the twins had taken to teasing each other good-naturedly, like siblings sometimes did.

But then Jacob clarified, for Benuel's benefit, "He means she's lost a *ton* of weight. Last summer Susannah was twice as wide as she is now."

Although he said it admiringly, Susannah's cheeks burned. She didn't know how to respond without drawing more attention to herself. Just when she thought she couldn't feel any more embarrassed, Benuel came to her defense when he said, "I doubt that's true. I can't imagine her being that overweight."

"It's true. She was really—" Jacob began, but Marshall cut him off.

"Let's clear out of the kitchen so the *weibsmensch* can finish making supper. *Buwe, kumme* wait on the porch with me."

"Benuel, you'll stay for supper, too?" Lydia asked, but it wasn't really a question. When she invited someone to stay for a meal, she didn't take no for an answer. In this case, Benuel didn't need any convincing.

"Denki." He looked directly at Susannah as he added, "It smells *appenditlich*."

The second the door closed behind them, Lydia whispered, "He seems like a nice young *mann*, don't you think?"

"Jah," Susannah replied distractedly, taking a stack of plates from the cupboard.

"And strong, too," Lydia insisted.

Aha. Now that she realized what Lydia was getting at, Susannah answered more cautiously, lest her own words be used against her. "That would explain why *groossdaadi* requested his help."

"I noticed *you* caught his eye." Lydia's silvery voice was too loud for Susannah's comfort.

She set the plates on the table, turned toward the oven and said, "I'd better stop gabbing and concentrate on finishing supper or I'll overcook this."

"What is it you're making?"

"Roasted vegetable casserole."

"That sounds *gut*. What kind of meat are you serving with it?"

"I didn't prepare meat. This is a very filling dish on its own."

"You're not going to win any *mann* over with nothing more than squash and brussels sprouts for supper," Lydia warned.

Her stepgrandmother's insistence that she should be trying to win a man over—winning him over with food, no less—was so exasperating that Susannah felt like screaming. But after a quick, silent prayer for grace, she was able to make light of the situation. She teased, "Then maybe I'll win him over with what I made for dessert."

Lydia narrowed her eyes. "I thought you said you didn't make dessert today."

Susannah snapped her fingers. "That's right, I didn't. Oh, well."

She giggled but Lydia just shook her head sadly, as if she didn't know what to make of a young woman who claimed little interest in having dessert and even less interest in having a suitor.

On Sunday morning, it took Dorothy so long to get ready for church that Peter considered suggesting she ought to stay home. But unless someone was out of town, in the hospital or seriously ill, an Amish person rarely missed church. Besides, Peter didn't want to discourage her, knowing she was doing the best she could to honor the Sabbath by gathering with others for worship. Still, by the time she got out the door, they were already late, and it was almost as much of a rarity for an Amish person to be tardy to church as it was to be absent from it.

Like the other settlements in that part of Maine, the New Hope district had constructed a building for their services instead of taking turns meeting in each other's houses, the way most Amish districts did. As the Lambrights approached the church, Peter felt self-conscious, knowing its large windows meant that everyone could see them. But at least the congregation was still singing hymns when his family tiptoed in, so they didn't disrupt the actual sermon.

The benches in the back of the room were filled, so Peter's family had to make their way to an empty bench halfway up the aisle. In their church, instead of the men and women sitting separately, as they did in some of the more conservative Amish churches, the families sat together. So once they took their places, Peter noticed Marshall and Lydia were occupying the bench two rows up from them. Two tall young men—presumably Lydia's nephews—were seated on the other side of Lydia, and Susannah was on the other side of the boys. To her right was a man Peter had never seen before; he would have remembered, as no man in their district had hair that color.

Did someone kumme *with her from Dover?* he wondered. *Her* bruder, *maybe?* But Susannah's brother was married with children; he wouldn't have come without them. Peter scanned the front half of the room but he didn't see any children he didn't recognize.

Then he caught sight of the Heiser family seated one row up from where Susannah was. Didn't Marshall mention that the crew member—Benuel, a bachelor Peter's age—was related to them? Peter deduced that there must not have been enough room for him on their bench, so he'd had to move back a row, joining Susannah and her relatives.

He tried to focus on the sermon, but Peter felt himself growing increasingly agitated to see Benuel and Susannah seated side by side. He wasn't troubled because it seemed as if they were a couple or because Peter himself wanted to be sitting next to her. He was troubled because he *used* to want to be sitting next to her. His favorite daydream used to be of the two of them going to church as husband and wife, and eventually filling a bench with their children. Seeing Susannah beside a man his own age made Peter keenly aware that he'd proved himself unworthy of being a husband and father by hurting the woman he loved in order to fulfill his own needs.

He sighed heavily, which startled his mother, who had fallen asleep against his shoulder. Dorothy jerked awake with an audible snort and Marshall glanced over his shoulder at her and scowled. Although it wasn't unusual for people to fall asleep during the three-hour Sunday sermon, usually those who dozed off were either teenage boys who'd been out late the evening before or elderly men. Dorothy covered her mouth with her hand, obviously embarrassed. And although he knew his mother really couldn't help falling asleep, at that moment, Peter was embarrassed by her drowsiness, too. He just wished he could disappear.

So when the service was over and Dorothy said she didn't think she could stay awake through lunch, Peter readily agreed they should go home, even though leaving church early was considered nearly as rude as coming to church late.

It was Marshall's turn to care for everyone's horses, so Susannah was relieved when he took Benuel, Jacob and Conrad outside with him. She'd felt self-conscious about Benuel's presence beside her throughout the worship service; single men and women virtually never sat together at church, even if they were courting, which they most definitely were not. However, no one else knew that and she was concerned people might jump to conclusions.

"I'll be more of a hindrance than a help in the kitchen," Lydia said as the women in the congregation began streaming downstairs to make lunch and the men stacked the benches atop of one another, transforming them into tables. "I'm going to go talk to the deacon's wife, Almeda Stoll, over there by the window. You'll be okay without me?"

"Of course." Susannah wasn't shy about pitching in. Besides, it would be nice to have a moment to catch up with Dorcas in private, if she could find her. She was so intent on scanning the room for her friend that she nearly bumped right into Eva Lambright, Peter's little sister, who was bending over to tie her shoe.

The summer Susannah came to New Hope, she and Lydia spent many afternoons picking wild blueberries with Eva and Dorothy Lambright in the field behind their house. She had treasured getting to know her suitor's family better, even though they were unaware she and Peter were courting. Despite how she felt about Eva's brother now, Susannah still had a soft spot in her heart for the girl.

"Oops. I'm so sorry. I didn't see you there, Eva," she said.

"Susannah? Susannah Peachy?" the young girl asked. Susannah braced herself for the inevitable comment about how much weight she'd lost, but instead, Eva excitedly called to her brother, "Peter, look who's back. You remember Susannah, don't you?"

That's when Susannah noticed Peter a few yards in front of them. He must have been trying to slink off without having to talk to her, because when he turned around, his face was red. Susannah used to love teasing him with sweet nothings and compliments until he blushed like that, but she certainly didn't feel like complimenting him now. *Please,* Gott, *help me to let go of my anger.*

"Hello, Susannah."

"Hello, Peter."

Their terse greetings were so stilted that Susannah was sure Eva would notice, but the girl seemed oblivious to their discomfort and continued chattering away. "I can't believe it's you. I was thinking about you this summer during *blohbier* season, but I didn't expect you'd *kumme* back to New Hope until *Grischtdaag.*"

The young girl's fondness toward Susannah was evident and she couldn't help but smile back at her. "I came here to help Lydia cook and clean during harvest season."

"Really? What a coincidence—Peter's going to be helping your *groossdaadi* with the harvest. It's too bad I have to go to *schul*, or I could help, too. I really enjoy picking *blohbier*, but I've never picked potatoes before."

As his sister prattled on, Peter shifted his weight, inching toward the door. "*Mamm* and Hannes are probably done using the restrooms now and are waiting at the buggy."

"It's too bad we have to leave. It would be so much *schpass* to catch up with Susannah," Eva said wistfully. "I heard there are pumpkin bars with cream-cheese frosting and apple crisp for dessert. We don't have any homemade sweets at the *haus*. Ever since *Mamm* stopped—"

"Eva!" Peter interrupted, as if he was trying to silence her from saying something embarrassing. "We have more than enough food to satisfy your appetite."

A blush rose across Eva's chubby cheeks and she looked down at the floor. Susannah understood from personal experience how humiliating it was to have someone else make a comment, directly or indirectly, about a woman's appetite or weight. She was so irritated at Peter for implying his sister needed to cut down that she offered, "If you'd like to stay for lunch, my *groossdaadi* could give you a ride home, Eva."

Meeting Susannah's eyes again, Eva said, "*Denki*, but I have to go… Maybe you could *kumme* over to our *haus* for lunch next *Sunndaag*?"

Susannah caught her breath. *That's what happens if I speak when I'm angry—I make a bigger mess of things,* she thought, racking her brain for a gentle way to decline the invitation.

Before she could come up with anything, Peter supplied an excuse for her, obviously as opposed to the idea of her visiting his house as she was. "Susannah's grandparents might have made plans to bring her on visits with them next *Sunndaag*."

"*Jah*," Susannah agreed. "I'm afraid I don't know what my schedule is like yet. *Denki* for the invitation, though. I'm sure our paths will cross again eventually. Meanwhile, please greet your *mamm* for me."

"Okay, but if you find out you have a free afternoon or evening, you're *wilkom* to join us for lunch or supper anytime."

As Susannah watched the brother and sister leaving the room together, she thought, *Eva is such a* schmaert, *sweet* maedel, *but I'd rather go* hungerich *than to have to eat at the same table with Peter.*

Chapter Three

On Monday morning, after Peter finished his third helping of oatmeal, Hannes joked, "Do you want to lick the pot clean, too?"

"Harvesting potatoes is going to make me a lot hungrier than working in the shop is going to make *you*," Peter replied pointedly. "Would you like to switch places?"

"*Neh.* I'm *hallich* you're the one helping Marshall instead of me." Hannes looked him in the eye and Peter knew his brother really valued the sacrifice he was making on his behalf.

Getting extra hungerich *because I'm working outside all day is the least of what my* bruder*'s antics have cost me.* As soon as the bitter thought popped into his mind, Peter dismissed it. While he *did* want his brother to appreciate the consequences of his actions so he wouldn't repeat them, he didn't want Hannes to feel indebted to him.

For one thing, making a sacrifice for his family was part of Peter's duty as the head of his household. For another, Hannes didn't know Peter had broken off a courtship in order to pay for the car he wrecked. So

Peter couldn't really blame him for that; he couldn't even blame Marshall. *I'm the only one at fault, because I agreed to it*, he thought.

"For lunch, I've packed you a couple of ham-and-cheese sandwiches, a container of broccoli salad and an apple," Eva announced, handing him a cooler. "I put several of those chocolate chip *kuche* in there, too."

Unfortunately, the cookies she was referring to were the kind that were wrapped in a plastic package and sold at the *Englisch* grocery store. Yesterday in church, Eva was being honest when she'd started to tell Susannah that they rarely had any homemade sweets in the house. Even though the meals Peter's sister put together usually didn't require much preparation time, going to school, keeping house, doing laundry and correcting papers kept her far too busy to make desserts. So she'd made a practice of buying cookies and cakes instead. Peter thought most of them tasted like cardboard coated in lard and sprinkled with sugar, and he rarely ate them, but today he'd likely be ravenous enough to eat almost anything.

"*Denki.* Please save something from supper for me, too, okay?"

"Are you sure you don't want us to wait to eat until you get home?"

"*Jah.* Sunset is around six thirty tonight and we'll have to make a final run to the potato *haus*, so I won't be home before seven. Maybe not even 'til eight."

Although Marshall was selling the potatoes to an *Englisch* buyer, he wouldn't allow *Englisch* technology on his property, including windrowers, tractors and trucks. So he'd be unearthing the potatoes with a horse-drawn mechanical digger. The crew would be "picking" them from the dirt and putting them in what they referred to as barrels, which were really cylindrical wooden containers that could hold sixty pounds of potatoes, since full barrels would have been too heavy for the men to lift.

After the crew had filled enough barrels, Peter and Benuel would load them onto the buggy wagon, which was a buggy designed specifically for hauling cargo instead of passengers. Then they'd take them to the *Englisch*-owned potato house, or storage building, for the *Englisch* buyer to transport them to the marketplace from there. The men would work in the fields from shortly after sunrise at six thirty until shortly after the sun set twelve hours later.

"That's going to be a long day. Maybe I should pack another sandwich to hold you over until you return?" Eva offered.

"*Neh*, that's okay. I've got to get going." Peter didn't want to reinforce Marshall's belief that he was irresponsible by showing up late to work. He reminded Hannes to check in on their mother a couple of times during the day, wished Eva a good day at school and then headed out the door.

I hope Mamm *is more rested today*, he fretted as he traveled toward the farm. Then his thoughts wandered to Susannah again. His second interaction with her had gone only marginally better than his first. He had tried to exit the church building surreptitiously so he wouldn't have to speak to her, but there had been no way to avoid it once Eva drew him into the conversation. And, in a way, it was a good thing she'd included him—otherwise his sister might have blurted out that their mother had been too tired or depressed to do any baking recently.

While Susannah had never been one to judge, Peter didn't want her to find out Dorothy had been struggling with fatigue this past year. Not only because it would have embarrassed his mother, but also because Susannah might mention it to her grandparents. *Marshall already holds a low opinion of* me—*I don't want him to decide* Mamm *is lazy, too. Especially because he noticed her sleeping in* kurrich *yesterday*, he thought.

So last evening, he'd gently reminded his sister that it was important not to discuss their mother's condition with anyone else. Eva had felt terrible for almost letting it slip in front of Susannah. "I'm such a *bobbelmoul*!" she'd lamented, explaining that she'd been so excited to see Susannah again that she'd rambled on without thinking. "I shouldn't have invited her over to the *haus*, either, just in case *Mamm* is having one of her really bad days."

"Don't worry," Peter had assured her. "It sounded as if Susannah's going to be too busy helping Lydia to *kumme* over here."

Even if Susannah didn't have a full schedule, Peter knew there was virtually no chance she'd be dropping in at their house. She may have invited Eva to stay and have lunch after church with her, but everything about her stance and tone toward Peter indicated she wanted to keep as much distance between the two of them as possible...just as he'd suspected.

As he neared the farm, his stomach tightened with apprehension and he silently prayed, *Lord, please bless my work in the fields and please keep me from seeing Susannah today. But if I do, please help me not to say anything to upset her.*

* * *

Susannah poured all of her frustration into scrubbing the greasy residue from a frying pan. On Saturday, after carefully preparing a menu, she'd gone shopping and bought enough groceries to last for three days, which was about all that would fit in her grandparents' small refrigerator. This morning's breakfast was supposed to include omelets, fresh fruit and yogurt with granola and a drizzle of honey. However, when Lydia learned what she was making, she insisted Susannah add pancakes and bacon to the meal, as well.

"Marshall and the *buwe* need more sustenance than that to keep them going until lunchtime," she'd insisted. "And we rarely eat yogurt, but when we do, it's the kind with fruit in the bottom, not that diet kind."

Since she felt it wasn't her place to object, Susannah had complied with Lydia's wishes. But inwardly, she'd argued, *It's not* diet *yogurt—it's plain. And the* buwe *will get plenty of sustenance from the protein in the* oier, *but I'm concerned about* Groossdaadi *having bacon—there's too much salt in it.*

While she was aware her stepgrandmother had only asked for her help cooking, not for her dietary input, Susannah's understanding of nutrition influenced what she made. Primarily because she cared about her grandparents and she had seen the effects of poor nutrition on her parents' health. Marshall and Lydia weren't overweight, but Lydia had mentioned Susannah's grandfather had high blood pressure.

Plus, Susannah had purchased groceries according to the menu she had planned. If her grandfather was going to expect to eat bacon every day, she'd have to go back to the store because Susannah had used up the last of what was in the fridge. *I can see if the store stocks reduced-sodium bacon. And at least the* buwe *will eat anything, so the food I already bought won't go to waste*, she thought.

After cleaning up the breakfast dishes, doing the laundry and sweeping the floors, she went into the living room, where Lydia was reading the Bible, and asked if she wanted to take a walk with her.

"A walk? Where do you want to go?"

"Just to the tree line out back," she suggested. Her grandparents' house was positioned on the western end of the farm, with the fields stretching to the east and north. Susannah figured if she walked across the grassy, unplowed meadow directly behind the house toward the tall pine trees, she wouldn't run the risk of bumping into the crew as they were harvesting the russets in the acreage closest to the house. More specifically, she wouldn't come within shouting distance of Peter.

"Why would we want to do that?"

Susannah anticipated the negative response she'd get if she told Lydia she wanted to walk simply because it was good exercise. Many of the Amish people she knew, especially those who were older, considered exercising for the purpose of exercising to be an *Englisch* pursuit. Physical exercise was a *result* of their lifestyle and hard work, but it wasn't considered the *goal*. So she carefully answered, "Because it's a pleasant way to enjoy the beautiful scenery *Gott* made. I don't get to see so many pine trees like this in Dover."

"That's why the windows are made of glass," Lydia teased. "Besides, it's a little chilly today. *Kumme* keep me company while I have another cup of *kaffi*. We haven't had a moment to chat in private since the *buwe* arrived. I want to hear what your friend Dorcas had to say when she saw you in *kurrich* yesterday."

"Dorcas wasn't in *kurrich* yesterday. She was spending the weekend with her *familye* in Serenity Ridge. I don't know if she's back yet." Susannah distractedly looked out the window and suddenly she was struck with an idea: she'd *walk* to the market to pick up more bacon and sausage for tomorrow's breakfast.

She thought she'd come up with the perfect way to get some exercise, but Lydia argued, "All the way on the other side of West River Road? That's too far and too dangerous. There's no shoulder on that road—an *Englisch* high school *bu* was recently hit riding his bike there. Your grandfather will insist you take the buggy."

Lydia was right; although most Amish men and women considered traveling by foot to be an integral part of their daily routine, Marshall had always been concerned about where and how far his granddaughter walked, especially in New Hope. Aware he wasn't going to budge on the issue, Susannah gave in. "Okay," she said with a sigh. "I'll take the buggy to the store."

"While we're talking about shopping, I noticed you didn't buy any beef. Weren't you planning on making sloppy joes for lunch?"

"*Jah.* But I'm using ground turkey, not beef." Susannah had memorized her favorite sloppy joe recipe, which also included a homemade sauce, carrots and green peppers.

"Oh, so that's what that turkey is for." Lydia wrinkled her nose. "I suppose that's okay, but it doesn't seem like you'll have nearly enough to feed five *hungerich menner.*"

"*Five?*" Susannah nearly shouted. "I didn't know Benuel and Peter were coming for lunch today!"

"They're coming for lunch *every* day. I thought I told you that you'd be cooking for the whole crew?"

What she'd thought Lydia said was that she'd be cooking for the out-of-town crew, referring to Conrad and Jacob, since Susannah hadn't known Benuel was coming from Serenity Ridge. "I guess I misunderstood. I figured Benuel and Peter would bring their own lunches."

"*Neh*. I can't let them eat a cold lunch while we're all in here enjoying a hot meal. I just wouldn't hear of it," Lydia declared. But her voice softened as she added, "We'll make do for this afternoon and you'll be going to the market later, anyway, so you can supplement what you bought on *Samschdaag*. There's no need to look so upset, dear."

Jah*, there is*, Susannah thought, close to tears at the notion of dining with Peter on a daily basis. But almost immediately, she consoled herself with the knowledge that there wouldn't be enough room at the table for all seven of them. So Susannah could claim she was too busy serving to sit down with everyone else. "I'd already planned to make a salad but I suppose I could supplement our lunch with more vegetables," she proposed.

"*Jah*—how about mashed potatoes?"

"I was thinking of roasted cauliflower and broccoli."

"*Neh*, potatoes are more filling. They're the perfect thing to have on the first day of harvest." Lydia looked out the window. "I see Peter and Benuel are loading the barrels into the buggy wagon—if you hurry, you can catch them before they leave and ask them to fill a basket for you now."

"That's okay. I'll go out and pick some myself after you've finished your *kaffi*."

"*Neh*, don't wait on my account—you've been itching to get outside. Besides, I told Marshall to *kumme* in for lunch at twelve thirty, so you've got a lot of peeling to do before then."

Susannah knew it was useless to protest once Lydia had made up her mind. *I'm going to have to see Peter every day at lunch, anyway. I might as well get used to it*, she silently conceded as she opened the door and stepped outside into the crisp autumn air.

Peter and Benuel finished heaving the last of the barrels onto the buggy wagon. It was Peter's turn to transport them to the potato house, where he'd unload them alone while Benuel would continue to help Conrad and Jacob pick in the fields. When Peter returned, he'd help pick, too. Once they had enough barrels to fill the buggy wagon again, they'd load it up together and then it would be Benuel's turn to go to the potato house. Because he was aware that an injured worker could significantly derail the harvesting schedule, Marshall insisted the two men alternate their transportation responsibilities like this throughout the day. He wanted each of them to have an opportunity to rest their arm and back muscles as they rode home from the storage building.

As he was checking to make sure the barrels were secure, Peter happened to notice something move in his peripheral vision. He glanced up to see Susannah approaching from the direction of the house.

"*Guder mariye,*" she said when she reached them and they greeted her back. Her tone was polite but cool as she explained, "Lydia sent me to get potatoes for lunch."

Since Peter was standing in the buggy wagon and he had easy access to the barrels, he extended his hand to take the basket from her. But Benuel intercepted it and hopped up into the bed of the wagon, too. "How many do you need?" he asked.

"That depends on how many you think you'll eat. I'm making mashed potatoes for lunch."

"In that case, I'll fill it up."

Marshall must have invited Benuel to eat with the familye, Peter thought. While he himself hadn't expected to have lunch with them, it seemed strange that he'd be the only one who was excluded. No matter what Marshall thought of him, it just wasn't the Amish way to leave one person out. *It's almost as if I'm being shunned,* he thought. But then it occurred to him that perhaps Benuel had forgotten his cooler today.

Whistling as he chose the biggest potatoes, Benuel placed them in the basket and then jumped back down from the wagon right beside Susannah. "This should be enough for me. Did you bring another basket for the rest of the crew?" he joked.

She chuckled. "*Neh*, just the one. And a word to the wise—you'd better take as much as you want the first time the bowl is passed, because with Jacob and Conrad at the table, it won't *kumme* around a second time."

"I'll keep that in mind." Benuel grinned and presented her the basket. Was Peter mistaken or did he deliberately touch her fingers before he let go of its handle?

"Denki," Susannah replied and quickly pivoted back toward the house.

Watching her go, Benuel remarked, "She might just be the prettiest *maedel* I've ever seen."

Surprised to hear his coworker openly express a sentiment most Amish men would consider worldly, Peter replied, "She's not a *maedel*—she's a *weibsmensch*."

"*Jah*, you can say that again," Benuel said. "A very beautiful *weibsmensch*. Jacob and Conrad said she used to be on the plump side, but she sure isn't now. Do you know if she's got a suitor back in Maryland?"

Peter was so appalled by Benuel's brazen references to Susannah's appearance—to *any* woman's appearance and especially to her figure—all he could think to do was correct Benuel, as he replied, "Delaware. She lives in Delaware."

Benuel snickered. "Okay, does she have a suitor in Delaware, then?"

"How would I know?" Peter snapped. He climbed down from the wagon bed, strode around to the front of the buggy and pulled himself up onto the seat, ready to depart. But at the last second, he decided he couldn't let Benuel's remarks about Susannah go unaddressed. Over his shoulder, he cautioned, "You'd better not let Marshall hear you talking about Susannah like that. You might find yourself out of a job."

"*Denki* for the tip," Benuel called as Peter steered the horse toward the lane leading to the road. "I'll make sure he's not within earshot."

Peter hadn't really been suggesting Benuel should be careful Marshall didn't hear him talking about Susannah—he'd been suggesting Benuel shouldn't talk about Susannah at all. Especially not in such a boorish, superficial way.

Admittedly, he could understand why Benuel found Susannah so attractive. Last summer, when Peter spotted her in church, he'd noticed her curly hair and fair, flawless skin, too. But it was her eyes had that made him go weak in the knees the first time they'd met. And it wasn't just because they were a striking, golden shade of brown; it was also because of the openness and warmth he'd seen in them.

Now she can't even bear to glance in my direction, he thought. Once again, he didn't blame her for that, but it bothered him that someone as bold as Benuel was vying for her attention. His comment about Susannah's weight was something he might have expected from an *Englischer*, not from a fellow Amish man. While it may have registered somewhere in the back of Peter's mind that Susannah seemed thinner than she had last Christmas, he hadn't given it a second thought until Benuel brought it to his attention again.

Maybe it was because he was too nervous in her presence to notice anything else, but the only thing that struck Peter as being different about Susannah's appearance was how rigid her posture was. It troubled him to know *he* was the reason she was standing as if her spine were a steel rod.

But at least I didn't say anything else dumm *to upset her just now*, he consoled himself. Of course, he hadn't said anything at all, but even that was an improvement from the last couple of times they'd interacted.

Once he reached the potato house, which was built into the side of a hill, half underground, half above, Peter emptied the barrels into a chute. Then he stacked the empty containers in the back of the buggy wagon and returned to the farm. His stomach had been growling for the last hour, so he was relieved when he saw the other four men going toward the house. *Must be time for our lunch break*, he surmised. It turned out just as well that Benuel had been invited to eat inside the house; Peter didn't want to have to listen to him make any more churlish remarks about Susannah while he was enjoying his own lunch.

After stabling the horse, he grabbed his cooler from his buggy and went to sit beneath a maple tree, leaning against its trunk. He closed his eyes to say grace and to pray for his mother's energy to return. But he opened them again when someone gave the sole of his boot a tap. It was Marshall.

Oh, wunderbaar. *He probably thinks I was sleeping on the job.* Peter jumped to his feet. "Sorry. I thought everyone was inside taking a lunch break."

"They are. And Lydia won't let us eat until you join us, so c'mon."

Peter understood: just as Susannah had made it clear it wasn't her idea to come and get potatoes from him and Benuel, Marshall was making it clear that it wasn't his idea to invite Peter to lunch. It was Lydia's. Susannah wasn't going to feel any more comfortable having Peter in the kitchen than he'd feel about being there, but he knew better than to insult Marshall's wife by turning down the offer of a good hot meal. He picked up his cooler and raced after the old man, who had already strode halfway back to the porch.

"I found him sleeping beneath a tree," Susannah's grandfather announced when he came through the door, with Peter lagging behind him, holding a cooler in his hands.

"I—I was saying grace. I didn't expect to be invited in for lunch. I brought my own," he said apologetically, wiping his boots on the rug.

"There's no invitation needed. It's expected that we'll

all eat lunch together every day, so you can leave that cooler at home from now on," Lydia said.

"*Denki*, that's very kind of—"

"Quit yakking and go wash your hands. We're *hungerich*," Marshall interrupted him.

Susannah noticed the color rise in Peter's cheeks. *Groossdaadi is too grumpy sometimes. I'm not* hallich *Peter is going to be eating with us every day, but at least he has the* gut *manners to express his appreciation...and to wipe his boots, which no one else took the time to do.* "The bathroom is on the right," she told him, pointing down the hall.

After he returned and they'd said grace, the men dug in to their food with gusto. For several minutes, no one spoke because their mouths were too full. Then, as their eating slowed, Marshall commented that he was pleased the crop seemed abundant so far and Lydia remarked how good the potatoes tasted.

"*Jah*, but next time, you should make more," Jacob told Susannah, scraping a spoon against the bottom of the serving dish to get every last trace of the white, creamy, mashed vegetable.

"Aren't you going to leave any for Susannah? She hasn't eaten yet," Benuel reminded the teenager. Then he caught her eye and offered, "If I scoot over, there should be room for you to squeeze in here."

Susannah was unnerved by his audacity; if she was going to sit at the table, she would have sat on the other side of Lydia, not next to Benuel. She'd found it awkward when he'd stood so close to her beside the buggy wagon and again when his hand had touched hers as she took the basket of potatoes from him. But she'd questioned whether he'd overstepped his boundaries accidentally or on purpose. Now that he'd suggested she should "squeeze in" next to him, she had no doubt he was behaving flirtatiously. And right in front of Lydia, too—what was he thinking? It was a good thing her grandfather had excused himself to the restroom.

"I don't want potatoes and I don't want to sit down next to you, either," she replied curtly. Then, seeing Lydia lower her eyebrows disapprovingly at her, she added, "*Denki*, but I'll eat later, after everyone has been served. Otherwise I'll be jumping up and down throughout the meal to bring things to the table."

"You mean like dessert?" Conrad hinted.

"I didn't make dessert but I thought you might like this yogurt, since no one ate any at breakfast," Susannah told him, placing the bowl on the table.

"There's a reason no one ate any of it for breakfast," Conrad muttered facetiously.

"It's not that bad when you add honey to it," his brother informed him, spooning a big swirl of honey into his bowl.

"I like yogurt. It's kind of like custard," Benuel said, but Susannah noticed he only took a small dollop.

"*Jah*, the consistency is the same. But the taste?" Lydia grimaced to demonstrate what she thought of it. Until Susannah started paying more attention to what she herself ate, she had never realized how finicky her stepgrandmother was about food.

"*What* taste? That stuff doesn't *have* any taste." Conrad's remark caused Lydia and Jacob to chuckle.

Susannah couldn't believe that they were making such a fuss over yogurt; it wasn't as if she'd served them one of the appetizers she'd read about in the *Englisch* cookbooks, such as escargot or baby squid. She was just about to tell them she wouldn't buy plain yogurt again if eating it was such a hardship, when Peter spoke up for the first time since sitting down at the table.

"I remember one time when I was a young *bu* and I complained that I disliked what we were having for supper. My mother said, 'At this table, mouths may be used for eating, conversing or thanking the Lord for what He has provided us. Since you want to use your mouth to complain, you may go out into the barn and complain to the pig until we're done eating our dessert.'" Peter licked his spoon and chuckled. "I didn't make that mistake twice."

His point taken, everyone laughed good-naturedly. As he plopped a second heaping spoonful of yogurt onto his dish, Susannah begrudgingly admitted to herself, *Maybe having Peter around at lunchtime isn't quite so* baremlich, *after all. At least he can have a* gut *influence on the others' manners, which might make it easier for me to serve healthier food.*

But that didn't mean she wasn't glad when her grandfather returned to the room and told the men it was time for all of them to get back to work, including Peter, who hadn't even finished eating his yogurt yet.

Chapter Four

On Thursday afternoon, when Lydia mentioned she was tired because her cast had interfered with her sleep the evening before, Susannah encouraged her to take a nap in the recliner. As she positioned a pillow beneath her stepgrandmother's arm, trying to help her find a comfortable position, she felt a bit guilty because she knew she had an ulterior motive for convincing Lydia to rest: Susannah wanted to sneak in a walk before it started to rain.

All week, Lydia had found one excuse or the other to keep Susannah inside the house with her, whether it was that she needed Susannah to do some mending or to write a letter to Lydia's sister, or simply to keep her company while she was drinking tea—and usually eating a snack—in the afternoon. Susannah didn't mind helping her stepgrandmother with whatever she needed; after all, that was her purpose in coming to New Hope. And she understood why Lydia felt frustrated and restless. However, after four straight days of being with each other virtually all the time, except during her solo trip to the market, Susannah felt frustrated and restless, too.

Several times she'd invited Lydia to go for a walk with her, but her stepgrandmother usually came up with an excuse for why they should both stay inside instead. Once or twice, she'd convinced Lydia to sit on the porch swing while she cleaned the chicken coop or did a little yardwork nearby, but Susannah was itching to really stretch her legs.

I'll take the clothes off the line and then I'll walk down the lane to the mailbox and back again, but instead of stopping at the haus, *I'll continue toward the far, southern edge of* Groossdaadi's *property. I can repeat the loop twice if I hurry,* she schemed as she picked up the laundry basket and crept out onto the porch.

To her surprise, Susannah found Dorcas climbing the stairs. She set down the laundry basket so she could greet her friend with a hug. "It's so *gut* to finally see you!" she exclaimed as they embraced.

"It's *wunderbaar* to see you, too. But your shoulders feel so bony." Dorcas stepped back and eyed her. "You've lost quite a bit of weight. Have you been ill?"

"*Neh*, I'm healthier than ever. I wrote that I've changed my eating habits and I feel a lot stronger and more energetic lately, remember?"

"I remember you writing that you'd made changes to your *familye*'s diet because of your *daed*'s diabetes, but you never said anything about losing weight yourself." Dorcas frowned and smoothed her apron over her stomach, as if to push her round belly flatter, too.

"It didn't seem like it was worth mentioning," Susannah said dismissively. In fact, it would have felt boastful. "But I can't wait to hear what's new with you. *Kumme*, let's walk to the mailbox and you can tell me what has been happening in your life since you last wrote."

"Can't we sit on the swing instead?"

Susannah had already descended the porch steps. "Lydia is inside taking a nap. I don't want to disturb her."

"I don't know how we'd disturb her—the windows are closed and we're not going to shout," Dorcas grumbled, but she followed Susannah, anyway. As they walked down the long dirt driveway, Dorcas told her about her recent trip to Serenity Ridge to visit her aunt, uncle and cousins. "My *gschwischderkind* Hadassah is three years younger than I am and she told me she's getting married this *hochzich* season. And my *gschwischderkind* Sarah is only seventeen and she's already courting. At this rate, I'm going to be the spinster of the *familye*."

"There are worse things in life than being single."

"*Jah*, I know that. But, *Gott* willing, I still want to fall in love, get married and start a *familye* of my own. You do, too, don't you?"

Susannah shrugged. "Not especially. Not anymore."

"Really?" Dorcas glanced over at her, raising an eyebrow. "That's a big change from when you and Peter were courting. You wrote that you could hardly wait to become a wife and a *mamm*. Don't tell me you gave up your heart's desire to be married just because one *mann* didn't think you were a *gut* match for him."

Neh, *what I really gave up was my hope that any* mann *would love me unconditionally, for who I truly am,* Susannah thought, but she didn't express her feelings aloud. Even though she and Dorcas had become close confidantes, as well as pen pals, there were some heartaches Susannah couldn't share with anyone else.

Instead, she said, "Speaking of Peter, did you know he's helping my *groossdaadi* and Lydia's great-nephews harvest the potato crop?"

Dorcas abruptly stopped walking. "He *is*?"

"*Jah*. There's another man on the crew, too. You might know him since he's from Serenity Ridge. His name is Benuel Heiser."

"*Jah*, I know him all right." Dorcas lowered her voice even though they were the only ones on the lane and explained that her cousins had told her Benuel had only ended his *rumspringa* last April, even though he was twenty-four. He'd spent several years living among the *Englisch* before finally returning to his family and being baptized into the church. Apparently, he'd made quite a bit of money by partnering with a couple of *Englischers* in buying houses, remodeling them and then selling them at a higher price in several of Maine's wealthier seaside vacation communities.

But after returning to New Hope for good, he'd made a commitment to work solely for Amish businesses as a way of completely cutting ties with his old *Englisch* lifestyle. Unfortunately, jobs within the small Serenity Ridge Amish community were difficult to come by, so Benuel took whatever work he could find. "I can understand why he'd help on your *groossdaadi*'s *bauerei*, but why would Peter join the crew when he has a business of his own to manage?"

"Peter knows a lot about harvesting potatoes. Before my *groossdaadi*'s *bruder*, Amos, died and left *Groossdaadi* the *bauerei*, Peter used to help with both planting and harvesting. He was a lot younger then, but I'm sure he still remembers. So I assume he agreed to help now as a favor because Lydia's *seh* couldn't *kumme* this season." Susannah tugged on Dorcas's sleeve to keep her moving; this was supposed to be a brisk walk, not a leisurely stroll.

"Maybe." Dorcas started forward again, but she still wasn't matching Susannah's pace. "Or maybe it's because he heard *you* were returning to New Hope. Maybe he wanted a second chance at courting you, so he thought this would be a *gut* way to be around you again."

"Ha! As if I'd ever accept him as a suitor again."

"You wouldn't? Not ever?"

"*Neh.* Never. But that's not why he's working on the *bauerei.* He didn't know I'd be here. He seemed as shocked to see me as I was to see him."

"You've already seen each other?"

"Not only have I seen him, but I've eaten lunch with him every day." Susannah told her that Lydia had insisted all of the crew members eat together. After the first day, she'd asked Marshall to add another leaf to the table so there would be room for Susannah to join them, too. As if that weren't awkward enough, Lydia had decided her granddaughter should sit in between Benuel, who was overly friendly, and Peter, who hardly said a word to her—nor did she speak to him unless it was absolutely necessary. Susannah thought the situation would have made her feel too flustered to eat anything at all, but instead she'd been nervously cramming food into her mouth, barely noticing how it tasted or how much she'd consumed.

"Was Peter surprised about your weight loss?"

"As I said, we've hardly spoken to each other. But judging from the fact he didn't even recognize me when he saw me, *jah,* I'd say he was surprised."

Dorcas gleefully rubbed her hands together. "That must have been so satisfying!"

Neh, it was actually quite hurtful, Susannah thought. "I didn't lose weight for other people's approval. I changed my *familye*'s diet so we'd be healthier. And because I've *kumme* to realize how important it is to take care of the bodies *Gott* has given us."

"I know, I know. But considering how devastated you were when Peter broke up with you because you were overweight, I'd think it would feel *gut* to show him how thin you've become. Admit it—didn't you feel a tiny bit smug?"

"You mean prideful? *Neh,* I can honestly say I didn't." Susannah used her chin to gesture toward the buggy coming up the road. "Shh. That might be him returning from the potato *haus* now."

But as the buggy neared, she saw it was Benuel, not Peter, holding the reins. He slowed the horse to a halt just before he reached them and gazed down at Susannah. "Hi, Susannah. Who's your friend?"

Before Susannah could respond, Dorcas said, "You know who I am, Benuel. We've met several times in Serenity Ridge."

He pushed back his hat and squinted at her. "Ah, right. Sorry, Naomi."

"My name is *Dorcas,*" Susannah's friend huffed.

Ignoring her disgusted reaction, Benuel addressed Susannah. "Do you need a ride somewhere?"

"*Neh.* We're enjoying our walk. Besides, my *groossdaadi* is paying you to transport potatoes, not passengers." Susannah intended to remind Benuel in a lighthearted way that he had work to do, but he seemed to think she was bantering with him.

"Maybe, but how can he blame me for wanting to take you for a ride when your eyes are so much prettier than a potato's?" Benuel replied with a wink.

Susannah's cheeks blazed from embarrassment. Speechless, she twirled and took off in the direction of the mailbox, with Dorcas in close pursuit. After hearing Benuel's wagon depart in the opposite direction, Susannah spluttered, "Can you believe how gutsy he is? He must have picked up that brash attitude from the *Englisch* during his extended *rumspringa*. They might think that kind of remark is complimentary, but I find it utterly offensive."

"You think *you're* offended?" Dorcas exclaimed. "I've been personally introduced to him at least three times in the past four months and he didn't have any clue what my name is. Plus, he flirted with you right in front of me. It's as if I'm invisible, which is *narrish*, considering I take up a lot more space than you do."

"Don't make jokes like that, Dorcas."

"Who's joking? It's the truth and you know it. Benuel acted as if I don't exist because he doesn't think I'm as attractive as you are."

"That's *lecherich*. Beauty is in the eye of the beholder."

"Exactly—and in *his* eyes, I'm too heavy to be beautiful."

Sadly, Susannah knew Dorcas was probably right about Benuel's perspective, so instead of denying it, she said, "If that's true, then I wish I was heavy again—it would be better than being the object of his flirtatious remarks. Or the object of *anyone's* remarks."

"You don't really expect me to believe that, do you?" Dorcas asked as Susannah retrieved the mail from the box. "I mean, I know Benuel comes on too strong, but I'm sure other people have complimented you on your weight loss and appearance. You have to admit, it must be encouraging to hear such positive comments."

"I won't admit any such thing because it's not true," Susannah countered defensively. "I wish people would stop talking about my weight altogether."

"Fine with me," Dorcas said, and Susannah recognized the edge to her voice. She'd heard it in other people's voices before, but she made no apology for her request. The women walked in silence until they almost reached the house again. It was beginning to drizzle, but Susannah figured if they hurried, they could make it to the tree line and back before the skies really opened up.

"Let's keep walking," she suggested. "I've been cooped up in the *haus* all week. Lydia never wants to go outside and she doesn't want me to go out, either."

"Shouldn't we take your laundry in first?"

"It'll be okay." Wheedling her friend, Susannah said, "When we get back we'll go inside for tea and you can have some of the oatmeal *kuche* I made, too."

"Oh, so you think you can bribe your chubby friend into exercising by offering her *kuche*?"

"*Neh.* That's not why I—"

Dorcas nudged Susannah's arm. "I'm only kidding. Of course, we can keep walking if it means that much to you. The extra exercise would be *gut* for me, too."

"*Denki.*" The tension between them dissolved, and Susannah admitted how challenging it was to spend nearly every minute of the day in Lydia's company.

"Then you ought to *kumme* to the work frolic my *schweschdere* and I are organizing for Elizabeth Hilty on *Samschdaag*. She's been in the hospital with pneu-

monia but she's coming home on *Muundaag*. So some
of the *weibsleit* from our district are cleaning her *haus*
and stocking her freezer with meals that we'll prepare
in her kitchen, since her husband will be away visiting
her in the hospital all day."

"That sounds like *schpass*. I'd love to join you, as
long as I can bring Lydia with me. She won't be able to
do much, but she'll probably appreciate being around
other *weibsleit* as much as I will."

As they discussed the details of the work frolic,
it began drizzling harder. Even though they hadn't
reached the tree line yet, Susannah conceded that they
should return to the house. They'd barely gone twenty
yards when the clouds burst, pelting them with a torrent of raindrops.

"The clothes!" Remembering the laundry on the line,
Susannah was delighted for the excuse to break into a
sprint. "We'd better make a dash for it."

"They're going to be drenched no matter how quickly
we get there," Dorcas objected. "And so are we. Wet
is wet."

"Dawdle if you want, but I'm going to run. I'll meet
you back there." Susannah charged forward, head down.
She loved running like this, her heart beating so hard
she could hear it in her ears, her breathing heavy, her
feet slapping the damp ground. Because she'd previously been overweight for so long, she hadn't run this
fast since she was a young girl, and as she barreled forward, she felt as vibrant and powerful as a wild horse.

"Whoa!" someone said just as that thought entered
her mind.

Susannah glanced up to see Peter standing frozen,
hands out, palms up, directly in her path. Attempting

to stop, she skidded across the wet dirt, almost as if on ice skates, before thudding backward onto her rump. Although she broke her fall with the palms of her hands, she landed so hard she bounced, but even that didn't hurt her physically as much as it wounded her pride.

"Are you all right?" he asked, towering above her.

"Jah," she replied, too abashed to look up at him. She reached behind her head to refasten her prayer *kapp*, trying to gather her composure. While she was pinning it into place, Peter opened the black umbrella he'd had tucked beneath his arm and held it above her, shielding her from the rain. He offered her his free hand but she rose to her feet without any help from him. A moment later, Dorcas joined them.

"Are you okay, Susannah?" She was either panting or laughing...or a little bit of both.

"Jah." Susannah couldn't say the same for the skirt of her dress, which was dirty, as well as wet.

Dorcas turned her attention to Peter. "Hello." She greeted him cordially, as if they were at a singing instead of standing in the pouring rain. "I'm surprised to see you here on the farm. I thought your business would keep you too busy to help Marshall with the harvest."

Susannah didn't appreciate Dorcas's line of questioning and she started walking—limping, actually—toward the house. She'd rather get soaked to the bone than walk beneath the umbrella with Peter. He and Dorcas followed closely enough that she was still within earshot of their conversation.

"I—I agreed last winter I'd help him. Hannes can manage the shop without me since this is a slow time of year for picnic-table orders."

"Oh. I see. Well, that's nice of you." Dorcas's voice

sounded sweeter than usual. Almost lilting. "Why did you *kumme* to this part of the farm? I didn't see anyone else out this way."

Susannah had wondered the same thing, but she'd been too humiliated from taking a spill to ask.

"Lydia saw me bringing some barrels into the barn and she called me over to take the umbrella to you two. She'd noticed it was drizzling and she was concerned you'd get wet."

"Ha!" Susannah sputtered. Lydia's matchmaking attempts were *so* obvious. Over her shoulder she remarked, "She should have been more concerned I'd get muddy. Why didn't you move out of my way when you saw me coming?"

"There wasn't enough time. I heard footsteps, glanced up and there you were, heading toward me like a freight train."

For as much weight as she'd lost, Susannah still bristled at being compared to a freight train. Dorcas, however, cracked up. "You really were running full steam ahead, Susannah. I didn't have time to call out a warning to either of you." She giggled again, then asked Peter, "Are you *menner* done picking potatoes for the afternoon?"

"*Jah.* The rain looks like it's going to keep up for a while and we don't want the potatoes to sprout or rot. So we'll wait until the sky is clear tomorrow and the ground has had a chance to dry."

"In that case, do you mind giving me a ride home? I don't have an umbrella and unlike my friend Susannah here, I get a little chilly from walking in the rain."

"We're going to have tea—that should warm you

up," Susannah reminded her. "And I can give you a ride home afterward."

"Won't you need to start supper, since your *groossdaadi* is coming in early?"

It almost seemed as if Dorcas actually preferred to go with Peter. "I'm sure *Groossdaadi* won't mind if I serve supper at our usual time."

"No need for that," Peter said. "Your *haus* is on my way, Dorcas. I'm *hallich* to give you a ride. I've got to help stable the *geil* and put away the equipment so it will be a few minutes before we can leave."

"That's fine. I'll be ready whenever you are." There it was again, that dulcet tone. Why was Dorcas being so sweet to Peter?

She must be trying to compensate for my brusqueness, Susannah thought as he walked away and the two women pulled the wet clothes from the line. Instead of feeling sorry for being inhospitable toward Peter, she resented Dorcas's affability. *It's easy enough for her to act so pleasant to him. She's not the one whose heart he broke. And she's not the one he caused to fall on her backside, either!*

When Susannah and Dorcas entered the house, Lydia was right there at the door with a dry towel for each of them. Apparently, she'd watched the entire scene unfold from the window. "Why didn't you walk beneath the umbrella with Peter and Dorcas?" she asked incredulously. "And why were you running in the first place? You're fortunate you didn't end up falling and breaking *your* wrist, too. Then what would we have done?"

I would have been able to go back to Delaware, Susannah thought. A broken wrist seemed like a small price to pay for the freedom of being able to take a nice long walk outdoors whenever she wanted—especially if it meant she could take that nice long walk in a state that was six hundred miles away from Peter.

"Where have you been?" Marshall asked when Peter reached the barn. Benuel was nowhere in sight and Conrad and Jacob were wiping mud and grease from the mechanical potato digger.

"Lydia asked me to bring Susannah and her friend an umbrella." Peter hoped that by mentioning it was Lydia's idea, he'd spare himself a lecture from Marshall, but he was wrong.

"You're not here to run errands or socialize with the *weibsleit*—you're here to help with the harvest," Marshall retorted. "The crew took care of stabling the *geil* and bringing in the equipment. You can gather the rest of the empty barrels, wipe them dry and turn them upside down. C'mon, *buwe*, let's go inside for a hot drink and something to eat."

Peter waited until they'd left to walk back out into the rain himself. The water dripped off the rim of his hat and ran down his back, but he didn't mind. *It's not as if I'm going to melt, the way Lydia seems to worry Susannah will*, he thought.

He didn't understand Lydia and Marshall's protectiveness toward their granddaughter. They coddled her as if she was an infirm child instead of a healthy adult woman. Except for when she was hanging out or taking in the laundry, Peter had rarely caught sight of her outdoors this week. She didn't even pick the potatoes she served at lunchtime—Benuel did it for her.

Up until this afternoon, Peter had entertained the possibility that she'd been ill; maybe that was why she'd lost weight. But seeing her bolting toward him faster than lighting a few minutes ago had eliminated that question from his mind. There was clearly nothing wrong with her health.

Is it that she's spoiled? Or...lazy? Although pride was considered one of the worst—if not *the* worst—character traits an Amish person could have, laziness was a close second. Peter felt judgmental for even contemplating whether Susannah lacked a strong work ethic. After all, he suspected that's how some people viewed his mother and nothing could have been further from the truth. Besides, the summer they were courting, Peter had seen Susannah at plenty of work frolics and she'd always been very industrious.

Whatever Susannah does or doesn't do while she's at her groossdaadi*'s* haus *is really none of my business*, he reminded himself as he stacked the half barrels on top of each other so he could make fewer return trips to the barn. But what *was* his business was how Susannah treated *him*.

Even though Peter knew he was at fault for having wronged her—for having broken up with her without giving her any real reason—it still bothered him that she clearly couldn't stand to be in his company. At lunchtime, she always inched her chair as far from him as she possibly could without bumping into Benuel on her other side. The most she'd ever spoken to him while they were eating was to ask him to pass the pepper.

And just now she'd demonstrated further evidence of her revulsion toward him by refusing to accept his offer to help her toward her feet. *She'd rather sit in the mud than touch my hand*, he thought. So much had changed since the previous Christmas, when they'd both walked three miles in twenty-degree weather just so they could spend one hour alone with each other at Little Loon Pond. As frigid as the weather had been, they'd removed their gloves to hold hands because it seemed more romantic that way…

Peter shivered and glanced up at the darkening sky. *If this rain keeps up, we won't be able to pick potatoes tomorrow, either,* he thought. While he'd appreciate giving his back and shoulder muscles a break from the arduous labor, Peter wished they could finish harvesting as soon as possible.

Dear Gott, *please help me have a better attitude about keeping my end of the agreement I made with Marshall,* he silently prayed. *I know that without his financial help, Hannes might have gone to jail. So please help me to be more grateful for this opportunity and to complete it in a way that honors You. And please show me what to do or say to help Susannah feel more comfortable about my presence on the farm.*

As it was, Peter hoped that by offering to take Dorcas home, he'd be sparing Susannah the inconvenience of hitching the horse and taking her friend home herself. In turn, Marshall's supper wouldn't be delayed. But twenty minutes later, when he went up to the house to tell Dorcas he was ready to leave, Peter regretted his offer of transportation.

"She'll be out in a minute," Marshall told him, stepping onto the porch. Once he'd closed the door behind him, he added in a low voice, "As long as you keep away from Susannah, it's none of my business who you court. But this is the last time I'll remind you that while you're on my *bauerei*, you're here to work, not to socialize."

Peter narrowed his eyes. What was Marshall talking

about? Then it dawned on him: he thought Peter was interested in Dorcas and that's why he was giving her a ride home. The notion was preposterous—not because Dorcas wasn't a perfectly kind and winsome woman. But because even if he didn't think of her in a sisterly sort of way, Peter had absolutely no inclination to strike up a courtship with her or anyone else, especially not under Marshall's watchful eye. Swallowing his indignation, Peter nodded his agreement, just as Dorcas came out of the house.

Whatever she chattered about on the way home went in one of Peter's ears and out the other; all he could think about was how wrong Marshall was about him. He'd been wrong about why Peter had needed money last winter and he was wrong about why Peter offered to give Dorcas a ride home this afternoon. And even though he'd just prayed that the Lord would give him a better attitude, Peter mentally wrestled with feelings of resentment all the way home.

By the time he arrived at his own house, he had half a mind to tell Hannes that *he* was going to have to finish harvesting the potato crop. If he didn't like it, that was just plain tough. As for Marshall's reaction, Peter supposed the old farmer would be pleased not to have to worry that Peter was going to waste valuable work time pursuing Susannah's friends. But he ultimately overcame the temptation to quit, knowing that it wouldn't have been the honorable thing to do, even if it seemed justifiable at the moment.

"Hi, Eva. Where are Hannes and *Mamm*?" he asked when he entered the kitchen.

"Hannes is doing the second milking. *Mamm*'s in bed."

"Already?"

"She's in bed *still*. Hannes said she stayed there all day. She was resting when I came home. I tried to get her to *kumme* into the kitchen and visit with me while I made supper but she didn't want to get up."

Peter went down the hall and knocked on his mother's bedroom door. When she didn't answer, he knocked again and then entered. "*Mamm?* Are you okay?"

She stirred but didn't sit up. "*Jah*. Just tired."

Although it was going to be dark soon, Peter raised the shades on both of her windows. "I know you are, *Mamm*, but it's important that you get out of bed each day unless you're actually physically ill."

"Mmm. I will. In a minute." But she pulled the covers over her shoulder and rolled over.

What would Daed *do if he were here?* Peter asked himself, rubbing his forehead. He supposed his father would have convinced Dorothy to go to the doctor. But Peter had no idea what his dad would have said to persuade her, and even though Peter was an adult, he believed it was still important to obey God's command to honor his parents. And right now that meant respecting his mother's wish to be left alone, so he turned and went to wash up before supper.

While the three siblings were eating their meal— fried fish Eva had purchased from the frozen-food section at the market—she asked, "What did Susannah serve today?"

Ever since Peter had told his sister that Susannah made lunch for the crew, Eva had become preoccupied with what she'd served them. Apparently, the summer he and Susannah were courting, she'd made blueberry crumb bars that had really left an impression on Peter's sister. "She called it cabbage-crust pizza."

"The crust was made out of cabbage?" Eva wrinkled her forehead. "Was it *gut*?"

"*Jah*. It was *appenditlich*." Everything Susannah had made was delicious. To be honest, her meals were the highlight of Peter's day on the farm. Which was saying a lot, considering how nerve-racking it was to sit at the table with her on one side and Marshall on the other. But once he began eating, Peter would forget about everything except the taste of whatever meal she had prepared.

Apparently, the same was true for the other men, because even though Jacob and Conrad had complained about eating yogurt on Monday, they hadn't voiced any dissatisfaction since then and neither had Lydia. Benuel was especially complimentary about Susannah's cooking, but in general everyone would devour the food until the serving dishes were empty. They rarely had enough time to lean back in their chairs and pat their stomachs before Marshall would rush them out the door and into the fields.

"There's going to be a work frolic at the Hiltys' home on *Samschdaag* to make food and clean house for Elizabeth. I don't mind walking there and back, so do you care if I go?" Eva asked her brothers.

"*Mamm* shouldn't be left home alone," Peter objected.

"But can't Hannes look in on her like he usually does when I'm in *schul*? She'll probably stay in bed most of the day, anyway."

Hannes chimed in, "That's fine with me. The shop's only open until two and I can take frequent breaks since we don't have any new orders to fill."

"None at all?" Peter had expected business to slow down at this time of year, but he didn't expect it to stop altogether. While they'd recovered from the financial setback after Hannes totaled the car, Peter hoped to pad their emergency-savings fund. Especially since they might need to dip into it if it turned out his mother had a severe health issue that required ongoing treatment.

"*Neh*. Not right now. But don't worry. I'm using our current supplies to get a jump on our next big order. I figure it's a way to save time without spending money."

While Peter was relieved that his brother was finally learning to take initiative, he still had qualms about Eva going off to a frolic and leaving their mother alone. Dorothy spent so much of the week by herself already and the weekends were a good opportunity for Eva to put in a little more effort to coax her out of bed.

"Please, Peter?" she pleaded, clasping her hands beneath her chin, her eyes filled with hope.

"Aw, you should let her go," Hannes commented to his brother. "You remember what it's like to be young and to want to socialize with your friends."

"*Jah*, you're right," Peter agreed, even though at the moment he felt so encumbered with concerns that he could hardly recall ever being young, and socializing was the last thing on his mind...no matter what Marshall Sommer believed about him.

Chapter Five

Susannah's grandfather had said he expected the rain to last until early Friday morning, but it kept up throughout the day, which meant the men couldn't harvest. In Delaware, Susannah lived with her father, brother, sister-in-law, and five nieces and nephews, so she was used to a bustling household. However, she hadn't realized quite how small her grandfather's house was until she had spent an entire day indoors with four other people. Not only was Lydia right there at her elbow every time Susannah turned around, but Susannah also felt as if she was constantly asking Jacob or Conrad to pull their feet in so she wouldn't trip as she passed by their chairs in the kitchen or living room.

Furthermore, even though they'd gotten far less physical activity than they would have picking potatoes, the teenagers were hungrier than they'd been all week. Susannah would just finish putting away the dishes from one meal when they'd ask if there was anything they could snack on until she made the next meal. Unfortunately, a couple of times she caught herself nibbling on the treats she'd prepared for them simply because she was antsy about being in such close quarters with everyone all day.

To add to her sense of the walls closing in, Lydia had said she didn't want to go to the frolic on Saturday. That meant Susannah had to stay home with her, as Lydia couldn't be—or wouldn't allow herself to be—left alone in the house for that amount of time.

So when Susannah woke on Saturday morning to the sound of drops pattering against the windowpanes, she was delighted. *This means I can go to the frolic after all, since* Groossdaadi, *Jacob and Conrad will be home with Lydia*, she thought.

She quickly got up and got dressed, but she noticed her skirt felt a little too snug around her waist. Like many Amish women, Susannah used straight pins instead of buttons to fasten her garments, so adjusting the closure for a more comfortable fit was easily done. However, it distressed Susannah that she needed to let out the skirt.

She went into the kitchen to begin making bread before anyone else woke up. As she was kneading the dough, she reflected on the meals she'd been preparing the last week. She had done her best to balance Lydia and Marshall's food preferences with healthier ingredients, and she'd been pleased that after Monday, they'd seemed content with what she'd served them. The trick, she'd learned, was to discreetly slip in or disguise the more nutritious substitutions—no small feat, considering Lydia shadowed her constantly.

However, she recognized from how bloated she'd become that she'd been eating too much. The lack of exercise didn't help matters, either. *Oh, well, at least I'll be walking to the Hiltys'* haus *today and I can just munch on vegetables for lunch, the way I'd do if I were home*, she planned.

She had zipped through her morning chores, including fixing breakfast, washing the dishes and sweeping the floors by nine thirty. She'd also prepared a cauliflower casserole that one of the boys could slide into the oven to bake for lunch, as Lydia wouldn't be able to manage the heavy pan on her own.

"I expect to leave the Hiltys' *haus* by three o'clock at the latest," she said as she put on her coat and grabbed an umbrella from the hook on the wall.

Her grandfather chuckled. "Slow down, Susannah. I haven't even hitched the *gaul* yet."

"No need to do that, *Groossdaadi*. I'm going to walk."

"In this weather?" Lydia asked, butting in. "We don't want *you* ending up with pneumonia, like Elizabeth did. Isn't that right, Marshall?"

"*Jah.* I'll go bring the buggy around."

Susannah was so exasperated she felt like screaming and stamping her foot, but then she would have been behaving as childishly as her grandparents were treating her. So she waited until she got into the buggy a few minutes later to discuss the subject in a calm, direct manner.

"You know, *Groossdaadi*, when I'm at home in Dover, I don't think twice about walking a few miles to the market or to my friend's *haus* if the buggy isn't available. I enjoy the fresh air and exercise. You really didn't need to trouble yourself to take me to the frolic."

"It's no trouble—it's my responsibility to take *gut* care of my *familye*. Our community is smaller and more spread out than yours is in Delaware and you aren't used to these roads."

Aha, I get it—Groossdaadi *isn't giving me a ride because he's treating me like a* kind *or because he's trying to stop me from doing what I want to do*, Susannah realized. *He's giving me a ride because he sees it as his responsibility as the head of his household.* Even though his perspective seemed old-fashioned to her, she appreciated his intentions. "*Denki* for looking out for me, *Groossdaadi*. I always feel very well-cared for when I *kumme* here."

Marshall cleared his throat. "Of course, there are more important ways of being a *gut* provider than giving a *weibsmensch* a ride in a buggy on a rainy day. Earning a decent living is one of them."

Now Susannah was perplexed. What was Marshall implying? He knew Susannah's father, a corn and soybean farmer, had frequently struggled to make ends meet. But while Susannah's family may have been among the poorer families in their district, she'd always believed they were one of the happiest.

Her grandfather looked straight ahead and adjusted his hat, as if he was embarrassed. "When it comes time for you to decide whether a young *mann* might make a suitable husband, I hope you'll consider his sense of financial responsibility, as well as his other qualities. For example, I happen to know that Benuel Heiser saved a good deal of the money he made while working with the *Englisch*. He may have made errors in judgment during his *rumspringa*, but he deserves credit for planning ahead about how to provide for a *familye* once he returned to the Amish."

Susannah couldn't help herself; she laughed out loud. "I don't know what Lydia has told you, but trust me, *Groossdaadi*, I'm not assessing any *mann*, rich or poor, to determine if he'd make a *gut* husband." She glanced over at him and noticed his cheeks were crimson. His wife must have put him up to having this embarrassing conversation with his granddaughter, the poor man.

By way of changing the subject, Susannah began humming one of the hymns they'd sung at church the previous Sunday. After a few bars, they both began singing, loudly and slightly off-key, just like when they'd travel by buggy together when she was a young girl. And by the time she arrived at the Hiltys' house, Susannah had forgotten about her tight skirt or how frustrated she'd felt about Lydia thwarting her plans to walk to the frolic.

"Hi, Susannah," Dorcas said, greeting her at the door. "*Kumme* into the kitchen. We're having a snack before we get started."

Susannah had met most of the other women and teenage girls at church. And as the rest of them introduced themselves, she was glad Lydia had decided to stay home after all. This was a younger group of mostly unmarried women and she probably would have gotten restless and wanted to leave earlier than three o'clock.

"Do you want a cinnamon roll?" a woman named Faith asked, extending a pan. "I just finished icing them."

"She doesn't eat sweets," Honor answered before Susannah could speak up for herself.

It was true that last Sunday Susannah *had* told Honor that she didn't usually eat sweets anymore, which was stretching the truth a little, since she did have dessert on occasion. The reason she'd told her that was because Honor had offered her a slice of pound cake that she'd brought to church…and Honor was a notoriously inept baker and cook. If Susannah was going to indulge, she wanted to thoroughly enjoy the treat. The cinnamon rolls that Faith had made smelled as tantalizing as they looked, so despite her expanding waistline, Susannah actually *did* want one.

"Oh, sorry." Faith turned and set the pan on the counter. "Is that how you got so skinny?"

"Susannah doesn't like it if you talk about her appearance," Dorcas interjected. She nonchalantly licked the top of her cinnamon roll as if it was an ice-cream cone. "She doesn't want people to think she's vain."

Susannah's mouth dropped open in surprise at her friend's remark. It almost seemed as if Dorcas was implying that Susannah *was* vain, but she didn't want people to *think* she was. *She still doesn't believe I'm uneasy receiving all of this uninvited attention.* Susannah thoughts were interrupted by a loud cracking noise in the hallway.

It was followed by the sound of a woman wailing. "Oh, *neh*! Look what I did!"

All of the women rushed into the hallway to find Hannah Miller scrutinizing a broken step on the staircase. Apparently, she'd brought her heel down on the edge of the board and had fractured the wood.

"David's a roof installer," Dorcas said, comforting her. "He'll be able to patch this up in no time."

"*Jah*, but he's been through such a hardship with his wife being hospitalized. The last thing he needs is to *kumme* home and have to mend something I broke. We're supposed to be making things easier for him, not more difficult."

"Listen." Susannah put a finger to her lips. "I just heard a buggy. I'll run out and see if one of the *menner* is dropping his *schweschder* or *dochder* off. Maybe it's someone who can fix the step."

She shot out the door and tore right past whatever young woman had been dropped off without registering who it was. Waving her arms as she pursued the buggy down the road, she hollered, *"Absatz!"* But the person at the reins didn't hear her and the horse increased its speed. Susannah increased hers, too, as well as her volume. *"Absatz!"* she shouted, chasing the buggy. She quickly realized whoever was in it couldn't hear her over the noise of the wheels and hooves on the pavement.

It wasn't until the buggy came to a halt at the intersection with the main thoroughfare that Susannah could make herself heard. Using the last of her lung power, she yelled, "Help!"

A man immediately hopped down from the carriage and raced toward her so swiftly that his hat flew off. It was Peter, of all people. "What's wrong? Is someone hurt? Are you all right?" he asked when he reached her, where she'd lost momentum some twenty yards behind his buggy.

She'd been galloping at such a fast clip and for such a long stretch she could hardly breathe. She bent over, pressing her palms against her thighs, and gasped in as much air as she could while holding one finger in the air to indicate she needed a minute.

"Take your time. It's okay. Take your time," Peter repeated, patiently waiting for her to catch her breath before she explained.

When Susannah peered over at him, she saw the look of concern in his steel-blue eyes matched the tenderness of his tone. She remembered that expression; most memorably, she'd seen it on his face last summer, when he'd confided he was worried his brother was becoming influenced by his *Englisch* friends during his *rumspringa*. The depth of Peter's concern about the well-being of others—especially his family members—was one of the things she'd found particularly attractive about him.

However, that kind of worry was unwarranted in this instance. Susannah felt sheepish as she told him, "Someone accidentally broke a board on the staircase. No one's hurt but we were hoping you could fix it before David comes home."

It seemed to take a moment for the meaning of her words to sink in, and when it did, Peter shook his head and asked, "You ran all this way to ask me *that*?"

It was kind of a melodramatic impulse, now that she thought about it. Susannah could have just asked her grandfather to repair the broken stair when he returned to pick her up at three o'clock. But she wasn't thinking as she was sprinting after the buggy. It was as if her legs were rebelling after a week of idleness—as if she was somehow breaking free from Lydia's restrictive behavior—but when she'd been running, all that had mattered was catching up to the horse. "I—I'm sorry if I alarmed you," she feebly apologized.

"It's fine. I'll look at the step to see what I can do. It'll take a couple minutes to reverse my direction." He turned and walked back down the narrow road. When he neared his hat, he lifted it from the ground, clapped it against his palm and got into the carriage. Even though Susannah knew it was utterly irrational, since she hadn't exactly been courteous to him, she felt the tiniest bit slighted that he didn't offer to give her a ride back to the house.

"Did you catch my *bruder* in time?" Eva asked when Susannah opened the door and stepped onto the small braided rug. Honor was standing behind her in the hallway and the other women's voices could be heard coming from the kitchen.

"*Jah*, he's turning the buggy around."

"I'll get a towel. You're dripping and dirty and we've already scrubbed the gathering-room floor," Honor said. "Don't go anywhere."

Eva left, too, so Susannah removed her boots, and as she was waiting for Honor to return, Peter came in, toolbox in hand. Susannah moved to one side of the rug so he could take off his boots. He'd barely untied his laces when Dorcas came out of the kitchen, smiling. "*Denki* for coming back, Peter. *Kumme*, I'll show you the damage."

Peter followed her down the hall, out of sight, but Susannah could still hear their voices. "This won't be any problem," Peter said. "I have some boards this size left over from when I redid our staircase. I'll go get one and *kumme* back a few minutes before I pick Eva up at two o'clock so I don't have to make an extra trip."

"You should *kumme* at noon instead. That's when we're taking a break for lunch and we've got lots of *gut* food here," Dorcas offered, to Susannah's dismay. Having made a fool of herself chasing Peter down for help as if the house had been on fire, she wanted a little more time to pass before she had to sit down at a table with him again. But he accepted her invitation and then Dorcas asked, "Would you like a cinnamon roll to take with you for now?"

Peter said something in a hushed tone that Susannah couldn't hear. However, Dorcas's melodic laughter rang out loud and clear. "Don't worry," she said. "It will be our little secret."

What will be their little secret? Susannah wondered as she heard footsteps coming down the staircase. Honor asked Peter if he'd take a look at the loose doorknob on the linen closet, too. A few seconds later, she came down the hall and handed Susannah a towel.

"You look like something the cat dragged in," she teased.

Susannah blotted her face, and the sleeves and hem of her dress, with the towel, then went into the bathroom. A glimpse in the mirror revealed her curly hair was fluffing up higher than ever, her prayer *kapp* was crooked and she had dirt smeared across both of her cheeks, which were blotchy from the exertion of running. *I look like something the cat* wouldn't *drag in,* she thought.

Despite claiming her appearance wasn't as important to her as it seemed to be to others, Susannah was disgusted with her reflection. She looked terrible and she *felt* terrible. Although she couldn't really put a finger on why, she suspected her low mood had something to do with the fact that her closest friend in New Hope had been laughing and sharing secrets with her former suitor. *Dorcas knows how deeply he hurt me,* Susannah thought. *Doesn't she have any sense of loyalty?* It wasn't that she expected Dorcas to ignore Peter, but Dorcas was being friendlier to him than she was being toward Susannah.

Then she wondered whether it was possible Peter and Dorcas liked each other. That didn't make any sense, though, because Dorcas was even heavier than Susannah had been at her heaviest. *Peter wouldn't have any romantic interest in a* weibsmensch *who weighs as much as Dorcas does and Dorcas wouldn't have any romantic interest in a* mann *who would reject a* weibsmensch *because of her weight*, she reassured herself. Not that she cared about who Peter courted, but Susannah didn't want Dorcas winding up feeling as crushed as she had felt.

When she emerged from the bathroom, she went into the kitchen. No one was in there; she could hear muffled voices coming from the rooms overhead. Noticing there was still half a pan of cinnamon rolls, she quickly pulled one of them from the loaf and took a huge bite. Icing dribbled down her chin. She dabbed it off and then licked her fingertip before taking another big bite of the roll. Three more bites and it was gone, but she'd eaten it so quickly she hardly tasted it, so she took another to enjoy at her leisure.

She'd only nibbled a third of the way through the cinnamon swirls to the sticky sweet center when she heard footsteps approaching. Panicked that she'd be caught eating the kind of food everyone thought she avoided, she shoved the rest of the bun into her mouth. Her cheeks felt as round as a chipmunk's, but her mouth was too full for her to move her jaw enough to chew the thick, soft dough.

As someone entered the kitchen, she twirled around toward the sink and picked up a clean glass, pretending she was washing it so she wouldn't have to face whoever had just come in.

Peter walked over and set his mug on the counter next to the sink. "Sorry," he said. "I know how frustrated my *schweschder* gets when she's almost done with dishes and someone brings her one more."

"Mmm." That was as close as she could come to pronouncing an actual word. Out of the corner of her eye, she saw him shift from foot to foot, but he didn't leave.

"I, um, I'm also sorry I caused you to fall the other day. I would have felt *baremlich* if you'd gotten hurt. I—I hope you'll forgive me since, you know, we'll be around each other on the *bauerei* for a few more weeks. I know things have been kind of awkward between us, but if there's anything that I can do to make you feel more comfortable about my presence there, I'll do it. Because I'd like it if we could be…more neighborly to one another."

Susannah couldn't answer him because her mouth was still too full, but how would she have responded, anyway? It would have been immature and unkind to tell him, *The only thing that would make me feel more comfortable about* your *presence on the* bauerei *would be my* absence *from it.*

There were too many people nearby, so she couldn't very well have added, *And you* did *hurt me, but not because you caused me to fall in the mud.* Besides, he knew how she'd felt when he'd broken up with her and he had already apologized that his decision had hurt her feelings.

Deep down, Susannah knew it was time to forgive him, to *really* forgive him. To ask the Lord to take the lingering hurt and anger she felt toward Peter and to help her to treat him in a way that reflected God's love instead of her unforgiving spirit. She still didn't think it was right for him to break up with her the way he had. But it was just as wrong for her to continue bearing a grudge against him…and for essentially expecting Dorcas to bear one, too. Especially since Peter had indicated he was willing to do whatever it took to make Susannah feel more comfortable around him for the duration of the harvest season.

She tried to say, *I'd like that, too.* Except her mouth was so full it came out more like "Erd wrikat ru."

In her peripheral vision, she could see Peter cocking his head and scrutinizing her. She managed to swallow a bit of the roll and then she covered her mouth with her hand and said, "I'd like that, too. I mean, I think we can be more neighborly to each other from now on."

"Gut." Peter nodded vigorously. He waited a moment, as if he expected her to say something else, but when she didn't, he told her he'd see her later and then he left the room.

As soon as she heard the front door close, Susannah went over to the trash bin and spat out the rest of the roll. She'd completely lost her desire for it, now that the Lord had replaced her bitter resentment with the sweet taste of forgiveness.

Denki, Gott, Peter silently prayed. He was so grateful that Susannah hadn't rebuffed him that he could have jumped up and clicked his heels together as he made his way back to the buggy. He'd asked the Lord to show him what to say or do to help her feel more comfortable around him. But until he saw Susannah standing alone by the sink, it hadn't occurred to Peter to ask *her* that same question.

It was such a relief to have directly addressed the awkwardness between them. Granted, he didn't expect they'd suddenly engage in long, meaningful conversations or anything like that, but at least now Susannah might not recoil at the sight of him. And he wouldn't feel quite so tense around her, either, always afraid he'd say or do something to upset her even more.

He journeyed toward the other side of town and when he reached his family's property, he headed toward the house instead of the workshop. He had left a note telling his mother where everyone had gone, but he wanted to stop in to try to urge her to get up and have something to eat. But, to his astonishment, she was sitting in the living room, reading her Bible and drinking tea.

When he explained why he had to return to the Hiltys' home, she said, "Oh, *gut*. This gives me the opportunity to write a note for you to take for Elizabeth. I might not have the energy to help at the frolic, but I can still let her know I'm praying for her recovery."

Recognizing his window of opportunity—and feeling encouraged by how well Susannah had responded when he'd broached a difficult subject—Peter replied, "You know, *Mamm*, a different *dokder* might be able to help you regain your energy again so that you *can* go to frolics. And, more importantly, so you can start to feel better."

"Shush, *suh*. You're ruining my concentration," she said, waving her free hand at him as she inscribed a note card with the other. But Peter was heartened that she hadn't definitively refused to see a different doctor.

Maybe with a few well-timed suggestions, she'll agree to make an appointment, he thought an hour later as he made the return trip to the Hiltys' home with the board and tools he needed. Even before entering the house, he heard peals of laughter and he smiled to himself, imagining the fun Eva must have been having with her friends. But when he went inside, he was surprised to find Benuel was the one making the young women giggle.

"Hi," Peter greeted him. "I didn't expect to see you at this frolic."

"I came to pick up Emily."

Emily Heiser, a year older than Eva, was Benuel's cousin. "*Jah*, I recently started a job babysitting for an *Englisch familye*," she said. "I don't have to be there until two o'clock, but I think Benuel showed up early because I told him about all of the *gut* food we were making."

"What can I say? It's true," Benuel admitted with a shrug.

"We're freezing or storing most of what we made for Elizabeth and David, but we've set aside plenty for all of us, too. It'll be ready in a few minutes, if you *menner* want to fix the stair in the meantime," Hannah suggested.

So Benuel followed Peter to the staircase, even though it was really a one-man job. "Can you smell that? It's potato stuffing and beef and noodles." He inhaled deeply. "I saw whoopie pies in there, too. One of the things I really missed when I lived with the *Englisch* was our food. Amish *meed* cook a lot better than the *Englischers* do. Well, except maybe for Susannah."

"What?" Peter asked as he pried the nails from the cracked board. Benuel had complimented Susannah after lunch every day. Had he just been flattering her? "I thought you liked Susannah's cooking."

"I don't *dislike* it. I just prefer my meals prepared the traditional Amish way." Benuel lowered his voice and added, "But I understand why she tries to cut back on calories or makes low-fat versions of what other *weibsleit* make. The *Englisch meed* I knew did the same thing to keep their weight down. Amish or *Englisch*, I suppose all *weibsleit* want to look their best—especially when they're single and they think it will help them attract a *mann*."

Benuel's reply surprised Peter for two reasons. Firstly, he hadn't realized Susannah had been cutting back on calories. The lunches she made were so tasty, especially in comparison to the processed food his sister usually bought, that Peter honestly hadn't noticed any difference between her cooking and the traditional Amish meals his mother used to make.

Secondly, although he'd noticed Susannah's weight loss, he hadn't suspected it was because she'd deliberately been on some kind of diet. Although in hindsight, he supposed that was more probable than her having lost weight due to an illness. Peter respected it if she was trying to take better care of her health, but Benuel had implied her real reason for losing weight was to catch the eye of a suitor. As becoming as she was, Susannah had never demonstrated that kind of vanity when Peter was courting her and he couldn't imagine that she'd consider her physical appearance worthy of so much focus. Yes, she'd always looked tidy and well-groomed, as was customary, but she wasn't the kind of woman who primped and preened in front of a mirror. She was more likely to be concerned about her inner character than her outer image.

Furthermore, her supposed desire to lose weight didn't seem like the kind of subject she would have discussed with a male acquaintance. Although it was possible she'd mentioned it to one of the women in the district and it had gotten back to Benuel, his perspective seemed to reflect *his* emphasis on outward appearances, not Susannah's. *It will take time for him to shake off the influence of the* Englisch *culture*, Peter thought.

Rather than respond to Benuel's remark, he asked for his help aligning the new board in the casing. Benuel quickly took over the entire installation and Peter was admittedly impressed by his adroitness and attention to detail. *At least the* Englisch *had a positive influence on him in regard to his craftsmanship*, he thought. Peter's mind immediately jumped to Hannes back at the workshop and he silently prayed that they'd receive at least a few orders this week.

Fifteen minutes later, when everyone was squeezed around the table or standing at the counter to eat lunch, Hannah asked if Peter and Benuel had been able to repair the board on the staircase.

"*Jah*. Except we didn't repair it—we replaced it entirely," Benuel answered. "It was splintered pretty badly. I've seen horses do less damage kicking a fence down than what you did to that board, Dorcas."

"Me?" Dorcas asked. "*I* didn't break it."

"*Neh?*" He scanned the room. "Oh, it was Eva?"

Eva paused with her fork in midair and she shook her head. "I wasn't even here when it happened."

It was clear to Peter that Benuel had assumed either Dorcas or Eva had broken the step because they were overweight, but he silently prayed the assumption would be lost on both of them.

"*I* was the one who broke it," Hannah admitted.

"You? But you're so thin," Benuel said and any hope Peter had that Dorcas and his sister wouldn't be embarrassed flew right out the window. Dorcas's cheeks turned bright red and Eva dipped her head and wiped her mouth with a napkin, as if she was trying to hide. Peter knew she was near tears.

He was just about to say that the stairs were so old and worn that a person much lighter than Hannah could have broken the step, too, when she diplomatically replied, "Thin or not, I can be a real klutz. I was running down the stairs really fast and I hit the last step a lot harder than I intended."

"*Jah*, it's amazing how powerful a slender person can be," Susannah chimed in. "When I first saw you, Benuel, I thought, 'He's so lanky, how is he ever going to lift those potato barrels into the buggy wagon?' Yet you slung them around like they were made of cardboard. I guess that's one of many reasons it's better not to make judgments or comments about someone else's size."

Because her tone was so pleasant, Benuel probably didn't know whether to feel insulted or complimented by Susannah's remark and he didn't reply. Peter wasn't quite sure how she'd intended it, either, until he saw her wink at Eva, who had dropped her napkin back onto her lap and smiled at Susannah.

As much as he appreciated how graciously Susannah had interceded, Peter was filled with nostalgia. Up until just now, he'd either been too nervous about offending her or too busy eating the meals she'd made at the farm to really reminisce about the reasons he'd liked her so much. The way she'd responded to Benuel demonstrated both her strength and her gentleness: she had effectively set him straight, without tearing him down. And it made Peter remember that he used to daydream about what a good mother she'd make one day.

She'll still make a gut mamm, *but not for* my kinner. The thought filled him with such remorse he could hardly finish his lunch and he didn't take any of the three types of desserts offered to him, either.

After everyone was done eating, he excused himself to go upstairs and tighten the doorknob on the linen closet. Because the women had finished preparing the meals for Elizabeth and cleaning her house faster than they expected, they were ready to depart as soon as they'd washed and dried the lunch dishes. As Peter was lacing his boots, Eva and Dorcas shuffled down the hall.

"I told Dorcas we can drop her off on the way home, Peter."

"Sure." He moved over to make room for Susannah, who had come to put her boots on, too.

"Is anyone giving you a ride?" Eva asked her.

"My *groossdaadi* was supposed to pick me up at three o'clock, but I don't want to hang around here until then. If I walk quickly, I can make it home before he leaves the *haus*."

"But it's pouring outside," Eva pointed out. "You should ride with us."

Peter winced, imagining how Marshall would react to him bringing Susannah home. He didn't want to tell her outright that she couldn't ride with them, but neither did he want to encourage her. He held his breath, hoping she'd decline his sister's offer.

"Oh, but Susannah enjoys exercising in the rain," Dorcas said. "She's been cooped up indoors all week, isn't that right, Susannah?"

Susannah looked so dejected that Peter decided he'd rather risk Marshall's ire than allow her to think that she was unwelcome, or that he hadn't meant what he'd said about being neighborly toward her.

But just then, Benuel came around the corner from the opposite direction. He must have heard their entire conversation because he said, "Unlike Peter, I'm going in your direction, Susannah. We'll have to drop Emily off at the *Englishers*' first, but we should make it to your *haus* in plenty of time to prevent your *groossdaadi* from heading out to get you."

Susannah glanced at the mechanical clock on the shelf and nodded. "I think that might be a better idea than walking. *Denki*, Benuel."

"No prob," he replied, just like an *Englischer*. And for some reason, the thought of Benuel giving Susannah a ride home alone disturbed Peter more than anything Marshall could have said to him.

Chapter Six

Since it was an off Sunday, Susannah worshipped with her grandparents, Jacob and Conrad at home in the morning. Afterward, they ate a light lunch, comprised solely of leftovers, since Susannah didn't cook on the Sabbath unless it was absolutely necessary. Then, since the sky was bright and sunny and it was the last opportunity to go fishing before the season ended for the year, the boys took off for Little Loon Pond.

Susannah wasn't sorry to see them go, but she was sorry they were taking the buggy because it meant she couldn't travel to the phone shanty. She had hoped to place a call to the phone shanty nearest her home in Dover, where she could leave a voice-mail message asking Charity to send the recipes for vegetable lasagna and a few other meals she intended to make. Iddo and Almeda Stoll—New Hope's deacon and his wife—were arriving later in the afternoon to visit Susannah's grandparents, so it would have been the perfect opportunity for her to slip away by herself. But since the boys took the buggy, out of respect for her grandparents' wishes,

Susannah wouldn't insist on walking to the shanty by herself.

So after a light lunch, she put on a pot of water for tea and sat in the living room with Lydia while it heated. Marshall was napping in the large chair at the opposite end of the room, next to the woodstove. At least, Susannah assumed he was napping; it was possible he was just closing his eyes because he didn't feel like being included in the women's discussion. Susannah didn't blame him; she didn't feel much like talking, either. She had a slight headache—she blamed it on eating either too much salt or too much sugar the previous day—and after the water came to a boil and she served tea, she hoped to go outside for a walk around the farm.

"Is Dorcas going to stop by today?" Lydia asked her.

"That would be nice, but I kind of doubt she will." Susannah had noticed Dorcas had been subtly cool toward her for the duration of the work frolic. And there was no question that she hadn't wanted Susannah to ride home with her and Peter and Eva. But Susannah realized she was probably the one at fault for that; it couldn't have been pleasant for Dorcas to be in the middle of the tension between Susannah and Peter. Now that they'd come to a truce of sorts, maybe Dorcas wouldn't have to try so hard to make up for Susannah's sour attitude toward him. "I'll have to apologize."

"Ach? Did you *meed* have a falling out?"

Susannah had been so deep in thought that she hadn't realized she'd voiced herself aloud. "*Neh*, not exactly. We just haven't been quite as close as we were last summer or at *Grischtdaag*," Susannah admitted. "It's probably because so much time has passed since the last time we saw each other. Writing letters is different than interacting in person."

"*Jah.* And I imagine she has to adjust to seeing you so thin. She might be a bit envious."

"*Neh*, I don't think so. She has never expressed being dissatisfied with her weight." On the contrary, she had sometimes commented that she was grateful she had a few extra pounds on her frame because she believed her stature helped her lift and carry the heavy trays of food at the Millers' restaurant more easily than some of the thinner waitstaff.

"Well, her *mamm* has told me she's been cutting back on what she eats, but she hasn't had much success losing weight."

Now that Lydia mentioned it, perhaps Dorcas was unhappy about her size. Susannah realized that might have explained some of her remarks. *If she wants to lose weight, I'd be* hallich *to share my recipes*, Susannah thought. *And I'll encourage her however else I can.*

Switching the subject, Lydia commented, "It was nice of Benuel to bring you home yesterday."

"I wouldn't have accepted a ride from him, but I didn't want *Groossdaadi* to have to *kumme* get me since Benuel was already there," Susannah emphatically explained, just as she'd done yesterday afternoon when she'd returned from the Hiltys' house.

"You know, your *groossdaadi* thinks he's got a *gut* head on his shoulders." Lydia lowered her voice. "I was surprised last night when he told me Benuel is a lot more financially responsible than Peter is."

Since when did other people's finances become such an important issue to Groossdaadi? *And what makes him think Peter isn't financially responsible?* Susannah wondered. While she agreed that it was important for men and women to be good stewards of the resources God gave them, she didn't believe it was her place—or her grandparents' place—to comment about how someone else handled their money.

"Whether that's true or not, it seems like a private matter between Peter, his *familye* and *Gott*."

Her response must have sounded sanctimonious, because Lydia quickly defended her husband, and said, "Marshall wasn't gossiping—he was telling me by way of saying how *hallich* he is that you're interested in Benuel, not Peter. I think he was even more delighted than I was when Benuel brought you home yesterday."

"I am *not* interested in Benuel!" Susannah exclaimed loudly. The fact that her grandfather didn't even flinch proved to her he was, indeed, only pretending to be asleep.

Lydia chuckled. "It's okay, dear. Your *groossdaadi* and I won't let on that we know, especially not in front of the *buwe*. We don't want them to tease you or make it uncomfortable for you to be around Benuel at lunchtime."

"Excuse me. I hear the kettle whistling." Susannah was so galled by Lydia's refusal to accept what she was telling her that she had to flee the room to keep herself from responding in an inappropriate manner. After turning off the stove element, Susannah went into the bathroom and splashed water on her face and then she opened the window. Leaning her elbows on the windowsill, she closed her eyes and allowed the crisp breeze to dry her cheeks and chin as she tried to think of a respectful way to tell Lydia and her grandfather that she wished they wouldn't meddle in her life so much. While she was resting there, she heard the familiar sound of a horse pulling a buggy up the lane. *It's Iddo and Almeda! Now I can finally go out for a walk alone.*

She straightened her prayer *kapp* and then returned to the living room. "I heard a buggy," she announced and this time her grandfather opened his eyes. "I'll fix a tray and say hello to Iddo and Almeda, then I'm going to take a stroll around the farm."

Susannah rushed into the kitchen before Lydia could insist that she ought to join her and Almeda for a visit instead of going outdoors. She pulled a plate from the cupboard and arranged several whoopie pies on it, as well as an assortment of cookies.

There were so many leftover desserts from yesterday's frolic that Faith had insisted she take home a bunch of goodies. "Since you don't eat desserts anymore, I suppose you don't bake them very often, either. But your household shouldn't have to suffer just because you're on a diet," she'd joked.

Conrad and Jacob had already polished off almost half of the sweets she'd brought home and Susannah hoped her grandparents, Almeda and Iddo would eat the rest this afternoon. Otherwise, Susannah might be tempted to overindulge. As she put teacups on the tray, Lydia shuffled through the kitchen with Marshall close behind.

"It's such a pleasant day that we're going to visit out on the porch," she told Susannah.

That's what I've been trying to get you to do all week, Susannah thought ruefully. She didn't understand her stepgrandmother's behavior lately. "I'll be right out with these treats."

When they got to the door, Lydia halted, almost as if

there was an invisible barrier keeping her from going any farther. Marshall reached to hold the door open for her with one hand, and with the other, he assisted her down the little ledge and onto the porch. Susannah had to admit to herself that her grandfather's watchfulness over his wife was rather sweet, even if she personally found it stifling for herself.

A minute later, she used her elbow to push open the door as she carried a tray outside. To her chagrin, it was Benuel, not Iddo and Almeda, who was conversing with her grandparents. "What are you doing here?" she asked without even saying hello. She set down the tray on the end of the bench next to the porch swing where her grandparents were seated.

Benuel held up a nine-by-thirteen-inch baking pan. "You left this in my buggy yesterday and I thought I'd better return it to you in case you needed it for breakfast."

Susannah had never heard such an implausible excuse in her life. She noticed even Lydia had turned her head sideways—was she trying not to laugh? "It's not mine. It must have been a pan Emily brought from your *ant*'s kitchen."

"Oh. Right. I should have asked her first."

"It was thoughtful of you to *kumme* all this way, Benuel," Lydia said, smiling. "Why don't you join us for a snack? We're waiting for Almeda and Iddo to arrive."

"Denki." Benuel stepped forward to take a seat on the bench, but when Susannah didn't move, he motioned to it and said, "After you, Susannah."

"Neh, I don't want to sit. I want to take a walk."

"That sounds *wunderbaar*," Benuel replied, nodding

as if she'd invited him to come, too. "Where do you want to go?"

Even without looking at Lydia, Susannah could feel the older woman's eyes on her and she knew she'd never hear the end of it if she told Benuel flat out that she didn't want him to come with her. She was about to say she'd changed her mind—that she'd prefer to stay there with her grandparents, the deacon and his wife. But then she realized Iddo and Almeda might get the wrong idea. Most, but not all, young Amish couples tried to keep their courtships a private matter, but a few made no concerted effort to hide their involvement with each other. And it wouldn't have been a stretch for the deacon and his wife to assume Benuel was at the house for the same reason Lydia had assumed he'd given Susannah a ride home.

Cornered, she was about to give in and allow him to saunter around the farm with her when she realized she could use this situation to her advantage. "I was just going to take a walk around the farm. But now that you're here, I wonder if you'd give me a ride to the phone shanty? Conrad and Jacob have taken the buggy and I need to call my sister-in-law."

Susannah would have been hard-pressed to determine who appeared most pleased by her suggestion: Marshall, Lydia or Benuel.

"Of course I will," Benuel said and practically danced down the porch steps.

"Don't hurry right back for my sake," Lydia called as Susannah reluctantly plodded after him. "If it gets late, Almeda can help me put supper on the table."

"We're only going to the phone shanty so I can leave a message for Charity. This isn't a leisurely outing,"

Susannah stated pointedly, so there'd be no question in anyone's mind about why she'd suggested Benuel give her a ride. But when she turned to wave goodbye, Lydia winked at her and held a finger to her lips, signifying she wouldn't disclose Susannah's "secret."

Unfortunately, Benuel didn't seem to take her at her word, either. "Since you wanted to go for a stroll, we could take a walk around Little Loon Pond after we go to the shanty," Benuel suggested as they headed toward the main road.

"Neh." As much as she loved the trail around the pond, Susannah didn't want to run in to Jacob and Conrad when she was out with Benuel, or else they might think he was courting her, too. Not to mention, Benuel might have interpreted her acceptance of the invitation as an encouraging sign. "As I told Lydia, my only purpose in going out is to make my phone call and then return home."

"Okay. But it sure is a beautiful day."

Susannah couldn't argue with him about that; the day was unseasonably warm. Peak fall foliage viewing for the elms, oaks and maples wouldn't happen for a few weeks, but the trees' colors were beginning to change and they provided a striking contrast with the abundant eastern white pines.

Since Susannah figured not even Benuel could misconstrue her comments about the weather or landscape as flirtation, she described the similarities and differences between this part of Maine with Dover. In turn, he told her about where he lived, too.

"There are some rigorous hiking trails leading up to the ridge, but the view of the lake from up there is well worth the effort. It's incredible," he raved. "There's a trail here in New Hope that's comparable—it goes through the gorge and up to Pleasant Peak."

"*Jah.* I know. I've hiked it several times." Technically, Susannah hadn't really *hiked* the trail. It was more like she and Peter used to amble through the woods in the same area, looking for a private, shady spot to picnic during the summer they'd courted.

One time they'd become so distracted talking to each other that they'd lost their way back to the parking lot. As they were trying to get their bearings, Peter had taken her hand in his for the first time. He'd apologized that the pads of his hands were calloused and his skin was rough from his work as a carpenter, but Susannah wouldn't have noticed; she was too giddy from the sensation of having her fingers intertwined with a man's for the first time in her life. *And for the last time*, she thought, quickly dismissing the memory.

"This is close enough," she said a minute later, hopping out of the buggy before it even rolled to a stop near the shanty. She didn't know why, but she didn't want Benuel to overhear the message she left for Charity. "I'll only be a minute," she promised.

But when she got through to the voice-mail recording for the phone in the shanty closest to her home in Dover, Susannah left a long, rambling message for her family. She hadn't realized how homesick she was until then and even though she knew they couldn't hear her, she felt as if she was talking directly to them. She mentioned she was praying about her father's medical checkup and that she hoped her niece was done cutting her tooth by now and was sleeping better. When she hung up, she realized she'd forgotten to ask Charity for the recipes, so she had to redial. She was so preoccupied with leaving her second message that until she hung up she didn't realize someone else had come from the opposite direction and was standing nearby to use the phone.

It was Hannah Miller and Dorcas. They must have walked from Dorcas's house; Susannah hoped nothing had happened to her horse or buggy. "Hello," she said, greeting them warmly. "What are you two doing here?"

"The same thing you're doing, *lappich*. Using the phone," Dorcas retorted.

Trying not to take offense at her sarcasm, Susannah clarified, "I just meant that I hope nothing's wrong... I mean, because you walked all this way to use the phone instead of coming by buggy. Your horse is all right, isn't she?"

"Of course." Dorcas sounded indignant. "I may not like to walk in the rain, but that doesn't mean I'm lazy, you know."

"I wasn't implying you're lazy," Susannah said softly. Given how sensitive Dorcas was about a thoughtful, straightforward inquiry, she was becoming more convinced that Lydia was right about her being envious of Susannah's weight loss after all. Still, it hurt to be the object of her friend's jealousy. And Susannah felt a little disappointed that Dorcas hadn't invited her to be part of her Sabbath recreation. *Hannah gets to see her all the time at the restaurant, but I'm only here for a few weeks and we had planned to spend as much time together on the weekends as we could.* "I'm just surprised to see you, that's all."

"Ooh—I think I know *why* we caught you off guard!" Hannah excitedly gave Susannah's arm a squeeze. She whispered, "Is that Benuel I see waiting for you in the buggy over there?"

Susannah glanced over her shoulder. "*Jah*. He just stopped by the *haus* to return a pan he thought was mine. I wanted to *kumme* to the shanty to call my *familye*, but Jacob and Conrad had taken my *groossdaadi*'s buggy, so Benuel gave me a ride." Even to her own ears, Susannah's explanation sounded as far-fetched as Benuel's excuse had originally sounded.

"Don't worry," Hannah said out of the corner of her mouth as she waved animatedly at Benuel. "You can trust us. We won't tell anyone, will we, Dorcas?"

"There's nothing to tell," Susannah insisted.

"Hi, Hannah. Hi, Dawn," Benuel called.

Susannah inwardly cringed because he'd gotten Dorcas's name wrong *again*, although at least he was getting closer. She thought her friend would deliver a snide comeback, but Dorcas plastered a smile on her lips and lifted her hand in a cheerful wave.

"*Neh*, we won't tell anyone about you and Benuel," she belatedly agreed with Hannah before following her into the phone shanty. "Have *schpass*, wherever you're going."

But Susannah *didn't* have fun; she had a headache. And the only place she was going was back to her grandparents' house, where she read alone in her room with a cup of tea, the last two cookies and half a whoopie pie left on the plate she'd set out for the guests.

On Sunday evening, Eva served reheated leftover cabbage-patch stew that Faith had sent home with her from the frolic.

"This is *appenditlich*," Hannes said. "Who made it?"

"Susannah Peachy. Do you like it, too, *Mamm*?"

"It's *wunderbaar*. I'll have another serving, please." Dorothy extended her bowl so her daughter could re-fill it.

For the second evening in a row, their mother had joined them for supper instead of retreating to her room early. Peter didn't know how long this spurt of energy would last, but he was grateful that the Lord had provided Dorothy a little more stamina than she usually had. Hannes and Eva seemed uplifted by their mother's health improvement, too. Eva was especially bubbly, repeating anecdotes and gossip from the frolic that she'd already told them about yesterday.

"Did you know that Hannah Miller and Isaiah Wittmer are getting married in December?" she asked her mother in a secretive tone.

Most, although not all, Amish couples in their district tried to keep their courtships private from their friends and family members. If they decided to marry, the announcement of their upcoming weddings were "published" or announced in church sometime in October. And then the weddings took place on Tuesdays or Thursdays in November and December. However, Hannah and Isaiah had been courting for a long time and there were few people in the district who weren't aware that this was the year they were finally getting married. But now that Eva was a teenager, she seemed more interested in discussing courtships and weddings than she had previously.

"I think you mentioned it yesterday," Dorothy replied. "Didn't you tell us that her *mamm* wanted to host the *hochzich* meal at their restaurant instead of at the *kurrich* or in their home?"

The majority of couples in other states got married in the brides' homes, since that's where the Amish met for worship. But because the New Hope district had constructed a church building for worship, some couples chose to hold their weddings there. However, no couple had ever considered getting married in a restaurant before, not even in an Amish one that was family-owned.

"*Jah.* Even though the *Ordnung* doesn't forbid it, Isaiah's *mamm* didn't want them to have their *hochzich* meals at the restaurant because it seemed too much like an *Englisch hochzich* reception."

"I can understand that," Dorothy remarked. "Although it's not as if Hannah and Isaiah intend to give the furniture away afterward."

Everyone chuckled at her comment, which was a reference to the *Englisch* picnic-table order Hannes had received on Saturday for a wealthy *Englisch* couple's wedding reception. The bride and groom had impulsively decided to get married outdoors at the end of October and they wanted brand-new picnic tables handcrafted just for the reception. The wood was to be inscribed with their names and the wedding date; afterward, they intended to give the tables to their guests as gifts, or donate them to local parks. In order to fill the order by the deadline, Peter would have to help his brother in the workshop in the evenings, but he was grateful for the way the Lord had provided for this need, too.

"I wish one of *you* would get married soon," Eva commented to her brothers. "Then we could have a wedding *and* I'd finally have a *schweschder.*"

"Peter will probably get married before I do since he's older," Hannes told her. "Although he's got to be a suitor before he can become a husband."

Don't hold your breath, Peter thought dolefully.

"Maybe he's already courted someone. And maybe *I* know who it is," Eva taunted.

Dorothy curiously tipped her head, eyeing Peter, and Hannes stopped slurping his broth and asked, "You're someone's suitor? If we guess who it is, will you tell us if we're right?"

"*Neh*, because I'm not courting anyone." Peter felt his cheeks burn.

Despite his obvious discomfort, his sister persisted, "Even if you're not exactly courting her right now, you *want* to court her, don't you?"

Peter didn't know how she'd found out he used to be Susannah's suitor, but he couldn't afford to have any rumors that he was interested in her again getting back to Marshall. He scowled and ignored her, but Eva persisted.

Addressing Hannes, she hinted, "I can't tell you her name but I *can* tell you she was at the frol—"

"*Absatz*, Eva!" Peter demanded. Seeing his mother flinch and his sister's eyes fill, Peter immediately regretted barking at Eva, especially because it was so rare for all of them to be engaged in such lively supper conversation. He rubbed his temples in slow circles and exhaled heavily. "I'm sorry," he apologized.

"That's okay, *suh*." His mother reached over and patted his arm. "You should go relax or read for a while. You seem tired."

"*Jah*. I think I'll hit the sack early tonight."

After he left the room, Peter heard Hannes as he scoffed, "Tired, nothing. Eva's right. Whether he's actually courting someone or not, he's got a *weibsmensch* on his mind."

As he got ready for bed, Peter mulled over his brother's comment. *I do* not *have a* weibsmensch *on my mind*, he silently argued. At least, not in the sense that Eva and Hannes were suggesting. Sure, over the weekend Peter had reflected on how relieved he was that he'd had a conciliatory chat with Susannah, but that wasn't the same thing as thinking about *her*. And, yes, he was looking forward to seeing her tomorrow, but only because he always got so hungry working on the farm and she was such a good cook.

Besides, even if he *had* entertained a fleeting notion about becoming her suitor again, Peter knew that a courtship with her was an impossibility. *Marshall would never allow it and Susannah would never want it*, he reminded himself. *Especially not if he told her why I broke up with her.* So as he lay down to go to sleep, he resolved to squelch any unprompted thoughts of romance as soon as they popped into his mind.

Chapter Seven

On Monday morning, Susannah woke with a stomachache. *Why did I eat supper last night?* she asked herself. *I was already full from the treats I had with my tea.* She'd only been in New Hope a little over a week and it seemed like the healthy habits she'd spent the past eight or nine months developing were melting away like whipped cream on warm apple pie…which she'd also eaten last evening, since Almeda had brought them two. No wonder her skirt felt tight.

Lord, please help me to exercise more self-control today, she prayed as soon as she'd gotten dressed, brushed her hair into a tight bun and pinned on her prayer *kapp*. Then she added, *And please help me to find a way to get together with Dorcas in private, so we can smooth things out between us.*

As she was making breakfast, Susannah mentally planned out her day. Like most Amish women, unless it was raining she considered Monday to be laundry day. Which didn't mean it was the only day they did laundry, but dirty clothes inevitably piled up over the weekend. Susannah intended to spend part of the morning running them through the ringer and then hanging them out to dry.

However, since she'd gone to the frolic on Saturday, she hadn't replenished their groceries for the first part of the week yet. *I guess I'll do that after lunch*, she decided. The thought of lunch put a smile on her face; maybe now that she wasn't at odds with Peter, she could relax and she wouldn't overeat. Perhaps she'd even enjoy conversing with him a little.

"Guder mariye," her grandfather said as he and Lydia came into the kitchen, where she'd just set a pan of meatless breakfast scramble on the table.

"You seem *hallich*. What are you thinking about?" Lydia questioned. "Or *who* are you thinking about that's lighting up your eyes like that?"

For a moment, Susannah felt as if her stepgrandmother had read the thoughts she'd just had about Peter. But then she realized she'd been referring to Benuel, so Susannah sighed. How was she going to convince Lydia she wasn't interested in him as a suitor?

"I'm just pleased it's sunny again today," she said as she poured coffee. "I need to go to the market. Would you like to ride with me?"

Lydia's countenance fell. *"Neh.* You go ahead without me. I'll just sit in the living room and read."

Her mewling reply grated on Susannah's nerves. Lydia had broken her wrist, not her ankle. Why was she acting as if she was almost completely incapacitated? "That's up to you, but I hope you don't expect me to hurry back," she snapped.

Lydia's eyes widened, but Susannah felt too cross to apologize. *I don't mind doing the housework and fetching her whatever she needs, but I'm tired of constantly*

entertaining her. She's acting as if she can't function un-
less I'm in the same room and I feel like I'm suffocating!

Susannah turned her back to arrange half a dozen
slices of bacon on a pan in preparation for broiling it,
which was somewhat healthier than frying. By the time
it was thoroughly cooked, both of the boys had come
in from doing the milking and everyone sat down to
eat. Susannah's grandfather seemed more talkative
than usual, perhaps because he was making up for the
strained silence between Susannah and Lydia.

"On *Dunnerschdaag*, Lydia and I are going to her
dokder's appointment," he informed Conrad and Jacob.
Because Lydia had suffered a severe compound frac-
ture, the specialist needed to take follow-up images to
confirm it was healing properly. If it wasn't, she'd possibly need surgery. "We'll be leaving at eleven o'clock
and not coming home until after supper, since we're
stopping to visit Lydia's *schweschder* in Serenity Ridge
on the way back. I'll have to make sure everyone knows
how to operate the digger, so someone can take my
place. The rest of you will need to pick and take turns
helping load the barrels onto the wagon. There's supposed to be rain coming on *Freidaag* or *Samschdaag*
again, so you're going to have to keep up the pace.
Keep your breaks to a minimum. Nothing longer than
five minutes."

Jacob nodded his agreement as he continued down-
ing his breakfast, but Conrad asked, "We only have five
minutes to eat lunch?"

"Don't be *lecherich*. Of course you'll take a full lunch
break," Lydia insisted. "Susannah will fix you something, as usual."

"Aren't I going with you to the *dokder*?" Susannah

asked. She had assumed Lydia would want her to travel with them, since she might need someone to help her with doors in the women's room or something.

"*Neh*. The driver charges per passenger and besides, the *menner* will be *hungerich*. They can't harvest potatoes on empty stomachs. We'll be gone for most of the afternoon, so you'll need to stay home to get supper started, too."

Susannah could hardly contain her glee. *I'll have half a day all to myself*—and *I'll have the buggy to myself, too! After lunch, I can go talk to Dorcas, since she said she's not working until* Freidaag. *Maybe we can even take a walk at the gorge.* Susannah was so invigorated by the prospect that she whipped through her morning chores.

After hanging out the laundry, she came in to make up a grocery list, a task she and Lydia usually did together. But her stepgrandmother wasn't sitting in her usual chair, nor was she in the bathroom. Susannah went down the hall and gently tapped on the bedroom door. "Lydia? Are you okay?"

"*Jah,*" she answered tersely.

"I'm going to make up a grocery list before I fix lunch. Do you want to help me decide what we need?"

"*Neh*. You go ahead. Whatever you buy is fine, since you're the one doing all the cooking, anyway." Lydia still didn't come to the door.

Susannah hesitated. It was difficult holding a conversation this way, but she had an inkling Lydia was angry with her, so she asked through the wood, "Are you sure you don't want to help me?"

"*Jah*. I'd just appreciate having a little time to myself."

Not half as much as I'd *appreciate it*, Susannah

thought, offended. She returned to the kitchen and checked the fridge and pantry to determine what items she'd need to restock. After making her list, she prepared lunch. When Conrad had asked at breakfast what she'd be serving for the noon meal, she'd told him they'd have French fries and fried chicken. But the fries were actually baked potato wedges and the chicken, which was coated with corn flakes, was also baked. She'd also serve steamed broccoli and salad, with a slice of leftover apple pie for dessert.

Although she thought she'd appreciate preparing the meal without Lydia sitting at the table talking the entire time, the more time that passed, the guiltier she felt. Whether Lydia had retreated to her room because she was annoyed with Susannah or not, she knew she owed her stepgrandmother an apology for having spoken so sharply to her. So after she'd put the meal in the oven and had set the table, she knocked on Lydia's door again.

Entering, Susannah found Lydia seated in the rocker near the window, an open Bible on her lap. She went over and sat on the edge of the bed. "I'm sorry I snapped at you earlier, Lydia."

Her stepgrandmother patted her knee. "I understand. You've been very patient with me and my demands. It must be difficult for you to take care of your old *groosseldre*, keep *haus* and make meals for everybody without anyone else to help you."

"*Neh*, it's not. I'm used to doing far more work at home. But even if I weren't, I *like* helping you however I can." Susannah chose her words carefully, trying to be kind yet direct at the same time. "I guess I'm used to being…a little more active."

"I'm being overbearing, aren't I?" She appeared so sorrowful that Susannah immediately consoled her.

"Not *overbearing*, it's just that… Well, *you're* usually more active, too, Lydia. I know there are a lot of things you can't do because of your wrist, but it's not like you to sit inside all day."

"*Jah*. You're right." She sighed, then confided, "I didn't tell you or Marshall this, but the evening we went out for milkshakes, I accidentally smacked my hand against the trash receptacle in the women's room and it hurt all weekend. Ever since then, I've been worried if I move around too much, I might fall again or do something careless and injure my wrist even worse. And the *dokder* said if it doesn't heal properly, they may have to put screws or a plate in it. I can't imagine having metal in my body. I'd feel like I was a piece of your *groossdaadi*'s farm equipment."

Although Lydia chuckled, Susannah's eyes welled with contrition. She couldn't believe that this whole time when her stepgrandmother had been sticking so close to her and wanting to sit down together all the time, it was because she was *afraid*. Susannah thought, *That's probably why she waited for* Groossdaadi *to help her out onto the porch yesterday, too. But at least he was sensitive about it, not impatient and snappish, like I was.* This morning she'd asked the Lord to help her exercise self-control about what food she'd put *into* her mouth, when she should have been more concerned about exercising self-control about the words that came *out of* her mouth.

"I'm sorry, Lydia. I didn't realize you were so worried about getting hurt again."

"I should have told you, but I didn't want to admit my fear because I felt like I wasn't trusting *Gott* enough."

"I'm *hallich* you told me. And I'm sorry for being impatient."

"I'm sorry I've kept you holed up indoors all week, listening to me nattering on and on. But I understand that a young *weibsmensch* needs to get out for a little *schpass* with her friends. Why do you think I'm so eager for Benuel to court you?"

Susannah chuckled. "I appreciate that, Lydia. But I'm honestly not interested in having Benuel as my suitor."

"Is it because you don't want a long-distance courtship?"

"*Neh*. It's because I don't want a courtship, period."

"You mean with Benuel...or with anyone?"

"With *any*one." Susannah didn't know how to make it any clearer than that.

"Why not? Don't you want to get married?"

Not unless I were to marry a mann *who'd love me for who I am, inside and out, no matter what. And I don't think a* mann *like that exists*, Susannah thought, but she answered lightheartedly, "*Neh*, because then I wouldn't be as free to *kumme* visit you and *Groossdaadi* whenever I want... And I really do love spending time with you." It was true; now that she'd had this heart-to-heart chat with Lydia, her resentment lifted and she treasured the opportunity to be in her grandparents' presence again.

"We love having you here, too... But I know two young *menner* who are going to be heartbroken to find out you're not interested in a suitor at all."

"*Two?*"

"*Jah*. Benuel and Peter."

Susannah guffawed. "I've already made it very clear to Benuel that I'm not interested in being courted by him, so if he's heartbroken, that's his own fault. And I'm absolutely positive that Peter has no interest in me."

"Trust me. I've seen how those two look at you. They're both smitten."

"*Neh.* They're just *hungerich*—they're smitten with the meals I make." Lydia's observation had caused Susannah to blush so she hopped to her feet to leave the room. "Speaking of lunch, the *hinkel* should be nearly done by now."

But when they went into the hall, Susannah could smell an acrid stench. The chicken and potato wedges weren't just done; they were burned to a crisp. After pulling the blackened food from the oven, she opened the windows to air out the room. That's when she noticed the broccoli she'd intended to steam was still in the colander in the sink. The men would be coming in any second now, so she decided to just serve it raw.

"The potatoes are unsalvageable," she admitted to Lydia as she disposed of them. "But I made a big salad and I think the chicken might be okay if we scrape the coating off."

"Do you need me to get a hose?" Conrad asked when he came through the door as she was talking.

"A hose? For what?" Susannah absently replied, peeking into the bread box; there was only a quarter of a loaf left, but they were so low on groceries they'd just have to make do with what they had.

"To put out whatever is on fire."

"*Voll schpass,*" she retorted and turned around to make a face at him, as they sometimes did in jest.

But Conrad had walked down the hall and Peter was

alone on the braided rug by the door, wiping his feet. When he saw her, he grinned and said hello, his eyes twinkling. Lydia's comment instantly flashed through Susannah's mind. Was she right; did Peter look at her as if he was smitten? *Neh. He's just amused because he caught me making a* lappich *expression*, she rationalized. As for the topsy-turvy way *she* felt, that was just because she was heady from the fumes of the burned food.

Yet a few minutes later, when they were seated at the table and their elbows bumped as they folded their hands to say grace, a tingling sensation buzzed up her arm and across her shoulders, making her shiver.

"Are you cold?" Benuel asked. Sometimes she felt like he was observing her as closely as Lydia had been for the last week.

"A little," she told him, so he immediately offered to close the windows for her.

"*Neh*, that's okay. I'd rather be cold than tolerate that *schtinke*." Lifting the lid off the serving dish she'd put the chicken in, she announced, "I'm sorry, everyone, but as you can see, I burned the main dish. But there's plenty of salad and half a slice of bread apiece. I set this *hinkel* out in case someone is brave enough to try it, but it's probably not edible."

"It's fine," Benuel contradicted, jabbing a fork into the biggest piece of chicken on the platter. "It's just a little brown."

Susannah noticed Lydia was smirking, just as she'd done yesterday when Benuel claimed he'd come to the house to return the pan, but fortunately, she didn't say anything aloud.

However, Conrad jeered, "If that *hinkel* looks a little brown to you, you need glasses, *mann*. Because that stuff is as black as sin."

But Benuel persevered, sawing into the chicken with a knife and then lifting the bite-size piece to his lips. *He didn't even scrape off the charred part*, Susannah thought, glancing at him from the corner of her eye. *What is he trying to prove?*

Peter must have been thinking the same thing, because before Benuel put the chicken in his mouth, he interrupted him as he remarked, "I thought you said you've done a lot of carpentry work, Benuel."

"I have. Over five years' worth."

"Then you should know you'd better sand that chicken down before you eat it," he mocked.

There was a half-second pause and then Susannah burst out laughing and so did the others. Even Marshall chuckled. Benuel set down his fork in defeat and Susannah got up and whisked the dish of burned chicken off the table.

"I shouldn't have even set this out. While you're eating your salad, I'll make scrambled *oier* to fill you up. It will only take a few minutes." Lifting a skillet from the bottom cupboard, she added brightly, "And we'll have apple pie for dessert."

"*You're* serving dessert at lunchtime?" Jacob teased. "Is it a special occasion?"

"*Neh*, there's no special occasion," Susannah replied, as she turned to smile at everyone. "Just special people."

Peter felt like Susannah was speaking only to him. Or was it that he *wanted* her to be speaking only to him? Was he already entertaining the very kinds of romantic thoughts he'd just resolved to put out of his mind the evening before?

No, he didn't think so. It was probably more that he just didn't want Susannah to consider *Benuel* special in a romantic sense. Not because Peter had any hope of courting her, but because Benuel was obviously trying to win her over with insincere flattery. She deserved someone more straightforward than that. *She deserves someone more straightforward than* I *was, too*, he reminded himself. Benuel's dishonesty about how he regarded her cooking paled in comparison with how Peter hadn't been forthcoming about the reason he'd broken up with her.

"I'll be away from the *bauerei* on *Dunnerschdaag* afternoon," Marshall mentioned as they were waiting for Susannah to finish scrambling the eggs. "So I'll need to make sure you all know how to gauge the digger point."

When Peter was a teenager, he'd helped Amos, Marshall's brother, during three consecutive harvest seasons, so he was aware that if the blade went too deep, it would slice into the potatoes, ruining them. He considered it a cinch to operate a mechanical digger, but Jacob, Conrad and Benuel had never harvested potatoes before, so it was understandable they'd need to receive Marshall's instruction.

"Who's going to be digging?" Benuel asked.

"I don't know. We'll have to see how each of you handles the equipment first."

Susannah placed two bowls of eggs at each end of the table, then prepared to take her seat again. Benuel was crowding her on her left side and as she sat down, she wobbled toward Peter, but caught her balance by placing her palm on his shoulder. It only took a second for her to steady herself and withdraw her hand, but her momentary touch warmed Peter from head to toe.

He dared not look anywhere except at his plate until the feeling passed. The problem was, it *didn't* pass, not even when he noticed out of the corner of his eye that Marshall was glaring at him. It was as if he thought Peter were the one who'd grasped Susannah's shoulder, instead of the other way around. His mouth went dry, making it difficult for him to swallow his food, and he'd only taken two bites of pie by the time everyone else had finished their dessert.

"Time to get back to work," Marshall ordered and the other men pushed their chairs back and started filing out the door.

"But, *Groossdaadi*, Peter's not done with his pie yet," Susannah pointed out. "And that's practically the main course of this meal."

Marshall glowered, but as he put his hat on, he told Peter, "We'll be in the north field."

"I'll be right out," Peter said, shoveling another bite into his mouth and triggering a coughing spasm.

"Take your time," Lydia told him once Marshall exited the house. "Sweet things are meant to be savored."

Susannah was still seated beside him and Peter thought he noticed her shake her head at her stepgrandmother, but maybe he'd imagined it. "This does taste *gut*," he agreed.

"*Jah*. But it's not as *gut* as the pies your *mamm* used to make," Susannah commented. "I mean, I really appreciate that Almeda made pies for us. But your *mamm*'s were extraordinarily *appenditlich*. Especially her *blohbier* pies."

"*Jah*. I remember that time you traded me your entire lunch for a second piece of her pie." Peter hadn't considered what he was disclosing until Susannah knocked her knee against his beneath the table. It was too late: Lydia's ears had already perked up.

"When was that?" she asked.

"It was on a *Sunndaag* last summer when some of us went on a picnic after *kurrich*," Susannah immediately said. Which was true, although "some of us" really meant "the two of us." Peter and Susannah never picnicked with anyone else when they were courting; Sundays were the only chance they had to be alone. They'd find a way to sneak to the gorge, which wasn't easy considering Susannah's grandparents didn't like her to walk anywhere on her own and she seldom had use of the buggy. Dorcas, the only person they told about their courtship, frequently dropped off Susannah at the gorge, where Peter would be waiting for her.

"Ah, that's right. You and Dorcas loved going out to the gorge on *Sunndaag*," Lydia recalled. "I didn't realize you'd gone with a group."

Susannah started coughing into her napkin. Or was she trying not to laugh? Peter couldn't tell. *How could I have been so* dumm *as to blurt out something like that?* he lamented. He wasn't particularly worried that Lydia would discover they'd been courting—for all Peter knew, Marshall had already told her. But he was worried what Susannah thought about him openly reminiscing about picnicking with her in the past.

After Lydia rose, put her plate in the sink and then excused herself to the restroom, Peter mumbled quietly to Susannah, "Sorry about that. It just slipped out."

"It's okay. Sometimes things spring to my mind, too, and I say them without really thinking them through."

It felt strange to be sitting side by side with her, with

no one else on the other side of the table. No one else in the room. It reminded Peter of when they'd sit on a rock by the creek in the gorge, dangling their feet into the water and chatting as they ate their sandwiches. And instead of pushing the romantic memory from his mind, Peter deliberately indulged it, lingering over his pie even though he knew Marshall would have something to say about his delay when he returned to the fields.

Susannah didn't seem in any hurry to get up, either. She was silent while he whittled his pie down to the last two bites. Then she asked, "How is your *mamm*? At the frolic, someone mentioned she's been...under the weather."

I'm sure they did, Peter thought and instantly the nostalgic connection he felt with Susannah was replaced by insecurity about whatever rumors she'd heard about his mother. Peter could bear it if Marshall thought ill of him, but he didn't want Susannah to think his mother was lazy. "She's okay," he said and abruptly stood up, even as he was scooping the last bite of pie into his mouth. "I'd better get going or your *groossdaddi* won't let me take any more lunch breaks after this."

He'd only been half-joking about Marshall, but Susannah replied, "Don't worry, Lydia would never let that happen." Standing, she caught his eye and added, "And neither would I."

Peering into her earnest golden-brown eyes, Peter was overcome with affection. *"Denki,"* he said and then forced himself to leave the house while his legs could still carry him out to the fields.

I can't believe he still remembers that time I exchanged my lunch for his pie, Susannah thought as she began gathering the dirty dishes. But what struck her even more was the fondness she'd noticed in his voice as he recalled the memory.

Then her thoughts jumped to the remark Peter had made to Benuel about sanding down his chicken, and she laughed aloud. One of the things she'd always appreciated about Peter was that when he said he liked something, she could trust he was telling the truth, not just saying what she wanted to hear. Unlike Benuel, whose compliments seemed insincere and excessive. *How could* Groossdaadi *and Lydia think I'd ever choose Benuel over Peter?* she wondered. Not that she'd ever accept Peter as a suitor again, either. But even as a friend, she definitely preferred Peter's company over Benuel's.

When she had cleaned, dried and put away the lunch dishes, Susannah got ready to go to the market for groceries. "Are you sure you don't want to *kumme*?" she asked Lydia. "I can help you get in and out of the buggy. We'll be very careful."

"*Denki*, but I'd prefer to stay home. I might actually take a walk to the mailbox in a few minutes."

Pleased that Lydia felt confident enough to go for a stroll by herself, Susannah happily set out for the market. Upon arrival, she hitched the horse in an area of the lot specifically designated for buggies, right next to another Amish buggy. She was almost at the entrance to the store when she spotted Dorcas coming out, pushing a cart filled with groceries.

"Look who's here," she exclaimed. "Hi, Dorcas."

Dorcas squinted against the sun. "Oh. Hi, Susannah," she replied flatly.

"I'm *hallich* we're bumping into each other. There's something I'd like to chat with you about."

"Okay, but you'll have to talk while I'm loading these into the buggy. I don't want to be late picking my *schweschdere* up from *schul*."

So Susannah followed her to the buggy and helped her place the groceries into the back of the carriage. As they were carrying out the task, she asked, "Would you like to go on a hike to the gorge on Thursday afternoon? I can pick you up, since I'll have use of the buggy that day."

"*Neh*, I don't think so, but *denki* for asking."

Susannah waited, expecting her friend to explain why she couldn't go hiking, but Dorcas just turned and rolled her empty cart to the trolley. Feeling slighted, Susannah waited for her to return and then she asked, "Is something wrong? I feel like there's tension between us and I don't know if I've done something to upset you."

Dorcas pushed her prayer *kapp* strings over her shoulders. "I just don't consider going hiking to be as much *schpass* as you do."

"Then we don't have to hike. I only suggested that because—"

"Because you like lots of outdoor activity and Lydia has been keeping you cooped up in the *haus* all week. I know—you already told me," Dorcas said. "But *I* get lots of outdoor activity. Every *Sunndaag* I take a long walk. The rest of the week I'm outside doing yard work and caring for the animals and making sure my little *brieder* don't get hurt when they're running around all over the place. And when I'm not watching them or helping my *mamm*, I'm on my feet at the restaurant. So if *you* need more exercise, you should ask your suitor to take you hiking."

Susannah had no idea why Dorcas sounded so defensive, but she could no longer bridle her tongue. "What I was *going* to say before you interrupted me was that I only suggested a hike because I was looking forward to spending time chatting with you, the way we used to. It wouldn't have mattered to me if we climbed Mount Katahdin or just sat on the porch swing. I just wanted to be in your company." Susannah was so upset, her voice was shaking. "And as I've already told you, I'm not interested in being courted by Benuel. Or anyone else, for that matter."

"So you've mentioned." Dorcas snickered. "But you're doing a lot of riding around together for someone who claims she's not interested in him."

"I've ridden with him two times. Two! On *Samschdaag*, I rode with him because it was raining. And yesterday I needed to get to the shanty," Susannah explained again. "To suggest that I want him to be my suitor when I'm honestly telling you I don't is as *lecherich* as—as suggesting you and Peter are interested in each other because he gave *you* a ride home!"

"Why is that idea *lecherich*?" Dorcas's cheeks reddened. "Is it so unimaginable that someone would want to be my suitor?"

"*Neh*, of course it isn't." Susannah could see the pained look on her friend's face, so she lowered her volume. "I think almost any *mann* would be thrilled to court you. But based on my experience with Peter, I'm just not sure he's one of them." She reached to pat her friend's shoulder, but Dorcas jerked her arm away.

"I have to go pick up my *schweschdere*." She headed toward the front of the buggy to unhitch the horse from the post. Coming around to the side when she was done, she glanced at Susannah and asked, "Did it ever occur to you that your weight wasn't the reason Peter broke up with you?" Then she climbed in without waiting for an answer.

Jah, it did, Susannah thought as Dorcas pulled out of the parking lot. Hundreds and hundreds of times. But if that wasn't the reason, then what was? *I can't start wondering about that again. I'll drive myself to distraction.* She briefly considered asking Peter about it directly. Now that so much time had passed and her emotions weren't running so high, maybe he'd be willing to offer her more of an explanation.

Neh, I'd better not do that, she decided as she wheeled a stray cart into the grocery store. *We've just gotten comfortable being around each other again. Knowing why Peter broke off our relationship won't change anything now, so it's better to leave the past behind.*

Chapter Eight

Tuesday morning seemed to arrive earlier than usual for Peter. He felt bleary-eyed as he journeyed toward the farm and reflected on the discussion he and Hannes had the evening before. They'd stayed up late planning the wedding picnic-table project in detail. They'd made a budget, determined what supplies they'd need to order, decided on a delivery company and wrote an estimate for the *Englisch* couple.

They'd taken on big orders before, but this one was challenging because the customers required octagonal tables, with angled attached benches. Because of the unique design of the table, the board lengths weren't standard, so Hannes was going to have to custom-cut them.

"So much for getting a head start on our next order," his brother had said in reference to the standard-shaped tables he'd been working on all week.

"It's not wasted effort," Peter had reminded him. "We don't want to turn down or delay any smaller orders that come in while we're working on this project, so it's *gut* you've increased our inventory."

"*Jah*. As it is, we're going to be hard-pressed to meet the deadline for the wedding."

"I'll help you in the evenings and on any day it rains. We'll get it done."

Now, as he directed his horse toward the farm, Peter wasn't feeling quite as confident about their ability to complete the order in time. The workshop had lights that were powered by a generator, so technically, the brothers could work as long as they needed to in the evenings. However, the work on the farm was grueling and Peter was exhausted by the time he got home.

Marshall really should have at least one additional person on the crew. And, ideally, he should have two or three, he thought. Once again, he wondered why Susannah wasn't helping pick potatoes, too, at least for some part of the day. Plenty of girls and women picked potatoes on *Englisch* and Amish farms alike. So it wasn't as if it was considered men's work by anyone's standards.

Out of the blue, it occurred to Peter that maybe Marshall wasn't relieving Susannah of any farm work responsibilities because he didn't want her doing such rigorous labor. *Maybe he's just trying to limit any interactions she might have with me.* If that was true, it seemed as if the old man was cutting off his nose to spite his face. *He's only making more work for himself and his crew*, he thought.

It was discouraging to suspect that Marshall thought so lowly of him that he'd rather risk not finishing harvesting before the first hard frost than to risk…what? Susannah *talking* to Peter in passing in the field when Marshall wasn't looking? *That's* lecherich, *especially since we sit inches apart from each other every day at lunch.* Of course, his invitation was at Lydia's insistence, so Marshall hadn't really had a choice. And maybe he felt as if nothing would develop between Peter and Susannah at the lunch table because he was right there to monitor every word Peter spoke to her.

However, he couldn't monitor every *thought* Peter had about her. Such as the one that ran through his mind later that afternoon when he entered the house and she turned from the oven to greet him. *I could go back outside right now without eating a single morsel and I'd still have enough energy to work for eight more hours, just because of her smile*, he thought.

Fortunately, he got to enjoy her smile *and* her cooking, a double blessing. After Marshall said grace, Conrad commented, "Oh, wow—beef Stroganoff. My favorite!"

"I'm *hallich* you like it," Susannah replied.

"You should hear him talking about your cooking," Benuel added. "He spends the entire morning wondering what's for lunch and then the entire afternoon guessing what's for supper."

Jacob joked, "He talks about food as much as Benuel talks about *weibsleit*. Especially about—"

Peter abruptly cut him off, and commented, "Sounds like you *menner* are doing a lot of talking when you should be working."

He knew it wasn't his place to admonish Jacob, but he hadn't wanted him to embarrass Susannah by announcing that Benuel frequently brought her up in conversation. He anticipated Marshall was going to be annoyed that Peter had usurped his position, but the old man simply said, "You're *all* doing a lot of talking when you should be eating."

So the group finished their meal in relative silence. Afterward, when Marshall had gone into the bathroom,

Lydia was standing in front of the sink as the other men were beginning their exodus out of the house, so Peter leaned over and whispered to Susannah. "Your *turkey* Stroganoff was *appenditlich*." He'd been able to taste that it wasn't beef and he actually preferred it the way she'd prepared it.

"Shh." She squeezed his forearm with one hand and put a finger to her lips with the other. "Don't tell anyone, okay?"

Just then, Marshall crossed the threshold into the room. Peter immediately lurched away from Susannah and toward the door, his heart pummeling his rib cage. But her grandfather clearly hadn't noticed that they'd been sharing a secret because he trailed Peter out to the fields without saying a word.

I've got to be more careful the next time I make a private comment to Susannah, he thought. And there *would* be a next time. Because he'd decided that no matter how hard Marshall had been trying to control what Peter said to her—and no matter how hard Peter had been trying to control his own thoughts *about* her—he wasn't going to stop trying to make Susannah smile.

Susannah couldn't help humming as she cleared the table; having a more harmonious relationship with Lydia and Peter again put a song in her heart. *Lord, please help Dorcas and me restore our friendship again, too*, she prayed. While she thought her friend's bitter attitude toward her was undeserved and the comments she'd made about Benuel and Peter were unfounded, she couldn't completely get them out of her mind.

Primarily, Dorcas's remarks made Susannah question whether she'd made it plain enough to Benuel that she wasn't interested in him romantically. *I've tried to communicate that to him, both indirectly and directly. I've ignored his flirting. I repeatedly said my purpose in riding with him on* Sunndaag *was so I could make a phone call. What else can I do?* she ruminated. It wasn't as if he'd actually asked to be her suitor yet. So it would have been vain and presumptuous to take him aside and say, "I want you to know I have no desire to be courted by you."

In addition to that dilemma, Susannah again found herself wondering if Dorcas herself hoped to start a courtship with Peter. She hadn't explicitly said that she did. But given that she'd claimed a woman usually only accepted a ride from a man if she was interested in him romantically, Susannah thought it was reasonable to infer Dorcas wanted Peter to be her suitor. Not only had she ridden with him twice, but her voice also became sugary sweet whenever she spoke to him.

The possibility that Dorcas was enamored with Peter troubled Susannah. And although she tried to tell herself it was because she didn't want Dorcas to get hurt the way she'd gotten hurt by him, in her heart Susannah knew that wasn't the only reason. It was also because if Peter *did* end up courting Dorcas, it would confirm that Susannah's weight had nothing to do with why Peter broke up with her. And it would indicate that he thought Dorcas was a better match for him than Susannah had been.

Dorcas wants a suitor and she wants to get married. So what is wrong with me that I wouldn't be hallich *for her—and for Peter—if it turned out they were* Gott's *intended for each other?* she asked herself. *It's not as if I'd want Peter as a suitor again...is it?* She wasn't so certain of the answer to that question any longer. But Susannah did know that she definitely wanted Dorcas for her friend and that they needed to resolve the tension between them.

She decided Thursday would still be a good day to seek her out, so she woke early that day to make a special treat to bring with her. Dorcas loved a dessert called funny cake, so-named because it was half pie and half cake. She also loved pumpkin pie. So Susannah made a funny cake that required pumpkin. Assuming Lydia was right about Dorcas trying to lose weight, Susannah reduced the amount of sugar and flour listed in the recipe. Since she had extra pumpkin, she used it to make muffins, which she added to the thermal bag she prepared for her grandparents to take on their excursion to the medical clinic.

"I put extra goodies in with your lunch in case your appointment runs long," she told her grandparents later as she walked them out to where the driver was idling his car.

"*Denki.* We should be home by around seven o'clock, but don't worry about us if we're not."

As Susannah watched Marshall help ease Lydia into the back seat, they both seemed so vulnerable to her that she silently prayed, *Please,* Gott, *watch over them on their trip. If it's Your will, give Lydia* gut *news about her wrist. And if the news is bad, give her grace and strength.*

After waving to them, she went back inside. The house felt oddly empty without Lydia in it, but Susannah didn't have time to dwell on any twinges of loneliness; she had to get busy making chicken-and-pepper fajitas for lunch. They weren't standard Amish fare and Susannah had never made them, but since her grandparents were away, she'd decided to give them a try. She wasn't sure the boys would like them, but she knew Peter would; the only time she'd ever eaten them was when he'd taken her out to a Mexican restaurant last summer.

Actually, it wasn't even a restaurant—it was a food truck that had parked in the lot by the large market. Peter had heard about how good the food they served was from Hannes, who'd been hanging out with a lot of *Englischers.*

Peter was probably relieved when his bruder *was baptized into the* kurrich *last spring,* she thought. *Hannes must have matured quite a bit since I knew him. Otherwise, Peter wouldn't be allowing him to manage the shop by himself.*

Suddenly, she remembered what Dorcas had said to her last week about how strange it was for Peter to be helping Marshall with the harvest. Susannah hadn't really thought twice about it, since she'd assumed he was just being a supportive community member. But now it struck her as odd that he'd put her grandfather's farm before his own business. Especially since yesterday, Peter had mentioned at lunch that the workshop had received a picnic-table order for an *Englisch* couple's wedding at the end of October.

I suppose he didn't count on his business picking up, she concluded. *I hope he doesn't regret offering to help* Groossdaadi, *though, because if he hadn't, we never would have become friendly to each other again.*

"What's that I smell?" Conrad asked after the men had come in, washed their hands and gathered in the kitchen about an hour later.

"*Hinkel* fajitas with peppers."

"Trust me, you'll love it," Peter told him, taking his usual seat next to Susannah's chair.

"Where's my plate?" Benuel asked.

"Oh, I put it there, where Lydia usually sits. I figured this would give us both a little more elbow room." What Susannah had really figured was that this was another opportunity to indirectly demonstrate she wanted to keep distance between them.

"But you don't need more elbow room from Peter, eh?" Jacob asked, and she could feel her face flush with embarrassment. She hadn't thought about how it would look for her to move one of the men farther away from her, but not move the other.

Thinking quickly, she said, "You know how strongly my *groossdaadi* feels about being the head of his household and at the head of the table. I didn't think it was right to put Peter in his chair."

Her answer seemed to suffice and Jacob dropped the subject. As usual, once they'd said grace and were served, hardly anyone spoke because they were all too busy consuming their food. But after they'd had seconds and their eating slowed, Benuel told her how much they'd enjoyed the meal.

"Es muy bueno," Peter added.

Susannah giggled. She silently recalled that the day they were waiting for their order at the food truck, the server had asked them how to say "It's very good" in *Deitsch*. Then she'd taught them how to say the same phrase in Spanish.

Benuel furrowed his eyebrows. He apparently didn't enjoy the meal as much as he'd said he did, because he'd only eaten a single fajita. Even more telling, he'd taken two helpings of salad, which was unusual for him. "What did you say?" he asked Peter.

"*Nada*," Susannah answered for him. *Nada*, meaning *nothing*, was another word the server had taught them.

"*Gut* memory," Peter said, complimenting her.

It was such a fun day, I remember everything about it, she thought wistfully.

Peter didn't know if Benuel's nose was bent out of shape because he was annoyed that Peter was joking with Susannah, or if it was because he hadn't gotten enough to eat. But Benuel glowered at him as he said, "If you're done making jokes, we should get back to the field. I'll dig—the *buwe* can pick."

"It doesn't make sense for you to dig. That's a job for someone who isn't as strong as you are. You and I need to load and transport the barrels. Let Conrad or Jacob dig. The other *bu* can pick until it's time to load. Then we'll take turns transporting and unloading, as usual."

"Who did Marshall put in charge? Me or you?"

Marshall had told Benuel he expected him to keep an eye on everything, but the notion of being "in charge" was more of an *Englisch* one than an Amish one. They were all supposed to work together collaboratively. Furthermore, Peter knew more about harvesting potatoes than Benuel did. But he also knew he had to tread carefully, since Marshall held Benuel in high regard. "I'm just concerned about being one *mann* short today."

"If you need another person to pick, I can help after I do the dishes," Susannah volunteered.

Peter thought that was an even worse idea than Benuel digging; he could imagine how upset Marshall would be. But Benuel was all for it. "*Jah*. That would be great. Like Peter said, Conrad and Jacob can take turns digging. Peter can do the loading and transporting, and the rest of us can pick."

How can he expect me to do all *the loading, transportation and unloading, just so he can be around Susannah?* Peter wondered, fuming inwardly. But he knew the more forcefully he resisted Benuel's instructions, the deeper Benuel would dig in his heels. So he offhandedly reminded him, "You know if one of us gets an injury, Marshall won't be able to finish harvesting on time, right?"

"*Jah.* So be careful out there." Benuel's scowl had been replaced with a grin.

Gott, *please give me patience*, Peter prayed as he headed out to the fields a few minutes later and began picking. Within half an hour, Susannah had come outside, too. Of course, Benuel suggested she work in the row next to him, while Peter and Conrad were picking in rows about fifty yards away. Jacob maneuvered the horse and digger, overturning the earth and bringing the potatoes to the surface.

Although Peter was too far away to hear what Benuel was saying, he could hear him jabbering to Susannah almost the entire time they were picking. On occasion, her voice could be heard briefly. After a while, Benuel's comments became less frequent and when Peter turned around, he understood why: Susannah had been picking so much quicker than Benuel that she'd moved up the row, too far away from Benuel for conversing. Peter grinned to himself. *I* knew *she wasn't lazy*, he thought.

In fact, a couple of hours later, when Benuel suggested it was time for another break, Susannah objected. "Already? We just took one."

"The *gaul* needs water and so do I," Benuel replied, and Jacob and Conrad agreed.

So did Peter. "*Jah*," he said. "I don't think we'll be able to fit any more barrels in the wagon. I should make a run to the potato *haus*."

"Okay, I know when I'm outnumbered." Susannah wiped her hands against her apron. As the five of them walked toward the barn, she asked, "Is anyone *hungerich* again?"

"*Jah*. Starving." Conrad was the first to reply, of course, but the other men quickly echoed his sentiment. So Susannah said she'd bring a treat out to them. After they'd walked out of the fields, she headed in the direction of the house while the men headed toward the barn. Peter was alarmed to see Hannes's buggy and horse hitched to the post and Hannes was heading in his direction.

Peter immediately suspected their mother was ill. But he waited until Hannes had greeted the other men and they'd gone into the barn, then asked, "What's wrong?"

"Nothing. I just need your signature on a few things for the project." Since Hannes wasn't eighteen yet, Peter had to sign off on all their legal documents, including purchase orders. "I wanted to put in the order for the wood today so it'll be delivered by *Samschdaag*. Eva needed me to take her to the grocery store, so I picked her up from *schul* on my way."

Peter glanced at the empty buggy. "Where is she?"

"She went up to the *haus* to say hello to Lydia and Susannah."

"Oh." Peter reviewed the paperwork to be sure his brother's figures were correct. Then Hannes handed him a pen and he signed it. "If you want to bring this to the lumber yard before it closes, you'd better go see what's keeping Eva." Peter always got a little nervous about what Eva might say to other women once she got chatting.

Just as he finished his sentence, he spotted Eva coming out of the house carrying a pitcher and some paper cups. Susannah was behind her with a basket.

"Hi, Hannes," she greeted his brother when she was within earshot. Her face was dirt-streaked and her hair was "poofing up," as she used to say about it, but she had a bright, warm smile. "Would you like a muffin and cider?"

So Eva and Hannes joined the others as they stood around the entrance of the barn, eating their snack. Peter noticed his sister seemed more reticent than usual and he wondered if her shyness had anything to do with meeting two new boys her age. She was such a smart, pretty and earnest young girl and Peter knew it wouldn't be long before she'd want to have a suitor. *But right now, she's far too young*, he thought. Fortunately, Jacob and Conrad seemed to be paying more attention to their muffins than to her.

"We'd better get going," Hannes urged Eva as soon as he'd finished eating. "I want to get to the lumber yard by four thirty."

Eva quickly popped the rest of her muffin into her mouth. Before leaving, she said to Susannah, "I'll see you on *Samschdaag*."

Peter's heart skipped a beat. "What happens on *Samschdaag*?"

"If Lydia doesn't mind being alone, Susannah wants to *kumme* visit *Mamm*." Eva's face was aglow. "And she's going to teach me to make one of her favorite recipes. Isn't that nice?"

Nice? It's baremlich! *When Marshall finds out, he's going to think this was* my *idea,* Peter worried to himself. *And who knows what Susannah's going to think when she sees* Mamm.

After saying goodbye to Hannes and Eva, Susannah realized there wouldn't be time for her to visit Dorcas after all; besides, she'd rather keep picking potatoes. Although her lower back was sore, she felt revitalized by the fresh air and hard work. Because she needed to use the restroom before returning to the fields, she started back toward the house with the tray and basket. Peter tramped toward the buggy wagon, while the men went back into the barn to fill a bucket for the horse and try to find the oil to grease the bearing components of the digger. She had gotten halfway to the house when she remembered to check the mail to see if Charity had sent her the recipes she'd requested, so she turned around.

Peter must have forgotten something, too, because she saw him heading back to the barn. Head down, he ducked inside the open barn door just as she approached it a few yards behind him. She was planning to tell the young men it would be a few more minutes before she joined them when she heard Benuel's teasing words. "I saw you eyeing Peter's *schweschder*, Conrad."

"If you did, it's only because I never saw a *maedel* eat anything so fast," Conrad replied, causing someone—Benuel? Jacob?—to laugh. "If she keeps that up, she'll wind up as big as Susannah used to be."

Susannah stopped cold in her tracks, a bilious taste rising in her mouth. She wanted to flee, but her legs felt as stiff and heavy as iron. Even though she hadn't reached the door yet and she couldn't see where anyone inside was standing, it was obvious to Susannah that none of the other men knew Peter had entered the barn. She was close enough to hear him loudly clear his throat.

"Er, sorry. I was just—" Conrad began, but Peter finished his sentence for him.

"You were just being unkind and ungodly, that's what you were doing." Peter's voice was deep and angry. "You were being self-righteous, too. Because if you want to see someone wolf down twice as much food in half as much time as my *schweschder*, you should look in the mirror, Conrad. Even more importantly, you should remember what the Bible says about people looking on outward appearances, but the Lord looking at the heart." He cleared his throat, then added, "And you aren't on your *rumspringa* anymore, Benuel. So if I hear another inappropriate comment about *weibsmensch* from you, no matter who it is, I will hold you accountable before the elders and deacon. Understand?"

There was a silence and then one or both of them mumbled something Susannah couldn't catch. Sensing the interaction was over, she sprinted toward the house as quickly as she could so when Peter came out, he wouldn't know she'd overheard everything.

She almost didn't make it to the kitchen before dropping into a chair, dizzy with emotion. Susannah felt hurt and humiliated by what Conrad had said about her and Eva. She also felt angry. *Really* angry. So angry, she could hardly see straight. Or maybe it was tears that blurred her vision. Closing her eyes, she buried her face in her dirty hands and wept.

Oddly, it wasn't just Conrad's words and the other men's reactions that caused her to cry; it was also Peter's response to them. As grateful as Susannah was that he'd confronted their attitudes, Peter's reaction left her feeling frustrated and confused. *I've never heard him speak so fiercely,* she thought. *If he really believes that it's ungodly and unkind to judge each other by our outward appearances, then he was being hypocritical to end our courtship because I'm overweight.* Either that, or she was wrong and their breakup had absolutely nothing to do with how heavy she'd gotten. In which case, she was determined to do whatever she could to find out his *real* reason for calling off their courtship.

For now, she was going to take a long, hot shower. *The men will have to finish picking potatoes without me,* she decided. *And if Conrad or Jacob wants dessert with supper, they'll have to bake it themselves, because I'm going to hide the funny cake on them.* But first, she was going to cut herself a nice, big piece.

Chapter Nine

Susannah had been overjoyed to hear that the specialist told Lydia her wrist was healing better than he'd expected and he didn't think surgery would be necessary. The news seemed to increase Lydia's confidence in her ability to stay on her own and to be more active. Still, Susannah was relieved when it rained on Saturday, because that meant Marshall and the boys would be home while she went to Eva and Peter's house.

However, to her surprise, Lydia announced at breakfast that she'd decided to spend the afternoon canning applesauce with Almeda and a couple other women in the district. "I'll probably be more of a nuisance than a help, but I'll enjoy chatting with the other *weibsleit* again." She asked Susannah, "What time will you be done at Eva's *haus*? Marshall or the *buwe* can swing by to get me after they pick you up."

Before Susannah could answer, Marshall asked, "Eva Lambright's *haus*?"

"*Jah*. Didn't I tell you? I'm going to visit her and Dorothy. And to show Eva how to make a few recipes."

"That's her *mamm*'s responsibility, not yours."

Susannah was startled by her grandfather's comment. Was he worried that Dorothy might feel like Susannah was taking her place by teaching her daughter how to cook? "*Jah*, but I don't think her *mamm* will mind. I've heard that Dorothy's been ill lately, so I think both she and Eva will be grateful to have a little help."

"What about your obligation to help Lydia? She's got a broken wrist. There's nothing wrong with Dorothy Lambright."

Susannah was so surprised she was speechless. She'd always known her grandfather was rough around the edges, but he almost sounded ruthless. How did he know whether Dorothy was genuinely ill or not?

"I'm going to be gone for most of the afternoon, so I won't need help, Marshall, but if I do, you and the *buwe* will be here," Lydia reminded him in a quiet but firm voice. "Susannah always considers her obligations to our *familye*. She already told me she'd prepare lunch for us before she leaves this morning. She'll be home in time to prepare supper, too."

Susannah added, "I don't mind walking if you're concerned about the *gaul* making too many trips in the rain, *Groossdaadi*."

"That's not my concern." Marshall stood up and put on his hat. "Jacob can take you and Conrad will pick you up. There's no need for you to walk or for the Lambright *buwe* to give you a ride home."

After he strode out to the barn, Susannah pondered why he seemed so stern. It was almost as if he had a grudge against Dorothy Lambright. *Maybe he thinks she didn't do a gut job raising Hannes, because he went through a rebellious phase during his* rumspringa. But that didn't make sense, because Benuel's wild running-around period had lasted a lot longer than Hannes's had, and Marshall had a lot of respect for the extended Heiser family.

Oh, well. It was frustrating enough that Susannah didn't know for certain why Peter had broken up with her; she didn't want to waste her time playing a guessing game about what Marshall was thinking, too. Collecting the dirty breakfast dishes, she concluded, *Whatever* Groossdaadi*'s concern about Dorothy is, it doesn't have anything to do with me and I'm not going to let it interfere with my relationship with her.*

"How is Susannah going to help you cook if you've got dishes piled up in the sink and on the counters?" Peter was unable to keep the annoyance out of his voice. The house was a mess—at least, compared to how orderly Susannah and Lydia kept their home. He should have tried to help Eva straighten it up earlier, but he'd half expected Marshall would have found a reason to prevent Susannah from coming. "You've also got *schul* papers spread around the living room."

"We won't be cooking in the living room," Eva retorted. "Don't worry, I'll clean everything up. Besides, this is my territory, not yours. I don't *kumme* into the workshop and tell you and Hannes how to organize your supplies."

"I wish you would," Hannes quipped. "We've got a big delivery of cedar coming today and we still can't figure out how we're going to fit all of it on our storage racks."

Peter ignored their kidding around. He lifted a dirty coffee mug from the counter and set it with the others in the sink. Then he rinsed a dishcloth so he could wipe up the brown ring the cup had left behind. "Is *Mamm* up yet?"

"Not unless she's hiding under the table," Eva joked, making Hannes laugh. "What are you so nervous about? Susannah is coming to see me and *Mamm*, not to inspect the *haus*."

"It's Susannah!" Hannes exclaimed and Peter's stomach dropped as he glanced toward the door, thinking his brother meant she'd arrived early. But then Hannes asked Eva, "*She's* the *weibsmensch* Peter wants to court, isn't she?"

"She is *not*," Peter objected, surprised by how menacing his own voice sounded.

"*Jah*, she is. Isn't she, Eva?" Hannes persisted.

Peter threw the dishcloth into the sink. "You two don't know what you're talking about and it's a sin to spread false rumors," he protested, glaring at his brother and sister. He knew how sanctimonious he sounded, given that they'd only been teasing him, but he couldn't risk that what they were saying in jest might somehow get back to Marshall.

Hannes rolled his eyes but Eva turned serious. "I may be a *bobbelmoul* sometimes, but I haven't spread any rumors, Peter. Dorcas's little *schweschder* is the one who told me you probably liked Dorcas. She said you gave her a ride home alone from Marshall's *bauerei* a while ago." Eva blinked her big eyes repeatedly, as if she was on the verge of tears. "That's why I suggested we should give her a ride home from the frolic last *Samschdaag*, too. I was trying to be helpful. I thought if you were courting someone, it would cheer you up."

Peter was so astonished he couldn't speak: his sister had made the same assumption about him and Dorcas that Marshall had made. And, apparently, Dorcas's sister had made that assumption, too. The question was, did *Dorcas* think he wanted to court her? *Neh, she can't think that...*she *was the one who asked* me *for a ride. I never* offered *her one*, Peter mused as he tried to reassure himself.

To his sister, he said, "*Denki* for being concerned about me, Eva. And I do trust that you wouldn't deliberately spread rumors, especially not about our *familye*. But you're too young to be thinking about romance and who's courting who. And I don't need a matchmaker."

"You mean because you and Dorcas are *already* courting?" Her lips instantly sprang into a smile.

"Neh!" Peter objected vehemently. "And I have no intention of courting her, either."

Eva's shoulders drooped. "When she finds out, she's going to be really sad."

"I doubt it. I don't think she's any more interested in our *bruder* than he is in her," Hannes said knowingly, which came as a relief to Peter. He didn't want to court Dorcas, but neither did he want to mislead her or hurt her feelings.

"What makes you say that? Are *you* courting her?" Eva asked.

"Neh, but one of my friends is. I'd tell you who, but then Peter would accuse me of sinning by spreading rumors." Even without naming names, Hannes's answer was all the confirmation Peter needed to put his mind at ease.

"What are you three whispering about over there?" Dorothy asked from the doorway. To Peter's astonishment, she was completely dressed and she'd brushed her hair back into a neat bun and pinned on her prayer *kapp.* If it wasn't for her pale skin and the dark circles beneath her eyes, she would have looked like she had a year or two ago.

"Why are you up already, *Mamm*?" he asked.

"You know why—Susannah's coming to visit your *schweschder* and me. She should be here shortly so we've got to tidy the *haus*. You *buwe* ought to get to work, too."

So the two brothers put on their hats and coats and stepped out into the rain. As he walked toward the workshop, Peter felt ashamed for having felt ashamed. For worrying about what Susannah might think of his mother or the state of their house. It wasn't exactly that Peter thought she'd be judgmental. But he was still worried that she might unintentionally mention something about her visit in front of Marshall. And then the old farmer would have another reason to judge Peter's family as unfairly as he'd judged Peter.

Who cares what he thinks of us? He doesn't really *know me. And he certainly doesn't know* Mamm, *either.* Because if he did, he'd understand that it had taken her more effort to get up and get dressed at this early hour than it took for Marshall to harvest his entire farm. And thinking about it like that, Peter's insecurities melted away and his chest swelled from all the admiration he felt for his mother.

When Eva brought Susannah into the living room to say hello to her mother, she was startled by Dorothy's appearance. *How can* Groossdaadi *say she's not ill?* Susannah wondered as she plastered a smile on her face and returned Dorothy's warm greeting.

"Will you make us a cup of tea before you *meed* start cooking?" she asked her daughter. When Eva left the room, she invited Susannah to sit down and then she said, "It's so *gut* to see you again. Tell me how you've been. And how is Lydia doing? Peter told me she broke her wrist."

Because Dorothy didn't start their conversation with comments or questions about her weight loss, Susannah immediately felt at ease in her presence and she shared openly. After telling her about her family back in Dover and her trip to Maine, as well as Lydia's good news about her arm, Susannah asked Dorothy how *she'd* been lately.

"As you can probably tell by looking at me, I've been a little out of sorts." Dorothy attempted to smile but her mouth slid into a frown and she teared up. "Ach, there I go again. I'm so moody. I pray about it, but…" Her voice trailed off.

Susannah was silent for a moment as Dorothy wiped her eyes. She didn't know whether Dorothy meant she was physically, emotionally or spiritually "out of sorts." But it wasn't really Susannah's business, so she didn't ask. Instead, she said softly, "I'm sorry you've been suffering… Is there anything I can do to help make things better?"

Dorothy audibly caught her breath in either a sob or a laugh. "You're one of the few people who has asked me what she could do to help me instead of telling me what I should do to help myself." A smile crept over her face as she said, "But the truth is, you've already done so much to help me."

"I have? How?"

"You've *kumme* here, to share some healthy recipes with my *dochder*. And you've prepared many hearty, *appenditlich* meals for my *suh* when I've been too tired to even pack him a lunch."

"It's my pleasure," Susannah replied. She told Dorothy that she'd learned about good nutrition when her father's health was failing and she listed the improvements he'd experienced since they'd changed their diets. "Not everyone is interested in changing what they eat, but I'm *hallich* that Peter appreciates what I make for lunch. And I hope Eva enjoys preparing the dishes I'm going to make with her today, too."

"I think she will. She works very hard to keep up with *schul* and take care of me and the *haus*. She cooks, too, but it's mostly frozen or canned food, so I think we'll all benefit from a change in our menu." Shivering, Dorothy adjusted her shawl around her shoulders. "You look as *wunderbaar* as ever but I notice you've lost weight since last summer. Is that a result of the healthy dietary changes you've made, too?"

"Jah." Dorothy's question was so matter-of-fact that Susannah didn't mind discussing her weight loss with her at all. "But I'm afraid some of my habits are slipping. I'd better get back on track soon, because I had so much more energy when I was eating well and getting enough exercise."

"Hmm. Maybe a change in diet is what I need, too," Dorothy mumbled thoughtfully.

Susannah nodded. "I was surprised how much it helped my *daed* and me. Although I was fortunate—the hospital connected us with a nutritionist first. She was a *wunderbaar* resource. I always thought we were eating healthy food, because we rarely bought anything from the store, but she taught me that even meals and desserts made from scratch can contain too much sugar or salt or carbohydrates."

Dorothy was a rapt listener and Susannah appreciated being able to share her excitement about what she'd learned without feeling she was being judged as boastful. "The nutritionist also emphasized that even though the *Englisch* lifestyle is much more sedentary than ours, it's still important for us to get aerobic activity for *gut* heart health. So my sister-in-law and I purchased a used stationary bicycle we put in the basement to use on rainy days when we can't take a walk outdoors."

"What a *schmaert* thing to do."

"That was also the nutritionist's idea. She thought it was worth a try although she told me most *Englischers* end up using their exercise equipment as clothes racks instead of for physical activity." Susannah giggled. "But I have to admit, sometimes Charity and I hang clothes on the handlebars of the bicycle, too."

As Dorothy threw her head back with laughter, Susannah was glad that her tearfulness had passed. Yet at the same time, her own mood momentarily flagged because seeing Dorothy again reminded Susannah how much she'd once anticipated being her daughter-in-law.

All morning as he restacked the shipment of cedar boards, Peter had been mulling over Hannes's suggestion that Susannah was the woman Peter wanted to court. His thoughts and feelings swung back and forth between hopeful wishing that he could become Susannah's suitor again to resentful acceptance of the fact that he couldn't.

So by the time he and Hannes walked up to the house for lunch, Peter's stomach was so jittery that he didn't know if he'd actually be able to eat anything. *That's lappich. I eat with Susannah every day. This is no different*, he reminded himself. *What's the worst that can happen—spilling my* millich *all over the table?*

No, the worst that could happen would be for Peter to say or do something that gave away the secret he could scarcely admit to himself: namely, that he was still in love with Susannah. He decided that the best way to try to prevent that from happening would be to say as little as possible. And given that his stomach was bouncing with anxiety, he decided he probably should *eat* as little as possible, too.

But when Hannes opened the door and a piquant aroma wafted through the air, he immediately felt hungry again. Then he heard his sister giggling at something Susannah said and Peter's shoulders relaxed, too. He grinned as he greeted them.

"Hi, Peter. Hi, Hannes," Susannah and Eva replied at the same time, which made them giggle again.

They act like two schweschdere, Peter thought. He immediately put the idea out of his head because it reminded him too much of Eva saying she wanted one of her brothers to get married so she could have a sister-in-law. He excused himself to go wash his hands and then Hannes took his turn. When Peter came back into the kitchen, Susannah was alone, peeking in the oven. She straightened up and turned to him.

"What are you looking at? The mess I've made?" she asked. "Usually I clean up as I go but we were having so much *schpass* I wasn't paying attention."

"I didn't even notice." Peter chuckled to think that he'd worried about a coffee-ring stain on the countertop. "Is my *mamm* reading in her room?"

"Actually, she's been taking a nap," Susannah replied nonchalantly, as if it was completely normal for an adult to take a nap before noon. "Eva went to ask if she wants to eat with us. If she's too tired, I'll keep something warm for her in the oven."

"Just make sure Hannes doesn't find it before she does," Peter warned her.

"Why? Does he eat as much as Conrad and Jacob?"

"He eats *more*."

"That's impossible."

"It's true," Peter insisted.

"I'll believe it when I see it," Susannah said in a saucy voice.

Peter didn't know how even the most casual conversation with her could make him feel so punchy, but if he didn't stop bantering with her like this, his butterflies would come back. And the food smelled too delectable for him to miss out on this meal.

Hannes returned to the room and a few minutes later, so did Eva and their mother. Dorothy looked much more tired than she'd appeared this morning. Or maybe it was just that her hair was mussed and her dress was wrinkled from lying down in it. They all sat down—Susannah was seated across from Peter—and he was about to say grace when he noticed his mother wasn't wearing her prayer *kapp*. He didn't want to embarrass her by drawing attention to her forgetfulness, but he knew she'd be upset if she realized she wasn't wearing it while they prayed.

Out of the corner of his eye, he noticed Susannah tug her own *kapp* strings, discreetly signaling Dorothy's oversight. It was such a small, simple gesture, but the amount of quiet dignity she extended to Peter's mother doubled his respect for Susannah.

"*Ach*, I forgot my *kapp*," Dorothy said, so Eva darted into her room to get it for her. When she had pinned it securely in her hair, Peter said grace. Then they passed around the platters of honey Dijon garlic chicken breasts, roasted vegetables and baked potato wedges that Susannah again referred to as French fries. Unlike during lunchtime at Marshall's house, this afternoon they ate slowly, simultaneously enjoying both the food and the pleasant conversation. Eventually, everyone but Hannes finished their meal. Peter caught Susannah's eye and gestured toward his brother with his chin, as if to say "See? I told you."

She glanced at the teenager. "I assume you liked the meal, Hannes?"

"*Jah*." His mouth was too full for him to say anything else.

"Didn't I tell you what a *gut* cook Susannah is?" Peter asked proudly, not caring if anyone picked up on his obvious appreciation for her.

"*Denki*, Peter…but I didn't make this meal. Eva did."

Hannes momentarily stopped eating. "Really?"

"Well, Susannah told me how to do everything," Eva quickly informed them.

"*Neh*, I just gave you the recipe. I couldn't have made this any better myself," Susannah said. "And, actually, if I had made it, the fries would have been burned to a crisp."

Peter chuckled and then the two of them recounted the story about the meal she'd ruined, how Benuel was going to eat the charred chicken, anyway, and what Peter had said to him about sanding it down. Everyone cracked up, especially Dorothy. *She may look tired, but she sure seems to be in a lively mood*, he noticed.

"Who wants dessert?" Eva asked.

"I do." Hannes popped the last potato wedge into his mouth.

Their mother's appetite was strong today and she said, "Me, too."

"Just a tiny sliver," Susannah told Eva.

"How about you, Peter?" his sister asked.

No, he didn't want dessert. Because that would mean their meal with Susannah was almost over. But since everyone was waiting for his answer he said, "*Jah*, please. Whatever it is, make mine a big piece."

After lunch, Dorothy offered to dry the dishes. Susannah could see how weak she was, but she didn't want to insult her by suggesting that she should go rest instead, so she gratefully accepted her help. However, as soon as they'd put away the last utensil, Dorothy admitted she needed to sit down in a comfortable chair in the living room. Close to tears, she said, "I *want* to help you *meed* cook, but I just feel drained."

"That must be frustrating," Susannah said, empathizing with the older woman. "But we did most of the prep work before lunch, so we don't have much left to do, anyway."

When Eva had stopped by the house with Hannes on Thursday, Susannah had given her some of the recipe cards she'd brought with her from Delaware so the young girl could purchase the ingredients they'd need ahead of time. Susannah had planned to help Eva make supper for their evening meal, which could be eaten again as leftovers on the Sabbath. She also wanted them to prepare a couple of dishes to refrigerate or freeze for later in the week.

As they worked together, it became clear to Susannah that, like most Amish girls her age, Eva was familiar with the basics of cooking. She just needed a few hints about the preparation and timing involved in making homemade meals, since she lacked experience cooking from scratch. The two of them had several pans sizzling on the stove when they discovered Eva had only bought half of the amount of ground turkey required for one of their recipes.

The Lambrights lived as far away from the main grocery store as Marshall and Lydia did, but there was a smaller, more expensive market nearby. Although it wasn't frequented by the Amish, Susannah suggested she could jog over there and pick up the turkey they needed.

"*Neh*, I'll go," Eva objected. "I'm the one who forgot to get it and it's raining."

From the other room, Dorothy called, "I'd go, but I'm too tired. Susannah, you should use our buggy and Eva can stay here and I'll help her keep an eye on the cooking. Take the black *gaul*. His name is Pepper."

Susannah agreed that was the best idea so she charged off to the barn. Pepper seemed a bit agitated and he had bits of bedding or dirt on his shoulders and flanks. Knowing that the harness could rub against the debris and give the animal a sore, Susannah decided to brush him off first. She spoke soothingly to him as she worked and he seemed more settled by the time she put on the harness.

As she was fastening the straps on the breast collar, Peter came into the barn, water dripping from the brim of his hat. He stopped short, as if surprised to see her. "Wh-where are you going? Is everything okay with *Mamm*?" he asked. There was a distinctly panicked tone to his voice and it occurred to Susannah that he must have been carrying an abiding concern about his mother's condition.

"Your *mamm* is fine." Having fastened the harness collar, Susannah paused to smile reassuringly at Peter. "We need something from the market over on Pine Street, so she told me I could take the buggy."

"Oh." He came closer and rubbed the horse's neck for a moment, then suggested, "Pepper can be a little skittish sometimes. The roads are slick and the *Englischers* drive pretty fast around here. Maybe I should go with you?"

Peter knew full well Susannah could handle the horse and buggy on her own. But he wasn't asking whether she needed help; he was asking whether she wanted his company. It reminded her of when he'd first asked if he could court her. The response she gave him now was the same as the one she'd given him then. "I'd like that. *Denki*." Then she added, "As long as it doesn't interfere with your work."

"*Neh*. Hannes ate three desserts. He has enough energy for both of us. I've just got to bring him that spare sawhorse over there and then I'll be right back."

Since the workshop was a good quarter of a mile away from the house and barn, Susannah had the horse and buggy hitched and was ready to go by the time Peter returned. After they got into the carriage and headed toward the small market, Susannah remarked, "It's been very pleasant spending time with your *mamm* and *schweschder* today. I'm sorry Dorothy hasn't been well, though."

"Denki."

Susannah didn't know whether his answer was so succinct because he was concentrating on the road ahead or because he didn't want to talk about his mother's condition. She'd gathered that their family was guarded about his mother's health and Susannah wasn't going to pry. But she did want him to know she cared, so she said, "I worried a lot when my *daed* was ill. But it helped me to know a lot of people were praying for him. I'll be praying privately about your *mamm*, too."

"I appreciate that, Susannah." Peter glanced over at her, his eyes more gray than blue in this light. His voice was husky when he added, "I—I'm sorry I wasn't a source of support for you when your *daed* was hospitalized. That must have been a very difficult time."

"Jah, it was," she admitted. *It was a difficult time because of my* daed*'s health and it was a difficult time because you'd broken up with me.* Sensing this might be a good opportunity to find out why Peter had called off their courtship, Susannah considered bringing up the subject. Asking him about it outright.

But she was torn. What if she found out her weight gain really *was* the reason? Or what if he still adamantly refused to say why he'd broken up with her one way or the other? It would put a damper on the delightful time she'd spent with him and his family. So as they slowed down, nearing an intersection, she just added, "But *Gott* is *gut* and His grace was—and is—sufficient for us."

"Jah," Peter solemnly agreed. They halted at the stop sign, opposite an *Englisch* vehicle, and waited for their turn to pull forward. As they started up, they passed

another buggy headed in the opposite direction. Peter craned his head in a backward glance. "Was that your *groossdaadi*?"

His voice sounded almost as alarmed as it had sounded when he'd asked her if his mother was okay. It occurred to Susannah that Peter might be worried that whoever was in the other buggy had seen them together and assumed they were courting. And it was fully possible that Marshall had been traveling down this street on his way back from dropping off Lydia at Almeda's *haus*. However, Susannah tried to reassure Peter, and said, "I didn't notice who it was. But if my *groossdaadi* mentions he saw us out today, I'll just explain the situation and he won't give it a second thought."

From the grim expression on Peter's profile, Susannah could tell he was unconvinced. *What's he so worried about?* she wondered as they pulled into the grocery-store parking lot. *We're not courting, so we don't have anything to hide. And even if we were courting and* Groossdaadi *saw us out together, what's the worst that could happen? It's not as if he'd try to prevent us from seeing each other.*

Chapter Ten

"The turkey meatballs we made for last night's supper turned out *appenditlich*," Eva told Susannah after church on Sunday as they were heading toward the staircase to go and help the other women prepare and serve lunch. "There was only one slight problem."

"What was that?" Susannah asked.

"Hannes and Peter liked them so much they didn't leave any for leftovers for today's supper!"

"*Ach*. I should have warned you. My *familye* enjoys those meatballs so much that I always set some aside ahead of time so there will be enough for a second meal," Susannah replied, chuckling. "Did your *mamm* go downstairs already?"

Susannah wanted to say hello to Dorothy, and to Peter. She also wanted to let him know that Marshall hadn't mentioned anything about seeing them on the road yesterday. Peter had been so uptight on the way home from the market, he'd hardly spoken two words to her, so she'd hoped to find a way to chat with him in private and put his concern to rest.

"*Neh*. She was tired so Peter brought her home as

soon as the sermon ended. But Hannes came in a separate buggy, so I get to stay for lunch for once."

"I'm *hallich* you get to stay, but I hope your *mamm* is okay."

Smiling, Eva assured her, "She'll be fine once she has a nap. And she told us last night that after speaking with you, she decided she's going to go see a nutritionist. She thinks her problem might be related to her diet—not that she's depressed." Eva clapped her hand over her mouth. Her voice was muffled as she said, "I wasn't supposed to tell anyone that."

"It's okay. I promise not to mention a word about it to anyone." Susannah was aware that some—but not all—Amish people she knew believed depression was akin to laziness, or that it was an indication that someone wasn't praying enough or was too self-focused. She even suspected that's why Marshall had claimed that Dorothy wasn't actually ill. Attitudes like that were probably why the Lambright family had been so secretive about Dorothy's condition, too. Susannah touched her young friend's arm. "It's *gut* that your *mamm* is going to consult a nutritionist, but no matter what her condition is, the important thing is that she receives help and starts to feel better. I'll be praying about that."

"Denki."

"For today, let's make sure the *weibsleit* send some of the lunch leftovers home with you. Just don't let your *brieder* see the food until suppertime," Susannah suggested, restoring the smile to Eva's face.

"Jah. Especially since I heard that some of the *weibsleit* made apple-butter pie for dessert today!"

A few minutes later, as Susannah was carrying a tray of bread, church peanut butter, cheese and homemade bologna from the basement to the gathering room, she passed Dorcas in the stairwell. To her dismay, her friend uttered a greeting, but barely glanced her way. However, when lunch was over and the last serving trays and dishes had been washed and put away, Susannah felt a tap on her shoulder.

"Can I speak to you?" Dorcas asked, still not meeting Susannah's eyes. "I thought we could walk to my *haus* together and I can give you a ride home."

Susannah was tickled that Dorcas wanted to spend the afternoon with her. "*Jah.* Of course. I just need to go tell *Groossdaadi* and Lydia they can leave without me." She raced outside and let them know, then circled back to where Dorcas was waiting for her beneath a large maple tree that was just starting to change from green to crimson.

Susannah thought she was seeing the reflection of its color on Dorcas's cheeks, but as her friend began speaking, she realized she was red-faced from embarrassment. "Oh, Susannah, I'm so sorry," she blurted out, as soon as they began walking. "My behavior toward you the past couple of times we've seen each other has been hurtful and unkind and I hope you'll forgive me."

"Of course I'll forgive you," Susannah told her. "And I'd like you to forgive me, too…except I'm not quite sure what I've done to offend you."

"You haven't really done anything. Nothing worth my getting so upset about, anyway."

"Even so, I'd like to know what's been troubling you."

"Well, I guess I was… I was annoyed because the day I came to the *bauerei*, I'd been on my feet at work all morning and then I walked all the way to your *groossdaadi*'s *haus*. Even though I was tired, I was so *hallich* to see you that I didn't mind taking another walk because you'd said you'd been cooped up in the *haus* for days. But then when it started to rain, it seemed as if you didn't even care if I got wet. All you cared about was getting exercise."

Now Susannah felt *her* cheeks turning as crimson as the maple tree's leaves. "*Ach*. That was so selfish of me. No wonder you were upset. I'm very sorry, Dorcas."

"It's okay. I should have said something at the time instead of holding it against you. I think I was also a little upset because, well, because when we first saw each other I was so *hallich* for you about your weight loss. But you didn't even notice that I've lost weight, too." She touched her stomach. "I still have a long way to go, but I'm trying really hard. I understand that you don't like anyone to talk about your weight loss, but I need encouragement."

She pulled her friend to a stop and looked into her eyes. "I'd be *hallich* to encourage you however I can, Dorcas. But to be honest, that day you came to the *bauerei*, the only thing I noticed was how *wunderbaar* it felt to finally see my friend's pretty face in person again after exchanging so many letters."

"That's really sweet, but you don't have to say that just because I've been feeling insecure about my outward appearance. Deep down, I know what we look like to each other isn't nearly as important as what our hearts look like to *Gott*."

"I know you know that. But I'm not complimenting you for any reason other than I'm telling you the truth about how I see you," Susannah asserted adamantly, peering into her eyes.

"Denki." Dorcas nodded, accepting the compliment. As the two women continued walking, she remarked, "I shouldn't have given you such a hard time about riding in the buggy with Benuel. I know you're not interested in him."

"It's all right. I've had to readjust to some of the customs and beliefs here in New Hope. In my district, it doesn't necessarily mean a *weibsmensch* is interested in being courted by a *mann* just because she accepts a ride with him." Susannah took a deep breath before asking the question she wasn't sure she wanted her friend to answer. "Speaking of accepting a ride with a *mann*... Are you interested in having Peter for your suitor?"

When Dorcas went silent and Susannah noticed she was blushing, she felt like weeping—a response that showed Susannah just how much she'd been wishing *she* could have Peter for *her* suitor again. She held her breath until Dorcas replied, *"Neh.* I'm not. I just rode with him out of envy. It was as if I was trying to prove that you may have lost weight, but I had a more attractive personality." She covered her face with her arm. "It was so childish of me...and I'm really sorry."

Susannah burst out laughing. "It's fine. And you *do* have a more attractive personality than I've had lately. Which is one of the many reasons I know you'll have a suitor like you've been hoping for very soon."

"Um. Maybe sooner than you think." Dorcas shyly dipped her head. "Samuel Wittmer, Isaiah's *bruder*, is courting me."

"Dorcas!" Susannah yelped toward the sunny sky. "That's *wunderbaar*! Why didn't you tell me?"

"Because he just asked me on *Dinnschdaag*. He said he wanted to ask me sooner but he heard a rumor that

Peter was my suitor. Which serves me right for asking for rides from him, I guess." Both women chuckled and then Dorcas remarked, "The idea of Peter courting me is unimaginable."

Susannah stuck her fists on her hips. "Now why would you say a thing like that?"

"Because of the way I saw him looking at *you*. I think he's enamored with you, Susannah."

Her heart pitter-pattered; Dorcas was saying the same thing Lydia had claimed. Both of them couldn't be wrong, could they? "I'm not so sure about that," Susannah replied. She wasn't so *unsure* about it, either. The only thing she did know for certain was that the idea of having Peter as her suitor again had become a lot more appealing ever since she'd heard him admonishing Conrad and Benuel for their comments about her weight. Yet, she still had her doubts, which she voiced to Dorcas. "Maybe he just likes me again because I've lost weight."

"*Neh.* The way he looked at you at the frolic the other day was the same way I used to notice him look at you the summer you were courting."

"*Jah*, but during the summer he was courting me I wasn't as heavy as during the winter he broke up with me," Susannah pointed out.

Dorcas shrugged. "I guess I can see why someone might draw that conclusion. But I've known Peter a long time and I've never fully believed that your weight had anything to do with why he called off your courtship."

"Uh-oh. Are you saying the real reason was because of my *baremlich* personality?" Susannah teased.

"*Neh!* I'm just saying I don't think it was your weight."

"The problem is, *Peter* isn't saying what the reason is." *And I'm not sure I can face his answer, anyway*, Susannah thought.

As they were chatting, a buggy slowed down and came to a halt on the shoulder of the road about twenty yards ahead of them. Benuel hopped out and exclaimed, "Hi, Susannah! You're just the *weibsmensch* I wanted to see."

"And *I'm* just the *weibsmensch* he apparently *can't* see," Dorcas muttered because he hadn't greeted her.

"Hi, Benuel," Susannah replied coolly as they neared each other. She didn't appreciate him ignoring Dorcas any more than Dorcas did.

"Can I talk to you privately?" he asked. "It's important."

"Now?"

"Dawn won't mind, will you?" he asked, grinning at Dorcas.

"*Neh.* I'll wait over there," she replied, graciously ignoring his error. She crossed the road and leaned against the split-rail fence bordering a meadow, which the women would cross as a shortcut on their way to Dorcas's house.

"This will only take *one minute*," Susannah called after her, emphasizing the words for Benuel's benefit. Then she turned to him. "What's so urgent it can't wait until tomorrow when we see each other on the *bauerei*?"

"Since you mentioned how much you like the trails at the gorge, I rounded up a group of people to go hiking together. I couldn't find you after *kurrich*, but Marshall told me you'd headed in this direction. We'll have to hurry to catch up with the others."

Susannah was incredulous that he'd assumed she'd want to go hiking with him without even asking her first.

Furthermore, it was rude of him to take her aside now, just so he wouldn't have to extend the invitation to Dorcas, too. "In case you didn't notice, I've already got plans for the afternoon—I'm taking a walk with my *gut* friend. I'm not about to just ditch her and take off with you."

He glanced across the road, to where Dorcas was leaning against the railing. "Okay, we can give Dawn a ride home first." He chuckled wryly. "Although it seems like she could use the exercise."

"Her name is *Dorcas* and she probably gets more exercise in a day than you do in three," Susannah replied hotly. "And my answer is still *neh*." She started to cross the street, but Benuel pulled on her hand and she spun back toward him.

"Wait," he urged her. Releasing her fingers, he whispered, "I didn't just search for you so I could ask you to go to the gorge. I wanted to ask to be your suitor."

Susannah had acquired a lot of experience turning down potential suitors in the last year, since she'd lost weight, so she knew a kind but firm response was the best way to decline. "*Denki* for the offer, Benuel. But my answer is *neh*."

His mouth dropped open in surprise and then he closed it again and his features turned hard. Narrowing his eyes, he shook his head at her, but he returned to his buggy and sped away without saying another word.

At least there's no doubt in his mind about whether I'm interested in him or not, Susannah thought. Which was more clarity than she had about Peter's feelings toward *her*.

On Sunday night, Peter was lying in bed, trying to focus on the blessings he'd received that weekend. Most notably, although his mother was as tired as ever—she'd fallen asleep during church again—her mood seemed to have improved. There was a spark of hope in her voice again, too. Peter attributed this to the conversation she'd had with Susannah about the health benefits she'd experienced after making changes to her family's diet. Dorothy was so excited about the possibility that some of these changes might benefit her, too, that she'd asked Hannes to use their business cell phone to schedule an appointment for her with a nutritionist. He and his siblings were encouraged that she was willing to seek medical help again.

The other blessing Peter was especially grateful for was that everything had gone smoothly with the lumber delivery. Sometimes they received the wrong amount of supplies, which caused a delay, but the shipment was exactly what they'd ordered. He and Hannes had organized the wood and other supplies in a way that it would be kept dry and allow them to work efficiently. So they were well-prepared to start crafting the tables beginning tomorrow.

Also, Eva was delighted to have tried out a few new recipes. Peter knew that Susannah's guidance had been a real confidence booster for his sister. It was a relief to know that if his mother's condition didn't improve soon and she still couldn't supervise Eva's cooking, the young girl had been emboldened to try new recipes on her own.

Yet in spite of these occurrences, Peter wrestled with worry and resentment. He was still deeply concerned about his mother's health, of course. *What if she goes to a nutritionist and finds out that changing her diet doesn't improve her health? Will that make her even more resistant to consulting a different type of* dokder *in the future?* he wondered.

He also fretted about whether or not he and Hannes would meet the deadline for the wedding project. Although Peter preferred to simply agree to a project and then keep his word, many *Englischers* insisted on writing up contracts. This particular couple stipulated that if Peter and Hannes didn't deliver the full number of tables on time, they'd face a steep financial penalty. Peter intended to work every evening with his brother, but what if one of them became ill? Even one missed day of work could jeopardize the entire outcome of their endeavor.

But what Peter struggled with more than anything else was his resentment about Marshall's disparaging attitude toward him. Even if he'd only meant it as a token gesture, Peter found it insulting that when Marshall had gone to the doctor with Lydia on Thursday afternoon, he'd asked Benuel to keep an eye on the farm and crew. It wasn't that Peter wanted to be put in charge himself. It was that the very notion of someone "keeping an eye on" him and the rest of the crew was demeaning.

While Jacob and Conrad may have needed occasional supervision or instruction, overall, they were diligent and skilled young men. And as a matter of fact, Peter had far more harvesting experience than Benuel and he was far more industrious, too. *If anyone needs someone keeping an eye on him and monitoring his behavior, it's* Benuel, Peter ranted to himself. *Not just because of all the breaks he takes when he should be working, but because of the way he speaks about* weibsleit. *Especially about Susannah.*

Granted, Peter had effectively put an end to those

kinds of comments when he'd confronted Conrad and Benuel in the barn after hearing them joking about Eva's and Susannah's weight. And both of the young men had mumbled apologies. So Peter knew it would be unforgiving to continue to hold their behavior against them. But what bothered him was that Marshall didn't seem to understand that Benuel was the kind of young man who still needed to be told to watch his mouth in the first place.

I don't want Marshall to think more highly of me than he does of Benuel just because Benuel is immature or because he's used inappropriate language, Peter told himself. *But I resent it that Marshall regards me as a lesser* mann *because he thinks I'm not a* gut *steward of the money* Gott *has given me. Especially since that's not even true!*

But it didn't matter what Peter wanted. The fact was, Marshall favored Benuel, probably because it was well-known in the district that Benuel had prospered financially when he'd lived among the *Englisch* and apparently he'd saved most of his income. *I'm sure Marshall would* wilkom Benuel into his familye *if he started courting Susannah and their courtship leads to marriage.* The thought made Peter's heart clench like a fist within his chest.

He would have liked to think the notion of Benuel marrying Susannah was a preposterous idea. However, at church this morning, as he'd been unhitching Pepper from the buggy, he'd overheard Benuel inviting Isaiah Wittmer to meet him and Susannah at the gorge to go hiking. "Bring Hannah," he'd said, referring to the woman Isaiah was going to marry soon. "We'll have a lot of *schpass* together—just the four of us."

"You're courting Susannah?" Isaiah had asked.

"Not yet, but I hope to ask her very soon. Who knows? Maybe by this time next year I'll be looking forward to my *hochzich,* just like you're looking forward to yours right now."

Their exchange had bothered Peter so much that he'd actually felt nauseated. So when his mother had said she wasn't sure she'd have enough energy to stay for lunch after church, Peter quickly volunteered to take her home. But his stomach never did settle down; he hadn't even been able to eat any of the leftovers Eva had brought home from church for their supper.

I doubt very much Susannah would accept Benuel as her suitor, he thought, but it was only a small consolation. Because whether or not Benuel courted Susannah, it didn't change the fact that there was absolutely no possibility that *Peter* could ever be her suitor again. It was so infuriating. So unjust. And it grieved him so deeply he almost wished Susannah hadn't returned to New Hope, so he wouldn't have to remember all he'd given up.

But the hard truth was, he'd made an agreement with Marshall and now he had to abide by his promise to not court his granddaughter. Peter rolled over on his side and was almost asleep when he was struck by a new realization: *I may have agreed never to court or socialize with Susannah, but I never promised I wouldn't talk with her, laugh with her and enjoy her company for as long as she's on the* bauerei.

He'd already been doing that to some extent, but he intended to do it more frequently and more fully. He was tired of hanging his head. Of flinching every time Marshall looked at him askance. Of acting like a teenager who was worried he'd get caught courting a girl in his father's buggy. *What's Marshall going to do about it? He can't tell Susannah about our arrangement—he'd be breaking his word. And he can't ban me from the* bauerei *because he needs my help too much*.

Suddenly, his stomach felt calmer than it had felt all day and he could hardly wait to eat lunch tomorrow.

Susannah sensed a certain frostiness in Benuel's attitude toward her during lunch on Monday afternoon. But having been rejected herself, she'd understood why it may have been uncomfortable for him to have to sit next to her at the table and make small talk after she'd just turned down his offer of courtship the day before. So she tried to ease the tension with lighthearted chatter.

"Eva told me you and Hannes enjoyed the meatballs we made on *Samschdaag*," she commented to Peter.

"*Jah.* I enjoy everything you make."

"*Denki.*" Susannah could feel her cheeks flush as Lydia raised an eyebrow at her. She was so flustered that she kept prattling away. "She said you *menner* devoured all of them and she didn't have any leftovers for your *Sabbaat* supper. That used to happen at my *haus*, too. I'd tell my little nieces and nephews how many they were allowed to eat and we'd count them out together as I put them in the serving dish. But then my *bruder* would take twice as many as he was supposed to and the *kinner* would get upset because he'd eaten some of their share, too."

Susannah stopped to take a sip of milk before continuing. "One morning, my youngest nephew must have heard me telling Charity that I was making meatballs for supper, because he brought home his number line from *schul* and set it near his *daed*'s place at the table. He wasn't being naughty—he thought he was being helpful. We laughed so hard we cried. Now when I make meatballs, I just set aside whatever I need for leftovers for the next day before I serve them. And my *bruder* is not allowed to have more than he can count on one hand." Everyone except Benuel and Marshall had a good laugh over Susannah's story.

"You should get a number line for Conrad," Jacob suggested. "That's his third helping of applesauce."

"Isn't it *wunderbaar*? Lydia made it at a frolic this weekend."

"I hardly helped make it—Almeda and Lovina did. I couldn't peel any apples with my broken wing here." She held up her arm. "But I did help whisk ingredients for the apple-butter pies they brought to *kurrich* yesterday."

"It was *appenditlich*," Peter said, complimenting her. "Eva brought home leftovers and I had a piece for breakfast this morning."

"Oh, that's right—I forgot apple-butter was your favorite autumn pie," Susannah said without thinking until she noticed Lydia shoot her an odd look. In an attempt to cover her slipup, she brightly announced, "My favorite pie is peanut-butter pie. Especially the way my *mamm* used to make it—Lydia's the only person who makes it exactly the same way. Last summer she used to make one at least once a week when I was visiting. Between my *groossdaadi* and me, we'd polish it off within two days, wouldn't we, *Groossdaadi*?"

Marshall barely grunted in acknowledgment of Susannah's question. At exactly the same time, Benuel remarked, "That must have been when you were still overweight."

Both responses stung, but at least Susannah understood why Benuel was making a wisecrack; she had no idea why her grandfather was being so prickly.

"That remark was inappropriate, Benuel," Peter stated in a low, controlled voice.

"What?" Benuel acted surprised, turning his palms upward. "I just meant that I can't imagine Susannah eating that much food anymore."

Marshall abruptly rose to his feet. "Time for work," he said and pointed toward the door. All of the young men scrambled outside, except for Peter, who finished the last three spoons of his applesauce first.

"*Denki*, Lydia and Susannah." He put on his hat and walked past Marshall.

As soon as Peter closed the door behind him, Marshall sat back down at the table. Susannah didn't understand what was going on, but it didn't take long for her to find out. "Has he asked to be your suitor?" her grandfather asked bluntly.

Most Amish parents or grandparents she knew didn't directly ask their children and grandchildren about their courtships. But Susannah figured her grandfather hadn't appreciated Benuel's comment and he was concerned about her having a suitor who was rude to her. So she openly admitted, "*Jah*. But don't worry, I turned him down. I think that's why he made the remark he made at lunch, but it's okay, *Groossdaadi*—I know how to handle it."

Her grandfather rattled his head, as if he hadn't heard right. "You mean *Benuel* asked to court you and you said *neh*?"

"*Jah*. That's right."

"Has Peter asked to court you, too?"

The answer just spilled from her lips. *"Neh."*

"*Gut*. Because I'd prefer you didn't socialize with him."

It was Susannah's turn to wiggle her head. "Why not?"

"I have my reasons," Marshall answered tersely and stood up as if the subject was closed.

Drawing her spine upward so she was sitting as straight as she could, Susannah stopped him when she said, "I respect your opinion, *Groossdaadi*, but I'm twenty-three years old and I'll make my own decisions about courting. If you'd like to share the reason you wouldn't want me to accept Peter for a suitor, I'll give it my full consideration. But otherwise, I can't abide by your wishes in the event that Peter asks to court me." Her legs felt shaky even though she was seated.

Marshall opened his mouth and then closed it again. Then he left. Susannah leaped to her feet and started clearing the table in a whirlwind of activity. "He is being *so* unreasonable," she complained, more to herself, under her breath. "And *so* controlling."

Lydia, who had been uncharacteristically silent during their discussion, spoke up now. "I know you're angry with your *groossdaadi* and you probably have *gut* reason to be. But his intention isn't to be controlling—it's to take care of you. He thinks he's asking you to do something that's for your own *gut*."

"I don't need him to take care of me. I'm twenty-three years old!" Susannah said for a second time, waving a dirty serving spoon in the air. "*I* can decide what's *gut* for me and what's not. And *I* can decide who I want for a suitor."

"I agree," Lydia said calmly. "And I'm not saying

you shouldn't make your own decisions about who to court. But you should keep in mind that your *grooss-daadi* has made concessions for your opinion, too. It might help you not to feel so angry."

"What do you mean? What concessions has he made for *my* opinion?"

"Well, he's been eating the kind of foods that *you* think are *gut* for him, even though he's certainly old enough to decide for himself what he wants to eat, isn't he?"

"But—but that's not the same," Susannah stuttered.

"Why isn't it?"

Because I'm right! Susannah wanted to retort. But then she realized her grandfather might have wanted to say the same thing about Peter. She rinsed a plate under the faucet before coming up with a better answer. "Because *I'd* explain to him why it's not healthy to eat a lot of fat or too much sugar. He isn't explaining *anything* to me."

"I suppose you're right." Lydia sighed. "How about this… I'll try to find out what his reason is—or to convince him to tell you what it is. In the meantime, it would be nice if you'd refrain from batting your lashes at Peter in front of Marshall during lunch."

Susannah was going to protest that she didn't bat her lashes. But she knew what her stepgrandmother meant; how she felt about Peter came across in the way she looked at him, as well as in the way he looked at her. So instead, she said, "*Denki*, Lydia. I really appreciate your help."

Not that Peter's going to ask to court me, anyway. But maybe if I find out why Groossdaadi *doesn't want him to be my suitor, it will give me insight into why Peter broke up with me in the first place.*

Chapter Eleven

After lunch, when Marshall approached Peter and Benuel as they were loading barrels of potatoes into the buggy wagon, Peter half expected the farmer to tell him to go home—that he didn't want him to help with the harvest anymore and that he wasn't welcome on the farm. Worse, maybe Marshall would even say that he'd told Susannah about the arrangement they'd made and that she never wanted to see Peter again, either.

He recognized that his behavior toward her during lunch today had been inappropriate. He may not have behaved as brazenly as Benuel sometimes did, but in some ways, Peter had acted as if he was Susannah's suitor. He'd complimented her, laughed at everything she'd said and come to her defense when Benuel made an inappropriate remark. None of Peter's actions was necessarily wrong, but his attitude while he was doing them had been one of defiance. It was as if he was saying to Marshall, "You can't tell me what to do." He'd even refused to immediately leave the house when Marshall ordered everyone to get back to work. But instead of making him feel more manly or powerful, Peter's actions had made him feel juvenile and rebellious. And he knew that in this instance he deserved whatever rebuke Marshall had in store for him.

Benuel must have been even more nervous than he was because Peter noticed his hands were shaking as Marshall approached. When the farmer cleared his throat, both of the young men immediately turned from their barrels to give him their full attention.

"My wife has invited you to share our lunch because she wants you to have *gut* hot meals in your stomachs when you're harvesting. But if your words or actions demonstrate disrespect for anyone—including each other—you won't be *wilkom* at the table again. Understand?"

"*Jah.* I'm sorry, Marshall," Peter apologized. But Marshall wasn't looking at him; he was staring at Benuel.

"*Jah.* Sorry." After Marshall walked away, Benuel blew all the air out of his cheeks, sounding every bit as relieved as Peter felt. Then they both resumed their work, eager to put the incident behind them.

When lunchtime rolled around on Tuesday, Peter made a point of *not* speaking to Susannah, who didn't say much to him, either. Which didn't mean he wasn't acutely aware of her presence; especially when she shifted in her chair and their knees bumped against each other's beneath the table.

But he didn't act on his impulse to tell her he'd never tasted roasted garlic potatoes before, but they were so good he hoped she planned to share the recipe with his sister so she could make them, too. And he didn't sneak a chance to confide that his mother had made an appointment with a nutritionist the following week, thanks to Susannah's encouragement. Nor did he say half a dozen other things he would have liked to tell her, such as that the dark green dress she was wearing made her eyes look more golden-brown than ever.

By Wednesday, the quietness at the table felt a little more normal again; instead of being a strained or awkward situation, they had the kind of silent meal that happened because everyone was enjoying their food too much to speak. Although, in Peter's case, he was so tired from working late at the workshop the evening before, he could hardly hold up his head, much less hold a conversation. It was probably the only time he would have preferred to spend his lunch break alone outside, or in the barn, where he could have slept instead of eaten. However, once he finished his second helping of ham and scalloped potatoes—something Susannah said she'd made especially for Marshall, since it was one of his favorite dishes—he felt invigorated again.

Two hours later, the buggy wagon was full of barrels and Peter headed out to the potato house. When he returned, he was surprised to see Susannah crossing the lane in the direction of the fields. She and Lydia had been taking walks around the property in the afternoons lately, but today she was alone. When she saw him approaching, she changed her direction and hurried toward him. Noticing the distraught expression on her face, Peter brought the horse to a halt and jumped down from the buggy wagon.

"Susannah, what's wrong?"

"It's my *groossdaadi*. He threw his back out and he's in agony," she said breathlessly.

"That's *baremlich*." Peter shielded his eyes to scan

the fields. "Where is he? Does he need help getting to the *haus*?"

"*Neh*. He's already there. The *buwe* helped him—it took almost half an hour because he was in such pain. We've given him muscle relaxants and ice packs and helped make him as comfortable as we could with pillows. I was just going out to take Jacob's place picking so he can do the digging." Susannah looked tearful and Peter had to fight the urge to wrap his arm around her shoulders to comfort her. "It's the only thing I could think of doing to help. I gave Lydia a cowbell so she could ring it if she needed me to *kumme* in… I don't know. Do you think I'm making the right decision? Maybe I should stay at the *haus* with them."

Peter considered her question thoughtfully before answering. "Your *groossdaadi* is probably going to be unable to work the next week, so unless you help us pick, we won't finish harvesting before the first frost. I think that's what Marshall would prefer that you do. But maybe today you could take a break every hour or so to run back to the *haus* to check on your *groosseldre*? That might help you feel a little less anxious, right?"

"*Jah*. So would prayer. Will you pray for *Groossdaadi*? I'm too wound up to pray for him myself."

"Sure." So they bowed their heads and Peter asked the Lord to ease Marshall's discomfort and Susannah's anxiety, to give Lydia patience and to give all of them strength and endurance. When he opened his eyes again, he saw that Susannah's forehead was no longer wrinkled with lines, and although she wasn't smiling, she didn't look as if she was about to cry anymore.

As she'd done when she'd helped pick before, Susannah quickly worked her way up the rows. For some reason—perhaps he was still embarrassed about the remark he'd made to her on Monday—this time Benuel didn't seem interested in conversing with her, so he kept up a good pace, too. And even though Susannah ran back to the house every hour, her help enabled the crew to pick and transport roughly the same quantity of potatoes they would have if Marshall hadn't gotten injured.

"How much longer do you think it will take us to finish harvesting?" Jacob asked as they headed toward the barn to put away the equipment for the night.

"At this rate, we should be done by next *Mittwoch*," Peter replied. "At least, we'd better be—there's a frost forecasted for Thursday."

"My muscles are so sore. I can't wait to finish," Jacob said.

Peter's muscles were sore, too, but that didn't mean he wanted the harvest to end…because now he'd get to see Susannah *all* day, instead of only at lunchtime or in passing around the yard. And now Peter knew that when he spoke and joked and even flirted with her out in the fields, he wasn't doing it with a spirit of defiance toward her grandfather; he was doing it with a sense of deep affection for Susannah.

Susannah lay in bed for a good half an hour after waking on Sunday morning. She was really looking forward to observing the Sabbath at home. Her aching body needed the rest and she was eager to spend time reading the Bible and chatting with her grandparents. She felt as if she'd barely seen them the last four days, since she'd been so tired in the evenings that she usually collapsed into bed right after finishing the supper dishes.

Yet, as dirty and demanding as picking potatoes was, Susannah valued the opportunity to be outside almost the entire day, to exercise muscles she didn't ordinarily use and to contribute to the urgent goal of harvesting the rest of the crop before the first hard frost.

And, of course, she relished the chance to work alongside Peter. Whenever he wasn't transporting potatoes to the potato house or she wasn't running inside to make a meal or check on Lydia and Marshall, Susannah and Peter would harvest neighboring rows, matching each other's pace. On occasion, Jacob or Conrad would pick close by, too, when they weren't operating the digger. The boys were hard workers, but once in a while they'd pull a prank, like tossing a rotten, smelly potato at each other. But more often than not, Jacob and Conrad picked nearer to Benuel, who moved down the adjacent rows from the opposite end of the field, out of earshot of Peter and Susannah. She figured Benuel was avoiding being around her because he still felt slighted that she'd refused him as a suitor.

She was happy to give him his space, as his distancing allowed her the privacy to converse freely with Peter, which they often did. He'd tell her about how he and Hannes had completed their first wedding picnic tables, or he'd repeat something Eva had said happened at school. Peter also confided that his mother had made an appointment with a nutritionist the following week and he thanked Susannah for being so encouraging to her. Susannah, in turn, told Peter about what Charity had written in her most recent letter, or she'd give him an update on how Marshall had fared the previous evening. Regardless of whether they were chatting or silent, Susannah treasured the experience of working side by side with Peter; it was how she'd once pictured them tending their own garden, or fields, as a married couple.

And sometimes, she *still* pictured them that way. Or, at least, she'd let her imagination roam to the possibility that Peter might ask if he could be her long-distance suitor again. She had made up her mind that if he asked, she wouldn't answer him until he'd told her the reason he had previously decided they weren't a good match.

I wonder if Lydia has been able to find out what Groossdaadi's *qualm is about Peter yet*, Susannah thought. But given how much pain Marshall was experiencing, Susannah doubted that Lydia would have added to his discomfort by bringing up an unpleasant subject. *Oh, well. It's not as if Peter has asked to be my suitor yet, so I don't need to consider Marshall's opinion right this minute.*

What she *did* need to do right this minute was get up and start breakfast, as the boys would be coming in from the barn shortly. But her mind was more limber than her body and it took her twice as long to get dressed, brush her hair and make her bed as it usually did. When she went into the kitchen, Lydia was struggling to lift a heavy frying pan from the bottom cupboard.

"*Ach*, Lydia, you shouldn't be doing that. I've got it. You should go enjoy a cup of *kaffi* with *Groossdaadi*."

"We've already had one."

Susannah didn't realize she'd stayed in bed *that* late. "Where is he?"

"I sent him to the barn with the *buwe*." Lydia wiped her forehead with the back of her hand and then confided, "I love Marshall dearly and I'm sorry he's in pain. But let me just say I have a much better understanding of how *you* must have felt when you were stuck inside looking after me all day."

Susannah giggled. "It's *gut* that you've been taking him on short walks around the yard, though."

"*Jah.* That's what the chiropractor told us to do the last time he injured his back."

Peeking into the fridge, Susannah remarked, "It looks as if we're awfully low on groceries. I'm going to have to take a break from picking to go to the market."

"I suppose I could try to do the shopping myself," Lydia suggested.

"*Neh.* It would be too difficult for you to get in and out of the buggy or to load the groceries into the carriage. I'll go tomorrow. But for this morning all we have to eat is eggs and toast. And bacon. Lots of bacon."

"That will make Marshall *hallich.*"

"It will make me *hallich*, too. My appetite has doubled since I've been helping with the harvest." *And my waistline has been increasing, too*, Susannah thought. Lydia had been helping with food preparation as much as she was able to, but it had been challenging for Susannah to make healthy, fortifying meals, while also working in the fields. They'd been eating more potatoes and bread than she usually served, simply because they were convenient options in abundant supply. But all the starch had left Susannah feeling bloated and she looked forward to replenishing the pantry and fridge with other types of food.

Maybe today I can plan a healthier menu for the next three days until we're finished harvesting, she thought. While she'd hoped to make a special dessert on Wednesday to celebrate their accomplishment, she realized now that she had to give up on the idea. She hardly had time to put together a simple meal as it was.

After they'd eaten breakfast and worshipped together, Susannah served a customary light lunch—cheese and homemade bologna sandwiches. Because it was drizzling out and she was too tired to take a walk, she suggested that they all do a jigsaw puzzle together. But the boys were undeterred by the weather and went off on a hike, and Lydia wanted to sit at the kitchen table and write a letter to her sister. "I guess it's just you and me, *Groossdaadi*," Susannah said. She brought him an ice pack and rearranged his pillows, then set up the folding table right above his lap so he wouldn't have to stretch or shift in his chair.

After sitting down opposite him, she began rummaging through the box for the edge pieces. After their disagreement on Monday until the time he'd injured his back on Wednesday, Susannah had noticed she and her grandfather were politer than usual to each other. It felt unnatural, as if they were acquaintances instead of relatives. Then, following his injury, he'd been in too much pain to say much of anything to anyone. He didn't even join the crew for lunch, presumably because he didn't want to have to make or listen to small talk. Instead, Susannah would bring a tray to his room for him. But now that they were alone, she hoped to rebuild their usual rapport.

"This is like old times, when you lived in Dover and you and *mamm* and I used to do puzzles on the *Saabbat* together, remember?" she asked. When Marshall didn't answer, Susannah wasn't sure if he hadn't heard or if he was ignoring her question. Glancing up, she was surprised to see his eyes fixed on her.

"*Jah*, I remember," he replied and he sounded so nostalgic that Susannah thought she might cry. But then he added, "Your *mamm* used to get frustrated with us for looking at the box cover."

"That's because she thought it was cheating," Susannah recalled with a laugh.

She and Marshall worked on the puzzle in comfortable silence for another hour, until he said he needed to lie down flat for a while. Lydia also retreated to their room to nap, so Susannah perused the recipes Charity had sent. *Even though these are simple enough, I still don't know how I'll have the time to make them and help the* menner *pick potatoes*, she fretted, just as she heard a buggy coming up the lane.

Hoping it was Dorcas, Susannah darted outside to greet her. However, as she stepped onto the porch, she recognized it was Peter's buggy that had arrived. He had never come to the farm on a Sunday before now. Was it possible he was here to discuss a courtship with her? The prospect made her feel wobbly, so she held on to the railing for support.

But instead of veering toward the hitching post, Peter brought the horse to a halt near the side of the house, which meant he didn't plan on staying long. Disappointment washed over Susannah as she waited for him to come around to the porch. To her surprise, it was Eva who walked toward her carrying two large, foil-covered pans. Susannah rushed down the stairs to help her.

The young girl explained that Peter had mentioned Susannah was doing all the cooking and cleaning, as well as picking potatoes. So on Saturday, Eva had made two casseroles for Susannah to serve to the crew and her family.

"I used low-sodium broth instead of canned *supp* because that had too much sodium," she informed her. "Hannes tried it and said it was *gut*, but he'll eat anything so I hope everyone else likes it."

Susannah couldn't have been more grateful. "Why don't you and Peter *kumme* in for tea?"

"Peter didn't bring me. *Mamm* did."

"That's even better—I'd love to chat with her. So would Lydia. I'll go wake her."

"Neh!" Eva exclaimed. Then she lowered her voice. "I'm sorry but *Mamm*'s… She's having a really bad day. That's why she didn't get out of the buggy. She didn't even want you to see her."

"I understand." Until now, Susannah hadn't really realized just how ashamed Dorothy was of her health condition. Or was it that she was fearful of being judged? "Please greet her for me and say *denki* for bringing you here to deliver these meals."

Later that evening, as she was lying in bed, it occurred to Susannah that maybe Dorothy's illness was the reason Peter had broken up with her. Maybe his mother didn't want anyone to find out she was depressed, as Susannah inevitably would have done if she'd ended up marrying Peter. *He's always been so loyal and devoted to his family—so that would explain why he couldn't give me a reason for breaking up with me.*

Certain she was right, Susannah whispered a prayer for the Lord to strengthen Dorothy. Then, out of the blue, she added, *And if it's Your will, please allow her to be my mother-in-law one day soon.* Because now that Susannah had finally figured out why Peter had broken up with her, there was nothing stopping the two of them from resuming their courtship.

* * *

On Monday morning, Peter traveled toward the farm feeling thoroughly energized. He'd spent the better part of the Sabbath either napping or praying for wisdom about his dilemma concerning the promise he'd made to Marshall. The more time Peter spent with Susannah, the more intense his desire to court her became. And he was confident that she would accept him as her suitor again if he asked. Yet he couldn't court her without breaking his word to Marshall, which was unacceptable to Peter. So his thoughts had kept circling around and around and ending up back at the same dead end.

However, as he was praying on Sunday it had occurred to him that there was *one* way he could court Susannah, and that was if Marshall released him from his promise. Until now, Peter couldn't have imagined the old farmer ever agreeing to do that. But because Marshall had injured his back and his crew had to take over the farm, Peter saw a perfect opportunity to show Marshall how responsible he was. To show him that he was a good steward—not just of his own money, but of a farm that didn't even belong to him. Maybe once the older man recognized that, he'd be more open to Peter courting Susannah.

The possibility was so exciting that as his buggy rolled down the lane on Marshall's property and Peter heard the birds' tuneful chirping, he couldn't resist whistling along with them. *It's already a* wunderbaar *day*, he thought. *And I haven't even seen Susannah yet.*

She always came out of the house a little later than Jacob and Conrad did in the morning, because she had to wash and dry the dishes and tidy the kitchen after breakfast. But he was surprised that Benuel hadn't arrived at the farm by the time the young men had hitched the digger to the horse and Peter had carried the barrels into the fields. When he commented about it to Jacob and Conrad, they shrugged.

"Last week he said he was going to take a long hike at the gorge yesterday, so maybe he got worn out and overslept," Jacob suggested.

Then Susannah came into the fields and Peter forgot all about Benuel's absence until she asked where he was. Peter said he expected him any minute, but a minute turned into an hour and then two more hours passed. Looking worried, Susannah suggested someone should ride out to the Heisers' house to find out what was keeping him.

"*Neh.* It's not worth the time we'd lose picking," Peter said, glancing toward the lane. "If he's not here by noon, I'll go over to the Heisers' *haus* during our break."

"You'd be willing to give up your lunch?" Susannah teased and hopped into his row to pick up a potato that she'd accidentally tossed over the barrel instead of into it. Standing inches in front of him, she playfully held up the spud. "I promise I'm not serving these again, if that's what you're worried about."

Knowing Conrad and Jacob had their backs turned and the view from the house was obscured by the barn, Peter closed his hand around hers and wrested the vegetable from her fingers. He tossed it into the barrel and said, "As I've told you before, I like *everything* you make. Even so, I'd sacrifice my lunch break if I had to for the sake of our crew." So she'd know he was completely serious, Peter peered into her eyes, then added, "But I'd really miss not sitting next to you at the table."

Beneath a residue of dusty dirt, a pink tinge rose in

Susannah's cheeks. "I'd miss that, too. I *will* miss that," she replied and Peter understood. She didn't just mean she'd miss him if he left this afternoon: she meant she'd also miss him once the harvest was over. It was all the confirmation he needed to decide he *had* to talk to Marshall about releasing him from his promise.

His heart thundering as Susannah gazed up at him, Peter wanted nothing more than to lean forward and put his lips on hers. But since they weren't courting, that would literally be akin to stealing a kiss—and Peter was no thief. It was agony, but instead of stepping closer, he took a step back. And he was glad he did because a moment later, someone shouted, "Hey!"

He and Susannah both turned their heads to see Benuel heading toward them and the boys. One of his coat sleeves was flapping loosely as he walked and he appeared to be hiding something beneath his coat.

"Hi, Benuel. What have you got there—a kitten?" Susannah asked, instead of immediately asking why he was so late.

"Neh." Benuel pulled open one side of his coat to reveal his arm was in a sling.

"Voll schpass." Because Benuel was smirking, Peter had assumed he was pulling a prank. Or feigning a broken arm as an excuse for being late, which actually seemed in poor taste considering Marshall's and Lydia's recent injuries.

"I'm not kidding. I dislocated my shoulder pretty bad when I was helping my *onkel* move a generator before work this morning. The *dokder* popped my arm back into place but the dislocation tore a ligament," he reported. "Anyway, I can't use my arm for the next two days at least, and no heavy lifting for two weeks after that."

Jacob clutched the top of his hat in consternation and Conrad muttered, "That's *baremlich*." But it was difficult to tell if they were upset on Benuel's behalf or because they were losing a coworker.

"I'm sorry you got hurt." Susannah furrowed her forehead, obviously concerned about his well-being. "Are you in a lot of pain?"

"Well, it doesn't tickle."

Even though Benuel seemed dismissive of Susannah's empathy, Peter also expressed his concern, and then asked, "I don't suppose you can steer the horses and digger using only one hand, can you?"

"Lydia might have a better chance at doing that than I would," Benuel quipped. Then his expression turned somber. "My *onkel* is waiting for me in the van. We asked the driver to stop here on the way home from the ER. So I guess I'd better go tell Marshall I can't finish harvesting now."

He said goodbye to everyone, but before he walked away, Peter offered, "If your arm feels better next week and you're looking for a job, Hannes and I could use some help making picnic tables. We've got an urgent order."

"Really?" Benuel's eyes widened.

"Jah." Peter had seen his carpentry; Benuel did good work. And Peter intended to pay him for every table he completed instead of by the hour, so that would keep him on his toes. As far as Peter was concerned, the arrangement might be the Lord's provision for both of them.

"Denki," Benuel said and started straggling through the fields toward the house.

"I should go with him and reassure *Groossdaadi* we can still finish the harvest by *Mittwoch* evening." Susannah bit her lip. "We can, can't we?"

"With *Gott*'s help, absolutely," Peter confirmed. *We'd better...because our future as a couple depends on it.*

Chapter Twelve

On Wednesday, as the sun was setting and Conrad and Jacob went into the house, Susannah lingered outside with Peter. After three days of arduous labor, they were grime-streaked and bone-weary, but also elated that they'd completed the harvesting.

"Are you sure you don't want to change your mind and *kumme* in for supper?" Susannah asked, even though he'd already hitched his horse and buggy. "There's plenty of food."

On Sunday afternoon, shortly after Eva and Dorothy had come by with the casseroles, Almeda and Iddo had dropped in for a visit. When Almeda had learned that Marshall wasn't able to work on the farm so Susannah was helping the crew, the deacon's wife offered to bring over a couple of meals. She also brought two more apple-butter pies, a batch of snickerdoodles and a container of pumpkin bars. On one hand, the extra food was terrific because it had meant Susannah didn't have to cook or go to the grocery store until tomorrow. However, it also meant she'd given in to the temptation to eat the treats more often than not. This morning she'd had to adjust the pins on her skirt again because it was too tight.

"*Denki*, but Eva is trying another new recipe and she'll be disappointed if I'm not home to taste it. Plus, I've got to help Hannes in the workshop as soon as we're done eating."

It was just light enough to see Peter's teeth as he turned toward her and smiled. Now that his horse and buggy were hitched, Susannah knew she should say goodbye and go inside and reheat her family's meal in the oven. But she figured Lydia was capable of doing that, and besides, this was probably the last time she'd see Peter until they went to church on Sunday.

"I'm sure if *Groossdaadi* was feeling better, he'd *kumme* out and thank you for all your help." At least, that's what she hoped he'd do. A breeze lifted her *kapp* strings and Susannah shivered, drawing her sweater closer around her torso.

"You're cold. I should leave," Peter suggested. But he didn't move away from her; he moved closer. Leaning down, he whispered into her ear, "If we were courting, I could give you a hug to keep you warm."

Susannah caught her breath. "If that's a question, the answer is *jah*."

"*Jah*, I can court you or *jah*, I can give you a hug?"

She giggled. "Both."

"*Denki*, Susannah." Peter wrapped his arms around her and held her close. "Is that better?"

"Much," she murmured into his chest.

As Peter journeyed home, he was aware that he'd put the cart before the horse by asking to court Susannah before speaking to her grandfather about their agreement. Yet despite acting in haste and against his better judgment, he didn't regret his behavior one bit. Holding Susannah in his arms for those few minutes had made Peter more motivated than ever to ask her grandfather to release him from his promise.

I'll talk to him before lunchtime tomorrow, he thought. Susannah had mentioned she was going to the grocery store late that morning, so he knew she wouldn't be at the house. He didn't know whether Lydia and the boys would be home, but he hoped if he told Marshall he needed to speak with him privately, the old man would oblige him and step outdoors.

That night he must have spent as much time praying about their upcoming discussion as he spent sleeping, and he yawned his way through the first few hours of the next morning. When it was finally time to leave, he informed Hannes, "I'm going to the farm. I'll be back in about an hour."

"The farm?" Hannes sounded surprised.

"*Jah.* And no complaints about working alone," Peter warned, scowling at him.

"I'm not complaining—especially not after all you've done for me, *bruder.* I just didn't think you'd be so eager to go back there now that harvest is over."

Realizing he'd been short with Hannes because he was anxious about talking to Susannah's grandfather, Peter said, "There's one last thing I need to discuss with Marshall. It's too important to wait."

Hannes clapped him on the shoulder. "Whatever it's about, I'll be praying the discussion goes smoothly."

That's another gut *change in Hannes's attitude this last year*, Peter thought. And for that reason, he gladly would have agreed to work on Marshall's farm for *five* harvest seasons…provided he didn't have to give up his courtship with Susannah.

Thankfully, when he got to the farm, he spied Marshall pacing very slowly in front of the barn, and the boys and Lydia were nowhere in sight. Whether or not the old man was surprised to see him, Peter was too nervous to notice. He greeted him and then launched into the speech he'd practiced several times on the way there.

"As you know, even though we were shorthanded and I had to do all the loading and transporting alone, we finished the harvest yesterday—"

He'd barely begun speaking when Marshall interrupted him. "*Jah.* You've held up your end of our agreement to bring in the crop. *Denki.* The *buwe* will take care of winterizing the equipment and any outstanding cleanup. There was no need for you to return to the *bauerei.*"

Despite Marshall's rare expression of gratitude, Peter understood he was being dismissed. But he wasn't leaving until he asked what he'd come there to ask. "Actually, there is a reason for me to return. I'd like you to consider whether I've been a *gut* steward of your farm and—"

Susannah's grandfather seemed to anticipate what Peter was going to say and he interrupted him again. "You've fulfilled your obligation to bring in the harvest. That was what you agreed to do, plain and simple. You also agreed not to court Susannah and I'm holding you to that, too." He started shuffling toward the house.

Isn't he even going to listen to what I have to say? Knowing this was his only chance to make Marshall reconsider their agreement, Peter was determined to speak his piece. He overtook the farmer within three strides and planted himself in his path. Staring him down, he announced, "I *love* Susannah and I believe she loves me."

Marshall's face didn't register any emotion, but he teetered ever so slightly, then growled, "Get out of my way and off of my property, *suh*."

Defeated, Peter stepped aside. How could anyone be so hardheaded? So hard-*hearted*? Peter's own heart was shattered and it took all of his strength to drag himself back to the hitching post. Before he could untie Pepper's lead, he spotted a buggy approaching. Knowing what he had to do, Peter waited for Susannah to stable her horse.

"Hi, Peter," she sang out when she emerged from the barn. "What are you doing here?"

He stammered, "I—I have to tell you something."

"It must be important if you left your workshop in the middle of the day," she said coyly, inching closer to him.

Aware he was about to crush her feelings the way Marshall had crushed his, Peter stiffened his posture and backed away from her. "It *is* important." He licked his lips. "And it's not easy to say. But I—I shouldn't have asked to court you last evening."

The color drained from Susannah's face and her eyes and lips drooped as the gravity of his words settled over her. "You don't want to be my suitor?"

I want to, but I can't, Peter inwardly wailed. Aloud, he apologized, "I'm sorry, Susannah, but *neh*."

"Why not?" Her tone was surprisingly gentle.

Forcing himself, he said, "I don't think we have a future together." *Only because Marshall won't allow us to have one.*

"But *why* do you think that?" When he didn't answer, she persisted, "Is it that you're worried about your *mamm*'s condition?"

"Her condition?"

"*Jah*. It's my understanding that she may be suffering from depression. But you must know by now that I wouldn't judge anyone for that. And I'd be *hallich* to help her any way I can, for as long as it takes."

Peter shook his head and closed his eyes before opening them again. "This has nothing to do with my *mamm*." Not at this point, it didn't. "I'm sorry, but I have to leave now."

He turned toward his horse, but Susannah grabbed his arm. Her nostrils flared and her cheeks ignited with color once more as she demanded, "If you're breaking up with me because I've gained weight again, then at least be *mann* enough to say the words to my face."

She could have knocked him over with a feather. "What are you talking about? That doesn't even make sense. You're a lot thinner now than you were when I asked to court you last summer." Peter had only meant to point out that she was being illogical, but her features turned as hard as her grandfather's.

In an icy voice, she said, "That just proves how attentive you've been to keeping track of my weight. Don't deny it. You broke up with me out of the blue last *Grischtdaag* when you saw how heavy I'd gotten. And when we embraced last night, you could feel that I'm not that thin. That I've been gaining weight again. You're probably worried I'll gain back every pound I've lost."

Peter was so affronted by her accusation, his voice rose when he asked her, "Are you kidding me, Susannah? The only person paying that much attention to your weight is *you*."

Thrusting her chin in the air, she challenged, "Okay

then, tell me exactly why you don't think we're a *gut* match or why we don't have a future together."

Peter was tempted to say "Because your *groossdaadi* is as wrong about me as you are, that's why." But he couldn't; he'd given him his word. Besides, it wouldn't be worth it. If Susannah truly believed he was the kind of man who valued her appearance over her heart, then maybe they *weren't* a good match for each other. And to think, less than five minutes ago, he'd claimed they loved each other. He looked at the ground and shook his head in disappointment and frustration.

"I knew it," Susannah uttered with disgust when he remained silent. "You showed me your true colors when you broke off our courtship after *Grischtdaag*. I should have paid attention to what you were like the first time."

"Well, if *you* had shown me *your* true colors the first time we courted, I never would have asked you a second time!" Peter countered. Then he got into his buggy and left the farm so quickly a cloud of dust rose in his wake.

"Are you ill?" Lydia had asked after the lunch dishes were done and Susannah announced she needed to go take a nap.

"*Neh.* I'm just tired. Those last three days of picking potatoes without Benuel on the crew wore me out. I'll be fine once I've had some rest," she claimed, heading down the hall.

Susannah had managed to keep herself from crying during their meal, but she couldn't hold back her tears for one more second. She closed her bedroom door and flung herself facedown on the bed, crying into her pillow as she relived the conversation she'd had with Peter near the barn.

How could I have been so naive as to think he truly liked me, inside and out? she lamented. *I should have been* schmaert *enough to learn my lesson the first time.* Not to mention, her grandfather had tried to warn her not to consider Peter as a suitor. Instead, she'd listened to Dorcas and Lydia. She had believed what she'd wanted to believe: namely, that Peter was as smitten with her as she was with him.

No. Not just smitten—that was too frivolous of a word. Susannah had wanted to believe that they were... falling in *love.* She wanted to believe that one day they'd commit their lives to each other. *Ha! He wasn't even my suitor again for one full day before calling off our courtship.* Susannah supposed she should have felt relieved that he'd changed his mind so quickly. At least this way she hadn't had time to get her hopes up even higher before dashing them with the words *I don't think we have a future together.*

How could he do something like that—*twice*—and then have the gall to act as if *she* was the one who was lacking character? It was all so hurtful and confusing and devastating that Susannah wept so hard her head ached. But even then, she didn't stop crying until she finally fell asleep.

For the rest of the day and on Friday, too, she withdrew to her room as frequently as she could, only coming out to make and serve meals or to do her other chores. Sometimes she spent her time alone napping, or in prayer. But most often she simply sat on the edge of her bed and stared out the window, with tears trickling down her face.

On Saturday morning, Marshall said he felt good enough to take the boys to the bus station, since they were returning to Ohio. After packing them a lunch and bidding them goodbye, Susannah slipped away to her room. She had just sat down on the bed when Lydia knocked.

"I'm resting," Susannah called.

Lydia entered, anyway. "Did you say *kumme* in?"

"*Neh*. I said I'm about to lie down. I didn't get much sleep last night." It was true; she'd been awake until almost three thirty…possibly because she'd spent too much time napping on Friday.

"Wouldn't you rather have a cup of *kaffi* with me, now that all the *menner* are out of the *haus*? Or we could take a walk—I noticed you haven't been getting as much fresh air lately."

"*Denki*, but I can hardly keep my eyes open."

"*Jah*. They look a little swollen," Lydia hinted and Susannah knew her stepgrandmother was aware she'd been crying.

But she just said, "I'm fine. Is there anything I can help you with before I take a short snooze?"

"*Neh*. I've got to start doing more things for myself since you'll be leaving us on *Dinnschdaag*." Lydia frowned. "We'll be sorry to see you go…and not just because of all the work you've done for us."

Susannah gave her a weak smile. "I'll miss you and *Groossdaadi* a lot, too." *But I'll be relieved to leave New Hope so I won't have to worry about running into Peter,* she thought, just like she had when she first arrived in Maine. Then she remembered tomorrow was a church Sunday, meaning the district would gather for worship in the church building. Her stomach knotted up at the thought of seeing Peter, so when Lydia left the room, Susannah decided rather than napping, she needed to pray.

Thankfully, the next day Marshall suggested they sit on a bench in the very back of the gathering room so he could stand against the wall if his back became sore. Susannah couldn't see anyone except the row of people immediately in front of her and Peter wasn't among them. And once the sermons began, she forgot about everything except what the minister was saying. When it came time to prepare and serve lunch, she made a point of staying in the kitchen to set up trays, instead of delivering them to the men upstairs.

When it was the women's turn to eat, Lydia told her they needed to finish their lunch quickly. Marshall was concerned about having back spasms and he was in a hurry to return home, which was more than fine with Susannah.

A few minutes later, she and her stepgrandmother were almost out the door when they bumped into Dorcas, who appeared positively glowing. "Oh, there you are, Susannah. I've been waiting for you. Some of us are going on a hike in the gorge. Do you want to join us?"

Susannah didn't feel like socializing; besides, she didn't know who else was going on the hike. For all she knew, Peter would be there, since he loved the area as much as she did. "I can't… I'm really tired."

"You should go," Lydia urged her. "This is one of your last chances to see your friends."

"*Neh.* But maybe you could *kumme* over for lunch tomorrow?"

"Sure. I'll bring a low-fat dessert," Dorcas offered.

Before they parted, Susannah whispered, "You look *wunderbaar*, Dorcas. Did you lose more weight?"

"Not a pound," she whispered back. "It's because I gained a suitor."

Susannah was genuinely happy for her, since she knew Dorcas wanted to be in a courtship. But all the way home she was troubled with misgivings toward Peter and as soon as she walked into the house, she told her grandparents she was going to her room for a nap.

"Wouldn't you like to do a jigsaw puzzle instead?" Marshall asked.

Susannah was surprised; her grandfather had never initiated a recreational activity, although he often participated when he was invited. Still, she felt too weepy to be around anyone right now. "*Denki*, but I need to rest."

"At least take a walk with me around the yard first. My back is tight and I might need to hold on to you for balance. Lydia's too unsteady to help me."

So they slowly ambled down the lane toward the mailbox. On their way, Marshall cleared his throat. "Lydia and I are concerned about you. Is something wrong?" he asked.

At first she was going to deny it, but she was so moved by her grandfather's open display of concern that she blurted out, "You were right to have reservations about Peter, *Groossdaadi*." Then she confided about their courtship and the reason he'd called it off twice. Finally, she admitted, "I'm sorry I got angry with you for trying to protect me. I should have listened to you."

By then, they'd reached the end of the lane and Marshall grasped the split-rail fence with both hands. Redfaced, he bent forward to stretch his back. "You're right, I was trying to protect you." He sounded short of breath. "You remind me of your *mamm*. I wanted *Gott*'s best for her."

Susannah understood the connection. "*Mamm* and *Daed* may have had their struggles, *Groossdaadi*, but they were *hallich*. They felt blessed."

"*Jah*. Your *daed* is a *gut mann*." Marshall stood up straight again. "Peter Lambright is, too. They both have a lot more character than I do."

Susannah felt stung. "How can you say that after what I just told you?"

"Because the reason Peter ended your courtship had nothing to do with you. He ended it because *I* told him he had to."

Susannah couldn't believe what she was hearing as her grandfather described the agreement he'd made with Peter and the conversation that he'd had on Thursday. She felt so hurt and angry and betrayed she could hardly look at her grandfather.

"How could you do something like that to Peter? And to *me*?" she cried.

"I thought I was doing it for your *gut*," he said. "But when I saw how miserable you've been and when I reconsidered Peter's character, I realized I was wrong. I'm sorry, Susannah, and I hope you'll forgive me."

Susannah hesitated before nodding. "*Jah*, I forgive you, *Groossdaadi*," she said. *I just hope Peter forgives* me.

"I'm going to take a walk over to the workshop and back," Peter told his mother as he lifted his coat from a hook near the door.

"Maybe you ought to take a nap instead," she urged him. "Not that I'm anyone to point a finger, but you've seemed more tired these past few days than you did when you were working two jobs."

Peter hadn't been tired—he'd been miserable. Dejected. Heartsick. So taking a nap wasn't going to help. Taking a walk probably wouldn't help him, either, but at least it would get him out of the house. He didn't want his cheerless mood to bring down his mother, especially now that she felt so hopeful again.

The nutritionist she'd consulted last week had suggested Dorothy get additional lab work done. When the results came back on Friday, they indicated she had a form of anemia that was severe, but manageable. Part of her health plan included receiving vitamin B-12 injections. Just knowing that she would receive effective treatment helped boost her spirit even before it was administered.

"Who would ever think I'd look forward to receiving an injection?" she had said, marveling after hearing the news. Although it was a doctor who had made the diagnosis, Dorothy credited the nutritionist for suggesting the lab work in the first place. And she said she never would have gone to a nutritionist if it hadn't been for her conversation with Susannah.

She was so grateful that on Saturday afternoon she'd baked a pie with the last of the blueberries Eva had frozen from the summer harvest. Dorothy intended to personally deliver it to the farm, so she could share her good news with Susannah. As Peter was leaving the house, she reminded him, "Eva and I won't leave for another hour. If you change your mind, you're *wilkom* to *kumme* with us."

"I won't change my mind," Peter replied, knowing that neither Susannah nor Marshall would welcome him on the farm. Nor did he want to see them. In time, he'd get over his hurt, but right now, he was still praying about it. And since he could pray as he walked, he me-

andered on the long road between his house and the
workshop for almost an hour. Finally, he decided it was
probably time for his mother and sister to leave and he
headed into the barn to hitch the horse so they wouldn't
have to do it themselves.

Pepper was friskier than usual and he took the time
to brush her coat and mane, hoping that would settle her
down. His mother had mentioned last week that she'd had
difficulty handling him. *It's too bad Hannes isn't home or
he could bring* Mamm *and Eva to the farm*, he thought.

At that very moment, he heard Hannes's buggy approaching, so he led Pepper back into his stall. When he
came out, he was dumbfounded to see Susannah standing in the doorway. "Hi, Peter." She tentatively moved
closer. "May I speak with you a minute?"

Speechless, he nodded. Although he didn't have anything else to say, he could at least listen to her.

"My—my *groossdaadi* told me about the loan," she
began.

Peter immediately saw red. *How dare Marshall not
hold up his end of the bargain after harping on* me *to
hold up mine. Is he really that vengeful? Or was he trying to make me look bad as a way of ensuring Susannah would never accept me as a suitor?* If that was the
case, he needn't have bothered; Peter didn't have any
interest whatsoever in courting her now.

"He shouldn't have told you—he broke his word.
Our arrangement is none of your business and I don't
want to talk about it. You'll have to excuse me. I'm
going inside." He started toward the door but Susannah blocked his path.

"Please, just listen to me," she pleaded, her voice
quavering. So Peter stood still, allowing her to continue.

"He only told me about it because he regrets how he treated you. He knows how much character you have. So do I, and I'm sorry for implying you were superficial. You were right—I was the only one who was focused on my weight. But that was just because I couldn't figure out what else had changed to make you break up with me…" Susannah covered her face with her hands and dissolved into tears.

So Peter took her by the shoulders and directed her toward a hay bale, where they sat down side by side, just like they used to do at lunchtime. "I can only imagine how confusing and frustrating it must have been for you not to know the real reason. I hope you'll forgive me for not being more honest from the beginning."

"Of course I forgive you. It wasn't your fault that you couldn't tell me—that was part of your arrangement with *Groossdaadi.*"

"*Neh*, that's not what I mean." Peter looked at his boots, unable to meet her eyes as he told her about Hannes wrecking the SUV and the *Englischers* demanding immediate reimbursement for the damage. He concluded by acknowledging, "I was trying to protect my *bruder* and my *mamm*, but I should have been more honest about why I needed a loan in the first place. I should have trusted the Lord to provide a way to help my *familye* without hurting you. Without *losing* you…"

Susannah nudged his shoulder with hers. "You haven't lost me—I'm right here."

Peter swiveled his head to see if she was serious. "You'd accept me as your suitor a third time?"

"*Jah*. I would—and I do."

Epilogue

"Have you seen my husband?" Susannah asked, surveying the crowded gathering room in the church. She and Peter had been married earlier in the day and the guests were enjoying supper and dessert, but Peter was nowhere to be found. "He said he had to do something outside, but he's been gone a while."

"*Neh*, I haven't," Lydia replied as Honor Bawell approached them, carefully balancing a plate of desserts.

"I can't believe you decided to have peanut-butter pies for your *hochzich*," Honor remarked.

Although a small number of Amish brides served large, bakery-made cakes similar to what might be found at an *Englischer* wedding, most did not. Instead, the Amish made their wedding cakes, as well as an assortment of desserts. Peanut-butter pie may have been included as one of the treats, but it wasn't usually the main offering, as it was at Peter and Susannah's wedding.

"It's my favorite," Susannah said. "Especially the way Lydia makes it."

After Honor walked away, Lydia asked, "Have you tasted it yet?"

"*Jah*. It's as *appenditlich* as ever. I was considering having another small slice," Susannah said. "*Denki* for making them. And for everything else you did to prepare for our *hochzich*."

"It wasn't difficult—I had a lot of help from Charity, Dorcas, Eva and Dorothy."

Throughout the course of her treatment during the past year, Peter's mother had increasingly experienced improvements in her health and mood. Now she claimed she had even more energy than she'd had before becoming anemic. Likewise, Lydia's wrist was completely mended—although she referred to it as her internal weather vane, because she felt mild pain whenever there was a storm coming.

"I have something to confess," Lydia whispered. "We used a lower-sugar, lower-fat recipe."

"I couldn't taste any difference," Susannah marveled. "But now I'm *definitely* going to have a second piece."

She went to the dessert table and took slices of pie for both her and Peter. *Where is he?* she wondered, scanning the room. She had endured being separated from him during their one-year long-distance courtship, but she didn't want to be separated from him on her wedding day, too. When she didn't see him anywhere among the guests, she edged toward the door and slipped out into the cool November evening. It was too dark for her to see very far and she was about to turn around and go back inside when Hannes came toward her.

"Are you looking for Peter?" he asked, and when she said she was, he led her to where Peter was standing beside a buggy wagon near the hitching rail.

"What are you doing out here?" she asked Peter as

Hannes walked away. "And why is this wagon here? You arrived in your buggy, didn't you?"

Peter chuckled. "*Jah*. Hannes brought this here for me. *Kumme*, I want to show you something." He took the two plates from her hand and set them inside the wagon. Then he climbed up and held out his arms to assist her into it, too.

Handing her a flashlight, Peter told Susannah to point it toward the bed of the wagon. She turned it on, illuminating an octagonal picnic table with separate benches, similar to the one he'd made for the *Englischers'* wedding last year. "I made this for you—for *us*. But I rounded the corners on the tabletop and the benches, so our *kinner* won't get hurt if they bump into the ends."

The words *our kinner* took Susannah's breath away. She couldn't wait to start a family with Peter. "*Denki*. It's *wunderbaar*," she said. Then she teased flirtatiously, "I notice you didn't engrave our initials and *hochzich* day on the table like the *Englischers* did."

"*Neh*. That would be superficial, when *Gott* wants us to look beneath the surface." Peter grinned as she crouched down. Pointing, he told her to shine the flashlight at the underside of the table. Susannah bent down beside him and aimed the beam of light where he'd indicated. She had to tilt her head to see it: Peter had inscribed their full names and today's date in the center of the table. Springing up, she clapped her hands together.

"I love it," she murmured. Clicking off the flashlight, she drew nearer to him.

"And I love *you*." Peter gently lifted her prayer *kapp* strings and placed them behind her shoulders. Cupping her face in his strong, calloused hands, he leaned down and kissed her until she was dizzy. She faltered as she pulled away, but Peter slid his hands to her waist and steadied her.

Relishing his touch, Susannah inched closer. "I have an idea. Let's eat our pie at our new table."

So they sat side by side in the near-dark atop of the buggy wagon, eating their dessert very, very slowly. And even after it was gone, the newlyweds lingered there a while longer. Because as Lydia had once told them, sweet things were meant to be savored.

* * * * *

HARLEQUIN
PLUS

Announcing a **BRAND-NEW** multimedia subscription service for romance fans like you!

Read, Watch and Play.

Experience the easiest way to get the romance content you crave.

Start your **FREE 7 DAY TRIAL** at <u>www.harlequinplus.com/freetrial</u>.